STAR TREK®
SEVEN DEADLY SINS

STAR TREK®
SEVEN DEADLY SINS

Dayton Ward & Kevin Dilmore
David A. McIntee • James Swallow
Keith R.A. DeCandido • Britta Burdett Dennison
Marc D. Giller • Greg Cox

Based on *Star Trek* and *Star Trek: The Next Generation*®
created by Gene Roddenberry

Star Trek: Deep Space Nine®
created by Rick Berman & Michael Piller

and *Star Trek: Voyager*®
created by Rick Berman & Michael Piller & Jeri Taylor

GALLERY BOOKS
New York   London   Toronto   Sydney

G

Gallery Books
A Division of Simon & Schuster, Inc.
1230 Avenue of the Americas
New York, NY 10020

First Gallery Books trade paperback edition March 2010

GALLERY and colophon are registered trademarks of Simon & Schuster, Inc.

For information about special discounts for bulk purchases, please contact Simon & Schuster Special Sales at 1-866-506-1949 or business@simonandschuster.com.

The Simon & Schuster Speakers Bureau can bring authors to your live event. For more information or to book an event, contact the Simon & Schuster Speakers Bureau at 1-866-248-3049 or visit our website at www.simonspeakers.com.

Cover art and design by Alan Dingman

Manufactured in the United States of America

10 9 8 7 6 5 4 3 2 1

ISBN 978-1-4391-0944-1
ISBN 978-1-4391-2342-3 (ebook)

Contents

Pride

The First Peer

Dayton Ward & Kevin Dilmore

Historian's Note

This story takes place in the year 2267 (ACE), less than a month after the *Enterprise*'s resupply mission to Gamma Hydra IV and her incursion across the Romulan Neutral Zone ("The Deadly Years" TOS).

"Pride, the first peer and president of hell."

—Daniel Defoe

Authors' Additional Notes

Commodore Robert Wesley appears in the original *Star Trek* episode "The Ultimate Computer."

Praetor Vrax was introduced as a senator in the *Star Trek Enterprise* episode "United."

The characters Toqel, Sarith, Praetor Vrax, and certain members of the Romulan Senate were established in the *Star Trek: Vanguard* novel *Summon the Thunder*.

Captain Thomas Blair was established as commanding officer of the *U.S.S. Defiant* in the *Star Trek: S.C.E.* novella *Interphase*.

Admiral Solow was established in Kevin Ryan's *Star Trek* trilogies *Errand of Vengeance* and *Errand of Fury*, and the authors would like to thank Kevin for his consultation during the writing of this story.

Romulan/Rihannsu Terms of Measure
(Comparisons are approximate)

dhaei—week
eisae—day
fvheisn—year (380 *eisae*)
khaidoa—month

1

"Pursuit course. Stand by to divert power from the cloaking field to the shields on my order, and place all weapons on ready status."

Standing among his subordinates on the confined bridge of the Romulan vessel *Revoth,* Commander Larael watched as his crew worked to carry out his orders. None of them spoke, focused as they were on their individual tasks, but Larael could sense the tension permeating the cramped room. He could understand their anxiety, and it rivaled his own rising excitement as the *Revoth* gave chase to the Starfleet vessel. For reasons that remained in question, the ship had crossed the Neutral Zone separating Romulan and Federation space, abrogating a treaty that had existed for generations almost without incident and thereby committing an act of war.

Of course, he mused with a degree of bitterness, *neither side is innocent in that regard.*

From where he stood at one of the four workstations positioned around the control hub at the center of the bridge, Centurion Bochir said, "Commander, the enemy vessel is proceeding without its defense fields, and its weapons do not appear to be activated."

Interesting, Larael mused as he moved closer to Bochir's station, peering over the centurion's shoulder in order to observe the sensor readings for himself. "Why would they travel in enemy space without their defenses activated?" Even while it towed the smaller, weaker vessel it currently held in its tractor beam, Larael knew that the Federation ship—a *Constitution*-class heavy cruiser and one of the most formidable ships in the Starfleet armada—was more than a match for his own vessel. Still, the *Revoth*'s primary plasma weapon, along with its cloaking technology, helped to balance the scales so far as any direct confrontation was concerned. Despite any apparent tactical superiority the Starfleet ship possessed and even if its captain felt he was not in any immediate danger, he had placed his vessel in a vulnerable position as it made way for the Neutral Zone and what he obviously presumed was safe harbor in Federation space.

"Commander," said another centurion, Odira, from where he stood next to the bridge's compact communications station, "we are being hailed by the Starfleet ship."

Frowning at the report, Larael circled around the control hub. "What?" He moved to stand abreast of the centurion. "How is that possible?" A glance at the status display mounted over the console confirmed that the *Revoth*'s cloaking field was still in operation. "Is he just broadcasting blindly?"

"I do not believe so," Odira replied as he reached for a control. The centurion pressed one of the panel's buttons, and an instant later the *Revoth*'s bridge intercom system blared to life.

"Attention, Romulan vessel. This is Commodore Robert Wesley, commanding the Federation Starship Lexington. *Our sensors have detected your ship following us on an intercept course. Your current distance is five point six million kilometers off our stern and closing."*

"He's lying!" Larael snapped, unwilling to believe what he was hearing. He glared at Odira, who turned from his station, and saw his own disbelief mirrored in the centurion's eyes.

Odira said, "Commander, he speaks the truth. I am not certain I have properly converted the distance measurements, but he is correct with respect to our angle of approach."

Unbelievable!

The thought echoed in Larael's mind even as stared at the status monitor. Rumors had circulated for quite some time—ones naturally unsubstantiated by higher command echelons—of Starfleet's apparent ability to detect a cloaked vessel—at least, one in close proximity. Larael had dismissed the unconfirmed reports. Some of the best scientists from across the Empire had collaborated over several *fvheisn* to redesign the proven technology and eliminate the acknowledged flaws in its design. As a result, this new incarnation was far superior to anything Starfleet might bring to bear in the way of countermeasures, even with the assistance of their longtime lapdogs, the Vulcans.

Current events, Larael conceded, *appear to undermine that conviction.*

If it was true, then it might well mean a shift in thinking on the part of the Praetor. By all accounts, the supreme Romulan leader seemed to be placing a lot of faith in this latest generation of the cloaking field. It was but one weapon in an already formidable arsenal, for which he had supervised one of the most costly and comprehensive replenishment and improvement programs in recent memory. Though no one would admit to having heard the Praetor speak the words aloud, there were many in the Romulan government who believed the aged leader might well be planning another war with Earth and its allies.

Might that war begin here, today?

Ignoring the unwelcome thought, Larael folded his arms across his chest and nodded toward the centurion's station. "Open the channel."

In response to his order, Odira pressed several controls on the console, each button pressed emitting a short, high-pitched tone. Then one of the station's three rectangular screens activated, a wash of multicolored static fading away as the communications circuit was completed to reveal a human male. Larael noted his gray hair as well as the creases along the human's forehead and along his jaw. He wore the simple, now-familiar Starfleet tunic, and Larael recognized its gold hue as that worn by personnel in command positions. Rather than some young, inexperienced, and perhaps impulsive or even reckless officer, this human affected the appearance of a man with significant training and experience.

On the screen, the human said, *"Romulan vessel, we regret our trespass into your space, but we are responding to a distress call. If you've scanned us, then you know the ship we're towing has lost all main power. It was unable to avoid drifting through the Neutral Zone and into your territory. At this very moment, the Federation's Diplomatic Corps is attempting to contact your government about this issue."*

"This is Commander Larael of the Romulan vessel *Revoth*." As he spoke, he kept his expression and tone neutral. "If what you say is true, then why not simply wait for our government to respond? I may well have been ordered to assist the freighter and its crew."

To his credit, the human also maintained his bearing even as he said, *"Commander, I think we're both aware that there have been a few unfortunate incidents on both sides of the border in recent months—unarmed vessels being fired upon and so forth. I didn't want this to be another such occurrence. I'm sure you know that wars have begun that way."*

"They have also begun after spies were captured committing espionage and sabotage," Larael countered.

Wesley nodded. *"Yes, and sometimes such tragedies were avoided, even when there was sufficient cause to proceed. Perhaps you're aware of a recent example or two."*

Larael bristled at the obvious, veiled accusation. From reading a series of classified reports, he knew of at least two separate clandestine missions undertaken by Romulan vessels into Federation territory. While one of the ships had been sent on a circuitous route to a distant area of largely unexplored space currently disputed by the Federation, the Klingon Empire, and the Tholian Assembly, a second vessel had been dispatched across the Neutral Zone to test Starfleet defenses. It was the first such mission since the ending of the war between the Empire and Earth more than eighty *fvheisn* earlier, and there was much to be learned about how far the enemy had advanced since that costly conflict. The lone vessel had carried out several successful attacks on Starfleet outposts stationed near the Neutral Zone, though it had not fared nearly so well after engaging another *Constitution*-class starship near the border. Its commander was forced to destroy the ship rather than allow it to be captured, a fate which many believed to have befallen the first vessel, as well.

As the human had intimated, the incident near the Neutral Zone, along with other, more recent encounters, might well have been enough to pull the Federation and the Empire into a new and perhaps protracted, costly war. Cooler heads had prevailed on those occasions, and Larael did not relish the prospect of any action being taken today that might not be handled with similar restraint.

Maintaining eye contact with Wesley and making sure his voice was loud enough for the human to hear, Larael said to Bochir, "Scan the smaller vessel again."

The centurion leaned over his console, peering at several of the displays and the data scrolling across them. "As before, Commander, the vessel appears to possess only limited defenses, which are not active. Its primary power generators are off-line. I am unable to determine the reason for the power loss, but there is no detectable external damage to the ship."

It certainly was possible that this was all a ruse designed to conceal espionage. Such a scenario was a likely if rather obvious cover for crossing the border and carrying out covert surveillance. If it was in fact an act of deception, then it lacked any manner of creativity, something Larael would not expect from the notoriously imaginative and unapologetically deceitful humans. There was also the fact that in addition to being a defenseless vessel, it as well as the *Revoth* was nowhere near any target of worthwhile military value. If the people on that ship were spies, Larael concluded that they might be better off pursuing some other vocation.

"You will continue on your present course at your current speed, Commodore," he said after a moment. "Any deviation, no matter how slight, will be considered a hostile act against the Romulan Star Empire. My further advice to you is to inform your superiors that future incursions into our space are unlikely to be indulged in similar fashion. Do I make myself clear?"

"Commander . . ." Bochir began, and Larael forced himself not to react to the centurion's questioning tone. A simple glimpse was enough to silence the subordinate.

On the viewscreen, Wesley nodded. *"You do, Commander. I appreciate your trust, and you have my word that it's not misplaced. Safe journey to you and your crew. Wesley out."* The image on the screen dissolved into static before being replaced by a display of the Federation ships continuing on their way.

"Helm," Larael said, "mirror their course and speed, but maintain this distance. Place weapons on standby." Turning to Bochir, he kept his voice low and steady as he regarded the younger officer with a hard glare. "Now, Centurion, what is it you wished to tell me?"

Bochir had the good sense to appear nervous as he replied,

"Commander, our orders are to protect the Empire's borders. How can our commitment to security be respected by our enemies if we do not answer their defiance with force?"

"Soldiers do not attack indiscriminately, Centurion," Larael said, allowing the merest hint of annoyance to creep into his voice. "The Federation ship was a match for us, and yet they did not raise their shields or bring their weapons to bear. They were at our mercy. I do not attack unarmed vessels, at least not until I have confirmed they are a threat. To do otherwise is to act no better than lawless thugs, and we hold ourselves to a higher standard. Do you understand?"

Nodding, Bochir replied, "I do, sir." He paused, as though weighing the potential risks of what he might say next, before adding, "I only hope that our enemies do not mistake your compassion for Romulan weakness."

The young officer had courage, Larael gave him that. Of course, being the son of a prominent senator tended to enhance one's self-confidence, whether or not such feelings were justified. Larael supposed he should be wary of how he treated Bochir, knowing full well that any dissatisfaction would inevitably be relayed back to Romulus and his father's sympathetic ear. The notion was as quickly dismissed. After nearly thirty *fvheisn* spent in service to the Empire, Larael had long since tired of looking over his shoulder and worrying how the wrong action or spoken thought might be viewed by those in power. He simply was too old for such games.

Still, he was forced to admit that young Bochir had made a valid observation. With encounters between Federation and Romulan ships increasing as both powers continued to expand into previously unexplored space, it was only a matter of time before a more violent confrontation resulted. The Empire would be forced to act, lest it find itself trapped within its borders and at the mercy of its rivals.

And on that day, will we once again find ourselves at war?

Larael took no comfort in knowing the answer to that question.

2

As it always seemed to be these days, at least so far as Proconsul Toqel could tell, the Senate was a hive of agitation.

Even before the towering, heavy doors to the chamber opened to allow her entry, the sounds of heated debate carried to Toqel's ears. No less than five senators, she judged, were talking at rapid pace over and around each other. None of them seemed content to pause for the shortest interval in order to comprehend or even acknowledge what their peers were saying. This sort of discourse had dominated the past several sessions, and not for the first time, Toqel frowned in private disapproval. Accounts of such decorum, should they travel beyond the confines of the Senate and to the citizenry of Dartha, would almost certainly instill at least some uncertainty within the very fabric of Romulus's capital city. How could those in power expect to hold sway over the populace if they could not even comport themselves with some small shred of discipline?

Is this how it was prior to our last war with Earth and its allies?

The question taunted Toqel as the massive doors opened and she, along with her assistant, Vice Proconsul Ditrius, stepped into the grand hall that was the Senate chamber. Once inside, she could not resist a moment's distraction as she took in the room's dignified splendor. Marble columns rose from the granite tile of the debate floor to support the translucent domed ceiling, through which the filtered light of the morning sun illuminated the gold and silver embellishments of elegant tapestries hanging around the room's perimeter. For generations, this chamber had been a focal point for some of the Empire's greatest minds and most fervent defenders. Many of the historic decisions and policies that had guided the Empire through prosperity as well as adversity had been born here. It was, Toqel believed, an almost divine place, worthy of solemn, unwavering respect.

Unfortunately, that grandeur was, in her opinion, spoiled by the unshielded, raucous dialogue that seemed poised to consume the storied hall. Seated at their ornate, ceremonial desks situated atop the raised dais that dominated the room's northern wall, most of the senators, along with Praetor Vrax himself, listened as Levok, one of the Senate's longest-serving and most accomplished members, stood before them on the debate floor. Stepping farther into the room, Toqel realized she and Ditrius were just in time to watch the veteran senator in the middle of yet another of his famed dramatic tirades.

"How much longer will we stand idle as our enemies intrude open our territory all but unchallenged? How many more incursions will we allow before one of their vessels finally reaches a vital target?" With what Toqel recognized as a practiced bit of zealous flair, Levok pointed toward the chamber's debate floor. Inlaid into the tiles was an elaborate star map representing the area of space claimed by the Romulan Star Empire, along with the border separating it from the United Federation of Planets. "How long after that until our enemy finally gathers the courage to cross the Neutral Zone and launch an all-out offensive? My friends, hear me well: The longer we wait to put the humans in their place, the weaker we will appear."

Seated at her desk on the dais, Senator Anitra said, "We know that the Federation has made their own significant technological advances since the war. That much has already been made quite obvious, just based on our most recent encounters with Starfleet vessels. It's quite possible that they are already more formidable an adversary than we are prepared to face."

Hushed murmurs filtered through the room, and Toqel watched as a few of the senators bowed their heads toward one another, exchanging remarks that were inaudible to her. Though younger than most of her colleagues, Anitra had in a relatively short period of time positioned herself as one of the Senate's most vocal, formidable members. She had garnered a reputation for holding no fears or reservations so far as conflicts with neighboring interstellar powers were concerned, though she almost always championed a deliberate, pragmatic approach to such matters. Indeed, working with Levok on several initiatives since her election to the Senate had allowed the two of them to forge an impressive tandem, with her providing reasoned counterbalance to Levok's more reactionary views and statements.

And, as it often had in the past, Toqel knew, the tactic once again was proving successful. Despite the seeming paranoia lacing the esteemed senators' words, the views held by Levok and Anitra were shared by several of their colleagues. Even the Praetor himself placed credence in at least some of what currently was being espoused, though he often presented a tempered response to the more inflammatory opinions.

"There is another facet to this situation that must not be overlooked," Levok said, his attention still focused on the Praetor and the other senators. "For some time, we have watched as the Federation and the Klingon Empire continue their efforts at extending their respective grips on the galaxy. Left unchecked, this growth may well result in our being surrounded by our enemies and at their mercy. While the Federation would entertain negotiations, I certainly do not believe the same to be true of the Klingons."

Sitting to the Praetor's left, Senator D'tran cleared his throat, shifting in his seat as he straightened his stooped posture. "While I might agree with your assessment of the Klingons, Levok, much of the public outcry about Federation expansion would seem to be misplaced. Let us be honest here. In all our dealings with the humans, have they ever shown a propensity for *initiating* hostile action?" D'tran's voice was subdued and gruff, owing to his extreme age. By far the oldest member of the Senate, he had always been a voice of wisdom and restraint even during the most tumultuous of debates. Toqel knew that his views on the Federation came with the credibility of direct, firsthand knowledge; as a younger man, while serving as an officer aboard a warship, D'tran had been one of the first Romulans ever to encounter people from Earth. As time passed, and given the overall lack of substantial information, D'tran and a few other individuals effectively had become the only real experts on humans, their worlds, and their culture. It was a distinction the elder senator had solidified thanks to his recent diplomatic work not only with the Federation but also the Klingon Empire.

Bowing his head in deference to the veteran senator, Levok replied, "You are correct, D'tran. However, is it not reasonable to assume that in response to our own reconnaissance missions into their space, the Federation has decided that more direct action is in order? It's likely that they remain as uninformed about us as we were about them. This might explain the rise of invasive incursions into our territory, yes?"

"Of course it might," said Ditrius from where he stood to Toqel's immediate left, his voice nearly inaudible.

"Silence," Toqel said, chastising her assistant in a hushed whisper as her eyes scanned the senators to see if anyone else had overheard the ill-considered remark. It had not been the first time she was forced to remind Ditrius of his place, particularly when in the presence of the Senate, to say nothing of the Praetor himself. The vice proconsul was an ambitious officer, hungry for advancement and at times careless in word or deed. Toqel had found that mentoring her young protégé was but one more full-time facet of the already demanding set of official duties entrusted to her. Without that guidance, she was sure Ditrius would one day say or do something that would set him at odds with a superior, and that would be the end of his brief, albeit impressive career.

Tread softly, my determined young friend.

Despite her disapproval of Ditrius's momentary loss of military bearing, Toqel released a small sigh, hard-pressed to disagree with his rash assessment. An effective and persuasive speaker, Senator Levok nevertheless was prone to stating the glaringly obvious, even if he tended to do so in grandiose fashion.

Though she was certain she had caught herself from reacting any further to Levok's remarks and instead succeeded in maintaining her bearing, Toqel straightened her rigid posture when she realized that Praetor Vrax was looking past the senator and directly at her. Seated in his chair at the center of the raised dais, the elderly leader seemed to smile—if ever so slightly—as their eyes met, and he raised his hand, indicating her with a wave.

"Proconsul Toqel," he said, his voice low and feeble. "Please, you and Ditrius, join us."

Toqel felt her stomach tighten as she withstood Vrax's measured gaze, which seemed at odds with the calm, genial manner in which he addressed her. A casual observer might wonder if her reaction, fleeting though it might have been, had angered the Praetor, but Toqel knew better. Indeed, she was no stranger to his personality, having seen it firsthand all her life thanks to her late father's association with him, which dated back to Vrax's often tumultuous career as a senator. Despite his public persona and the cloak of mystery and even fear that came with the Empire's highest office, Vrax had always fostered an air of spirited, diverse debate within the confines of the Senate chamber, even from appointed military representatives such as Toqel herself.

"My Praetor," she said as she and Ditrius stepped to the edge of the dais, offering a formal bow as she observed the stringent, traditional protocols. "How may I be of service?"

His left hand toying with the polished wooden cane that had all but become an extension of his body as he inexorably succumbed to advancing age, Vrax regarded her with that subtle, amused expression Toqel had come to know all too well. "What is your assessment of this issue, which has consumed so much of the Senate's time in recent days?"

Toqel clasped her hands behind her back before replying, "As I'm sure Senator D'tran will attest, the Federation has never shown a propensity for attempts at peaceful negotiation while simultaneously employing tactics of deception and betrayal. It's possible, even likely, that espionage is being conducted, but at this time I suspect it's of a limited nature. Whether any such clandestine activities continue or escalate will almost certainly be dictated by the outcome of various diplomatic initiatives currently under way."

The most prominent of such overtures had only recently been set into motion, thanks to the efforts of Senator D'tran. Through means Toqel still did not quite understand, D'tran had been in contact with a Federation ambassador, who had convinced the aged senator that some form of aggressive diplomatic communication was required if the interstellar neighbors were ever to secure lasting peace. Responding in his normal, unconventional manner, D'tran had left Romulus on a personal mission, eventually meeting with the Federation envoy with whom he had been corresponding as well as an ambassadorial representative from the Klingon Empire. Together, the three politicians had forged the beginnings of an agreement to establish a joint colony on the third planet of the Nimbus system, located within the Neutral Zone separating Federation and Romulan space. As presented to the Praetor and the rest of the Senate by D'tran, the settlement was intended to demonstrate that the disparate governments could work together and reap benefits from such willing collaboration. Even now, a Romulan diplomatic cadre, as well as a group of scientists and colonists, was preparing for transport to the arid world that had been chosen for the historic, if atypical, endeavor.

Toqel had her doubts that the venture would succeed; however, she had chosen to keep such opinions to herself.

Leaning forward in his chair, Vrax said, "With all of this in mind, I'm confident that you've given the matter sufficient thought to formulate an approach that will serve us in the event these various high-minded undertakings should prove less than successful?"

"Indeed I have, my Praetor," Toqel replied, stifling an urge to smile. She already had discussed this matter in his private chambers, soon after her promotion to Senate proconsul in the wake of her successor's retirement from military service. It was during this privileged conversation that Vrax had given her authorization to conduct further analysis to determine the feasibility of the plan she would now explain. While she had yet to make significant progress, the Praetor had decided that the time was right to present her ideas to the Senate for consideration. "Though we have agreed to meet with the Federation and the Klingons in an attempt to broach a peaceful accord, prudence demands that we continue to ready ourselves in the event such efforts fail."

As she spoke, Toqel moved from where she stood before the dais, pacing from side to side and crossing before the assemblage of senators, making eye contact with each member of her audience. "Extended analysis of both Starfleet and Klingon starships indicates that from a tactical standpoint, we are at best evenly matched. Our cloaking technology gives us some advantage, but as we have seen from recent and costly examples, it is not a full-proof measure. Despite our advances, the technology must be further improved."

"It's my understanding," Levok said from where he had resumed his seat on the dais, "that a new generation of the cloaking technology is currently in development."

Toqel nodded. "Quite correct, Senator. However, our studies have shown that in order for the cloak to achieve true stealth, the new prototype requires more power than can be generated by the majority of our vessels. New classes of ships are also being designed and a few are even under construction, but a test craft will not be ready for some time."

The last words caught in her throat, but Toqel was able to maintain her composure even as she thought once more of her daughter, Sarith, who had commanded one of the very vessels that had proven inadequate to the task of providing for its cloaking device's demanding power requirements. Her ship, the *Bloodied Talon,* had been dispatched to a distant region of space known as the Taurus Reach, in which the Federation had taken an unusual interest. Sarith and her crew had been ordered to determine what had attracted such attention, not only by Starfleet but also the Klingons and the Tholian Assembly. In the midst of its investigation, the *Talon* had suffered massive damage after being caught in the shock wave of a planet destroyed by a heretofore unknown weapon, the nature of which remained the subject of much consternation within and beyond the boundaries of the Romulan Empire. Adrift in space and with no reasonable hope of rescue, Sarith had eventually been forced to destroy her own ship once it became obvious that its presence had been detected by a Klingon battle cruiser.

Might she and her crew have avoided that fate? Toqel had pondered that question more than once, wondering perhaps if Sarith and her crew could have found a way to survive until rescue arrived, had the *Bloodied Talon* been equipped with a more efficient cloaking device. As a military liaison to the Senate, Toqel had always been committed to using her influence as a means of seeing that those who served the Praetor in uniform were provided the proper resources to ensure the safety and security of the Romulan people. In the time since her daughter's death, her resolve had only strengthened in this regard.

Despite her convictions, Toqel knew that the Senate's more

conservative members would likely view her next words and the ideas they conveyed as controversial, to say the least. Glancing to Vrax for affirmation, she saw the Praetor offer a slight nod for her to continue

"The truth of the matter is that while the Klingon Empire may well prove to be the more formidable enemy, besting them yields no tangible long-range results. We all know that their warrior ethos demands that they subvert weaker enemies to their rule, but the harsh reality is that the Klingons pursue their program of subjugation simply to survive." It was common knowledge that the space currently controlled by the Klingons was lacking in planets with sufficient natural resources to sustain enduring growth, and their efforts at expansion had been hampered by the Federation. As with the Romulan Empire, the Klingons also faced the prospect of having to combat the Federation as both sides continued to move toward the denser regions of the galaxy, where allies and resources awaited whoever should make it there first.

D'tran held his hand to his mouth in order to stifle a raspy cough before asking, "You're suggesting the Klingons may have more in common with than the Federation, and less reason to fight us if we were to reach some form of agreement?"

"Not simply an agreement, Senator," Toqel replied, unable to keep a slight hint of satisfaction from creeping into her voice. She then smiled, if only slightly. "I'm proposing an alliance. According to data obtained by spies we've placed within the Empire, their newest class of battle cruiser is capable of meeting the power requirements for our new model of cloaking field generator. If a pact can be reached, we might avail ourselves of such vessels, at least long enough to study them and use that knowledge to design ships to meet our own needs."

"Why would the Klingons enter into such a pact?" Senator Anitra countered, her expression one of undisguised skepticism. "What do they gain from it?"

Before Toqel could reply, Ditrius interceded. "We will of course have to offer something of value to them, Senator. It may be something as simple as unobstructed passage through our space to an area they wish to explore for potential conquest. They may well want access to our cloaking technology."

"We have not yet refined this part of our proposal," Toqel said, suppressing the urge to rebuke the vice proconsul for his brash interjection in front of the Praetor and the Senate. "But these are Klingons, after all. Surely we are capable of standing up to them at the negotiating table?"

"Take care, Proconsul, that you don't underestimate our enemy," Levok said, making no effort to hide his disapproval at what he was hearing. "Such thinking led to our defeat at the hands of the humans during the war. By sharing such a major tactical advantage with a sworn enemy, what does this mean for the security of Romulan territory and interests? The Klingons are conquerors, not collaborators. It is what they've always been. Mark my words, Proconsul; time and history will bear this out."

"Despite the generally constructive nature of my meeting with the Klingon ambassador on Nimbus III," D'tran offered, "I am forced to agree with you, Levok. That said, perhaps there is an opportunity here for us to gain even a temporary advantage, which we can then exploit for further, lasting value." Turning to Vrax, he added, "My Praetor, you know my stance with regard to the Federation. While I believe there is potential to build an enduring peace, I do not expect it will happen in our lifetimes. There simply is too much resentment and distrust on both sides to be ignored. With that in mind, it is in our best interests to continue developing effective measures should we find ourselves once again on a war footing with our old adversaries."

Vrax nodded toward his old friend. "Agreed, and now seems the perfect time to test the goodwill fostered by your efforts at Nimbus III." To Toqel, he said, "Very well, Proconsul. Let's see where this curious notion of yours takes us."

As the other senators nodded and spoke to one another in subdued tones, Toqel was able to sense their general agreement. Some of that consensus naturally was offered with no small measure of hesitation or doubt, but Toqel would not concern herself with such negativity. She had all the approval she required.

Once more standing before Vrax, Toqel bowed as she took her leave. "Understood. Good day, my Praetor." Nodding to Ditrius for him to accompany her, the two of them departed the Senate chamber. As she exited the room, she was unable to suppress the rush of anticipation she felt as her mind began reviewing and refining the next steps she already had plotted days earlier. Unusual though it might be, her proposal stood poised to solidify the security of the Romulan people.

"You are not worried about dealing with the Klingons?" Ditrius asked once they had emerged into the hallway and allowed the doors to close behind them. Not for the first time since she had shared her ideas with him, the vice proconsul sounded skeptical.

Toqel replied, "To a point. However, they've repeatedly shown themselves incapable of employing anything resembling an adequate grasp of subterfuge, which lies at the heart of all successful negotiations. It is this weakness that we will exploit, Ditrius. Once the Klingons no longer are a viable concern, I will be ready to show the Senate how best to deal with the Federation, once and for all."

And if, along the way, she was able to do something that might at least reduce the chances of another's child suffering the same fate as her beloved Sarith, that also would be satisfactory.

3

Toqel inhaled crisp, cold air as the transporter beam released her. A low, steady wind rocked the barren branches of the trees towering overhead as she squinted against sunlight reflecting from the snow-covered ground. She shoved her bare hands into the deep pockets of her protective thermal coat, blinking as minuscule pellets of ice carried by the wind prickled her cheeks. Turning to Ditrius, she asked in a low voice, "Readings?"

The vice proconsul removed a handheld scanner from the pocket of his own heavy coat. His boots crunching in the ice-coated snow pack, he stepped toward her as he studied the portable device's display readout. "Two Klingon life-forms, located inside that structure." He gestured with his free hand toward a small, one-story building nestled among the trees. White smoke curled from a chimney on one side of the weathered, stone-walled cabin, and Toqel was able to make out two sets of footprints through the snow, both of which terminated at the cabin's only visible door.

She nodded in approval. "Just as we agreed. Anything else?"

"Nothing," Ditrius replied. "With the exception of indigenous animal life, we are alone here, Proconsul."

Excellent, Toqel mused. Given the evening's agenda, privacy would most certainly be preferred. "Then let's proceed," she said as she started toward the cabin.

The soles of their boots punched through the slick crust of the snow, white powder coating the leggings of their thermal trousers as they approached the building. Toqel could not recall the last time she had found herself in such weather conditions, as she rarely left her home planet and her travels into the subarctic regions of Romulus were infrequent at best. She would have preferred this first clandestine meeting be held elsewhere, but after weeks of negotiations conducted via encrypted subspace communications, Grodak, her Klingon counterpart for tonight's activities, had been immovable as to the choice of location. It would be held here, at Grodak's remote residence deep in the forests of Narendra III, a Klingon colony planet located near the Romulan border, or not at all. Toqel finally had relented, deciding she could endure the world's inhospitable climate if it facilitated matters with the reclusive Klingon official.

Despite her best efforts, she had been unable to collect much in the way of meaningful information about Grodak. His name had been given to her by D'tran himself, and according to the senator he was a minor official within whatever association of worn-out or failed warriors passed for a diplomatic corps so far as Klingons were concerned. His military career was undistinguished, and his service as a politician appeared to carry no distinction among his peers. If not for D'tran's recommendation, Toqel would have believed that Grodak carried nothing approaching the influence needed among actual decision-makers to make him worth her effort.

We shall soon see if D'tran's judgment remains untarnished.

Drawing closer to the cabin, Toqel could now hear bursts of raucous laughter amid pseudo-melodic shrieks and stringed musical instruments that grew louder as they approached. She looked over her shoulder at Ditrius.

"Is someone in pain?" she asked.

"It's Klingon music," the vice proconsul replied, shaking his head. "If Circassian plague cats could sing, they too would find such disharmony most unpleasant."

Bracing herself for the coming auditory onslaught, Toqel proceeded to the cabin's only apparent entrance. The door was constructed of heavy wooden planks cross-braced with metal bands, and once Ditrius stood beside her, she pounded loudly upon it with her fist.

"nuqneH!" A gruff voice she thought she recognized as Grodak's called over the music, which quickly decreased in volume.

Toqel understood the Klingon greeting and grasped the door's metal handle, feeling its sharp chill against her bare hand. Pushing the door open, Toqel felt a rush of heated air against her face.

"Proconsul Toqel, I presume?" bellowed a portly Klingon with short-cropped graying hair and a matching beard as he rose from his seat at a rather expansive wooden dining table. "Welcome to my humble domicile." Grodak waddled toward them, illuminated only by an oil lamp on the table as well as the flames of a fireplace along the cabin's far wall. Stepping through the doorway, Toqel schooled her features so as not to display her reaction as her nose detected a displeasing combination of old grease, wood rot, and Klingon sweat polluting the air inside the cabin.

"Thank you for inviting us into your home," Toqel said, making an earnest attempt at sincerity as she stepped aside and allowed Ditrius to enter. This was the Klingon who could obtain what she sought? He seemed ill-equipped to carry out any action that did not involve lifting food to his face. A quick glance at Ditrius told her that the vice proconsul was harboring similar thoughts, but he fortunately had elected to keep his doubts and any related observations to himself.

Gesturing toward the table and indicating the other chairs situated around it, Grodak replied, "Merely my home away from home, if you will. I come here to hunt, and to rediscover what it means to be a true warrior."

"I see," Toqel said, masking her lack of interest.

Grodak laughed, clapping his hand on Ditrius's shoulder as they gathered around the table. "Perhaps you understand," he said. "The need to hunt alone and kill to survive. You against the world."

"Indeed, sir," Ditrius said, his near-mocking tone prompting a quick scowl from Toqel. The vice proconsul offered a slight nod in return, communicating that he comprehended her desire to temper his responses.

Detecting movement from the corner of her eye, Toqel turned to see another Klingon, this one decidedly younger and more physically fit than Grodak. He emerged through a doorway, beyond which Toqel saw the familiar trappings of a lavatory. A most unwelcome odor assailed her nostrils, and she once more forced herself not to wince.

"Kopok," Grodak called to the other Klingon, "the cold appears to disagree with our guests. Bring something to warm their bones."

"That's hardly necessary," Toqel said, her eyes widening as Kopok moved to the fireplace and retrieved a large metal bowl. Wondering idly if the Klingon had even bothered to wash his hands prior to exiting the lavatory, she watched him lower the bowl into a small cauldron suspended over the flames, lifting it away as chunks of some unidentified substance smeared paths down its sides and onto the floor. He repeated the move with a second bowl before turning and walking to the table, upon which he unceremoniously sloshed portions of the concoction onto its pitted, stained surface.

"We have serious business to discuss this evening," Grodak said, offering a wide smile, "and it simply wouldn't do for you to begin with such a disadvantage." Toqel paused, holding her response long enough that the Klingon seemingly recognized she might be considering his choice of words. "I mean, *we've* already eaten."

"Ah," Toqel said, examining the bowl before her and its unappetizing mixture of what appeared to be brown animal flesh and orange vegetables stewed in a thick, grayish stock. "We are here to discuss our proposition, not impose upon your . . . hospitality."

"You eat. Then we talk," he said, his voice less jovial and more insistent. "I did not demand that you cross the Neutral Zone or risk my superiors' discovery of our new friendship just to kill you with my cooking. You honor me when you share a meal in my home." To emphasize his point, Grodak leaned over the table and plunged two fingers into her bowl. Toqel forced herself not to recoil as he hoisted several dripping chunks from the bowl and stuck his fingers into his mouth. Loudly smacking his lips on the morsels, he wiped a line of gray gravy from his bearded chin and lowered his hand out of view, seemingly to rub it against his pants leg.

"That was hardly necessary," Toqel said. "I trust you when you say you have not poisoned this food." In truth, she had considered the possibility, though she found herself forced to agree with the Klingon's dismissal of the notion.

Grodak laughed. "Then eat." He offered a mischievous grin as he repeated his two-fingered scooping gesture. "You'll never have to prove your courage in any other way."

Seated to her right, Ditrius refrained from mimicking the Klingon's method, opting instead for the large spoon resting on the table next to his bowl. Using the oversized implement, he sampled his meal before leaning back in his chair and regarding her with a bemused expression.

"I am not certain, Proconsul, but I believe the addition of a nerve toxin might well enhance the flavor."

Throwing back his head, Grodak released a laugh so boisterous that Toqel was certain the cabin's windows might shatter. "Well played, Romulan. I appreciate a sense of humor."

Shrugging, Toqel brandished her own spoon. If Ditrius could stomach the foul brew, so too could she. She retrieved a portion of the stew and brought it to her mouth, ignoring the unsavory odor as she chewed in a controlled manner. The gravy's slimy texture coated what tasted like vinegar-soaked roots and meat much spicier than she was used to eating. It took physical effort not to gag. How had Ditrius so easily managed his own reaction? The foul concoction tasted as though Grodak had attempted to duplicate *t'lea'checha,* but with ingredients long soured and spoiled. She finally was able to swallow, after which she realized she had no drink with which to cleanse her palate.

"Some bloodwine?" Grodak asked, offering a self-satisfied smirk.

Toqel shook her head. "Thank you, but no." It was obvious that the Klingon was playing with her, hoping to elicit reactions of disgust and perhaps even frustration. Unwilling to allow him even the smallest victory, Toqel continued to eat her meal as though nothing were amiss. "Shall we proceed with the purpose of our being here?" she asked before chewing on another mouthful of the mystery stew.

"Ah yes," Grodak replied, nodding. "This proposal of yours. You're serious."

"Completely. I also have the support of the Romulan Senate," Toqel said. Her statement was not altogether true, of course, but nor was it wholly a lie. She ate another spoonful of her meal. Was it her imagination, or was she getting used to it? "What about your people?"

Grodak released another bout of unrestrained laughter. "Do you believe for even a single moment that the High Council would respond to this outlandish fantasy of yours with anything other than disdain? Offer a sworn enemy access to some of our fleet's most powerful vessels?"

"Most powerful? Come now, Grodak, we both know that's not at all what I've proposed." Reaching for a stone carafe at the center of the table, Toqel peered inside and saw that it contained water. As there were no drinking vessels in plain view, she decided to play the Klingon's game and drank straight from the pitcher before handing it off to Ditrius, who repeated her technique. "I know that the Council as an entity would have to voice opposition to such a notion, but surely you know of at least *one* member with *some* authority who might see the benefit of what we propose. After all, I'm told you're someone of great influence."

Her words were having the desired effect, as Toqel watched Grodak frown, then emit a low grunt of irritation. He obviously was not someone accustomed to having his status questioned, which Toqel knew in Klingon circles might earn her a ritual challenge to the death.

"Perhaps," Grodak said after a moment, punctuating his reply with a long pull from his goblet of bloodwine.

Toqel nodded. "We know that development is under way for a new class of battle cruiser to replace the D7s you currently employ." Romulan intelligence agents working within Klingon territory had confirmed the effort to design and construct a test flotilla of twelve new ships, named *K't'inga* class by her creators, which eventually would replace the stalwart D7 class of cruisers within ten *fvheisn*. This naturally troubled higher officials within the Romulan government, but Toqel saw it merely as another opportunity. After all, the Klingons would not be so quick to deploy their new warships against Romulan targets if it could be decided that the two powers had a mutual enemy in the Federation, and even more reason to pool their resources and their efforts.

Focus, she reminded herself. *Those are not your concerns now.*

His eyebrows twitching as he regarded her, Grodak replied, "I do not have access to information on military developments such as those you suggest." Shifting forward in his chair, he leaned his large, flabby arms on the table, and Toqel noted that his left sleeve tracked through whatever sauce he had used to dress the meat on his plate. "Even so, D7 battle cruisers remain superior in every regard to the vessels you possess."

Toqel shrugged. "Offensively, you have some minor advantages. Upon that much, we can agree, but defensively? Our cloaking devices give us the tactical edge."

"*va!*" Grodak sneered and held up the palm of his hand to her. "Cloaks are for cowards and *taHqeqmey*. No commander with the slightest shred of honor would ever allow the installation of such a loathsome construct aboard his ship."

Instead of replying, Toqel turned her attention to the remainder of her meal. By the time she was skimming the sides of the bowl with her spoon, Grodak was studying her with an expression of both grudging respect and anticipation at whatever she might say next.

Now, she thought as she pushed aside the empty bowl, *if only it will stay down.* As she reached once more for the carafe, she saw the expectant look on Ditrius's face. Knowing that Grodak was again trying to bait her and curious as to what the vice proconsul might add at this juncture, she nodded for Ditrius to proceed.

"Grodak," he said, setting his spoon down on the table and folding his hands before him, "we have no wish to impugn the honor of any Klingon warrior. However, would such formidable commanders not want to study the technology, perhaps in the hope of gaining some measure of tactical advantage? If not how best to utilize the field aboard his own vessel, then at least how to go about penetrating a cloak being employed by an enemy ship?"

"We can already do that," Grodak replied, waving the words aside with a nonchalant brush of his hand and appearing pleased with himself for revealing that bit of information.

Toqel leaned forward, glaring at the Klingon. "Yes, we know the limitations of our technology, but that will soon be resolved." Of course, telling him that such a resolution might entail the use of Klingon vessels, at least until such time as a Romulan vessel of comparable power completed construction, was neither an option nor a sound negotiating strategy.

"Perhaps that's true," Grodak replied, reaching up to stroke his beard. "Shall we be honest here, my friend?"

"I have endeavored to do so from the beginning," Toqel replied without a moment's hesitation. After all, lying came so very effortlessly to politicians. Scrutinizing his face with a practiced ease, she decided that he was the sort who could be persuaded to offer up more information than might be considered wise in discussions such as this, owing to nothing more than a desire to be perceived as important or powerful. Grodak did not strike her as one to act in such a manner without sufficient coaxing, but for the first time since her arrival, Toqel was sensing that she finally was beginning to take charge of the situation.

"As you've probably guessed," Grodak said after a moment, "I have indeed spoken of this to members of the High Council, and as I suspected would happen, their initial reaction was to dismiss the idea as coming from the drink-addled mind of a broken warrior. However, I was able to bring them around after much convincing. They put their trust in me because I have never failed to deliver on my promises, and I now put my trust in you, Toqel."

"I understand," Toqel replied, forcing down rising anticipation at what the Klingon might reveal now that a rapport seemed to have been established.

"There are those on the Council who welcome this alliance," the Klingon said, "precisely for the reasons you believe would appeal to them. They see uses for this cloaking technology, even though they know it will meet resistance from hard-line followers of the old ways. Still, not every Klingon follows the ways of Kahless or, at the very least, not all of his teachings. Others are content to reinterpret his words to suit their own ends." He paused as though lost in thought before waving his free hand in the air. "None of that is your concern, Romulan. Suffice it to say that there is interest in an exchange of technology, including your cloaking field. However, if you were to offer something that better fits Klingon sensibilities—tactical sensors or weapons advances, for example—such cooperation might very well sway the negotiations in favor of this alliance."

"Interesting," Toqel said, feigning surprise even though this was the sort of counteroffer she had expected from the outset. "And if you were able to report that your initial refusal to discuss this venture led to my offering this additional information, as though it were a show of good faith and the Romulan Empire's commitment to ensuring the success of our partnership . . ."

Grodak nodded with no small amount of enthusiasm. "Well, that would certainly make this seem like an opportunity we would be shortsighted to ignore."

Rising from her seat, Toqel nodded. "Then it would seem we have an arrangement. Shall I expect terms of this agreement in your next transmission?" She paused, looking around the room. "Or should I plan for another clandestine meeting, perhaps this time at a location of my choosing?"

"No need for that," Grodak said, smiling. "I called you here because I prefer to see my allies as well as my enemies face-to-face. It's far easier to gauge them when you can look directly into their eyes." As though unable to resist one last attempt at riling her, he added, "It is something only a warrior would understand."

"My loss, then," Toqel said, keeping her expression neutral and resisting the urge to laugh in his face. Turning to Ditrius, she instructed him to contact their transport ship, which still orbited Narendra III, before returning her attention to the Klingon. "The path we start down today may well lead to lasting change for both of our peoples, Grodak, to say nothing of the positions we hold in the galaxy."

"It will be glorious," Grodak said, his wide grin exposing his jagged, yellow teeth.

What a trusting fool you are, Toqel thought, feeling her vessel's transporter beam beginning to envelop her. If more Klingons had shared such bad judgment, their empire might have fallen to Romulan rule generations ago.

All in good time.

4

Holding the cup to her nose, Toqel settled into her chair and released a contented sigh as she allowed the tea's aroma to tickle her nostrils. She had savored this particular blend since childhood, having inherited a taste for it from her mother and her grandfather. She had attempted without success to pass on her love of the beverage to Sarith, but her daughter had always preferred a more potent variety. During her offspring's tumultuous youth, Toqel had on many occasions and with great amusement wondered if Sarith's choice of tea might have been yet another means of rebelling against her mother.

She did inherit her headstrong nature from you, after all.

As she gazed out the window of her office in the main Senate complex and over Dartha's sprawling cityscape, Toqel caught her reflection in the glass and realized that she had been smiling at the fleeting memory of her daughter. Rather than allowing her thoughts to turn to regret and grief, she instead cherished those happier times, enjoying them as a respite from the stresses of the two *khaidoa* that had passed since putting her plan into motion.

She was tired, yet satisfied. There had been much to accomplish, and little time in which to do it. The challenges of keeping veiled in secrecy an effort of the scope she currently oversaw were numerous. Still, the people under her command had performed with distinction, meeting or exceeding every deadline she had set. In time, she hoped to reward her teams' accomplishments and validate their efforts in the eyes of the Senate and others who doubted the ideas she had put forth.

Soon, she decided, catching once more her smile reflected in the window.

A chime alerted her to someone outside her office. Turning to her desk, Toqel reached for a control panel embedded in its surface and pressed a button, unlocking the door and allowing it to slide open. Standing at the threshold was Ditrius, carrying a portable computer interface pad in his left hand.

"Ditrius," she said as the vice proconsul entered the office and approached her desk. It was well before the start of the day's Senate sessions, but her aide had been assigned many of Toqel's normal duties while she concentrated on her current tasks. To his credit, Ditrius had accepted the additional responsibilities without complaint and performed admirably in his expanded role. "What brings you here at this early hour?"

Holding up the handheld pad, he replied, "The latest testing status reports. So far, the retrofitting of cloaking generators aboard the six ships is more or less on schedule. There have been some difficulties, owing mostly to various compatibility issues with respect to different onboard systems." He paused, tapping on the handheld and consulting the reports before adding, "The design itself does not appear to be at issue, but each of the ships has been subjected to overhauls, refits, and other post-construction modifications that all have to be taken into account. There's also the fact that much of a Klingon ship's power generation and routing systems are designed for maximum effectiveness of weapons and defenses."

Toqel nodded, already quite aware of the issues. "Our engineers have done excellent work navigating these obstacles." The progress reports she had read were quite impressive. Most of the installation work had already been performed on one of the six vessels, the *I.K.S. Kretoq,* and the battle cruiser had served as a test bed for working out problems with the modifications before proceeding to the other ships. So far, tests of the field generator installed aboard the *Kretoq* had exceeded expectations. Not only was the cloak more effective at masking the vessel from outside detection, the generator itself operated at a level of energy efficiency that was several percentage points higher than engineers had estimated. Apparently, the disparate aspects of the two empires' technologies possessed some benefits as well as challenges.

"And what of our information exchange with the Klingons?" Toqel asked. "I trust Grodak is satisfied with that aspect of our new partnership?"

Grunting in what to her ears sounded like mild amusement, Ditrius replied, "According to him, engineers are already poring over the technical schematics for the cloaking generator, as well as the prototype we provided." He paused, uttering a small, almost mischievous chuckle. "They will spend *khaidoa* learning to understand it all, even with our able assistance."

What Toqel had naturally not shared with Grodak and his compatriots was the simple fact that the provided schematics were for the older, less effective version of the cloaking generator. The technical information she had given him—both for the cloak as well as a few weapons systems—had been modified so as to appear to be the product of more recent developments. Klingon vessels operating with such technology could still be tracked, albeit with proper scanning equipment operated by technicians who understood what they were seeking. It was a minor deception, Toqel knew, and one likely to be discovered, but probably not for some time, and by then it would not matter.

"Given the favorable progress with the *Kretoq,*" she said after a moment, "it may almost be time to proceed with next phase of the project." Once modifications were completed on the *Kretoq* and the other five vessels, her plan was to deploy them on trial runs into both Klingon and Federation space. After a series of seek-and-destroy exercises with a handpicked cadre of Romulan ships and tested commanders, Toqel would conduct similar war game scenarios with Klingon vessels reporting to Grodak. The true challenges would come after that, when the new ships were tested against the formidable scanning and detection capabilities of Starfleet outposts and starships stationed near the Neutral Zone.

Tapping a key on the handheld pad, Ditrius looked up from the device. "Our latest intelligence reports show the current positions of observation outposts along the Federation border, and recent patrol patterns of their vessels moving through the region. We will soon have a comprehensive analysis of traffic patterns and sensor coverage that will assist in preparing navigational data for the tests."

"Excellent," Toqel replied, nodding in approval. "I'll want any route we use to take us through Klingon space." She smiled. "If Federation sensors do detect our passage, it will give them something unexpected to worry about." While this new partnership was by no means politically entwining, the idea of a technological exchange between two of the major military powers in the sector would certainly merit the interest of the Federation. They would then spend inordinate amounts of time contemplating the ramifications of a Romulan-Klingon alliance.

"Praetor Vrax and the Senate have received some new information," Ditrius said, his attention once more on his pad, "which may impact our schedule. It seems Starfleet has been busy again." Reaching across her desk, he offered her the handheld device, which she took and turned in order to read its display.

"Mav'renas," she read aloud.

"What the humans call Theta Cobrini," Ditrius replied. "It's a rather unimpressive system located on the fringe of the Avastam."

Toqel was familiar with that area: a region of space wedged between the borders of Romulan, Klingon, and Federation territory. The Avastam itself contained few planets of worth to any of the major powers, though Orion pirates and other parties used the region to conduct all manner of business, legitimate and otherwise.

Scanning the data Ditrius had provided, Toqel reached up to rub the bridge of her nose. "They are constructing a base in the Mav'renas system." The report contained computer-enhanced imagery captured by unmanned drones operating at the extreme limits of their sensors, and she called those up for study. Magnifying the images revealed unmistakable signs of construction on an impressive scale, likely the beginnings of a permanent installation with several sizable structures.

"Starfleet is known to build support facilities for its ships patrolling the fringes of their territory," she said, "so that in itself is not surprising." Pointing to one image, she attempted to enhance it, quickly exhausting the handheld's capabilities. "This structure, set away from the primary construction zone, appears to be a large-scale sensor array."

Ditrius nodded. "That is the assessment of the Tal Shiar," he said, and Toqel noted the way the vice proconsul's lips almost formed a sneer at the mention of the feared branch of the internal security division. "They do not think construction has been completed, but once operational, they believe it will offer unprecedented capability to monitor activity far into our territory. Their intelligence gathering ability would far exceed the levels they now enjoy."

"That would definitely present an issue," Toqel said, considering the ramifications of this new development.

"Politically, we have little recourse," Ditrius said. "Despite its proximity to the Avastam, Mav'renas does lie in Federation space." By mutual agreement reached the previous *fvheisn*, the Federation, Klingon, and Romulan governments had endorsed a policy of not installing any tactical assets within the border region, effectively rendering it a demilitarized zone. However, of the three major political entities, only the Federation contained a planetary system in close proximity to the Avastam that would support an operation such as the one seemingly under way.

"Regardless of its being in their territory," Toqel countered, "it will be viewed as an aggressive action. I suspect that installation's defenses and any sensor apparatus in operation there will be quite formidable."

Ditrius said nothing for a moment, but then his mouth curled into a knowing smile. "Quite a test for our new ships, I'd think."

"Indeed," Toqel replied, pleased with the vice proconsul's deduction.

She returned the pad to him, and Ditrius keyed another string of commands into the device before saying, "The system's location offers a vantage point to observe some Klingon space, as well, though it's obvious the installation's primary mission would be observing us."

"Still," Toqel said, "the Klingons may well find the presence of such a base as alarming as we do."

"Even the Klingons are not so foolhardy as to strike a target so clearly in enemy territory," Ditrius said. "At least, not without direct provocation. They would see no true advantage in such an action."

Clasping her hands before her, Toqel steepled her fingers and rested them under her chin. "We don't need the Klingons to strike the base. All we need are a few Klingon battle cruisers."

Ditrius widened his eyes as he processed the thought. "Attack the outpost ourselves, and let the Federation hold the Klingons responsible?" He paused, considering that notion. "What prevents the Klingons from redirecting the blame to us? They would almost certainly reveal our alliance, and cast doubt on their culpability."

"By then, it might not matter," Toqel replied. "It may well be enough to get the Federation and the Klingons bickering with one another across their border. With tensions heightened and their focus elsewhere, opportunities might arise for other parties not directly involved in the matter." Considering her words, Toqel knew the idea she had presented was not flawless. "Obviously it's not something that can be done in the short term, nor is it something that should be rushed. There are too many variables to consider before formulating a cohesive strategy." Indeed, such planning would require the best tactical minds the Romulan military had to offer, for a single attack as well as a coordinated campaign to face the likely response from both the Federation and the Klingon Empire.

Toqel would probably not be involved in such strategizing, which she found acceptable. Grand schemes of that sort had nothing to do with the mission she had levied upon herself, and her goal of finding ways to strengthen the fleet. What happened after that was beyond her influence and, ultimately, not her concern.

"What does Vrax want us to do?" she asked, dismissing the thoughts that seemed determined to affect her focus on the work still before her.

"Just as you've suggested," Ditrius replied. "Once you feel the test ships are ready, you are to take them to the Mav'renas system and investigate this new facility. He shares your belief that such an exercise is vital to determining the effectiveness of the new cloaking generators, and an unparalleled intelligence gathering opportunity. Imagine the surprise on the faces of the Federation Council when they learn our ships can assume orbit over their worlds and either scan or destroy them at the push of a button?"

Silence hung in the air between them for a moment. Her plan, which Toqel knew would require much consideration and refinement, was bold—one Sarith would have appreciated. Her daughter would not only have approved of such a daring scheme, but she also would have wanted to play an active role.

Perhaps I can make you as proud of me as I always was of you.

"Well," she said, forcing her thoughts back to the business at hand. She tried without much success to ignore the possibilities she now faced with regard to changing the course of Romulan history. "It seems we have much work to do."

Much work, indeed.

5

Captain Thomas Blair stepped from the turbolift and onto the bridge of the *U.S.S. Defiant,* pausing to allow the circulated air to cool his sweat-dampened skin. Wiping his face with the towel draped around his shoulders, he glared at the main viewscreen, upon which was displayed the now-familiar Alamedus asteroid field. The region had been the target of the *Defiant*'s survey assignment for the past two weeks, but the asteroids currently visible on the viewer, varying in size from meters to kilometers in diameter, were not his concern. Instead, it was the metallic, cylindrical object at the center of the screen that demanded his attention.

"What's the story?" Blair asked, nodding toward the viewer. Letting the towel fall back around his neck, he made his way around the upper deck toward the science station.

Rising from the command chair at the center of the bridge and turning to face him, Commander Kamau Mbugua eyed Blair and his exercise attire, which consisted of perspiration-dampened gray sweatpants and a matching shirt emblazoned with the *Defiant* insignia. "Apologies for disturbing you, sir, but I thought you needed to see this." The first officer was a large, imposing man of African descent, broad-shouldered and muscled beneath his gold uniform tunic and presenting the very epitome of physical fitness if ever Blair had seen such a specimen. Just looking at the younger, robust Mbugua caused Blair to recall the days when he too could take pride at being in top form.

That was twenty years and thirty pounds ago. Happy fiftieth birthday to you.

Indicating his state of dress with a dismissive wave, Blair reached to pat his midsection. "I already promised Doctor Hamilton that I'd make up the abdominal drills later." With a wry grin, he added, "Not that it won't stop her from denying me my slice of birthday cake and consigning me to dietary salads for the next month." Putting aside the pleasantries, he nodded toward the viewscreen. "What've we got?"

Nodding toward Lieutenant Commander Erin Sutherland, who stood waiting at the science station and holding a data slate at her side, Mbugua said, "You're on."

Sutherland pointed toward the viewscreen. "It's a communications buoy, sir. Older model, in common use until about ten years ago or so, mostly by civilian colony and freight-hauling ships. They turn up on secondary and black markets from time to time, as the internal components are useful in all sorts of other equipment. The crews on Orion ships in particular tend to like them." Pausing, the science officer reached up to brush away a lock of red hair that had fallen across her eyes. "We detected it about five minutes ago, sir, when it began broadcasting a transponder signal on a wide band."

"How long has it been here?" Blair asked.

Her eyes shifting to glance at Mbugua in an expression the captain realized was one of nervousness, Sutherland replied, "About five minutes, sir."

Blair frowned. "Come again?"

"There are no other ships or artificial constructs anywhere in the system, sir," Mbugua said, folding his arms across his chest. "No background radiation or electromagnetic fields interfering with sensors, either. The place is a graveyard, Skipper."

The captain nodded, already knowing this based on Sutherland's initial report on the Alamedus star system as well as the scant data collected by unmanned sensor probes more than a decade ago and culled from the *Defiant*'s library computer banks. A notable lack of properties that might impede the effectiveness of sensor equipment was one of the prime reasons Alamedus asteroids were receiving further scrutiny. If all went according to plan, several of the larger bodies would be selected and ultimately relocated to predetermined coordinates along the border separating Federation and Klingon space. Once moved into position by teams of *Ptolemy*-class towing vessels equipped with heavy-duty tractor beam systems, the asteroids would become the foundations for new observation outposts, similar to those currently in use along the Federation-Romulan Neutral Zone.

"Is the thing carrying some kind of shielding to hide it from sensors?" Blair asked, turning his attention back to the main viewer and the image of the communications buoy. "Or was it just powered down until now?" Even as he asked the questions, he knew what his science officer would say.

Sutherland replied, "No odd shielding that I could find, and even if it had been drifting inert for however long, our sensors should still have picked it up." She nodded toward the viewscreen. "That thing wasn't here five minutes ago, sir."

"Then where the hell did it come from?" Mbugua asked from where he stood at the bridge railing, looking up at Blair and Sutherland.

Her attention attracted by an indicator light flashing on her console, Sutherland turned and once more peered into the workstation's hooded sensor viewer. "Okay, this is starting to get annoying." When she looked away from the console, a frown clouded her features. "Sensors have just detected *another* buoy, seventeen million kilometers from our present position, toward the system's outer boundary."

Not liking the implication of what he was hearing, Blair said, "And you're sure it wasn't there before, just like this other one?"

"Absolutely, sir," the science officer replied. "Sensor logs show no record of it."

From behind Blair at the communications station, Ensign Ravishankar Sabapathy said, "Captain, the second buoy is now transmitting its own signal."

Blair gestured to Sutherland. "Feed those coordinates to the helm," he said as he stepped down into the command well and moved to the center seat. "T'Lehr, take us there, safest speed."

"Aye, sir," replied Lieutenant T'Lehr, and the Vulcan began inputting the appropriate instructions to the helm console.

Settling into his chair, Blair said, "Sutherland, let's have a full-spectrum sensor sweep of the system. Give me everything you've got."

From where he still stood at the railing near Sutherland's station, Mbugua said, "What are you thinking, sir?"

"That somebody's screwing with us," Blair replied as he again used his towel to wipe his face. It was a gut call, nothing more, but an instinctual feeling he had learned long ago not to dismiss out of hand.

Mbugua frowned. "We're a long way from Romulan space, if that's what you're thinking." He nodded toward the viewscreen. "The Klingons are just down the block, but cloaking technology doesn't strike me as their cup of tea."

"Don't believe everything you've heard or read," Blair countered. "There are plenty of Klingons in the Empire who'd happily use a cloaking device if they thought it could get them close enough to cut your throat with one of those ceremonial daggers they love so much. That said, a Klingon ship commander wouldn't play games like this." Pausing, he shook his head, regarding the image of asteroids sliding past the *Defiant* as the starship made its way through the field. "No, this is something else." Would a Romulan ship venture so far into enemy territory, even with the ability to shield itself from sensors? Blair held no illusions about such a scenario, provided the vessel's commander had good reason for such an act.

So, the question—assuming it is the Romulans—is: What's the point of all this?

"Captain!" Sutherland called from her station, and Blair looked up to see the science officer alternating her gaze between her hooded viewer and other screens and readouts at her console. "I think . . . wait . . . that's not right." When she frowned, Blair was sure he heard the science officer mutter a particularly colorful Andorian oath before she turned to face him. "Sir, I thought sensors registered some kind of spatial distortion, just for a second, but it's gone now."

Rising from his seat, Blair moved to the edge of the command well, placing his hands atop the red railing. "What kind of distortion?"

Sutherland shook her head. "I'm not sure, sir. I've never seen anything like it, natural or artificial. According to sensor logs, it reads almost like background ionization, but there's nothing here that could be the cause of something like that." Drawing what Blair took to be a calming breath, she added, "It has to be artificial, sir."

"Another ship," Blair said, at almost the exact instant as Mbugua offered an identical declaration. The two men exchanged a knowing glance before the first officer turned from the railing.

"Red Alert," he called out, his voice booming across the bridge. "All hands to battle stations."

Moving back to his chair at the center of the command well, Blair said, "Shields and weapons, T'Lehr. We're going hunting."

Even as he gave the orders, Thomas Blair gripped the arms of his chair and felt a knot form in his gut, his anxiety increasing as he considered the nature of the quarry they might be seeking.

Happy birthday to me.

The bridge of the *I.K.S. Kretoq* was dark and all but silent. The battle cruiser's primary power generators had been taken off-line, with reserve power being channeled only to systems absolutely required to operate the vessel. Those consoles that were active were muted, their controls casting a pale red glow only just visible in the room's subdued lighting. From where she sat in the command chair, Toqel sensed the anxiety all around her as she and everyone else on the bridge watched the image of the Starfleet vessel on the main viewscreen. Drifting among the asteroids of the Alamedus system—labeled the Dar'shinta system on Romulan star charts—it rotated in space as it altered its trajectory and began drawing closer to the *Kretoq.*

"Maintain position," Toqel ordered. The chair's high, unpadded backrest was uncomfortable, designed for Klingon physiology as well as a mindset that viewed concepts like ergonomics as crutches for the weak. Despite the ache at the small of her back, Toqel forced aside the compulsion to rise from the seat, not wishing to appear frail in the eyes of those few Klingon warriors present on the bridge.

"Range ten thousand *mat'drih* and closing, Proconsul," reported Rezek, the young centurion standing alongside his Klingon counterpart at the tactical station. "They know we are here."

"They *suspect* something is here," Toqel corrected without turning her attention from the viewscreen, tapping the nail of her right forefinger on the arm of her chair. Casting a glance toward Rezek, she asked, "What's the status of the cloak?"

Pausing to study one of the tactical station's status displays and to confirm with the Klingon officer assigned to him, the centurion replied, "Operating at full capacity, Proconsul."

Toqel nodded in approval. The integration of cloaking mechanisms into the onboard systems of six Klingon vessels had gone surprisingly well, even when accounting for the often radical differences in Romulan and Klingon technology. Her cadre of engineers had negotiated those obstacles in fine fashion, leaving Toqel to test the newly equipped vessels in the only manner that was of any tactical importance. Entering foreign territory and attempting to thwart the sensors of an enemy ship would quell any lingering doubts held by the Senate. Once all such uncertainty was laid to rest, Toqel knew the senators would give her the latitude she needed to further strengthen the Romulan fleet, eventually forging it into a weapon against which no enemy of the Empire would be able to defend.

First things first, however.

"Proconsul," Rezek said after another moment, "the Starfleet ship is engaging its full array of sensors." When he spoke this time, Toqel thought she detected a hint of anxiety in his voice. "They appear to be conducting an expansive scan of the immediate area."

Seated at the helm before Toqel, Centurion Nilona turned in his seat. "Should we cut all remaining power, Proconsul?"

Toqel's immediate response was to arch her right eyebrow as she regarded him. "That would hardly be conducive to our experiment." Though the new cloaking field was able to conceal the ship's motion—an ability lacking in earlier versions—it could not completely mask plasma emissions generated by the impulse engines. Still, the output from the *Kretoq*'s maneuvering thrusters was easily shrouded. Provided no undue spike in power generation took place while the enemy vessel's scanners probed for her ship, Toqel had been assured by her engineers that the cloak should withstand even the most intense sensor sweep.

The Starfleet vessel was growing larger on the viewscreen, its maneuvering thrusters propelling the enemy vessel ever closer.

"They detect us!" Nilona said.

Toqel did not agree. Engaging the *Kretoq*'s impulse engines to give them some distance after depositing the last communications buoy—itself a means of baiting the Starfleet ship and seeing how its commander would react to the mysterious appearance of the objects—likely had triggered an alarm to the enemy vessel's sensors. It was a calculated risk, but in addition to being a further test of the cloak's abilities, Toqel also wanted maneuvering room if it became necessary to retreat, or even to turn and fight.

Forcing her voice to remain calm and measured, she ordered, "Stand by to route power to weapons and shields at my command." Glancing toward Rezek, she called out, "Range."

The centurion replied, "Sixty-three hundred *mat'drih,* and closing." After a moment, he added, "Proconsul, their current course heading indicates they will pass close enough that collision is a danger."

Very close, Toqel conceded, but still distant enough to suggest the Starfleet vessel's sensors had not actually locked onto the *Kretoq.* "Helm," she said, "lay in a course out of the asteroid field along our current orientation. Adjust your course to utilize the largest asteroids along our flight path for cover. Engage when ready."

"Understood, Proconsul," Nilona replied as he leaned over his console and set to work. The only indications of the *Kretoq*'s acceleration were the telltale movement of a status indicator Toqel noted on the helm console, followed by the image of asteroids passing the edges of the viewscreen as the ship pushed forward.

Stepping away from the tactical station, Rezek moved until he could lean close enough to Toqel to speak without being overheard by other bridge personnel. "Proconsul, that heading will take us to dangerous proximity to them."

Toqel nodded. "Yes, it will. What better way to test the cloak than from point-blank range?" Her engineers had boasted that the cloaking field would be effective from as close as one ship length away from an enemy target. She intended to test that claim to the fullest extent possible.

"We should attack the Earther ship now," said Mortagh, the Klingon officer manning the tactical console and the *Kretoq*'s designated liaison to those members of the original crew who had been retained in order to assist Toqel's people with the transition to the vessel's onboard systems. "They do not suspect that we lie in wait, ready to slaughter them like the helpless prey that they are."

Turning from the viewscreen, Toqel glared at the Klingon with undisguised contempt. "And what point would that serve? If I'd wanted to destroy them, I could have done that long before now."

Mortagh sneered so that she could see his yellow, uneven teeth. "This childish game wastes a ship of the *Kretoq*'s stature. Do you know how many glorious victories this ship has achieved in battle? Of those, none were earned by sneaking around like cowards in the dark."

"I'm not interested in glory," Toqel countered, returning her attention to the screen. "I care only about defeating the enemies of the Empire." Glancing at Mortagh one last time, she added, *"My* empire, not yours."

Though still uncomfortable with the evolving situation, Rezek had returned to his station without further comment. Once more hovering over the tactical displays, he called out, "They are passing abreast of us, range three hundred *mat'drih.*" Nothing else was said for the few moments it took for the underside of the Starfleet ship to fill the viewscreen. It now was so close that Toqel could make out the seams in its hull and the markings of its registry number, NCC-1764, rendered in Federation Standard text.

"Proximity warning," Nilona called over his shoulder, pointing to an alarm indicator mounted above the viewer. It had begun to flare fiery crimson an instant before a dull tone droned from the intercom system. The helm officer returned his attention to the task of guiding the ship through the asteroids, a task now compounded by the need to avoid a collision with the enemy vessel. "Our distance is less than five ship lengths," he added, his tone laced with caution. "Any closer and we risk making contact with their deflector shields."

Toqel nodded, feeling as though she could reach through the screen and brush the hull of the other ship with her fingers. "Maintain course and speed." Glancing around the bridge, she saw the worry on the faces of her crew, and even clouding the stoic countenances of Mortagh and the other Klingons assigned to assist her people. This was probably as close as any of them had ever been to a Starfleet ship. On any other occasion, this would be an unparalleled opportunity to subject the vessel to intensive sensor scans and other means of gathering data on its construction and capabilities. Despite her earlier chastising of Mortagh regarding the need for stealth, Toqel privately admitted a desire to unleash the *Kretoq*'s weapons. At this distance, the battle cruiser would still inflict massive damage even with the enemy vessel's defensive shields activated.

No, she reminded herself. *This is not the time.*

Another moment passed, and then the ship moved beyond the screen's frame, leaving nothing but a scattered collection of asteroids and open space.

"Hold position," Toqel ordered. "Put it on-screen." On the viewer, the Starfleet vessel now was moving away from the *Kretoq*. "Status?"

"They appear not to have detected us," Rezek replied, sounding both relieved and impressed. "The cloak is functioning perfectly."

Toqel smiled in approval. "Well, Rezek, as it seems we will survive the day, please pass along my compliments to Doctor Vaniri and his team."

A collective murmur of satisfaction circled around the bridge, and Toqel did nothing to quell the newfound confidence. Even Mortagh and his fellow Klingons seemed duly awed by what they had just witnessed. Listening to the reactions taking place around her, Toqel sat in silence, content and yet disheartened to a small degree as she considered what had taken place here.

I am sorry, Sarith, thinking as she did each day of her late daughter, *that we could not have accomplished this sooner.*

"Maintain course until we're out of the field," she ordered, setting aside the sobering thoughts. "Then, set a course for Klingon space and engage at maximum warp." Sensing a presence near her right side, she turned to see Mortagh standing there, and noted that the liaison maintained his dismissive attitude as he once more glared at her.

"An effective toy you have devised, Romulan," he said, his arrogance and bluster firmly in place, the heel of his left hand resting atop the pommel of the dagger suspended from the belt at his waist. "And what will you do with it? Attack your enemies, or cower from them?"

Offering a wan smile before returning her attention to the viewer, Toqel replied, "Consider that knife with which you feel the need to assure yourself. In the hand of a savage, a blade can do little but kill, but when wielded by a gifted surgeon, it might save a life. As your knife is a tool, so too is the cloaking field. It can save lives, or be used to take them. The difference, Klingon, is the intention behind its use."

Mortagh loosed a snort of derision before turning and leaving her. Once more alone with her thoughts, she considered the report she soon would file with her superiors. The cloaking field was ready for a more stringent series of tests: trials in which the risks were far greater and accompanied by rewards of equal merit.

"Rezek," she called over her shoulder, "prepare a secure communiqué to Romulus. I want to speak to Ditrius." Her next actions would require soothing the troubled, feeble minds of the senators, and in her absence the vice proconsul would find himself burdened with that thankless duty. It was necessary, if she was to continue with her mission, and she could only hope that the headstrong officer was up to the task.

Yes, Toqel decided, the time for bolder, more decisive steps was fast approaching.

6

It was going to be one of those days, Admiral H. Franklin Solow decided as he peered through the expansive picture window of his office. The view of early morning sunlight illuminating the calm waters of San Francisco Bay was spectacular, even with the hint of dark gray beginning to discolor the horizon and promising rain in the hours to come. He already could feel the first dull pangs of a headache beginning to take root beneath his temples, radiating inward and settling in behind his eyeballs. Normally, it would take until late afternoon on a Wednesday—Thursday, if he was lucky—for Solow to begin feeling these initial assaults on his mind and his sense of well-being. When it started before lunch on a Monday morning?

I should've called in sick.

Forgoing his normal beverage of choice, black coffee, Solow instead had ordered a tall glass of chilled orange juice from the food slot in his well-appointed office. The juice had aided in swallowing a pair of analgesic tablets he had taken more from habit than with any real hope of alleviating his headache. Releasing a sigh that signaled his surrender to whatever personal discomforts chose to visit him on this day, Solow turned from the window and moved toward the high-backed chair situated behind his wide, polished oak desk. On the desk's surface was a collection of reports, files, memoranda, and other administrative flotsam which was part and parcel of a Starfleet flag officer's job.

Not for the first time, Solow wondered how quickly the Headquarters building would burn to the ground with the aid of the considerable amount of flammable materials housed just in his office.

And here I sit, with no marshmallows. Truly a tragedy if ever there was one.

Lowering himself into his chair with something less than ideal professional decorum, Solow eyed his assistant, Lieutenant Commander Cheryl Allen, who sat in the middle of three chairs positioned before his desk. The woman's pale skin contrasted sharply with the bright red of her uniform dress, and, as he often did since the commander had begun working for him, Solow wondered if she might burst into flames when subjected to direct sunlight. "Okay," he said, pausing to drink from his glass of juice. "Let's have it."

Allen, long ago having grown accustomed to the admiral's relaxed demeanor when working in the confines of his private office, nodded as she held up the data slate that had been resting in her lap. "We're still compiling the latest information and readying the newest set of reports for you, sir."

"Anything new?"

"No, Admiral." When the commander shook her head, the action was so animated that it caused the locks of her dark blond pageboy hairstyle to swing from left to right. Solow had commented on it early during their working relationship, fearing that Allen's head might actually detach from her body and fly off to parts unknown. "Starfleet Intelligence is cross-referencing Captain Blair's report against what we know of Klingon ship upgrades, but there's been no chatter about anything like this. Whatever they're up to, they're keeping it very well hidden."

Nothing bothered Solow more than a Klingon acting in anything other than the brusque, uncompromising manner that characterized their species. One of the benefits of attempting to understand a culture so predicated on a military mindset or warrior ethos was that—after a time—such an adversary became predictable, at least to some extent. The Klingons, when they remained brash and brutal, were consistent. It was when they chose subtlety or cunning over direct confrontation that they became enemies to be watched and feared.

This, Solow had realized upon first reading the report submitted by Captain Thomas Blair, commander of the *U.S.S. Defiant*, was looking to be one of those times.

"A cloaked Klingon vessel," he said, shaking his head as he leaned back in his chair. No matter how many times he had read Blair's report during the past three weeks, the words simply did not sound correct or even believable to his ears. "And I thought I'd seen it all when it came to dealing with the Klingons."

Now referring to whatever notes she carried on her data slate, Allen replied, "Comparative analysis of the *Defiant*'s sensor logs showed that the ionized plasma emissions they detected, while faint, were a definite match for the impulse engines of a Klingon D7 battle cruiser." She looked up from her notes. "The Klingons aren't in the habit of trading or selling military hardware, are they?"

Solow smiled, knowing the question was rhetorical, from her tone as much as the fact that Commander Allen was well-versed in the machinations of the Klingon military. Indeed, she was one of Starfleet Command's foremost experts and advisers. Still, the notion was not without merit.

"Maybe not," he said, "but if that was a Klingon ship playing games with the *Defiant,* then they had to get that cloaking technology from somewhere." He let the sentence trail off, watching as Allen's expression melted into a frown.

"The Romulans?" she asked. "Working with the Klingons?" She shook her head. "That's going to keep me up nights."

Offering a slight, humorless chuckle, Solow nodded. "It's one possible explanation, but I'll be damned if we've got the slightest hint of anything like that going on." None of the reports he had been reading from Starfleet Intelligence had provided even the most inconsequential evidence to support the notion that the Klingons and the Romulans—or representatives who might or might not be operating with the authorization of their respective governments—had entered into some sort of alliance. While the very idea might be laughable to the casual observer, Solow knew that Starfleet Tactical had among its vast library of simulations and strategic planning more than one scenario featuring Federation starships pitted against combined fleets of Romulan and Klingon ships. So far as Solow was concerned, the results as provided by computers devoted to the execution of seemingly endless tactical war games were, to say the least, rather less than encouraging.

"For the Klingons to partner for any reason with the Romulans would suggest something's upsetting someone somewhere," Allen said, "perhaps for both sides. Are they that worried about us?"

Solow nodded. "Anything's possible. After all, we're not exactly overflowing with useful intelligence data so far as our friends across the Neutral Zone are concerned."

Despite the period of isolation the Romulan Star Empire had imposed upon itself for decades following its defeat at the hands of Earth and its small band of allies, Starfleet Intelligence had made a handful of attempts to insert covert agents into the Romulan government and military. Most were never heard from again, and those who had survived detection had done so only by immersing themselves in Romulan society to the point of invisibility. Contact with such agents was sporadic at best, and with the care nearly every citizen of the Empire seemed to employ in order to safeguard information, reports offered by the operatives often were of little use.

"It certainly doesn't make any sense on the face of it," Allen said. "Romulan and Klingon cultures are so different, it's hard to imagine them ever agreeing on anything, let alone getting along to the point of working together for some common goal."

Leaning forward, Solow rested his arms on his desktop, reaching up to run the fingers of his left hand through his thinning, gray hair. "From what we know of how the Romulans go about things, they might be interested in seeking such an alliance, but only if they had something to gain, and felt they were in the superior negotiating position." Assuming this theory of a partnership between the two enemy powers was correct, the natural question was what the Romulans felt the Klingons had to offer that justified handing over technology as advanced as a cloaking device. Solow wondered if seeking such a partnership, particularly with the Klingons, might create more problems than it solved.

Sounds like wishful thinking.

"Why do I feel like we're on the outside looking in?" Allen asked.

"Because we are," Solow replied, rising from his chair and retrieving the juice glass from his desk before making his way to the food slot situated in the wall to his right. "Or, we will be, if there's any truth to this." Starfleet had been attempting to develop their own version of a cloaking generator for years, or at least create sensor technology that might penetrate such a field, with no tangible results. When the Romulans disappeared deep into their own territory, seemingly never to be heard from again, that research slowed and eventually faded to nothing as other priorities took precedence. With the reappearance of Romulan ships during the past year, efforts had begun anew, but the progress to this point did not look promising. According to the reports Solow had read, new teams of undercover agents were at this moment being prepared and trained for insertion behind enemy lines, in the hope that they might eventually uncover information pertaining to the cloaking technology, as well as other military secrets. Such operations required time and patience to carry out with any degree of success, and Solow now doubted the Federation had that kind of time.

Turning from the food slot with a fresh glass of juice, Solow returned to his desk. "When can you have the updated reports ready?" he asked, reaching up to rub his temples. Was it his imagination, or were the analgesics actually working?

"Eleven hundred hours today, Admiral," Allen replied.

"Good," Solow said. "I want a package encrypted and readied for secure transmission to Starbase 47. Nogura's our foremost expert on the Romulans, and if they're getting into bed with the Klingons, we need him looking over the data we've collected." Pausing, he shook his head. "Figures Starfleet would ship him out to the farthest point of known space that doesn't require you to speak Kelvan."

Admiral Heihachiro Nogura was one of Starfleet's leading tactical minds and a key player in much of the strategic planning that had been put into motion during the previous year when war with the Klingon Empire had seemed inevitable. For over a year, he had been stationed at Starbase 47, a remote installation on the fringes of Federation space. Overseeing a massive—and highly classified—research and military operation taking place in that region, Nogura still had been called upon to weigh in on the escalating situation with the Klingons, even after the mysterious Organians had put a stop to the pending hostilities between Starfleet and the Empire. If the Romulans were emerging from their figurative shells and seeking renewed conflict with the Federation—and asking the Klingons to participate—then Starfleet once again would require Nogura's keen insights.

"What do we do in the meantime, sir?" Allen asked.

Releasing a heavy sigh, Solow settled back in his chair, turning it so that he once more looked out over the bay. To the west, storm clouds were gathering.

Was it an omen? If so, then it most certainly was going to be a very long day.

"For the moment," he said, not liking the way his words sounded, "we wait."

7

"Transition from warp drive complete, Proconsul. Now proceeding at impulse power."

Toqel swiveled the captain's chair at the sound of Centurion Nilona's voice, feeling a slight twinge in her stomach as the *Kretoq*'s inertial dampers compensated for the battle cruiser's deceleration to sublight speed. Looking up from the handheld computer interface pad containing the latest reports delivered by her lead engineer, she said, "Excellent." She rose from the chair, moving to stand behind the helm officer and take in the image displayed on the bridge's main viewscreen. "What about the *Vo'qha*?"

From behind her at the tactical station, Centurion Rezek replied, "It has just dropped out of warp, as well." A status indicator flashed on his console, and after turning to consult it, he added, "Coded burst message from Commander Lajuk, Proconsul. He awaits your orders."

"What is the status of our cloak?" Toqel asked.

Rezek said, "Fully operational." He reached for one bank of controls at the tactical station. "Sensors detect no trace of the *Vo'qha*."

As it should be. Toqel smiled at the thought. She had been waiting for this moment since receiving approval from Praetor Vrax to undertake this clandestine survey mission. Having proven the success of the technological exchange she had championed, the *Kretoq* now was crewed solely by loyal Romulans, with Captain Mortagh and his contingent having been returned to Klingon space after the completion of the exercise in the Dar'shinta system.

"Continue on course to the fifth planet," she ordered. In accordance with the instructions she had been given by Praetor Vrax himself, the first order of business would be to determine the full capabilities of the outpost's sensor array. During the *khaidoa* that had passed since the Tal Shiar's initial report on the installation being constructed here, covert reconnaissance had been conducted by vessels operating at the very edge of the border separating Romulan and Federation space. As a result, most of the new information was limited in details and quality, but one thing had been determined: the base—while still largely under construction—was operational, including the massive sensor array that appeared to be its most prominent feature.

"Sensors standing by," Rezek said, and Toqel nodded at the report. Stepping around the helm console, her attention was fixed on the image of Theta Cobrini V—as it was listed in Federation data banks—growing larger on the viewscreen. According to the long-range scan data originally collected *fvheisn* ago by sensor probes, the planet was unremarkable in nearly every measurable sense. It possessed no useful mineral deposits in any amounts to justify establishing a mining operation. Its atmosphere, just like the system's other four planets, was poisonous to most humanoid species. Indeed, the world's only redeeming feature was that it was the outermost planet in a system that sat adjacent to the territory of an enemy. Its orbit around the Mar'venas star would allow for ground-based sensors to collect detailed scans of Romulan ship activity in the vicinity of the border. If Starfleet followed its usual pattern, a series of satellites and other unmanned drones would augment that sensor coverage, making this system a key location in the Federation's early warning and defensive reaction strategies.

Assuming it's allowed to remain here unmolested.

"Proconsul, we are inside the planet's orbital trajectory," Nilona reported from the helm.

"Activate sensors," Toqel ordered, casting a glance over her shoulder at Rezek. "Inform Commander Lajuk to do the same." According to the information gleaned from the unmanned drone scans, the outpost's sensor array should have been powerful enough to detect an uncloaked vessel while still light-years away at warp. Pinpointing such a vessel within the system's perimeter should be child's play. Despite the known limitations of the new cloaking generator to fully mask impulse emissions, detecting such readings normally required specialized sensor components. The likelihood of the outpost's possessing such equipment was small, Toqel knew, therefore increasing the odds of a successful reconnoiter prior to departing the system and returning to Romulan space.

"All sensors active," Rezek reported after a moment. When Toqel turned from the viewscreen, she saw the expression on the centurion's face change. "We are detecting only residual energy signatures coming from the planet's surface."

Frowning, Toqel asked. "What do you mean?"

Looking up from the sensor displays, Rezek replied, "All power generation systems are off-line. Sensors are recording traces of discharges from particle beam weapons as well as high-yield explosives. Proconsul, the outpost appears to have been destroyed by orbital bombardment."

"What?" Even though she had suggested just such a scenario scarcely a *khaidoa* ago, the words still sounded alien to her ears. "Are there any survivors?" Perhaps someone still alive down on the surface might be able to offer some clue as to what had taken place here.

Rezek shook his head. "I am detecting no life-forms, Proconsul."

Total destruction? How was that possible, and who was responsible? The questions raged in Toqel's mind as she turned once again to face the viewscreen. "Helm, take us into orbit. Rezek, disengage the cloaking device, and route that power to scanning. I want a full-spectrum sweep of the surface."

"Redirecting sensors," Rezek replied, his voice taut. For several moments, the only sounds on the bridge were those of the various control consoles, with the occasional chatter of a disembodied voice speaking through the ship's intercom system. "We have visual."

"On-screen!" Toqel snapped, the first hints of dread beginning to worm their way into her mind. The image of Theta Cobrini V was replaced by an orbital view of what to her eyes appeared as an opaque ghostly smudge against the craggy, orange-gray terrain of the planet's surface. Without being asked, Rezek increased the image's magnification, bringing into sharp relief what Toqel could see were vast craters, from which emerged remnants of artificial constructs—twisted structural supports, fragments of blackened hull plating, and other detritus littering the scorched earth. Turning from the screen, Toqel saw Rezek looking back at her, the centurion's expression one of confusion.

"Well?" Toqel asked, all but shouting the question.

"Residual energy readings are consistent with those of plasma torpedoes," Rezek answered. "Romulan plasma torpedoes, Proconsul. I am confirming my findings with the tactical officer aboard the *Vo'qha,* and she corroborates the readings."

How in the name of the Praetor is that possible?

Had Vrax, or someone in the Senate, authorized a separate mission, and left her uninformed? To what end? None of this made any sense. Was someone pursuing another agenda, one at odds with her own? Had she been betrayed? If so, by whom, and for what purpose?

No answers presented themselves, and then she had no time for further reflection as an alarm klaxon wailed across the *Kretoq*'s bridge.

"What is it?" she asked, talking to Rezek's back as the centurion bent over the tactical displays.

"Sensors are detecting four vessels," he said. "Klingon D7 battle cruisers. They were on the far side of the planet. I don't know where they . . ." He paused, and before he spoke again Toqel heard the frustrated grunt escape his lips. "They were *cloaked,* Proconsul."

"Cloaked?" Toqel's thoughts turned to the four other ships traded by the Klingons as part of the exchange initiative. According to the last report she had received, those vessels were still conducting tests near Galorndon Core, nearly a *dhaei*'s travel at maximum warp.

Another warning alarm sounded on the bridge, and Rezek shouted to be heard above its wail. "The vessels are assuming attack postures, increasing speed and powering their weapons!"

"Shields up!" Toqel ordered, lunging around the helm console and reaching for the captain's chair. "Stand by all weapons. Helm, make ready for evasive maneuvers." All around her, Romulan centurions turned to their stations, carrying out whatever frantic preparations they might complete in the precious little time remaining to them. Toqel tried to ignore her racing heartbeat. It had been a very long time since she had faced ship-to-ship combat, and only once as a vessel's commander.

Sarith, I wish you were here now.

"They're locking weapons on the *Vo'qha*," Rezek called out, and on the screen, Toqel saw the leading Klingon vessel enter the frame, its weapons ports glowing a harsh, vibrant jade. Then a pair of writhing green balls of energy spat forth, crossing the void separating the ships before disappearing past the screen's right edge. "Direct hit on the *Vo'qha*!" Rezek reported. "Their weapons are passing through the ship's shields!"

"Fire all weapons!" Toqel called out, an instant before something struck the *Kretoq*. The deck shifted beneath her feet and she all but fell into the captain's chair. Alarm sirens blared again, and she saw several alarm indicators flashing on workstations around the bridge.

Behind her, another centurion, Santir, said, "Direct hit to our secondary hull. Engineering reports damage in their sections."

"Proconsul," Rezek said, "Our attackers are pulling back, but Captain Lajuk is broadcasting a distress signal. They're under continued assault."

"On-screen," Toqel ordered, and the image changed to show the *Vo'qha* being pummeled by repeated weapons blasts from two of the four newly arrived Klingon ships. Hull breaches were evident, and a cloud of debris surrounded the wounded vessel.

"The enemy ships are firing Romulan weapons, Proconsul," Rezek said, his tone one of shock and disbelief. "Plasma torpedoes."

We have been betrayed!

The blunt statement hammered in her mind, defying her efforts to ignore it as she took in the scene on the viewscreen. Everyone on the bridge watched as the *Vo'qha* shuddered beneath the brunt of multiple hits, and an instant later the ship disappeared in a brilliant burst of white-hot energy as its warp engines overloaded. A sphere of superheated plasma expanded outward from what had been the secondary hull, swallowing the ship and everything in the immediate vicinity. The image on the viewer automatically lowered its brightness and reduced its magnification so that Toqel could see the pair of Klingon warships that had slain the *Vo'qha* making a hasty retreat.

"Evasive!" Toqel shouted over the disorderly cacophony threatening to engulf the bridge. "All weapons, fire at will! Helm, plot a course out of the system, and stand by to engage at maximum warp." Still reeling from the loss of the *Vo'qha,* Toqel forced her mind to consider her options. Her ship, already damaged and alone against four adversaries? Those were very poor odds indeed.

From the tactical station, Rezek said, "Proconsul, the ships are retreating." A moment later, another indicator tone sounded at his station, and he added, "One of the ships is hailing us."

"Open a channel," Toqel said, turning toward the viewscreen. The image jumped and broke up in response to the frequency shift, and then Toqel beheld the pudgy, irritating visage of Grodak, seated in the command chair aboard the bridge of a Klingon ship. No longer the disheveled, unclean brute she had encountered in that repellent cabin on Narendra III, Grodak now sat before her well-groomed and alert, and wearing a ceremonial ambassadorial sash over his crisp military uniform.

"Greetings, Proconsul."

Her anger already mounting, Toqel rose from her chair and pointed an accusatory finger at the loathsome Klingon. "Grodak, you worthless piece of filth! What is the meaning of this?"

The Klingon shrugged. *"I should think that much was obvious by this point, my dear. I have been given the singular privilege of testing our newest advances in weapons and stealth technology. The information provided to us by your military with respect to plasma torpedo launchers was most illuminating, even if the technical schematics were a bit—how shall I say it—lacking? Thankfully, we possessed the resources to make up for the gaps in our information. What do you think of our results?"*

Imagining her hands around Grodak's throat, Toqel hissed through gritted teeth, "We had an agreement—an understanding."

"Quite true," Grodak replied, *"and one we may have honored, but it seems that trust remains an issue for both sides of our arrangement. This business you conjured about attacking this outpost and leaving the blame to fall to the Klingon Empire—did you truly believe you would accomplish such folly?"* When he leaned forward, his lips curled to reveal his uneven, stained teeth. *"And did you honestly believe we would give you vessels from our fleet, without some means of defeating them in the event we ever faced them in battle?"* He used one hand to indicate the bridge of his ship. *"It's quite a simple thing to retune our weapons and thwart the frequencies on which deflector shields operate, particularly if you have access to the enemy vessel's main computer, as I did. Deactivate your weapons, or I will demonstrate this ability again."*

Forcing herself to stand rigidly still, Toqel called over her shoulder to Rezek. "Do as he says." To Grodak, she growled, "So much for Klingon honor."

Grodak waved away the accusation. *"I told you before that not all Klingons subscribe to the teachings of Kahless. I merely happen to be one such Klingon."* He pointed at her. *"Besides, I'll not be lectured about honor by the likes of you. After all, you did have spies sneaking about in our midst. We found one such rodent, and he proved to be most cooperative once he was subjected to some of our more effective interrogation techniques."*

Of course, Toqel realized. Bitterness enveloped the thought, but she allowed no visible reaction. "No doubt you have spies among us, as well."

"Indeed. That is the way of things, after all. If the Klingon Empire is to thrive, we need to adapt to our enemy, even when that enemy prefers cowardly skulking in the shadows rather than direct action. Regardless of where you choose to fight this battle with us, Romulan, you will lose."

Toqel wrestled with the repercussions of what Grodak had admitted. Surely, Starfleet vessels already were on the way here, once it was realized that contact with the outpost had been lost. They would investigate the remnants of the base, and conclude Romulan culpability, just as Toqel would have engineered Klingon blame if she had been allowed to go forward with her original plan to attack the outpost.

"I can see it in your face, Toqel," Grodak taunted. *"So far as the Federation is concerned, Romulus will have much to answer for in the days to come. We are content to leave the details to you, but I think we both know the correct course of action if we are to preserve the secrecy of the alliance we've forged."* Once more, he offered another repulsive smile. *"Good luck with that, Proconsul. Perhaps in the future, your unchecked arrogance will not blind you to the possibility that your enemies are not fools."*

He vanished from the viewscreen, his image replaced by that of the quartet of Klingon battle cruisers, which immediately began to veer off and move away from the *Kretoq.*

What have I done? The question rang in her ears, even as she became aware of the bridge crew standing at their stations, watching her and waiting for new orders.

"Proconsul?" Rezek prompted, his voice low and uncertain.

"Prepare a message to Romulus," Toqel replied, her gaze shifting to the deck plates at her feet. "I need to speak to the Praetor at his earliest convenience. Helm, set a course for home. Everyone else, return to your stations." The tension on the bridge was palpable as her people turned to whatever tasks awaited them, leaving Toqel alone with her own tortured thoughts. Her mind and body were only now beginning to feel the stresses of what had happened here today, as well as what it might mean once they returned to Romulus.

"I'm sorry, Sarith."

Turning in his seat, Nilona regarded her with an expression of concern. "Proconsul?"

"Nothing," Toqel snapped. Then, in a calmer voice, she added, "See to your duties, Centurion."

As I will soon see to mine.

8

Eschewing any of the chairs adorning his opulent private office, Praetor Vrax had instead chosen to pace across the room's ornate carpet. Flanked by a security officer as well as Vice Proconsul Ditrius, Toqel stood at the center of the supreme leader's sanctuary, her hands clasped behind her back. She watched the Praetor, who, in apparent defiance of his age, moved with a determination belying his years. Despite the room's cool temperature, Toqel felt perspiration beginning to dampen her back.

"A most distressing problem we have here, Proconsul," Vrax finally said, breaking the silence that had all but engulfed the room since Toqel's arrival under guard several moments earlier. He spoke with a deliberate cadence, each word channeling a portion of the frustration and disappointment Toqel knew he now felt toward her.

"Yes, my Praetor," she replied. There was no point in attempting to deny or mitigate what had happened. It would be insulting, both to Vrax as well as herself, and ultimately do nothing to alter the current situation.

"Both the Federation and Klingon diplomatic envoys are quite upset," Vrax continued, "though obviously for different reasons. The Federation naturally believes the attack on their outpost to be an act of war, and we may one day find ourselves at odds with the humans and their allies as we did generations ago. Still, I prefer it to be on my terms and at a time of my choosing, rather than being manipulated into a war I do not yet believe our people are prepared to wage."

While being held in custody, Toqel had been allowed to review the latest reports detailing how the Federation had communicated its displeasure to the Romulan government. At this moment, deliberations were under way that might force the ejection of Romulan ambassadors and their staff from the recently established embassy on Earth. Elsewhere, both Klingon and Federation officials were calling for the removal of Romulan representatives from the still-developing joint colony venture on Nimbus III. It had been difficult for Toqel to contain her own anger while reading reports of how Klingon leaders were decrying the recent "Romulan" action at Mav'renas.

"My Praetor," she said after a moment, "I do not understand. Why do we not show the Federation that the Klingons are responsible for the attack on their outpost? Our sensor logs of the battle we later fought, including the destruction of the *Vor'qha,* could speak for themselves." While such a confession almost certainly would require revealing the Romulan-Klingon cooperative effort she had helped to forge, the price of that admission surely would be enough to quiet the political turmoil Vrax currently faced.

Though he did not offer an immediate answer, Vrax released a small, humorless chuckle as he leaned on his cane, as close to piercing the cloud of irritation that had hovered over him since Toqel's arrival. Finally, he shook his head. "It is quite simple, actually. The Senate, and I am forced to agree with them on this point, is unwilling to reveal to the Federation that we were so easily duped by the Klingons. Fortunately, the Klingons, for their own reasons, are quite willing to continue our budding alliance, and would prefer not to alert the Federation to its existence. For that to occur, we must accept total responsibility for the incident in the Mav'renas system. Needless to say, doing so at this time presents its own unique set of problems, much like the last time we found ourselves facing such a situation."

Toqel nodded in agreement. Barely a *fvheisn* had passed since the Praetor's authorization of the covert mission into Federation space and the subsequent destruction of those Starfleet observation outposts along the Neutral Zone. Several lengthy negotiations between political representatives from both sides had calmed the humans' initial outrage at the unprovoked attacks, which the Romulan contingent had explained as a tragic misunderstanding of the outposts' purpose. Whether the Federation diplomats truly had believed the reasoning—a mistaken perception that the outposts were to be the focal point of a new offensive by Starfleet forces—had been a matter of much debate in the Senate chamber in the time immediately following the matter's resolution.

"We were able to come to an accord on that occasion," Vrax continued, "forestalling hostilities at least for a while, to say nothing of the promise of renewed talks between our governments. Even that colony on Nimbus III, which I originally opposed, might still prove useful." He paused, his brow furrowing as his gaze locked with hers. "Contrary to what the citizenry may or may not believe, I am quite content to bide our time until we can learn more about Starfleet's strengths and weaknesses, and to allow for our ships and personnel to prepare for the day when war might well come. If we are faced with such a conflict now, I am uncertain as to how we might fare."

Coming from any ordinary citizen, such a remark, if made in the presence of the Tal Shiar, would be considered treason against the Empire. Indeed, even though Toqel was aware of the current status and capabilities of Romulan forces better than any other military officer, it still alarmed her to hear the Praetor speak in such stark, unflinching terms.

"So," Ditrius said, speaking for the first time since escorting Toqel into the Praetor's chambers, "the Romulan people will have to stand in silence while the Klingons make fools of them."

The Praetor shook his head. "No, not the Romulan people, Vice Proconsul. So far as they, the Federation, and perhaps most Klingons will be concerned, what happened was the grave overreaction by a single overzealous ship commander."

Of course, Toqel realized. Drawing herself up, she nodded. "I understand, my Praetor." Duty demanded no other response.

Rather than appearing grateful for her reply, Vrax instead released a small, sad sigh. "Hubris, Toqel, was your undoing. You were warned not to misjudge the Klingons. Make no mistake: while you certainly were not alone in that regard, the Senate is not so eager to stand up and accept responsibility for their failure of imagination."

I suppose it was foolish to expect anything else from that herd of simpering opportunists, Toqel mused, though she forced her expression and body language to reveal none of her disapproval. She had known from the beginning that her plan carried with it significant risks were it to be exposed to any degree—risks not only to her career but also to political relations with both the Klingons and the Federation.

"What is to happen now, my Praetor?" Ditrius asked, and though Toqel was not certain, she thought she sensed just a hint of anticipation in the vice proconsul's voice. That was only natural, she supposed, seeing as how her assistant likely would enjoy a promotion if she was removed from her position. There was no quelling the younger officer's determination, it seemed.

Vrax cleared his throat, suppressing a congested cough before replying, "As we speak, our diplomats are once again engaged with their human counterparts, attempting to mitigate the situation. The Federation is requesting your extradition to stand trial, which they promise will be fair, in keeping with their rather quaint, broad-minded concepts of justice. As disagreeable as I find that notion, there are those in the Senate who see it as necessary for the long-term diplomatic relations between our two peoples. If such an offer is to be tendered, I would rather it be genuine, rather than a ruse designed to elicit temporary trust while we pursue some other agenda." He paused, his gaze softening a bit as he studied her, his expression taking on an almost paternal quality. "You are like one of my own children, Toqel. Your family has served the Empire for generations, and your father was a trusted adviser to me from a time before you were born. Nevertheless, I must put first the interests of the Romulan people."

"I have no desire for my fate to be decided by humans," Toqel replied, her voice firm and steady, "or the Senate, for that matter. Still, I will face whatever punishment you deem appropriate." Even before being summoned to the Praetor's office, she had made the decision not to shirk from whatever pronouncement Vrax ordered. While she all but recoiled at the thought of being offered up as a sacrifice to protect the cowardly fools occupying seats in the Senate chamber, her loyalty to the Praetor was and remained absolute. She also was fueled by the example put forth by her beloved Sarith, who had honored her oath and her service to the Romulan people until the very last moment of her life. Toqel vowed she would do no less, if for nothing else than to honor her daughter's memory.

Vrax nodded. "I know you will." Looking past her, the Praetor said to Ditrius, "Vice Proconsul, you are hereby promoted to proconsul, and you will immediately assume Toqel's duties. Your first task will be to return her to security confinement until such time as I have made my final decision." He returned his attention to her. "It is unfortunate that events have brought us to this point, Toqel. I truly wish it were otherwise." Releasing a tired sigh, he stepped away from her and headed to the door leading from the office to his private study. Toqel watched him until the door closed behind him, leaving her alone with Ditrius and the security officer. Turning to face Ditrius, she offered him a formal nod.

"Congratulations, Proconsul."

Ditrius replied, "Thank you."

As she studied his face, Toqel noted that the younger officer was unable to keep a slight hint of satisfaction from creeping onto his features. "It seems your efforts have finally been rewarded. If you are open to some unsolicited advice, I would caution against letting that ambition allow you to lose focus of the greater responsibilities you now carry. You owe that much to the Praetor, as well as the people of the Empire."

Drawing himself to his full height, the newly installed proconsul looked upon her with a barely disguised expression of disdain. "Much like your own overconfidence blinded you as you pursued your goals. Did you truly believe the Klingons would allow themselves to be manipulated? They are not simply warmongering animals, contrary to what the Senate and the Tal Shiar would have the public believe. They are an enemy to be feared, they have spies here on Romulus, and their military strength, along with their audacity, will only grow now that they have obtained cloaking technology. Quite an impressive legacy you've crafted for yourself, Toqel. Your daughter would be proud."

Toqel stepped forward, her anger rising. "You pathetic *veruul.*" She stopped when the security guard moved toward her, his hand reaching for the holstered weapon on his right hip. Ignoring him, she instead leveled her gaze on Ditrius. "If ever you manage to trap a mate long enough to bear your child, then you'll understand why I want to kill you just now. Pray I never have the opportunity."

In response to her threat, Ditrius merely shrugged. "I welcome the challenge, but I suspect it will never come." Looking to the guard, he said, "Centurion, take her into custody."

Still fuming as she glared at Ditrius, Toqel did not move as the centurion stepped toward her. His left hand retrieved the pair of prisoner restraints at his belt, which he had removed from her wrists at the Praetor's order upon their arrival. As he moved to stand behind her, a high-pitched whine echoed in the room and the guard's body stiffened, his face twisting into an expression of shock and pain as he collapsed to the floor. Stepping back, Toqel could not contain her own confusion and disbelief as her eyes moved from the smoking hole in the guard's back to the disruptor pistol Ditrius held in his hand.

"What have you done?" Toqel asked, still reeling from the sight before her.

Ditrius moved to stand over the fallen guard. "He was a traitor, working for an undercover Klingon agent. He had received orders to kill you, thereby preventing any chance of your revealing to Starfleet our alliance to the Klingons, should the Praetor opt to surrender you to the Federation."

Shaking her head, Toqel could not believe what she was hearing. "How could you know this?"

"Actually, I don't," Ditrius replied. "I simply require a cover story so that I can carry out *my* orders."

Fury and betrayal boiled within Toqel as she realized just how much her own arrogance and single-minded drive had prevented her from seeing Ditrius for the traitor he was. No, not a traitor; a Klingon spy, now serving at the Praetor's side.

She had no time to reflect on the severity of her failure, for the last thing Toqel saw was the muzzle of the disruptor pistol Ditrius pointed at her face.

Greed

Reservoir Ferengi

David A. McIntee

Historian's Note

This story takes place in 2377 (ACE) during the admistration of the Grand Nagus Rom ("Dogs of War" DS9).

For the late Mursya,
one of the Cat Collective
who inspired my previous story, "On the Spot"

Today

War between the planets of the Urwyzden system didn't show in the vast field of empty black between them. The vacuum wasn't deformed by warfare; there were no craters and no trenches. There was only the occasional quick flare of hard radiation, or the brief flash of oxygen-rich atmosphere igniting and being snuffed out as a starship split open and died.

Missiles were too small to be visible to the naked eye as they clawed their way up from the surfaces of Urwyzden Alpha and Beta, looping in long arcs from one planet to the other. Lunar and asteroid facilities crumbled and erupted into dust that dispersed gently across the heavens.

The turquoise-and-white face of Urwyzden Alpha was blotched and streaked, as mushrooming clouds wept fallout across half the southern hemisphere. Small shuttles and winged craft tore through those filthy tears, stabbing out phaser and disruptor beams and depleted-uranium slugs at each other. They dodged and darted, jinking in and out of sullen storms, and cutting contrail scars into the blue where the clouds hadn't reached yet.

The losing aerial duelists tumbled haphazardly from the skies. Some plummeted like meteorites into the forests and the fields, gouging craters into the earth. Other pilots tried to avoid the remaining inhabited residential areas of burnt-out towns. Occasionally one would burst through the layers of smoke and rip into buildings, spraying startling eruptions of dust and concrete.

People on the ground, be they soldiers, or civilians huddling in their shelters, flinched at any sound from the sky. Some flinched because they expected death to fall, and others because they feared that no more refugee launches would follow, and they and their families would be trapped in this hell for the duration of the war.

In the quiet hours, when the fighting had moved on, the refugees emerged, choking on the dust and smoke as they clambered through the rubble-strewn avenues. The capital, at least, still had a functional spaceport, and every approach to it was thronged with people trying to get out on one of the vessels that were leaving soon.

There weren't enough mass-scale transporters to beam people to the few neutral or private ships in orbit, so there was a ragged schedule of shuttles and smaller vessels ferrying large groups back and forth. Most of the Urwyzden who were backed up all around the entrances were poor, since the rich and powerful had been able to arrange to be beamed up in ones or twos. Other species, who were still waiting for transport, towered over the wrinkled and gnarly natives, wishing they had never come to this planet. The ships picking people up belonged either to worlds with citizens living in or visiting the system, or to the United Federation of Planets, which was doing its best to provide evacuation for those with no other recourse, as well as for its own citizens.

Even at the fringes of the capital's spaceport, the sounds of phaser and disruptor fire were audible, carrying across the flat expanses in between the cracks and rumbles of photon grenades going off.

Fighting still raged throughout the squat pyramid at the heart of the spaceport. Soldiers scrambled across the ruined VIP departure lounge's floor, trying to dodge streams of agitated particles fired by the enemy while also shooting at shadows and smudges that could easily be camouflaged enemy soldiers. It was nightmarish, and any soldier involved in the room-by-room clearance on either side would have been glad that their adaptive camouflage armor included faceplates that hid their fear and confusion.

At first it was just like training in a holosuite: acquire targets, get the job done, and watch your mates' backs. But once people got hit, it became a different matter. Modern warfare was usually conducted at a distance, and since Urwyzden had been left alone during the war with the Dominion, most of the soldiers had never seen a dead body before. The last Alphan soldier to enter had been watching for any attempts to outflank them, and belatedly dashed across the rubble-strewn floor as his confederates gave covering fire. A phaser blast cut him down, and he fell forward into cover behind a shattered wall. His body slammed into one of the troopers who had been covering him and knocked him down.

That soldier had the wind knocked out of him by the impact. He put a hand up to wipe the seared blood from his face before he realized that the blood was on the faceplate of his armor, and not on his skin. The soldier could tell that the straggler was dead, no tricorder needed. All the troops were shaking with every breath they took, but there was nothing from the fallen body. The soldier shuffled as far away from the corpse as he could without breaking cover. He didn't want a dead body touching him.

Glass walls and plaster partitions exploded into dust. Monitors burst with big enough pops to make them dance on their desks. Soldiers ducked and leapt, slid and ran, all the while releasing hell from their hands.

Suddenly, a stout figure, larger than any Urwyzden native, appeared, running the gauntlet of flying plasma and phased energy. He ran in a crouch, heading for a breach in the wall through which the gentle slope of the pyramid was accessible. His clothes were once fine and multicolored, his frame round and unfit. His large ears, almost as big as an entire Urwyzden head, were torn and bloodied.

He turned and aimed a hand phaser at a doorway just in time for a second figure to charge out. The second was a little taller and fitter, but was clearly a member of the same race, and just as battered. He froze, eyes wide, as he realized his nose was about three inches from the phaser muzzle, and he let out a little yelp. For a moment, both of them stood there, and then the stouter gunman paled and looked at the phaser. He shook it. "Oh . . ." The leaner one roared in anger and lunged forward, propelling them both across the floor.

Troops on both sides paused, watching this strange fight, as the pair wrestled each other for control of the phaser. The phaser wasn't working, but each man tried to smack the other in the head with it.

Whispers were transmitted across the comm frequencies of both groups of soldiers. "Isn't that—"

"Yes, I think it is."

"They're not with you?"

"We thought they were with you!"

The pair reached the lip of a hole that had been blown in the terminal wall by a photon grenade, and tumbled through it with startled cries.

Outside, the aliens—two Ferengi—rolled down the slope of the pyramidal terminal while hanging desperately on to each other's throats and lapels. Jagged chunks of rubble thumped repeatedly and randomly into bone and flesh, always in the least expected and most painful places.

Black fingernails tore at skin, and bruised knuckles bruised themselves some more against jaws and cheeks. The two combatants butted up against a handful of Urwyzden corpses; soldiers lay sprawled around, with blood-slicked weapons lying on the tarmac.

The stouter Ferengi leapt on top of his enemy and started to throttle him, while trying to keep his face out of range of the fists that were coming up in an attempt to dislodge him. He jerked his head back away from one punch, and that was when he saw the most beautiful sight on this miserable slime-hole of a planet: a warp-capable shuttle, impulse drive idling, with its hatch open and a fully powered but mercifully uninhabited cockpit inside.

Pieces of rubble clattered down from farther up the sloping wall of the terminal, and both Ferengi looked up to see armored Urwyzden soldiers scrambling down in pursuit. Both then looked back to the shuttle.

The distraction was just enough to allow the leaner Ferengi to roll, throwing the other off. They broke apart on all fours, scrambling for the weapons lying near the hands of the fallen soldiers. Then they were on their feet again, both trying to get the business end of a hand phaser into the other's face first.

Neither won.

Beaten and bloody, their eyes blackened, their clothes torn and bloodstained, each found himself pressing a phaser to the other's lobes at arm's length. The pursuing soldiers were gathering around them, weapons raised, cutting them off from the shuttle. "Gaila," the leaner Ferengi said smugly. "Oh, if only you were Quark . . . that's the only way this moment could possibly be any more delicious. Or profitable."

Gaila tried to look less bowel-looseningly terrified than he felt, consoled only by the thought that he couldn't look *more* terrified. "You're finished too, Brunt! It's a mutual loss scenario!"

Brunt, formerly of the FCA, just sighed as the troops closed in. "How did my life come to this?" he asked.

One Year Ago

This looks like the beginning of a beautiful friendship." Brunt nursed a bottle in his own home.

He wasn't actually sure what it was a bottle of, beyond that it was strongly alcoholic. The label had long since smeared away, but he had preferred to drink here rather than go to a properly licensed establishment. Bars reminded him too much of Quark's continued . . . *Not success,* he thought, *but mere existence.* His visitor also reminded him of Quark's infuriating existence, by dint of being a member of Quark's infuriating family.

"That's what I said," Gaila agreed.

"It's not a Rule of Acquisition I'm familiar with," Brunt said pointedly. "In fact, as I'm given to understand the term, it's a hew-mon expression. What do hew-mons know about profit? Hew-mons are the kind of people who would secure a speculation against a debt instead of an asset!"

"Can any Ferengi really have a friendship with an FCA Liquidator?"

"No," Gaila admitted, "but you're not 'Brunt, FCA' anymore."

Brunt glowered, his beady eyes focusing on some future vengeance. "Liquidator for the FCA is who I am, Gaila, not just a job I did."

"The Economic Congress thought differently when they expelled you."

"They took away my job," Brunt corrected him, "but not who I am."

"And that's why there's such an opportunity for profit in a business alliance between us," Gaila said. "Your ruthlessness and drive, coupled with my lobes for tracking down good opportunities . . . Failure is impossible. Liquidator Brunt, the most driven man on Ferenginar, and not a man for whom any chance to earn a slip of latinum will be an improvement on where you are now." Brunt didn't respond; he didn't want Gaila to think he was a charity case or, indeed, that Brunt might owe him a favor. Favors were always more expensive things to owe than mere currency, and repaying them always ate more into one's profits than paying money did. "You know I work in the steadiest market in the galaxy."

"Arms dealing," Brunt agreed, trying out the words for size. They rolled off the tongue nicely.

"I prefer the term planetary security retail specialist, actually. But you've already heard the most important element: my business is in the steadiest market that has ever . . . " He paused. "Second steadiest. I don't sell females, after all. Not usually, anyway."

"I feel reassured already," Brunt said dryly. "But don't worry, I fully appreciate the point you're trying to make." He was beginning to sound hungry. "War is a universal constant—"

"And people at war always need the latest and best weapons. Which means a retailer specializing in such a market always makes profit. Always," Gaila reiterated.

"All right," Brunt agreed, "I'm in."

"You know it makes sense," Gaila replied. "I'll be leaving Ferenginar first thing in the morning. I'll have space cleared in in my shuttlebay for your shuttle. As a matter of fact, perhaps we can travel together—"

"Five slips."

"Done. I'll meet you in the morning."

When Gaila had gone, after that first meeting, Brunt opened a panel in the wall and withdrew a data chip. He clipped it into a padd and activated it, first making sure to switch in a dampener to prevent anyone from accessing the padd remotely. He doubted anyone would dare, but it was definitely better to be safe than sorry.

Certain that he had the electronic privacy he needed, Brunt scrolled through the files on the chip. They were all tagged with the FCA's data seal. They had been highly classified files accessible only to Liquidators, but Brunt had never seen the necessity to delete his copies when he was expelled from the Economic Congress. The Congress would have seen it differently had they known that he had hung on to the files, which is why he had never seen the necessity to mention that he had them. Most of the data was material he himself had collated and reported anyway. It was, as far as Brunt was concerned, his to do with as he pleased.

He stopped scrolling at the entry on Gaila, and began to read and to think. Gaila was a relative of Quark's, of course, which was a massive strike against him, but he was also a frequently successful and profitable businessman. He had become rich enough to buy his own moon; most impressive, even in Brunt's opinion.

Gaila's known contacts included the likes of a hew-mon called Hagath, and the Regent of Palamar: callous murderers with no regard for the number of exploitable lives they wasted for fun rather than profit. Brunt was repulsed by the idea. All those wage-earning people no longer putting their currency into the system . . . It was appalling. And yet Gaila had made enormous profits over the years, dealing with such people. Enough profits, in fact, to buy that moon he was so famous for. Brunt felt an involuntary thrill run down his spine at the thought of enough personal profit to buy a moon.

Why stop at a moon? he asked himself. He was Brunt, FCA—in his heart and soul if not in actual profession at the moment. *Why not a planet?* After all, he had once been acting Nagus, presiding over the whole of the Ferengi Alliance.

That sort of investment would require a lot of profit, but, as Gaila had said, no one had ever gone broke selling weapons. War wasn't just a universal constant, it was an infinite source of profit. Brunt grinned to himself; this was his chance, to get it all back. He would make his profit and buy his way back into favor. It had always worked before.

The next morning dawned with a lightweight western drizzle, and Brunt and Gaila took shelter in Brunt's tiny shuttle as quickly as they could. After paying take-off fees, they were soon flying high and away from their drab homeworld.

Hunched over the controls, and still pretty much brushing shoulders with Gaila in the cramped cabin, Brunt said, "So, where are we going?"

"Right there." Gaila pointed out the viewport toward a large cruiser ahead. "Now, we'll need venture capital to begin a new trading company. If we are going to invest in selling major arms—"

"I've been thinking about that," Brunt agreed. "What we need is a suitably small but vicious conflict to begin with."

"My thoughts exactly. One in which we can raise the maximum amount of capital quickly by selling to both sides."

Brunt thought carefully. "It would take a lot of preparation to set up such a deal. So much, in fact, that it would require a number of people to run smoothly."

"You're not wrong."

"A number greater than two," Brunt added.

Gaila smiled troublingly. "Right again. And, as luck would have it, the crew of my ship is just the right small group of people."

The ship was an aging light marauder, of similar shape to the *D'Kora*-class ships of the Ferengi Alliance's military, but much smaller. It was no larger than that Federation ship that the hated Quark used to hitch rides on. *What was it called, again?* Brunt asked himself. *The* U.S.S. De-*viant?* Something like that; the name certainly sounded appropriate for something connected with Quark.

"Welcome aboard the *Golden Handshake*," Gaila said proudly, once the shuttle had settled into place in the hangar. It didn't take up as much room as the cargo sled next to it. He and Brunt got out and stretched their legs. "The ship is all mine."

"As are its contents," Brunt agreed. The ship was, after all, Gaila's home away from home. Gaila led the way to a wide corridor. Almost immediately, six Breen soldiers stomped out of a side passage, in full sand-colored armor and helmets over their environmental suits. Brunt froze, the contents of his gut turning to lead.

"Oh, don't mind them," Gaila said breezily. "They're just body-guards."

"Bodyguards?" Brunt recovered his superior demeanor. "And whyever would you need bodyguards?"

"For one thing, people who need an arms dealer usually have that need because they're embroiled in some sort of violence." Gaila looked uncomfortable. "Which means sometimes, to make a profit, one has to visit violent places."

"And the list of enemies I should watch out for . . . ?"

"When a beetle-snuff salesman, for whatever reason, ends up with a dissatisfied customer, he can just ignore the lobeless little pest. But when a supplier of top-grade military technology and armaments ends up with a dissatisfied customer . . ."

Flanked by the Breen, Gaila and Brunt made their way up to the bridge. Two Breen halted to stand guard on either side of the doors, and the others disappeared somewhere into another corridor. The bridge was small but comfortable, with a plush command couch on a raised platform. A small minibar was built into it. There were consoles on either side, and a flight console at the narrow nose of the bridge, with a reclining chair set into a cockpit-like enclosure sunk slightly into the floor. There was also a console standing free, having been pulled out from the wall. Sounds of clattering and indistinct cursing indicated that some sort of repairs were in progress.

A short, slim Ferengi sat in the sunken cockpit, making preparations to leave orbit. He looked to be rather small-lobed, and Brunt was surprised that Gaila had employed someone without real business lobes. Then again, perhaps a pilot didn't need such business acumen, so long as he had worked out a good deal on fares.

Another Ferengi came in, carrying a large container of tools and parts. Brunt paled; this was the biggest Ferengi he had ever seen—even larger than the Klingon that he used to see occasionally on Deep Space 9. "Where do you want these, Gaila?" he asked in a deep yet mild voice.

"Take them down to engineering, Bijon."

"Oh, right."

"Bijon, wait." Gaila said quickly. "I want you to meet someone. This is Brunt, my new partner."

Brunt stepped forward. "Brunt, FC— just Brunt," he finished uncomfortably.

"Hallo, Brunt." Bijon put the box down and pressed his wrists together, cupping his hands. Gaila cleared his throat and jerked his head toward the door. Bijon took the hint, picked up his box, and left.

"Bijon is a useful . . . factotum," Gaila said, "but he needs constant direction to remain focused." He went over to the cockpit and looked down. "Pel, are we ready to leave orbit?"

What Brunt had taken to be an effeminate young Ferengi at the helm turned around and rose. He was simultaneously repulsed and intrigued to see that the lobeless pilot was actually female. A clothed female, wearing a sporty pilot's jumpsuit. He didn't try to hide the scowl of disapproval that crossed his face. "Just about," she said eagerly. She had the tone of voice of someone who loved their means of earning profit; Brunt had to give her that. "Voloczin is just installing a few more hardware updates that he picked up while we were here." She looked in the direction of the console that had been uprooted from its position. "Voloczin," Pel said, "is the initializer linkage fixed now?"

"It's kushti," a somewhat mechanical voice said from below. A thick tentacle, covered in parchment-like skin, reached up from the access hatch and around the console. It looked like an agglomeration of all the braised slugs Brunt had feasted upon when he was a regular patron of Ferenginar's finest restaurants. For a moment he thought he was hallucinating. Then another tentacle joined the first, and another, and another . . . The tentacles tensed, and levered up a fluked torso from the crawlspace below. If a hew-mon had been on board, he might have described it as something between a spider, a crab, and an octopus.

"Wotcher," it said. The translator that gave its voice a noticeable mechanical bent flickered on a beak, half hidden under a fold beneath its one baleful eye. There were belts of tools, wide enough to go around a hew-mon waist, around the thickest parts of the tentacles, nearest the body. "Fresh meat, eh?"

"My new partner," Gaila agreed.

"Another one?" Pel exclaimed. Gaila glared at her.

Brunt finally found his voice again. "What is . . . that?"

Pel looked studiously blank. "An engineer. What else would he be, with all those tools?"

"I meant, what sort of . . . What species is he?"

Gaila looked at Voloczin and opened his mouth to express his pride in the quality of his employees, but then closed it and shrugged. "Actually, I haven't a clue. Nobody's ever asked before." He shrugged off the question. "Anyway, welcome to our little enterprise. My associates are, as I said, the right small group of people." Pel and Voloczin returned to what they were doing.

Brunt lowered his voice. "Females making profit . . . wearing clothes." He gave a theatrical shudder. "This is what happens when the Nagus is kin to the likes of Quark. No offense."

"None taken. At least you don't have to stand having that blood in you." Gaila said darkly. "I can almost feel it poisoning me as I speak."

"Might as well turn the whole treasury over to a hew-mon and be done with it."

"Urgh. Hew-mons invented subprime!" Gaila spat.

"Give that idiot Rom time, and he'll probably manage it."

"Don't even joke about that. Besides, Pel may be allowed to earn profit, but who do you think invests it for her?"

"Ah." Brunt grinned understandingly, as did Gaila.

"The hew-mons have a saying: 'A sprat to catch a mackerel'— they're some kind of aquatic food animals, I think. So I use Pel's little bit of profit to bring myself more." Brunt merely nodded; that was how a proper Ferengi should behave, after all. "Come on, I'll show you your cabin, then we'll discuss where we make our first deal."

Gaila took Brunt down one deck and past three doors to a suite of rooms that were even more richly appointed than his home on Ferenginar had been at the height of his powers as FCA Liquidator. Objets d'art were on display, and there was a gleam of gold and latinum everywhere. There was a little office filled with accountancy paraphernalia, and a bedroom with a massive fur-strewn bed. "Nice little home from home, eh?" Gaila said.

"It's passable," Brunt said quickly.

"Get freshened up if you want, then meet me on the bridge and we'll decide on a course."

An hour or so later, Brunt returned to the bridge. Bijon was standing by a console, watching the displays, while Pel was seated in the cockpit. Gaila, on the command couch, beckoned Brunt to sit. "Snail juice?" he offered, replicating Brunt a glass from the minibar next to him. Brunt took it. "Now, I've been orbiting Ferenginar for too long. It's time to get back out there and seek out new profits."

"Rumor has it that there's been a coup on Fonnam II," Brunt said. "No doubt the original government will be looking to counter it and dispose of their traitors. And of course the new government will want to strengthen their hold and dispose of their traitorous counter-plotters . . ."

"That's the kind of level we want," Gaila agreed, "to offload the last of last season's product and raise capital. Fonnam is not such a good option, though; they're notorious for wanting long credit terms."

"No good for raising capital, then," Brunt agreed. "No, we want a planet with hard latinum to spend." His mind was working furiously. Was there anything in his stolen FCA files that could help? He took his padd from his pocket and looked at it, keeping its display away from Gaila's view. "Kalanis Major," he said hungrily. "They recently converted a lot of escrow into latinum, and there is a civil war running, with no sign of an end in sight."

"Perfect!" Gaila exclaimed, rubbing his hands. "Pel, set course for Kalanis Major, and engage."

"Kalanis Major . . ." she echoed. "It'll take four days at warp seven."

"Good enough."

Four days of travel meant Brunt had time to get to know the ship. The first thing he learned was that his bedroom shared a bulkhead with the ship's computer core. Computer cores were solid state, of course, with no moving parts above the subatomic level, but the one that shared a wall with Brunt's cabin still somehow contrived to make occasional noises. They were small sounds—a crackle here, a distant metallic pop there—but just random enough to be unpredictable and therefore annoying.

As a result he couldn't sleep on the first night, and found himself touring the ship. Occasionally the Breen soldiers would look at him silently, but they didn't challenge him, and he hoped—if not prayed—that Gaila had told them he was on their side. He wondered how many Breen there were on board; their identical uniforms and face-covering helmets made it impossible to tell them apart or count the number of individuals.

He found that the ship had a large engineering deck, but Voloczin was the only engineer on board. There were vast cargo holds taking up most of the volume of the ship, and several large-scale replicator units programmed for weapons production.

There were a lot of automated systems overall, so the ship clearly didn't need a large living crew. Brunt didn't think that much of it. In his opinion, profit-making needed an audience. There just didn't seem to be as much fun in being surrounded by automatic systems that couldn't admire you or feel inspired to earn their own profit or, indeed, be jealous of how profitable and ruthless you were.

The only audience aboard most of the ship was the Breen, and they didn't seem to care. Brunt caught up with Gaila at breakfast in the gilded dining chamber to ask him about them. The chamber was reminiscent of a good Ferengi restaurant, but with replicators.

"Do you trust the Breen?"

"Of course," Gaila scoffed. "They're utterly incorruptible."

"Really?" Brunt wondered whether this was an opinion worth testing.

"Well, for one thing, nobody wants to hire soldiers who fought on the wrong side of the Dominion War. Secondly, they're not easy to communicate with, without specialized equipment. Thirdly, I pay them more than anyone else could afford."

Brunt nodded. That, he could understand; it was the best way to secure loyalty. He still didn't like them, though.

"You're a pilot," Brunt asked. He was trying, more or less, to keep the disdain out of his voice, and as a result, the question came out as something of a squeak.

Pel looked up from the cockpit. The ship was on course on its own, so she was there merely to check that the instruments were working correctly and to see whether any gravitational fluctuations had necessitated a course change.

"I am now."

"I didn't think females were allowed to—Well, until recently."

"I wasn't always a pilot."

"Ah, that's good to hear. You used to be a proper female?"

"I used to be in the service industry. Trying to make my way up to becoming a proper businessperson. I had the confidence of—" She chuckled, ignoring Brunt's rictus of a smile. "Well, one day I had to give all that up."

"How did you become a pilot?"

"By necessity. Necessity is always the mother of profit." She relaxed, her eyes focusing on something only she could see. "I was stranded on Solamin Prime during the Dominion War. Everyone had to do something to keep things running, and I ended up catering for the shuttle pilots. One of them liked me enough to want to show me how to fly the shuttles. At first I wasn't interested. There was no profit in it. But then I tried it, and found I was a natural. And when I qualified, people would pay for side trips or deliveries. . . . It was more profitable than I ever imagined."

"How nice for you."

"Now I couldn't imagine doing anything else."

"Not even being a—"

"A skivvy? A servant? Oh, you were going to say 'a traditional Ferengi female,' weren't you?"

"Maybe," Brunt said, sounding defensive. She smiled to herself, knowing that she was everything a man like Brunt hated. She knew who he was, of course; his feud with Quark had become legendary among Ferengi. It was true that Brunt was a good if somewhat inflexible Ferengi, but he was no Quark. It was easy enough for Gaila and Brunt to make profit when everything was weighted in their favor, but Quark could make profit out of absolutely nothing. There would never be another like him.

After four days in flight, the *Golden Handshake* dropped out of warp and swept into a parking orbit around Kalanis Major. The planet was an average Class-M world with three moons. Sensors had no difficulty picking up the signs of conflict on the surface.

Thankfully, they also had no difficulty making contact with the leaders of three factions. The existence of a third faction had come as a surprise, but Brunt, Gaila, Bijon, and Pel all took it as a sign that their venture was looked upon favorably. The Great Material

Continuum was flowing their way, and they need only enjoy the cruise.

Gaila had set up a meeting with the government faction for first thing the morning after they arrived in orbit. Brunt then contacted the old Loyalists and arranged a meeting with them for lunchtime. Since there was a third faction, and Bijon had trouble counting that far, they reluctantly let Pel arrange the rendezvous with the counterrevolutionaries that evening.

When the Minister of Procurement and his entourage materialized on the transporter pad, Gaila stepped forward to greet them. They were humanoid, roughly the size of a hew-mon or a tall Ferengi, but reptilian, with armored foreheads and scaly skin. They wore red armor and harness. "Greetings, Minister. I'm Gaila, representative of Gailtek Armaments and Technologies. This is my partner, Brunt, and our clerk, Pel. Whatever you require, we at GAT will do our best to fulfill the order."

"We need weapons." The minister had a female voice, though it was hard to tell if this was truly indicative of its gender.

"Obviously, or you wouldn't be contacting an arms dealer."

"Quite so." She—Gaila decided to think of her as she—hesitated. "We'd prefer the most efficient killing machines possible."

Gaila pursed his lips for a moment. "I probably shouldn't try to influence a client's choice," he began slowly, "but it strikes me that you don't really want weapons of mass destruction."

"We don't?"

"You can't exploit what you've destroyed," Gaila said reasonably. "No, what you need in order to deal with your undesirable rivals"—as if there was ever such a thing as a desirable rival—"is urban pacification equipment. Crowd control." He led the delegation first to a display room, filled with both physical specimens and holographic images of Klingon weaponry. Disruptor pistols and rifles of various designs filled the racks and tables.

The minister picked up one, a rifle with a three-pronged barrel and a heavy stock. "This disruptor rifle . . ."

"Ah," Gaila began silkily. "Klingon Type 47, the very best there is. When you absolutely, positively have to disintegrate every mother-creditor in the room . . . accept no substitute!"

The minister hefted the rifle. It was finished in black, rather than the red and silver more typical of Klingon weaponry. "It doesn't look Klingon."

"We've commissioned this upgraded variant to have a seamless outer casing that dampens the weapon's energy signature, making it less detectable by scanning devices. . . ."

Brunt tuned out Gaila's excellent pitch as his communicator buzzed. He stepped away from the group and brought it to his ear. "What?"

"The Loyalists are at the transport site," Bijon's voice came over happily. Brunt was immediately alarmed; the last thing he needed was two rival groups on board at the same time. *"I'm bringing them up now,"* Bijon went on.

"No!" Brunt called frantically. The others looked around at him. Cursing Bijon for being even more stupid than Quark's miserable tribe, Brunt smiled weakly and addressed Gaila. "That was Bijon," he said meaningfully. "He has acquired some more . . . credit." Gaila's eyes widened, and he paled.

"Go and see to it," Gaila hissed. Brunt practically ran out the door.

Gaila smiled back at the minister, knowing all too well what might happen now. He still had nightmares about the time Quark caused the Regent of Palamar and General Nassuc to meet at a deal he was brokering with the Regent. It had taken months to shake off the Purification Squads.

"A matter of paperwork that is due," Gaila said silkily. "My junior partner will deal with it so that we can continue our negotiations. If you'll come this way, we can take refreshments in the dining hall, and see what we can do for you." He indicated another doorway than the one by which they had entered, and turned to Pel. "Have Voloczin reset the chamber for Cardassian weapons," he whispered. She stayed behind, opening her communicator, as Gaila ushered the minister's group out.

Brunt tried to smile as the Loyalist group marched toward him, their green armor making them look half naked. "I am Commander Lotral of the Kalanis Defense Arm," the leader said, also in a female-sounding voice. Somehow this fit with the slightly nude impression given by the color of their armor, and Brunt felt a tiny bit more comfortable.

"I'm Brunt, GIT. Sorry, GAT."

"G—?"

"Gailtek Armaments and Technologies." Brunt said. "You're a little early, but that's not a problem, is it? The early investor reaps the most interest, after all."

"Really?"

"Rule of Acquisition number thirty-seven. It's the code we Ferengi live by."

"Good for you." The commander followed Brunt into the corridor. The door to the transporter room had only just closed when Brunt heard the worst sound he could imagine right now: Bijon's voice, too muffled to make out the words, and the whine of the ship's transporter. Brunt felt as if the contents of his stomach were about to fall out and go clean through the floor. Thankfully, none of the commander's group seemed to have heard the sound, and Brunt was grateful that not every species had Ferengi ears or Ferengi hearing. He hastily opened the nearest door, which turned out to be the door to his own quarters. "This is . . . the ex-ecutive lounge," he said hurriedly, and opened up the replicator and bar that were against one wall. "Please make yourselves at home, while I check with my secretary that the display models have been prepared."

He ducked back out and locked the door, praying that none of the commander's people would try to leave and find this out. He ran back to the transporter room, and sure enough, a third group of Kalani were just stepping down from the pads. This lot wore a mix of differently colored armor and harness, presumably acquired from wherever they could find them.

"Bijon," Brunt snapped.

"They were ready," Bijon said mildly, "so I thought we don't want to keep them waiting—"

"Bijon, don't you know what an appointment is?"

"I've never been to . . . Appointia." He shrugged.

"Where is Pel?" one of the Kalani demanded. None of them were armed, but they flexed their hands threateningly, and Brunt suddenly saw that the four digits on each hand had extended a thick black claw as long as one of his own fingers.

"Pel is just setting up the display models for you to browse. She sent me to greet you while she finished."

Wondering whether Bijon even had a share in the profits, of which he could be stripped, Brunt gritted his teeth. "Would you call Pel and ask her to come here, and tell her that—" He looked at the Kalani questioningly. "I'm sorry, I don't know your name."

"I don't know yours either, so we're even."

Brunt decided not to bother introducing himself. His former reputation as a Liquidator wouldn't intimidate them, and he was in no mood to be nice to this one. "That a representative of the Kalani Republican People's Democratic Front is waiting for her." Brunt hurried out as Bijon made the call and ran all the way to the dining chamber on the deck above.

Gaila looked around from the head of the table as Brunt came in. "Ah, Brunt, you're just in time to witness the signing of—" He halted, seeing Brunt's harried expression. Brunt leaned in close. "They're all here."

"What?"

"The Loyalists are in my quarters, under the impression it's a lounge, and the People's Front are in the transporter room!"

"How?" Gaila hissed through his suddenly frozen smile.

"That half-Pakled factotum of yours!"

Gaila groaned. "I should have sent one of the Breen to supervise."

"Who'd have thought operating the transporter was a two-man job?"

"Anyone who knew Bijon." Gaila sighed. "Is Pel with them?"

"She better be, by now."

Gaila nodded. "You entertain your group, and let the People's Front browse the Cardassian products. While the KRPDF are doing that, I'll escort the minister and her people off the ship. Then Pel can bring them here, and you can sell the Federation weapons to Commander Lotral. There's no reason any of them should meet up on board."

It sounded suicidal to Brunt, but he could do nothing else but nod.

★ ★ ★

Five minutes later, Pel was showing off Cardassian pistols and rifles to the KRPDF, and Brunt was in his suite, insisting on sharing a drink with Lotral. It stung to be so free with his supply. Brunt wasn't incapable of generosity, but he much preferred it to be in the context of giving a little to recoup a greater return. He forced himself to remember that the sale of Federation phasers to the KDA was a greater return.

When Pel buzzed his communicator to let him know that she had taken the KRPDF contingent to the dining hall, Brunt magnanimously opened the door to his quarters and stepped out, followed by Lotral and her group.

Movement out of the corner of his right eye caught Brunt's attention, and he tried to look in that direction without turning his head. Three of the minister's aides were still in the corridor, not yet in the transporter room.

Brunt hastily leapt in front of the door to his quarters, and pointed down the corridor to the left. "Right along there. I mean, not right, straight. Straight along there to your left." Miraculously the six reptilian soldiers all did as they were bid, without looking the other way along the corridor. Perhaps it was because being soldiers made them more receptive to commands, or maybe it was because the drinks in the impromptu lounge had made them relaxed and suggestible. Brunt hoped it was the latter, as this would make for an easier sale.

Just to be on the safe side, he looked into the demonstration room to be sure that there were none of Pel's clients still inside. It was unoccupied, the racks and tables filled with Federation phasers of a design a few years old. Relieved, he escorted his charges inside.

Gaila felt a percentage of panic recede as soon as the minister and her entourage had returned to their planet. That was a recession he could appreciate, almost as much as the price they had agreed to pay for a shipment of disruptors. He hurried back to the dining hall to make sure that Pel was still there with the KRPDF group.

She had their leader's thumb on her padd even as Gaila walked through the door. It was unfortunate that she was now legally allowed to keep some of the profit, but, at the price Gaila was charging, he could afford to indulge her.

He exchanged a few pleasantries with her and the clients, and then went back down to the hall in which Brunt was showing off phasers to Commander Lotral. "Commander!" he exclaimed volubly. "I'm Gaila, president and CEO of Gailtek. Has Brunt been showing you these prime weapons?"

"He has indeed. They are quite fit for our purpose." And with those words, Gaila knew he had another sale. All three groups would receive their chosen quantity of the specified weapons, and none of them would ever see the weapons they had bought in the hands of any of the other factions. They would never know that they were one of three customers today, or that Gaila, Brunt, and the others had just made three times as much as they had paid.

He barely restrained himself from laughing outright. A short time later, when the last Kalani had returned to their planet, all the Ferengi laughed themselves silly. Lok, the leader of the Breen soldiers on board, and Voloczin, who came to investigate the sound, merely looked at each other.

Eight Months Ago

We'll celebrate," Gaila announced brightly one morning as they all took a delicious breakfast in the dining hall. "I've had reservations made on Risa for us to unwind after all these negotiations." It had taken a couple of trips to deliver all the arms ordered to Kalanis Major, but they had completed the delivery with no problems. They had even made a few side deals on the way.

Brunt was happier than he had been in months; he had profit now, and that bought him contacts and information with former colleagues at the FCA. Or, at least, with former subordinates who were still in awe of him. Through them, he could keep his files updated as he planned his eventual triumphant return. Brunt didn't think much of the idea of wasting their profits at Risa. Who knows where the money spent there actually ended up? Not among Ferengi, that was for sure, and that meant he'd never be able to charge it back someday. He said as much.

"Profits are there to be enjoyed," Gaila said. "Besides, it's the best place in the Alpha Quadrant to pick up tips for future ventures, isn't it? All those people vacationing, drinking, letting themselves go wild . . . and letting their tongues slip! Their nondisclosure agreements forgotten." He gave a conspiratorial grin. "Now do you feel the urge—"

"For a celebratory vacation? Now that you mention it, I suppose I do."

"Good. We also need to invest our profits, and I have no intention of doing so through a former FCA Liquidator. No offense intended."

"None taken. I don't trust you either."

"I don't imagine any of us are stupid enough to trust any of the others to invest their shares for them," Gaila said pointedly.

"I don't mind," Bijon said.

"I'll see to yours," Pel said quickly. Gaila and Brunt both glared at her. A female earning her own profit was bad enough, but tricking a man out of his . . .

"Where's that Romulan ale?" Gaila asked. "Didn't I have it opened to breathe?" He looked around the room.

Voloczin blinked his huge eye, slowly and deliberately. "I opened it half an hour ago," he grated. "Where do you *think* it is!?" His skin flushed a pastel-blue shade, making Bijon laugh uproariously. It just made Brunt feel that the *Golden Handshake*'s dining room was colder than it really was.

Lok stomped up behind Gaila, rumbling a question. Gaila waved him away. "Of course you don't have to accompany us. Remain on board and conduct security drills."

A few days later, Brunt was sitting on a beach, bored out of his lobes. Water was brushing against sand in an irritatingly dry atmosphere. It was a nice enough view, if you liked that sort of thing, but it was all free. There was no charge he or anyone could make for it. Even the Risans themselves didn't charge extra for lodgings in the area.

There were, however, one or two ways in which Brunt was enjoying himself in spite of his disapproval of the Risan way of doing things. He was moderately surprised to find that most females on the planet, of whatever species, went mostly unclothed, as females should.

On the one hand, this meant there were some strange and distressing types of alien flesh on show, but on the other hand, even Pel had changed into a skimpy two-piece affair resembling hewmon undergarments. Not only did this suit her, but it suggested to Brunt that there was hope for her yet. She could still be persuaded to be like a proper Ferengi female, if the circumstances were right. Brunt himself still wore his hand-tailored suit and latinum around his neck.

"You've never been to Risa before?" he had asked her.

"I've heard of it, but never imagined I'd ever go there."

"I've tried to avoid it myself," Brunt agreed. Before he could say anything else, or even compliment her on her state of undress, a hew-mon bumped into him. "Watch where you're going," Brunt snapped.

"Hey," the hew-mon said, "it's okay. I just slipped is all. It's the bloody sand, you know. It twists your feet under you when you try to turn around." Brunt had noticed this himself.

"Another reason to hate Risa."

"Nah," the hew-mon said. "Just the beachfront properties, you know?" He shook his head, with its short copper fur glinting in the sunlight. "Me, I like the mountains better. Though they're not as good as the ones on . . ." He frowned in thought. "That banking planet. You must know the one; you're a Ferengi."

Brunt looked sidelong at the hew-mon, Pel all but forgotten. "Banking planet?"

"There's a three-planet system, mainly does corporate banking and investments, bonds, that kind of thing . . . But their mountains are fantastic. Best in the galaxy for climbing."

"What sort of people are they?" Brunt asked, suddenly interested.

"Pacifists, same as here. No wars, no military. Just lots of banks and lots of mountains."

Brunt grinned in what he hoped seemed like a friendly manner. "Tell me more . . ."

"A three-planet system?" Gaila echoed, later that night. Brunt had called to arrange to meet at a dabo club. It was noisy and smelly and a lot more fun than the beach. Gaila smiled, and nodded to himself. "It's a sign."

"A sign?" Brunt didn't believe in supernatural aid.

"Three always was my lucky number."

"They're called the Urwyzden." Brunt frowned, stroking the bar of gold-pressed latinum he wore around his neck. "I've never heard of that place described as a vacation paradise until today."

"But you have heard of it?"

"I've seen FCA records, and communicated with some of the governmental officials on Urwyzden Alpha."

"When you were a Liquidator for the FCA?"

"Exactly. I've had cause to deal with Ferengi who have invested their profits with the Urwyzden."

"Invested?"

"It's a banking center," Brunt said. "Mainly for governments and interplanetary conglomerates. A lot of small single-planet or single-system governments deposit escrow with the Urwyzden, and use the place to broker deals and holdings. And sometimes, the most . . . lobe-less of Ferengi do so as well."

"Offworld banking?" Gaila said, disbelievingly. "There are Ferengi who trust aliens to hold their assets? Inconceivable!"

"Oh, but it happens," Brunt went on, warming to his subject, and, as always when that happened, sounding personally affronted. "There are Ferengi out there who like nothing better than to rob the Nagal treasury of its cut of the banking charges." Brunt's hands subconsciously curled into claws, as if to wring the payments out of someone. "When a Ferengi collections agency charges a debtor"—he spat the word—"ten slips for the communication telling him that they're charging him, one of those slips goes to the Nagus."

"As is his right."

"But when an alien bank does the same thing, there is no profit for the Ferengi. That's precisely why Grand Nagus Lifax made it a crime for Ferengi to bank offworld."

"Lifax? Ha! He was the biggest idiot the Nagal throne has ever had. A man who thought that harassing people and stopping them earning profit would make them better able to invest that profit with him."

Brunt fixed Gaila with a warning look. "Biggest idiot until now," he corrected him. "But it doesn't matter. The law is the law, and we should be proud to uphold it."

"Of course," Gaila said. "That's why I allow Pel to wear clothes and earn profit. The laws passed by our idiot-in-chief are, as you say, the law." He broke off as a cheer of "Dabo!" erupted at the next table. The interruption seemed to have derailed Gaila's train of thought. He frowned and said, "So, Urwyzden . . . Why are pacifists of interest to us?"

Brunt thought for a moment. Truth to tell, it was the opportunity to search their files for the identities of Ferengi who banked there illegally that he had first thought of. "Because they have something that others may want to steal, and no way to defend themselves from them."

Gaila nodded slowly. "Interesting . . . The riskier the road, the greater the profit."

"My thoughts exactly," Brunt said, insincerely.

"Let's hit the road, then."

Six Months Ago

Urwyzden Alpha was a turquoise ornament set into the velvet heavens. Deep oceans formed a band around the equator, separating continents that reached up to the clouds with beautiful razor-edged mountains. Where the mountain slopes fell away toward the more extreme latitudes, the rich green of the forests blended into the crisp white of the polar caps.

As the *Golden Handshake* entered orbit, a white Federation ship was peeling away from the planet. Brunt couldn't see all of the ship's name or registry on the view shown on the main screen, but it ended with an E. *"Sovereign* class," Pel said. "Wish I could take one of those for a spin. More transporter rooms, faster engines; think of the profit we could make with one of those. . . ."

Gaila looked out at the vast, sleek form as it rode proudly forward. It didn't need to be streamlined like a creature built for racing in order to travel in a vacuum, but it was beautiful. "I wonder . . ."

"What?" Brunt asked.

"How much it would cost to commission the hew-mons to build me one of those as a private yacht," Gaila said dreamily.

"Can't cost more than that moon used to cost you to run." Gaila looked at him piercingly, and Brunt smirked. "Did you imagine the FCA didn't know exactly what its income and overheads were?" He could tell from Gaila's conflicted expressions that he had thought exactly that. Which in turn meant he had set out to make that the case, which meant the FCA's figures weren't necessarily correct. Brunt made a mental note to find out how much Gaila's moon really had cost to run. One never knew when some tidbit of fiscal information could open a door or two.

Someday, Brunt promised himself, his old office door would be opened to him again.

Gaila continued giving instructions. "Lok, scan for locations of military bases and defensive weapons emplacements."

Lok snapped an affirmative and began working the sensor controls. "According to the latest open-source Federation database," Pel advised, "Urwyzden has no armed forces."

"No armed forces?" Gaila echoed. "Do you mean no military at all? Do you mean that hew-mon Brunt spoke to was actually correct?"

"That's what the Federation have listed."

"If I was the Urwyzden," Brunt said darkly, "I'd hide my military from the Federation. And anyone else." He shook his head. "I can't believe such an important and fiscally sensitive planet would have no protection at all."

Lok straightened up from the sensor console and made a surprised-sounding comment. Gaila looked at him. "It sounds unbelievable, but Lok says there are no military installations detectable."

"That just means we need new sensors," Brunt scoffed. *Or new bodyguards,* he thought. He didn't dare say that aloud, since, even though he didn't understand anything Lok said, Lok clearly understood everyone else in the room.

The biggest cultural museum on Urwyzden Alpha was a banking museum. The second through seventh biggest museums were also museums of banking. The eighth biggest was a general cultural museum, which, unlike the banking museums, seemed aimed at an offworld audience rather than a native one. Brunt and Gaila had taken Brunt's shuttle down to the central spaceport and parked as closely as they could to the sprawling pyramid of its terminal.

Much as both Ferengi would rather have visited the banking museums to compare Urwyzden development with that of Ferengi culture, they took a tour of the general history and culture exhibits.

The Urwyzden were small humanoids, perhaps the size of a prepubescent or teenaged Ferengi, and had slate-gray skin, gouged with wrinkles and studded with thick patches. There were, however, plenty of visitors to the planet, and so the Ferengi didn't stand out that much from the hew-mons, Tellarites, and others who were visiting. The hew-mon Brunt had met on Risa had been right about the mountains, and it was clear that as many people came for them as came to do financial business.

The museum was a sprawling complex detailing Urwyzden evolution, and it was singularly lacking in displays of weapons and famous battles, either in the halls of preserved artifacts or the holosuite reconstructions of important events. Even the tour guide, who was so diminutive that she would have made Pel look as massive as Bijon, explained when asked that "Urwyzden has never had a war, in its entire history."

"But, don't conflicts lead to new inventions?" a hew-mon tourist asked.

"Perhaps among other races," the guide said. "It's true that Urwyzden civilization was ancient before it progressed enough to discover space travel. This is in comparison to other species' development, but we could point out that several civilizations had risen and fallen on, say, Earth, before space travel was discovered there. Only one civilization rose here, and it never fell. But, when the time was right, we did develop the technology, and colonized the other Class-M planets in the system." The guide smiled, showing tiny teeth. "It is true, as you said, that necessity is the mother of invention, but there are other necessities. When we needed space travel, it was invented. But we never needed to kill ourselves to do so."

On their way back to the spaceport, Brunt and Gaila passed every kind of expensive luxury transport. It was said that some bankers had private homes on floating mountains tipped upside down and supported over the oceans by massive gravity lifters. A quick call to the *Golden Handshake*, and the download of some imagery from orbit showed that this was true.

"This is the richest system I've ever seen," Gaila said hungrily. "They could afford to pay top prices for any weapons systems imaginable."

"If only they had a need for them," Brunt pointed out.

"I can't believe for a moment that any civilization, let alone one that is so steeped in finance and brokering, could have no use for weaponry. There must be some people out there who want to deprive them of all those funds in all those currencies."

"People other than us, you mean?"

"Exactly. And I don't mean businessmen either. There must be robbers and pirates who know about this place. If even hew-mons on Risa know about it, the Orions must."

"They have never had a war," Brunt said, thinking aloud, "but war and protection are different things. Urwyzden must have a use for defensive and security weapons systems to protect their financial complex from ordinary criminals, surely?"

"Let's find out," Gaila suggested. "I've arranged a nice, quiet meeting with very discreet representatives of the Urwyzden Confederacy's government."

The Urwyzden government people were a trio of almost identical middle-aged officials in the latest funereal fashions, with black suits and high collars.

They were meeting with the Ferengi in a very old gaming club built into the side of a mountain. The carpets had borne the footfalls of centuries, and ancient clocks ticked and occasionally sang creakily in the darkest corners of the room. "What you have heard is true," the Minister of the Interior was saying. "We have never had need of weapons. We maintain an attitude of strict neutrality, even with the Romulans, the former Dominion . . ."

Brunt looked sidelong at them. It was almost inconceivable that a place so steeped in money and profit could be forever unmolested. War was rare in the Ferengi Alliance, but it had been known, and surely there were criminal elements who would find the Urwyzden's vaults and information far too valuable to be unattractive.

"But what about Orion pirates? The Korth? These worlds of yours are such ripe targets for robbers and raiders . . ."

The minister's gnarled features twisted and flowed into what passed for an Urwyzden smile. "Without naming names, gentlemen, I suspect that you will find that many of the backers and investors in such . . . entrepreneurial endeavors trust the Urwyzden fiscal system to ensure that their own assets remain liquid without any outside interference."

"You mean the Orion Syndicate—"

"The what? I'm sorry, I must have misheard; for a moment I thought you were about to suggest that a purely fictional organization of doubtful integrity really existed."

"Orions in general then . . ."

"It's certainly the case that a number of Orion conglomerates place funds in escrow with us. I believe they prefer the convenience of not having to wait for Federation bureaucrats to go through the motions as they would, say, with the Bank of Bolius. We can facilitate that."

"And what about those races with a lust for conquest instead of profit?" Brunt asked.

"A race that was truly geared for conquest—say, the way the Cardassians were a few decades ago—would be so geared for war that, yes, they would conquer us easily. But the other races, who would then be left in difficult circumstances, would, I'm sure, find it in their interest to make things right." The minister's smile widened. Brunt felt the opportunity slip from his grasp, and he could see the same reaction reflected in Gaila's expression. Then the minister blinked slowly. "Nevertheless, you do bring up an interesting point, and it has been considered in the recent past—what with the Dominion War and the Borg invasion—that some orbital defense platforms would be a wise investment. These would allow . . . others time to recognize the importance of their decision . . ."

"Oddly enough," Gaila said quickly, "orbital defense drones are Gailtek's specialty."

"Oddly enough, I thought they might be."

Within the hour, Gaila had sealed a deal to supply the three Urwyzden planets with orbital drone networks. *He was good,* Brunt thought with grudging admiration. He hadn't even noticed when Gaila passed the minister the bribe.

Once back aboard the *Golden Handshake*, Gaila had Pel take the ship off to the vicinity of his old moon, claiming that he could pick up the orbital drones there, among other things. At first, the crew were delighted with the news of a decent sale, but Brunt could only see the downside: "It's a good sale, but a one-off," he said. "We need a regular source of capital that offers good dividends. Profit is for life, not just for a holiday."

"You're absolutely right," Gaila agreed. "That's one of the reasons I brought you onto our team. You think like a profit machine. You're smart."

"Perhaps if we introduced deliberate flaws into the drone software, forcing the Urwyzden to continually purchase updates—"

"An excellent idea, but somewhat limited to a minor product line." Gaila paced around the bridge. "But you inspire me, Brunt! You inspire me . . . Now . . . There are three planets: Urwyzden Alpha, Beta, and Gamma."

"Three planets, three opportunities."

"Yes . . . But not for defense against outside attackers." Brunt wondered where this was leading, and felt that Gaila's speech was sounding a little more rehearsed than it should for a sudden, budding idea. "What if the Urwyzden planets fought among themselves," Gaila began, "for political control of the fiscal services? There'd be potential for massive profit then, all of which would need to be banked somewhere . . . else."

"Then there might be a demand for regular weapons shipments—"

"Might?! It would be a profit farm! An ongoing struggle, kept at just the right level, would make for a perfect regular income."

"Regular." Brunt shivered with anticipation at the thought.

"And if we could then control the level of product use—limit the amount of charge a weapon could hold, even the means by which it is used—we could have a going monopoly. Our own private war."

"How much more profitable could we get? It would be a big, ongoing job, with plenty of up-front investment needed."

"I know just the people," Gaila said, and Brunt wondered how long it would be before he finally got used to hearing Gaila say that.

Brunt was less annoyed to be back at Risa than he had been to visit it before. Partly it was the thought of Pel properly undressed, and partly it was because this time he and Gaila were visiting a Tongo parlor inland.

They had both played well, ending up as the last two players in the game they had joined, and walked away with three times as much latinum as they had originally bought in with. "My lucky number," Gaila had reminded Brunt, when the subject was raised.

After a long and satisfying game, they had retired to a holosuite to relax. The setting was ancient Ferenginar, and there were mud baths and all the finest food they could eat. "I thought we were supposed to be meeting your so-called business contacts," Brunt said.

"This is where they said to meet. They didn't say we should starve ourselves or sit like Bajoran prylars while we wait."

"Good." It wasn't long before two stunning Ferengi females approached Brunt and Gaila. They were as naked as the most traditionalist Ferengi female, and moved as seductively as the most alluring Risan hostess. It was a heady mixture, and Brunt found himself almost having to gasp for breath. Gaila sat up from his lounger, his eyes almost bulging out of his skull in some attempt to reach the females before the rest of him.

"What are the two most interesting arrivals to Risa in weeks doing playing around with holograms?" the first one asked. She sat beside Brunt, laying the softest, smoothest fingertips on the edge of his right ear.

The second female took Gaila's hand in hers, guiding it toward her own ear. "Especially when there are real females who've been waiting here for you."

"That depends—" Gaila squeaked, then cleared his throat and spoke more normally. "That depends on the rates of remuneration for . . . for . . ."

"Why? Aren't you looking for something to invest your profits in?" the first female asked. "You're businessmen, by the look of you, and with the lobes for success."

"We are," Brunt agreed, "but a successful businessman always looks for an investment that promises good returns."

"Oh, we can guarantee that." She tugged on Brunt's wrist, and he found himself rising to his feet and following her. Gaila was doing likewise. "Returns and highly favorable bonuses." The two females led them appreciatively and expectantly toward the exit, but before they got there, they stopped. "Oh, there is just one other thing."

"What's that?" Gaila asked impatiently.

"This." The female with Gaila did something Brunt had never seen a Ferengi do before: the Vulcan nerve pinch. He was so stunned to see Gaila fall that he didn't realize the same was happening to him. Then everything went black.

The blackness came and went a few times. Brunt felt himself return woozily to consciousness, and realized that he was being carried by burly men wearing gauntlets. Then there was the searing electric buzz of a neural stunner, and more blackness. He thought he felt the tingle of a transporter beam at one point, then came around as he was slammed roughly against a wall. Gaila was pushed in with him, and the two were squashed uncomfortably into a cramped space. Brunt could hardly breathe for Gaila's weight against him.

Everything went black yet again. Brunt was almost getting used to it. He could feel movement, and was sure they were on board a ship in flight. After an hour or two, he felt a vibration through the walls and floor, and knew the ship had docked. The vibration felt the way he imagined a disruptor blast would feel, and he fully expected to be proved right at any moment, because people didn't knock you unconscious, kidnap you, and stuff you into access panels just to give you a rebate.

The access panel was removed and allowed to clank onto the floor, and blinding light flooded in. Strong pairs of hands grabbed Brunt and Gaila by the lobes and dragged them out into the companionway, and then out of the ship altogether. On legs turned to jelly by the sensations coursing through their nervous systems from the painful grips on such sensitive areas, Brunt and Gaila were frogmarched through the main lounge of a private yacht. All the viewports were black with privacy filters, and a force field shimmered slightly just inside.

The lounge was filled with low tables covered in goblets of the finest slug juice, and platters of plump tube grubs. "Here's an irony," the thin-faced Ferengi sitting opposite them said cheerily. The thugs who had brought in Brunt and Gaila shoved drinks into their hands and forced them to sit in comfortable chairs. Perversely, this made the chairs uncomfortable. "A stalwart agent—no, actually more of a fixture, like the furniture—of the FCA now comes to me looking for help—"

"I do?" Brunt yelped. "I mean, I do, sir . . ."

"You don't know who I am, do you?" He pinched his almost long nose between finger and thumb, stroking it. "Not a clue?"

"You're . . . Gaila's contact?"

"Well . . . yes and no. Actually, Gaila's contact couldn't make it to-night; he was unavoidably detained for the rest of his life." Gaila paled, and Brunt swallowed, feeling a sudden near-fatal chill. "Ah, don't be like that, boys; life for him was only a couple of minutes. Now, the most important thing is that all his projects, shall we say, passed on to me. You got me?"

"You?" Gaila managed to say at last.

"All right, let me introduce myself. I am Daimon Blud. And don't make any fancy remarks about how that sounds compared to a similar word in Federation Standard."

"Blud?" Brunt echoed. "The head of the Shadow Treasurers?"

Blud nodded gracefully, and Brunt was even more certain that he and Gaila were about to die horribly. The Shadow Treasurers were the bane of the FCA, even more so than Quark and his ilk. They were an organized gang of offworld bankers, thieves, money launderers—the underworld. Brunt couldn't help the snarl of disgust that twisted his face. "If I was still in the FCA . . ."

"You'd have been left outside the ship," Blud said. "You still might be, if I think you are still with the FCA." He clapped his hands once. "You're not drinking, I see. Are you trying to insult me? It's not poisoned, I assure you. If I want you dead, my boys will blow your heads off. Poison's too unreliable." He added, more conversationally, "You never know if someone's inoculated or immune, or what. A good point-blank disruptor blast to the head is really the only way to be sure." He indicated that they should drink up.

"Now, what does a treasurer do?" Brunt and Gaila exchanged a look, each mentally willing the other not to use words like *terrorize*, *blackmail*, or *murder.* "Looks after latinum," Blud said. "Banks it, invests, borrows, lends, and so on." He pointed at them. "That's why I've allowed you to come here. I've thought about your plan, Gaila, and it's interesting."

Gaila brightened immediately, though Brunt could still smell the stink of fear on him. Brunt decided that Gaila would tell Blud whatever he thought Blud wanted to hear. He doubted that he himself would do any differently; imminent death had that effect on most Ferengi.

"You see, like yourselves, we—I mean, my friends and I—have had our disagreements with those irritating creatures who inhabit the Urwyzden system." He took a sip of his drink. "Oh, wait, I'm sorry, did I say 'disagreements with irritating creatures'? I'm always doing that." He laughed lightly. "I meant to say that the sooner those SOUL-SUCKING MOTHER-CREDITORS ARE ALL DISEMBOWELED AND SERVED TO THE SLUG FARMS, THE HAPPIER I'LL BE!" He took a long, shuddering breath, and a drink to soothe his undoubtedly strained throat. "Sorry."

Brunt's ears were still ringing, but he knew better than to be less than respectful to someone who could kill him—or worse, bankrupt him—on a whim. "You are clearly a man of great feeling."

"That he is," Gaila agreed. "And it's so understandable."

"We have had dealings with the Urwyzden before," Blud admitted. "Well, when I say 'had dealings,' I mean we've offered to have dealings with them, and they've replied by insulting me. I sent the prime ministers of all three planets a hundred bars of gold-pressed latinum each. They sent it back. I killed their best friends, and they actually had the gall to complain to Grand Nagus Zek. This was a couple of years ago.

"So, if you're going to make a profit out of them, I'm willing to invest, for a forty percent cut of the dividends." Blud held up a hand to stave off any haggling. "Don't try to negotiate. I like you, and I hate having to disembowel people I like. But it doesn't stop me doing so."

"Forty percent," Gaila echoed, mortified.

"I'm glad you agree. Now, enjoy your drinks, and then go and show those twisted little dwarves what a real financial power can do. We'll teach them a lesson about messing with the Ferengi!"

Five Months Ago

"The same procedure as at Kalanis Major?" Brunt asked.

"Same procedure as every deal," Gaila confirmed. Daimon Blud had arranged the rental—at a surprisingly reasonable rate—of a holoship, a vessel dedicated to holosuites for training purposes. This smaller vessel had been slaved to the *Golden Handshake*'s helm. Brunt and Gaila walked through the empty holodecks. "The prime ministers of Urwyzden Alpha, Beta, and Gamma will be brought here in that order. They've already had deliveries of their drones, but we can use an inspection tour for each as an excuse to make our pitches."

"Let's hope Bijon knows to wait between appointments this time."

"Just to be sure," Gaila said grimly, "I've made the arrangements for three different days. And to be doubly sure, one of Lok's troops will beam them directly to the holoship."

As they walked, Voloczin stretched his tentacles down and descended from the hologrid. "How does it look?" Gaila asked.

"Like gold-pressed latinum," Voloczin said cheerily. "All the goodies on offer to each bunch are detectable by sensors we can sell to the other. I gave each planet's gear a different casing and color."

"Perfect. Let's do it."

"I think I'll stay a moment," Brunt said, "and get a feel for our products."

"You'll enjoy them, I'm sure," Gaila promised. With that, he called back to Lok, and he and Voloczin beamed away.

Left alone, Brunt selected a Klingon disruptor and hefted it. The last time he had held a weapon in anger, things had not gone well. There had been Jem'Hadar then, and a Vorta, and he had intended to fight. Well, more accurately he had intended to escape, but if that meant shooting a few Jem'Hadar, then that was what he would have had to do.

It had all been the fault of Quark's family, of course. His mother had let herself get captured by the Dominion, and Brunt had been willing to help rescue her for a share of fifty bars of gold-pressed latinum. Except that this had been on Quark's promise, and that was hardly trustworthy. It had even been Quark's fault that Brunt's own star had sunk so low that he had had to accept such a demeaning job just to hope to earn some profit.

At least Gaila had, on that occasion, proved himself the most redeemed of Quark's family, by trying to shoot Quark. Sadly, he had not proved himself any more competent than the rest of Quark's discount-rate kin.

It always came back to Quark, Brunt thought. Quark's schemes, and Quark's impossible luck that haunted Brunt and drove him to penury. If only it had been Brunt who had been quick enough to fire a shot at Quark on Empok Nor. The loathsome welcher would have been as overcooked as hew-mon food.

Looking at the holographic target, Brunt didn't even see it as a circular targeting matrix. It was Quark's smug, leering face! He blasted it. Immediately another target was generated; Brunt saw Quark again, and was only too happy to oblige by firing again. Two more targets flashed in from the flanks. Rom's and Nog's faces spun wildly across the room, but Brunt got them both with a single shot each. And then there was Zek . . . Yes, sure enough, he could see Zek's wrinkled jowls laughing at him on the surface of the next target globe, and he smoothed them out with a disruptor beam right between the beady little eyes.

"*Simulation complete,*" a computerized voice stated mildly. Brunt was surprised, and looked down at the rifle in his hands. He had actually enjoyed that, he realized, and much more than he had expected to.

"You're a good shot," Pel said from behind him. He jumped, almost dropping the disruptor. "I don't think I could have hit all of those target globes, especially not those last two."

Brunt was rather impressed himself; he hadn't expected to hit them all either. He wasn't going to tell her that, of course. There was always more profit in keeping your assets or debits secret and letting others draw their own conclusions. "It's just about hitting what you see," he said truthfully, and with not a little relish.

"I could see the targets, but . . ."

"Let's just say I have good motivation."

"I could never do that."

"But you must have good hand-eye coordination to be a pilot?" If not, Brunt thought, he would never step into the group's ship again until they got a new pilot.

"That's true. It just feels different flying a ship, though. You're not pointing at something; you're having your whole self carried along. It's like you're using your whole body." Brunt tried not to think about her whole body. It was difficult, what with its being so temptingly clothed and therefore invitingly mysterious. "I don't like those Breen that Gaila has taken up with."

"I know what you mean," Brunt agreed. "Dominion soldiers. At least with a Jem'Hadar you could see his face, and what he was thinking."

"You've met Jem'Hadar?" Pel asked admiringly.

"Yes," Brunt admitted. He decided not to tell her that the meeting was in the context of trying to swap a Vorta for the Nagus's mate—who also happened to be Quark's mother.

"I'm impressed! What did they do?"

"They . . ." Brunt hesitated. On that occasion most of them had simply been withdrawn, and two had been killed, by Rom and Leck. "They died," he said at last.

Pel nodded slowly. "So the famous Liquidator does have lobes, eh?"

Brunt looked at her. After the past few months, he had even stopped noticing that she was clothed. "Oh yes."

"I never imagined I'd say that to a Liquidator."

"We're not all monsters. We try to be, but we're only flesh and blood. Something shows through."

"You're actually a pretty decent Ferengi," she admitted. "Strong, resourceful." She was standing closer to him now. "Profit-driven."

"We should keep out of the way of those Breen. I mean . . ."

"You mean you have a reputation to uphold?"

"I do? I mean, I do." Brunt smiled nastily, suspecting that Pel might actually like that kind of expression. It would fit his reputation as the nasty FCA Liquidator, after all, and she had brought up that reputation. "I don't like the way they look at me."

"I don't like the way they look at me either," Pel admitted. "In fact, I don't like the way they look at anyone other than Gaila and Voloczin." She pulled herself up proudly to her full height, such as it was. "I especially don't like the way they look at people talking together."

"Then we shouldn't let them look at us talking."

Pel began to giggle, then stopped. "They'd probably assume we're conspiring together against Gaila, or them."

"I don't trust any of you enough to conspire with you, about anything." *Not yet, anyway,* he thought, and the thought surprised him.

"That won't stop them," Pel said. "I was one of the first females to earn profit, and I want to keep earning profit, but . . . I sometimes wonder if Gaila's way of doing things is really . . . well, if it's really the best way to get the maximum profit."

"You don't trust Gaila?"

Pel gave him a disbelieving look, then her expression cleared, and she laughed. "Oh, you were making a joke! Sorry. It's a long time since I've seen irony or subtle humor. The Breen don't laugh, Bijon only thinks people falling over is funny, and Voloczin . . ."

"Is just a little too different," Brunt observed.

"You're right. Of course I don't trust Gaila; nobody trusts Gaila. Frankly, you've been his partner for seven months. That's not a record, but it's not that far off."

"He's always been a profitable man," Brunt reminded her. "Everything he does is so beautifully geared toward increasing profit. Not just for himself, but for all of us."

"I suppose it is, as best he can think of it. But, you know, sometimes I think he just does it for fun—or for practice. And profit comes second."

Brunt shivered at the very thought of profit coming second. Yet he had seen Ferengi behave that way before. "Perhaps it runs in the family."

"The family?"

"His cousin does that a lot."

Three times, Gaila marched around the racks of supplies in the holo-ship, stroking a hand along the edges. He gave the same speech to each of the three prime ministers; it was well-rehearsed and care-fully honed to sound off-the-cuff, heartfelt, and believable. "We have everything for the growing military defense force." He paused and lifted a hand phaser from a row of them. "Hand weapons with vari-able stun and kill settings. Concealable, and ideal for enforcement and protection." He moved to the next rack. "Sidearms for troops in the field. More powerful, with a longer-lasting power pack, which is easily removable for charging while in the field. Again, very reliable. Accurate up to over a kilometer, variable power, and can fire in pulse or beam mode."

"What about larger weapons?" each prime minister had asked. "Anti-air, for example," the Alphan had suggested. The prime minister of Urwyzden Beta wanted "orbital defense." The man from Gamma had requested "air superiority."

"I'm glad you asked that," Gaila said with undisguised delight in each case. He moved his customers into another chamber and acti-vated it. A moving cradle clanked into life, bringing out a mechanism roughly eight feet tall, made of two linked canisters with an array of folded solar receptors and sensor packages. It looked vaguely like a giant, hibernating wasp of some kind. "These are my most . . . deli-cious offers," Gaila went on. "They are drone weapons. Unmanned automatic probes that are fully user-definable. You can program them as passive guardians, to detect and interdict unauthorized approaches, or as offensive weapons that can be sent in waves to overwhelm enemy defensive positions."

"Armaments?" everyone asked, during their separate visits.

"Kinetic energy missiles are standard, but—for a small fee, of course—they can be replaced with plasma pulse weapons, photon mortars, or even an antimatter payload with a self-detonation yield of up to two hundred and fifty megatons." Gaila grimaced. "Though, if you don't mind my saying so, that option tends to be more for consumers who wish the destruction of planetary ecologies along with their enemies. For the urban pacification you are interested in, I'd recommend the standard or photon mortar options."

"Fully customizable?"

"Of course. My engineer will make any complex adjustments necessary to fulfill your specifications before delivery, and supply comprehensive manuals."

Brunt decided it was time to add his voice, to help seal the deal. He could almost feel those bars of latinum brushing against the skin of his fingertips already. "And, as well as automatic systems, they also have—"

"Brunt!" Gaila snapped. "Please! Our customers don't want to be bored with meaningless technobabble. They want to see their potential purchases in action!"

Why, Brunt wondered, *did Gaila not want to advertise the remote-control options on the drones?* It was unthinkable that he didn't know about them, as he was always very knowledgeable about his products, and it was equally inconceivable that he didn't see the option as a selling point. Maybe he wasn't immune from the stupidity that characterized his cousins after all.

Of course, it wasn't just the sales pitch that Gaila was enthused about. There were the bribes, the little words of worry, and the outright lies. The words that spread tension and unease. The suggestion to each prime minister that the others had approached the Ferengi in search of offensive weapons, but been turned down.

By the time the prime minister of Urwyzden Gamma had visited the holoship, he was desperate to buy, because he was so certain that Alpha and Beta were plotting against his holdings.

All three planets bought in heavily. And, a month later, they asked Gaila and Brunt to return with more.

By the time of the second visit, there were three Breen guards on the drone production unit. Gaila waved them aside and went through.

Voloczin was curled in the rack, several tentacles twisting their way into access panels on a drone. Lok was at a console, monitoring readings from the drone.

"How are my special babies today?" Gaila asked.

"Happy as Larry, squire," Voloczin grated. Lok gave a short agreement.

"Good. Business, my friends, is about to be booming." He laughed. "And booming business is the best kind!"

Three Months Ago

Orbital traffic around Urwyzden Alpha was light when the war started. Most of the vessels arriving and departing belonged to other governments or private corporations, but there were enough intrasystem transports ascending and descending. A corporate shuttle was the first to explode, speared by a burst of kinetic energy missiles from a drone. Several more Betan shuttles were hit in the moments following. A few vital cargo vessels strayed too close to a drone armed with pulsed phase cannon, and it came to life and peppered the entire flight with fire.

Passenger vessels weren't immune, and Urwyzden women and children died in many crashes after being shot down. Pel looked on in horror as another ship exploded on the *Golden Handshake*'s main viewer. "Unbelievable . . ."

"In what way?" Gaila asked. "We did come here because of a most profitable ongoing military escalation, didn't we?" He laughed again.

The prime ministers were enraged, screaming at each other over the system's communications network. "You are murderers!" the Betan yelled at the Alphan. "This is unprecedented and unacceptable! No Urwyzden has ever declared war on another!"

"Declared war!?" the Alphan replied. "We are the victims of your madness. Is this some kind of attempt at a takeover of the Board?"

"We are clear that some members of the Board of Premiers need to be let go!"

"And the sooner the better. Urwyzden Alpha is now in a state of war . . ."

In his palatial quarters aboard ship, Gaila listened to the arguments, accusations, and counteraccusations. They were the finest opera he had ever listened to. This was the kind of situation he had long dreamed of, and knew that his idiot cousin Quark would never have been able to stomach. Thankfully, he had had the sense to have Brunt as his partner; Brunt was a strong man, and would do what it took.

The door chimed, and when he opened it, Lok stepped in, buzzing a report. Gaila raised his glass to the Breen. "Exactly as planned, Thot Lok. Here's to exploiting the weak for fun and profit."

Outside in the corridor, Brunt was on his way back to his suite, and overheard Gaila's comment. It was a strange thing to say, he thought. He continued onward and into his suite, helping himself to a stiff drink. He had profits to count, and it would take time to work out how to invest them all. These profits were stacking up quite nicely.

On their next trip, having arranged for slightly upgraded weapons software and longer-lasting power packs, they approached the Urwyzden system cautiously. Ships were departing on a regular basis, but there was no large-scale exodus yet. Fighting was rather neatly confined to skirmishes in orbit, and things didn't look that much different on the surface. Nevertheless, the Ferengi took care, because, while they wanted to be welcomed as customers, they didn't want any of the three governments to take exception to their visiting the others.

"The Beta and Gamma governments may not be pleased to see us visiting Alpha," Brunt pointed out.

"That's why we've got this." Pel patted a bulging addition to the flight control panel.

"Ah," Brunt sighed appreciatively. "A cloaking device?"

"It's Klingon," Pel explained. "It came from an old *B'rel* class. Gaila bought it from an old Duras clan captain who was trying to raise funds to pay his bar bill in exile. The cloak was just about the only part of his bird-of-prey that still worked. And, being on the wrong side of the civil war, he couldn't really take it back and exchange it for a new ship."

★   ★   ★

"Welcome, my friend!" the Alphan prime minister enthused, when Brunt and Gaila visited him. This time they had beamed down to his office, which was a crisp white-and-chrome affair overlooking a deep blue lake. "It seems I was wise to make those purchases."

"You know it makes sense," Gaila said.

"And continues to do so. I shall have ongoing business with you, I think. Our own military productivity is still in its initial stages . . ."

"How goes the war?" Brunt asked. "We didn't see much sign of it."

"Obviously we are doing our best to ensure that it doesn't interfere too much with business." Both Ferengi nodded understandingly. They could appreciate that. "For the most part we're concentrating on inhibiting the colony worlds' ability to take hostile action against us. We're eliminating their satellite weapons, and so forth." Brunt felt a warm glow around the money belt. That would mean the other worlds' prime ministers would be ordering replacement drones during this trip. "We have also," the prime minister went on, "begun interning Beta and Gamma citizens in conditioning camps to be sure of their loyalty."

"I like that," Gaila said. "I like when a people take their responsibilities seriously." That pleased the prime minister. Brunt was less enthusiastic. Once they had returned to the ship with a new order and contract, he said so to Gaila. "They're running the war properly, and taking it to heart," Gaila told him. "They'll be the best customers because they're giving themselves wholly to their responsibilities. They'll keep us rich for life."

"The only problem with anything that's for life, is that it's only for the living," Brunt muttered.

"You're not going all hew-mon on me, are you?" Gaila asked suspiciously.

"Of course not! Who better to rip off than—" Somebody you hate? He had no problem with it. Yet.

Two Months Ago

Gaila looked up as the ranking leader of his Breen mercenaries stomped onto the bridge, while he was alone there. Pel was delivering hardware to Urwyzden Gamma, and Brunt to Beta. Bijon was helping Voloczin to fetch and carry aboard the holoship. "What is it, Lok?" It occurred to him that, were the Breen to switch rank markings between their uniforms, he could find himself addressing the wrong one. That led him to wonder if they occasionally did this to amuse themselves by making a fool out of him. He dismissed the idea; Breen were cold, heartless killers who did what they were told. They didn't have a sense of humor.

Lok rumbled a warning, describing what he had been observing for some time.

"Brunt and Pel?" Gaila scoffed. "You must be joking." Lok buzzed a short reply. "Er, yes, I was just thinking that . . ."

Lok leaned forward and slipped a data chip into a padd. Immediately, the screen came to life, and a miniature Brunt and Pel were walking across the bridge of the *Golden Handshake* a few days earlier. Brunt seemed strangely laid-back as she showed him the innermost secrets of the Klingon cloaking device that Gaila had once gone to such lengths to covertly acquire.

As Gaila watched, he felt a mix of anger and dismay, but at the same time he felt a strange relief. He had always expected to be betrayed by his partners, and at least now he didn't need to worry about when Brunt or Pel would do so. He couldn't blame Pel, of course; she was only a female, and the freedoms of wearing clothes and earning profit had clearly gone to her head. It was bound to happen eventually.

Brunt, on the other hand, had been a Liquidator, and had spent a lot of time in the past trying to think like Quark. This was one of the reasons why Gaila was always so reluctant to return home: his relatives were idiots and it was a contagious idiocy. Leaving and buying his own moon had saved his intellect, just as stalking Quark seemed to have whittled Brunt's intellect down. "Ah well," Gaila said. "What am I to do with them, eh?"

Lok made a dark, almost subsonic, suggestion.

"You took the words right out of my mouth." Gaila grimaced. He hated having to do this kind of thing, but sometimes it was unfortunately necessary. He was a weapons dealer, not a soldier, but he recognized the need for the use of weapons, and for the occasional death, and that was why he employed soldiers as well as selling to them. He didn't like the necessity for killing, but he accepted it as an infrequent price to be paid. A tax, in a manner of speaking. He had even tried to kill Quark once or twice, by sabotage.

Anger began flooding through Gaila. Brunt's betraying him was one thing. Pel's betraying him was a little different. But Brunt and Pel colluding in order to betray him . . . that stung. That wasn't the sort of personal ambition or mere incompetence that he accepted. "They're conspiring! Against me!" He blinked. "I can hardly believe it, Lok. How could anyone conspire like that?"

Lok growled something suggestive.

"Brunt? He doesn't have a heart any more than . . . any more than a Breen does." Lok didn't answer this time. "I suppose," Gaila sighed, "it's that time again. Time to lay off workers, and start cutting overheads."

Lok's response was tinted with a powerful joy. Gaila wasn't surprised; those with ice instead of flesh and blood were capable of anything.

Pel's hands moved quietly over the controls of a small, crab-nosed shuttle. She prided herself on doing a professional job as she guided it into a neat glide path toward Urwyzden Alpha, on what felt like the hundredth cargo run since the Urwyzden conflict had started. She didn't think about the crates of disruptor rifles secured safely in the hold. She just wondered about Brunt, and what had driven him to join their merry little band. She also wondered if he was really as misanthropic as he appeared—not through any sense of friendship, but simply because she had difficulty believing that anybody could be quite as misanthropic as he seemed.

She noticed a sensor blip approaching, and checked it. It was one of the drone satellite-killers that protected the Alphan southern hemisphere from overflight by the probes of other Urwyzden factions. She paid it no more heed. She had a transponder clearing her for transit, and there was no profit in paying anything more attention than it needed.

The shuttle swept toward the drone, growing clear in its sensors. Inside, the drone's computers registered the shuttle as nonthreatening, and passed the telemetry on to the various recorders and data-saving equipment that were monitoring it.

This data also played in real time across a set of monitors watched over by a Breen soldier on the holoship. Lok stood behind him, awaiting just the right instant. When the shuttle was at the optimum distance and angle of approach, Lok pointed an index finger at its image, and barked the fatal order.

The soldier touched a control.

Pel never saw the shots coming. The drone simply flashed into life, hitting the shuttle with a volley of kinetic energy missiles at point-blank range. The viewscreen shattered and the console died. Air was streaming out somewhere, and Pel was slammed against the bulkhead behind her as the shuttle lurched.

She fought to reach the controls, thumping a fist on the restart pad. The controls glowed back to life, and she struggled to keep the shuttle level. It was going down fast and hard, and she had no illusions about keeping it flying. She wasn't sure she would want to anyway, if it was venting atmosphere. There was still the problem of the intense heat caused by friction with the atmosphere, but she raised the shields, modulating them to take most of the heat energy.

Pel had no idea where she was heading, other than down, and just had to hope that the Great Material Continuum would provide a soft bedding for the vessel.

The shuttle screamed through the air, and clipped some hillside treetops as it plowed into a series of thick sandbars in a shallow river. A shielded power plant overlooked the river from the hilltops, but Pel didn't have much of a chance to notice it before the shuttle flipped and seemed to implode around her. Then there was only blackness, and it was a far deeper blackness than that of the mere void.

Lok congratulated his subordinate on his shooting, and moved away to report the result to Gaila. The Breen soldier paused for the briefest moment to acknowledge the compliment from his commander, and then returned the drone to self-control, and purged its memory of the event.

A group of half a dozen or so Urwyzden Homeland troops emerged from the tree line and observed the crash site. "Is it a Beta shuttle?" one of them asked.

"No. It's alien. Ferengi, by the looks of it."

"There are some Ferengi who are important to the prime minister and the Board of Directors. If any of them are harmed . . ."

"I hear you. Let's check it out." They walked cautiously down toward the smoking shuttle, keeping their tricorder on it. They wanted to be sure it wouldn't suddenly explode as a result of whatever damage it had taken. When they reached the stricken vessel, one trooper felt around the edges of one of the hull breaches. "KEM hits, sir."

"Betan?" another asked.

"Can't tell. Ours or theirs . . ."

"Let's hope it was theirs." The second soldier saw something tubular in the dark, and reached for it. He had to wiggle partway into the hull breach, and stretched out his arm until it hurt. For a while he could just feel his fingertips brush the surface of the object, but with a final agonizing twist, he managed to drag it forward just enough to get his hand around it.

When he drew it out through the hull breach, he found that it was a disruptor rifle. It wasn't the same as the phaser rifle he and his comrades carried, but identical to the weapons carried by the Betan factions.

"Sir," he called out. The rest of the troops came to see. "Look at this."

The officer in charge took the disruptor. "Betan . . . yet this is one of the people who supply us with phaser rifles."

"Who says they supply only us?"

The Alphan prime minister and his Board of Directors were gathered in his office. A large hologram of an unconscious Pel and a soldier holding one of the Betan weapons was flickering in the center of the room.

"Contact Gaila," the prime minister ordered.

"He's already on the line," one of his aides said, surprised.

"Gaila—"

"Prime Minister," Gaila said urgently from thin air. *"I must warn you! I have uncovered evidence that one of my crew has been stealing from me, and may be trying to sell to one of the other factions. I'm transmitting the details of her shuttle to your military—"*

"No need," the prime minister interrupted. "We have already shot down the vessel to which you refer."

In his suite, Brunt listened in to the communications channel. Eavesdropping was a vital skill in the FCA, if one was to uncover evidence of fraud, illicit unionizing, and so on. It was always a good way to retrieve salable information.

So, he thought, *Gaila is beginning to betray his crew.* He wondered how long it would be before it was his turn. It was time to take action, he decided. Time to look after number one. Time to visit Bijon.

"Bijon," Brunt began, oozing false camaraderie. "You look tired. Haven't you had a lunch break today?"

"I'm all right," Bijon protested bashfully. "I'll just get this manifest loaded, then I'm done for a while. I can have lunch then."

"If you say so." Brunt hesitated, as if just thinking of something.

"Oh, do you know . . . they do serve the most exquisite tube-grub casserole in the dining room. It's the best I've ever tasted outside of Ferenginar itself."

"Oh, that sounds good," Bijon replied. "I like tube grubs."

"Everybody likes tube grubs," Brunt told him. "You wouldn't be a Ferengi if you didn't like tube grubs."

"My father doesn't like them."

Brunt bit his tongue before it could run on ahead and say something along the lines of his not having expected a Pakled to like tube grubs. "Well, almost everyone," he said at last.

"That's true enough," Bijon agreed. "Are you coming as well?"

"Not at the moment. I already ate, less than an hour ago."

"Aw. Oh well."

"Oh, and Bijon?" Brunt put on an expression of having just thought of something. "Why don't you check with Voloczin that the remote control for the Alphan drone weapons is working correctly. I'm sure I noticed some degradation in their performance over the past few days."

"Oh, right." Bijon nodded slowly. "I'll ask."

Voloczin was draped over the entire surface of a table at one end of the dining hall when Bijon entered. Lok and a couple of his soldiers were seated at another table, consuming something from canisters through flexible tubes that fitted directly into their faceplates. Bijon went to the replicators and ordered the tube-grub casserole. It was very nice, just as Brunt had said it would be.

"Oh, Volo," Bijon said, "are the—what are they called, the remote control for the drone things. Are they working all right?"

"The what?" Voloczin demanded, startled.

"The remote-controlled drone things."

"Oh, er, those . . . Ah, well, you see, matey, me old mucker . . ." Lok stepped up behind the octopoid engineer and barked a command. "Righty-dokey, skip!" Voloczin suddenly scooted forward, two incredibly strong tentacles reaching out and whipping around Bijon. One grabbed him in a rib-crushing grip, while the other tied itself around the large Ferengi's neck. Bijon tried to squeal in shock, but the tentacle around his throat had already crushed his windpipe. Turning a deeper shade of purplish orange, Bijon grabbed at the tentacle and exerted all of his not inconsiderable strength to try to tear it away, but the tentacle was like a welded steel cable, and simply would not move.

In a matter of seconds, Bijon's arms fell limply, and Voloczin let him go.

While Bijon was talking with Voloczin, and Gaila was on the bridge, Brunt used a site-to-site transport to beam into Gaila's suite of rooms. That was another skill that had often proved its worth during Brunt's long career with the FCA, and at least this time he didn't materialize in a wardrobe.

He established a link between his padd and Gaila's computer. The cracking tools in the padd made short work of Gaila's security, and Brunt began to browse. He gave the computer the word *Urwyzden* to play with, and sorted the files by date. They went back years, giving the lie to the idea that Gaila hadn't heard of the place until Brunt himself had spoken of it.

Stranger still was a communication with a hew-mon just before they arrived at Risa. Gaila had primed that hew-mon to approach Brunt! From there, Brunt went into Gaila's private communications links, but found nothing openly or clearly suspicious to him. He then did the same with the Urwyzden Alpha computer net, and explored it thoroughly. He didn't find anything there to indicate what might be going on either, but he did see tracks of mass deletions. Gaila had been deleting records as he went, meaning there was something he needed kept secret.

It occurred to Brunt to compare the files he had just copied from Gaila's computer with the Urwyzden Alpha network and look for matches in files. There were dozens.

Gaila had invested heavily in Urwyzden hiking and mountaineering resorts—well, Brunt thought, that explained the hew-mon's mentioning them—over the past several years.

There was a sound at the door of the entry hall, and Brunt hurriedly disconnected his padd from the computer, and initiated another site-to-site transport. This time he materialized in the hangar bay.

Gaila, Voloczin, and Lok moved swiftly into Gaila's quarters. "Bijon would never have asked such a thing on his own," Gaila was saying.

"He was a few Borg short of a collective," Voloczin agreed.

"Which means Brunt is betraying me! Damn the FCA! He probably still works for them after all." How could he have been so stupid? He should have listened to Quark all along; his cousin was an old enemy of Brunt, and knew him a lot better than Gaila. Brunt would take all the profit now, and probably waste it on the legal cut for the Nagus. Greed was good, but Brunt had the wrong type of greed. "Where is he now?"

Brunt climbed into his shuttle, and flew it out of the *Golden Handshake*'s hangar. Setting course for the Urwyzden Alpha capital, he felt much more comfortable alone in the shuttle. It was just the right size for him, and it struck him that it just wasn't big enough for both him and Gaila.

Just as the *Golden Handshake* wasn't.

He had made sure to program the shuttle's transponder with Gaila's personal signal, and so faced no challenge as he descended toward the city that clung to the Alpha's largest mountain like serrations on a blade. He called ahead and asked to speak to the war minister, who answered promptly.

"This is Brunt, GAT. Gaila has asked me to check over the wreckage of the shuttle that crashed in your territory recently. He wishes to be sure of the pilot's condition."

"*Brunt,*" the war minister replied. "*The shuttle you refer to has been taken into custody. The pilot survived, but we have her interred at Conditioning Camp Seven. Does Gaila want her executed for her betrayal of him?*"

"Of course he does! How could he not? That's why I'm coming to collect the worthless cretin, so he can have the pleasure himself. Can you have her ready for me?"

"*Of course. We're sending coordinates and clearance. Just follow the instructions.*"

Conditioning Camp Seven was far to the north, bordering the arctic snow fields. It was situated in a network of deep crevasses, whose sheer cliff faces were slick with black ice. The inmates were housed in caves with force-field projectors at the openings instead of doors. Since the fields let air molecules through freely, they also let the cold through.

Stacks of twisted little bodies were piled at one end of the north-ernmost crevasse, and there was no sign of any real activity for the inmates. Brunt couldn't understand the purpose of such a place. Intel-lectually he knew it was a place to dump the unwanted and be rid of them, but he couldn't comprehend why there was no manufacturing industry at least. The inmates simply froze to death or rotted away. Even the Cardassians, when they had set up such camps on Bajor and other worlds, had seen the profit in putting their unfortunates to good use.

The Urwyzden, for all that they were an economic force to be reckoned with, clearly knew nothing about generating profit.

He was reluctant to leave his shuttle, which he had landed on a pad kept clear of snow and ice. He'd rather let the Urwyzden bring Pel to him than have to set foot among the walking dead. They gave him the creeps, and, worse, their condition made him feel as angry as Quark's allowing his employees to unionize had. Was this what the Federation types called a conscience pricking at him? He hoped not.

Two Alphan soldiers dragged a figure toward him. At first he thought it was another Urwyzden, but he realized with a wave of re-vulsion that it was Pel, shrunken to the point where she looked smaller than her usual eager self. Her tailor-made pilot's jumpsuit hung from her in shreds. She was shivering, which wasn't surprising, considering the cold, but somehow Brunt felt that it was caused by a deeper chill.

The soldiers shoved her toward him, and she fell at his feet. "There you go," one of the soldiers said. "She's sold weapons to the Betans."

"So I heard. That's stealing profit from me and Gaila." Brunt knew he sounded harsh, and the soldiers laughed.

"And means the Betans can kill our folks. Make it slow and painful for her. Maybe cut off her ears, eh?"

Brunt's lips pulled back, showing sharp teeth. "I can promise you, I'll be getting dividends out of my anger. Every last slip." He looked around, and spotted a few other inmates standing nearby, shaking and trying not to be noticed. "I'll tell you what, lads . . ." He took the bar of latinum from around his neck. "Gaila and I like to see a full program of executions. What would you say if I offered you this bar of latinum to take, say, these half-dozen along as well. The Breen could do with some target practice, and a holographic shooting range is never, you know, quite the same thing." He grinned evilly.

The soldiers grinned back, and began shoving other prisoners toward him. In a few minutes, his shuttle was filled with shivering, stinking prisoners. "Thank you," Pel managed to say.

"Don't thank me," Brunt grumbled. "I'm just doing what an FCA Liquidator should do to a Ferengi who banks offworld and robs the Nagal treasury of its lawful share."

Last Month

Brunt had had more sense than to return to the *Golden Handshake*, or even to Urwyzden Alpha itself. Vouched for by some of the prisoners whom he had flown out of Conditioning Camp Seven, he had been allowed to land safely in a settlement on Urwyzden Beta.

The town clustered under an overhang at a bend in a river, and the marshes all around reminded Brunt and Pel of Ferenginar, though it didn't rain nearly as much. It was also better protected from Alphan drones, and Brunt felt safer there.

Agents from all three colonies were waiting for him when he took a simple room in one of the town's largest hotels. None of them were looking to buy weapons, and he had half expected them all to want to kill him, but they weren't that stupid. They all had the same question: "What did you sell to the other factions, and what do we need to counteract those purchases?"

"Let's talk prices," Brunt had said.

"No," the Betan had said.

"Ten bars of latinum," the representative from Gamma had offered.

"Name your price," the Alphan said bluntly. "And it's yours."

Brunt thought long and hard. The Alphans had been building the death camps. Selling to them would be selling only mass death, which, in the long run, would be counterproductive. The dead couldn't pay.

"The dead can't pay," he said aloud.

"What?" Pel asked.

"The dead can't pay. There's no profit in them." He sighed. "Call the three contacts we've seen. Tell them I'm going to give them what they want. And, Pel?"

"Yes?"

"Have all three appointments made for here, tomorrow at noon."

The next day, three rather uncomfortable Urwyzden sat beside the pool on Brunt's private patio. "Ten bars," he said to the one from Gamma, and got it. He got the Alphan's thumbprint on his padd, for a fee of two hundred bars of gold-pressed latinum. Then he grinned at them all. "And now comes the part where you all wish you had made a deal for exclusivity."

"Gailtek sold you all the same resources for the same price. All of you. And to be sure that Gaila kept earning, he started this war." He paused to let that sink in. "There are Breen troops with Gaila, who control all your satellite drones by remote. They fired the shots that began this war, and they continue to manipulate it."

"This is valuable information," the Betan agent said slowly. "Worth more than you've been paid. Very generous of you."

"This is not generosity—it's a price, and we Ferengi believe that prices are . . . sacred. Profit doesn't always come in latinum—and neither do fees that must be paid."

When the Urwyzden had gone, Pel looked thoughtfully at Brunt. "You're really not what I'd expected. I was thinking . . . Gailtek is surely doomed."

"Not necessarily, but we are not going to be part of it anymore, are we?"

"The thought occurs that you need a new partner."

"So do you, if you want to keep"—Brunt still could only say it through gritted teeth—"being a profit-earning female."

"So . . . if we're partners, what do we do next?"

Brunt knew the answer to that with every fiber of his being. It was instinct. "As our business rival, we want to ruin Gaila and outdo his profits. As a loyal retired Liquidator of the FCA, and partner, we want Gaila brought to justice. As the people he tried to kill, we want him . . . dealt with." Brunt kept the final answer as a thought to himself. As Gaila was a member of Quark's family, Brunt wanted him humiliated as well as dead.

Last Week

Shuttles converged in the darkness between worlds, hurtling toward a minor moon caught in the gravitational eddies between Urwyzden Beta and Gamma.

They didn't arrive undetected. Voloczin, checking over the systems of the holoship, which was parked in a deep crater, noticed the blips on the sensor screens. "You what?" he said to himself, flushing an orange tinge. The sensor returns were coming from both of the colony planets, but they weren't forming up to engage each other. Voloczin couldn't understand that; the two groups were enemies, weren't they?

The first strafing run convinced him otherwise. A considerable chunk of the drone perimeter set up around the moon was destroyed in a second. "We're under attack!" Voloczin shouted, summoning Breen soldiers to the controls.

The Breen began returning fire, but it was too late; the Urwyzden forces had made a breach and had begun descending toward the parked holoship. Voloczin immediately started to power up the engines, ready to leave, but before they were warmed up a thump rang through the hull. An Urwyzden shuttle had docked. A second vessel joined it in a matter of moments.

Two of the holoship airlock hatches exploded into the corridors, and space-suited soldiers flowed into them. Breen troops began firing immediately, and battle was joined.

"Bugger this," Voloczin muttered. "I'm offski." He pulled himself into an upper level, making for the holoship's shuttle. Halfway there, a group of Urwyzden ran right into him. His tentacles immediately snatched up two of them, crushing their fragile bodies in a trice. The others opened fire as soon as his victims' screams were silenced.

Struck by multiple phaser beams, Voloczin's skin ripped apart. Being mostly gaseous inside, he exploded like a burst balloon.

It took less than an hour for more arriving Urwyzden to subdue the remaining Breen. None surrendered, and none survived.

The news reached Urwyzden Beta within the hour, and Brunt found himself summoned to a secure military office. The Betan prime minister was there, with several generals and other advisers. Representatives of Gamma were there too, as was someone Brunt vaguely recognized as one of the inmates he had brought out of Conditioning Camp Seven. It turned out that he was a high-ranking civil police officer.

Brunt felt uncomfortable with so many eyes on him, all masking mixed emotions. Mostly hostile emotions, at that. "You were right," the prime minister said at last. "We've taken control of a vessel midway between our worlds, and there is a mass of computer data showing how this war came about as the result of the Ferengi desire for profits." He hesitated. "Did you start the war for profit?"

"The crew of which I was a part did," he admitted, "and I did my part in it. The camps and the . . . the rest of it, weren't part of my personal intention. I can't sell to the dead."

"Then why? Why did this happen?"

Brunt had expected that question as well. "Gaila invested here. This whole project has been set up to allow him to cash out without anybody—especially Daimon Blud or the Nagus—knowing what he's doing. The war is a distraction for a massive insider trading scam!"

The police officer nodded slowly. "Many of us are indebted to you," he said, "but you must understand there'll have to be a reckoning about your part in this abomination."

"A Ferengi always pays a fair price," Brunt promised.

"Can you bring us Gaila?"

"Yes."

Last Night

Brunt materialized in the *Golden Handshake*'s engine room. The place was darkened, running on minimal power to avoid detection, just in case. It had occurred to Brunt that Gaila—or more likely Lok, as Gaila wouldn't have the expertise—might have changed the transporter protocols. For that reason he had come alone, rather than risk bringing up an Urwyzden, which might set off an alarm when the biofilters noticed it.

Brunt was no expert at demolition, but he didn't have to be. With access to the computer, all he needed to do was override the autodestruct system. It was a simple enough task, and just as simple to make sure that his override couldn't be overridden by Gaila or Lok. It was impossible, however, to avoid the loud alarms and vocal warnings that the computer would give, and Brunt had to move as quietly as he could to get where he wanted to be before Gaila and Lok heard them.

Gaila woke with a scream when the alarm started blaring. *"Autodestruct in five minutes,"* a voice was calling.

He knew it was Brunt, of course. Brunt with his FCA snooping skills. "Computer, cancel autodestruct sequence. Authorization Gaila four four two seven nine omicron."

"Autodestruct sequence cannot be canceled. Autodestruct in four minutes thirty seconds."

Gaila swore in several languages, then called upon Lok to try to deactivate the autodestruct. By the time he ran onto the bridge, Lok was thumping a console with his gauntleted fist. Obviously he was having no luck either. The only thing to do, it soon became clear, was evacuate the ship.

The transporter room was pitch dark when Gaila and Lok ran in. "Set the coordinates for the spaceport on Urwyzden Alpha," Gaila ordered. "We'll blend in with everyone else who's leaving the—"

A phaser blast cut down Lok where he stood, and he fell with a mechanical gurgling sound.

"Hello, Gaila," Brunt said. "Brunt, FCA . . . ish." He grinned, waving a phaser before him as he emerged from the shadows. "You're about to become notorious as the first ever Ferengi war criminal, you know. And I must say, it gives me great pleasure to arrest you as a war criminal, as a member of the Shadow Treasury—"

"If I'm a war criminal, then so are you!"

"As an offensively poor example of Ferengi morals, and as a personal threat to my own profit and opportunities."

Gaila just laughed. "What profits? Once you ran out, I made sure to sequester your share of the company profits."

"Then I can add breach of contract."

"You can add what you like, but if we're still here in fifteen seconds . . ."

"Step onto the pad."

Gaila did. Brunt touched a control on the transporter console and stepped up onto the pad. Immediately, Gaila grabbed for the phaser, and the room dissolved around them.

In orbit, the *Golden Handshake* exploded, and Gailtek Armaments and Technologies was, in all possible ways, dissolved.

Now

At the Urwyzden capital's spaceport, Brunt and Gaila rolled down the slope of the pyramidal terminal while hanging desperately on to each other's throats and lapels. Jagged chunks of rubble thumped repeatedly and randomly into bone and flesh, always in the least expected and most painful places.

Black fingernails tore at skin, and bruised knuckles bruised themselves some more against jaws and cheeks. The two combatants butted up against a handful of Urwyzden corpses; soldiers lay sprawled around, with blood-slicked weapons lying on the tarmac.

Gaila leapt on top of his enemy and started to throttle him, while trying to keep his face out of range of the fists that were coming up in an attempt to dislodge him. He jerked his head back away from one punch, and that was when he saw the most beautiful sight on this miserable slime-hole of a planet: a warp-capable shuttle, impulse drive idling, with its hatch open and a fully powered but mercifully uninhabited cockpit inside.

Pieces of rubble clattered down from farther up the sloping wall of the terminal, and both Ferengi looked up to see armored Urwyzden soldiers scrambling down in pursuit. Both then looked back to the shuttle.

The distraction was just enough to allow Brunt to roll, throwing Gaila off. They broke apart on all fours, scrambling for the weapons lying near the hands of the fallen soldiers. Then they were on their feet again, both trying to get the business end of a hand phaser into the other's face first.

Neither won.

Beaten and bloody, their eyes blackened, their clothes torn and bloodstained, each found himself pressing a phaser to the other's lobes at arm's length. The pursuing soldiers were gathering around them, weapons raised, cutting them off from the shuttle. "Gaila," Brunt said smugly. "Oh, if only you were Quark . . . that's the only way this moment could possibly be any more delicious. Or profitable."

Gaila tried to look less bowel-looseningly terrified than he felt, consoled only by the thought that he couldn't look *more* terrified. "You're finished too, Brunt! It's a mutual loss scenario!"

Brunt just sighed as the troops closed in. "How did my life come to this?" he asked.

Gaila licked his lips. "If you want us to cross each other, then fine, but we should at least get offworld first, and then do it in a proper Ferengi fashion." He spoke calmly and as rationally as he could manage. "There's no profit in getting ourselves killed by these troops."

"Profit?" Brunt echoed. "Profit can still be profit even if it's coming as something other than latinum. Information. Matériel. Females." He nodded. "But you're right—we're Ferengi together, and should put that first."

The pair turned to aim at the approaching soldiers, raising their weapons. . . . Then suddenly, before anyone could fire, Brunt turned back and clubbed Gaila down with his weapon. He disarmed Gaila and shoved him toward the troops.

"What are you doing?" Gaila demanded as the soldiers forced him to his knees and wrapped restraints around his limbs.

"I have a new partner. The Rules of Acquisition say there's profit in peace, and profit in war, and in each of those conditions you must prepare for the other. You didn't understand that. There's no ongoing profit in genocide and death camps. You can't exploit someone you killed. It's just . . . un-Ferengi." Brunt was wholly incapable of letting such un-Ferengi behavior slide. That's why he was so well-suited to the FCA. "Oh, I didn't mind the insider-trading scam, but the genocide that will cut off all opportunities for future profit, that's not just un-Ferengi, it's unnatural." Brunt leaned in more closely. "And, of course, there's the fact that you are a member of the detestable House of Quark, as well as being guilty of all the things that the FCA was devoted to rooting out. And I will always be 'Brunt, FCA.'"

"And where's your profit? Your nonlatinum profit?"

"Well, let's see," Brunt said smugly. "By exposing you, I will stop the war, preserve opportunity for future Ferengi profits, and thwart a member of Quark's detestable family. That's worth a lot. Oh, and did I forget to mention that I've negotiated a license to operate as a consultant/enforcer who is a properly legal authority in the region, albeit one operating on private and government contracts and commissions. It's not the same as being in the FCA, but it's the closest thing—especially since the diplomats for such a fiscally important exchange planet will exert pressure on Ferenginar to allow me to earn profit from non-Ferengi. That's my profit: not in latinum, but in opportunity for more latinum. I won't be in the FCA, but I will be doing the same job in the private sector—for more money!" He laughed at Gaila's horrified expression.

While the soldiers dragged Gaila away, Brunt could hear him trying to bargain both for his life and for the rights to holonovels of his life and this scheme. It was almost more than he could take.

Then again, he didn't have to. He had a shuttle just the right size for himself and Pel, and a new, profitable job in the career he had always lived with.

The three Urwyzden prime ministers met on Urwyzden Alpha, to make a joint declaration of peace. The war was over.

"Now we know who our enemies are," the Alphan said.

"And we will never forget," the Betan agreed.

The prime minister from Gamma nodded. "The Ferengi."

"We must look into this matter," the Alphan continued. "We must protect ourselves in future, proactively if need be." He looked out across the smoldering capital. "Next time, we will teach the Ferengi how to conduct business."

Tomorrow

Quark had a long day. His brother Rom and family were visiting the bar on a stopover at Deep Space 9. This wouldn't normally be cause for a long day, even with his niece, little Bena, teething and being a royal pain, but now that Rom was Grand Nagus, and the bar the official Ferengi Embassy to Bajor, it was a different matter. Now there were security people, and advisers, and businesspeople looking for an audience with the Nagus, and innumerable other annoying hangers-on.

Quark pretended not to mind too much, as he was glad of the chance to see Rom and Leeta again for a proper family dinner. He pretended not to be too glad either, but they were family, and he was charging premium prices for Ferengi dishes and drinks while there were so many Ferengi visitors among the crowd following the Nagus. This was looking like his best month so far this year, as far as the takings were concerned. If he could persuade Leeta to take a shift on the dabo table, he could increase profits further by casting it as a nostalgic grand return . . .

Quark had mostly tuned out the sound of FCN. The net was playing on a large display next to the staircase to the upper level. It was a screen similar to the main viewer in ops, but Quark rarely had it put up, as it tended to distract patrons from the dabo tables and other attractions. Rom liked to keep an eye on it now that he was

Nagus, however, and so Quark had had a couple of waiters install the screen.

He had just sat down to dinner with the group when there was a sudden crash from upstairs and a horrifyingly familiar voice roared triumphantly: *"Brunt, FCA!"*

Rom let out a howl, causing Bena to wail as well. When Quark turned, his guts filling with ice and his throat with fire, he was all ready to unleash the full diplomatic fury of an ambassador's ire.

There was nobody there. There was nobody on the stairs, and the only faces visible on the upper gallery were Morn and his Klingon date. *"That's right!"* Brunt continued. *"I'm back, and debtors and deal breakers everywhere are in for their worst nightmares."* Rom squealed again, and Quark stepped back, looking up.

Brunt's face leered out of the large screen, the bar of latinum around his neck looking as if it was about to crack Leeta in the back of the head. "I don't believe it," Quark muttered. "What is he doing there?"

"I don't know, brother," Rom answered. At least he had stopped yelling. Quark wished Bena would too.

On the screen, Brunt grinned his oiliest and most repulsive grin. *"Only on FCN!"* A title slammed down over his face: "BRUNT THE BOUNTY HUNTER: ALL NEW!"

Quark and Rom exchanged a glance, and then both of them screamed.

Envy

The Slow Knife

James Swallow

Historian's Note

This story is set in early 2362 (ACE), during the Cardassian-Federation conflict while Miles O'Brien was serving aboard the *U.S.S. Rutledge* ("The Wounded" TNG).

For Sean Harry, with thanks

The deck plates rose up to meet her and she felt the impact of the fall vibrate through her duty armor, felt the gridded metal slice into her right eye-ridge. Sanir Kein swallowed a reflexive cough and tasted the earthy wash of new blood in her mouth, where her teeth had cut the inside of her lip. Dimly, she was aware of alert sirens howling and the cloying, spent stink of curdled electroplasma.

It was the smell that propelled her back to her feet, up in a shaking, wavering motion; that stench was an engineer's worst nightmare. As the cry of a child would always rouse a mother to action, so the venting of a power conduit did the same for a Fleet-trained systems specialist. Kein found herself moving through her daze with the wooden motions of muscle-memory. She saw Enkoa across the *Rekkel*'s smoke-choked bridge, and he gave her a momentary look. The tactical officer seemed as shocked as she felt.

Someone else was trying to get up ahead of her, and Kein bent to help; the officer angrily shook off her grip, and with a shock she realized it was her commander.

Gul Tunol stood. Her slicked black top-knot had come free from its band, pooling around the taller woman's shoulders like an oil slick. Tunol glared past Kein at the main viewscreen and lurched toward her command throne.

"What in space happened to my ship?" snarled the gul. "Arlal?" She glanced around, searching for her executive officer. "Arlal!"

Enkoa moved a weighty man-shape on the deck, the haze of low gray smoke parting around it. He said nothing, just drew a single finger across the line of his neckthreads, miming a dagger's edge. Dal Arlal's sightless eyes stared up at the ceiling, glassy and dull.

Tunol swore under her breath, and Kein caught the gutter oath as she reached the engineering console. She had never heard the gul stoop to such a thing. Kein knew the stories, that Tunol was from a commoner family and had clawed her way up the ranks with a mix of dogged obedience and ruthlessness, but that single utterance was the first sign that had confirmed it. Not that Sanir cared where Gul Tunol came from; in a military as dominated by patriarchs as Cardassia's Great Fleet, to be a woman and reach gul's rank was to be admired, and origins be damned.

Enkoa crossed to the upper tier of the bridge, stifling a cough. "Talarians," he husked, speaking the name like a curse word. "Concealed below the rings of the gas giant. They must have been drifting in quiescent mode—"

"Where are they now?" demanded the gul. She shot a look at Kein. "Sensors, Dalin."

Kein nodded, her hands already crossing back and forth around the discs of her keypad. "Severe loss of parity," she reported, blinking as blood pooled around her eye. "But I have them." She brought a fuzzy tactical plot to a tertiary screen and revealed three Talarian raiders in an unkempt V-formation.

Tunol's face soured. "They dare?" she asked of no one in particular. "Enkoa, disruptors."

He was denied the chance to respond. White light flared suddenly on Kein's panel. "Weapons discharge!" she shouted. "They're firing again!"

Tunol called out for evasive maneuvers, and the engineer felt her gut twist. The meters on her panel told the tale before it unfolded; some lucky shot by one of those barbarian gunners had caused a cascade discharge through the *Rekkel*'s power train, sending spikes of malfunction into every primary system. The ship's main guns were cycling through a reset phase and the shields . . . The shields were sluggish, rebuilding themselves too slowly to block the full force of the next assault. The trickle of Kein's blood became a sluggish line down her cheek, and for the first time she wondered if she might die today.

The enemy had spent what little tactical acumen they had on the first strike; the next was as artless as it was brutal. In some small mercy, one barrage of particle beam fire missed *Rekkel* entirely as the helmsman put the light cruiser on its port fin, impulse grids flaring yellow-orange with the effort. The other two warships did not make the same error. Kein felt the first hit through the soles of her boots as a discharge ripped away hull plating down the dorsal surface of the Cardassian craft. The second, a heartbeat behind, drove a spear of energy straight into the wound still smoldering from the initial surprise attack. Systems that had only just reset themselves, breakers newly refreshed and ready for action, were abruptly awash in a murderous overload surge. The Talarians dug in the knife and twisted it.

A wall of heat swept over Kein and she cried out as it buffeted her. She rocked forward, clinging to her console for support, and dared to glance back.

Plumes of hot gas backlit by electric discharges coiled overhead. The command throne was gone, crushed beneath a fallen section of armored ceiling wreathed in blue-tinted flames. She could see nothing of Gul Tunol; one moment there, and the next . . .

The concept was barely formed in her thoughts when a new realization crowded it out. *Tunol was dead. Arlal with her.* That meant that Kein and Enkoa, both sharing the rank of dalin, were now the senior officers. She searched and found him staring back at her, the same understanding in his eyes. And more there as well, she sensed. Fear. A moment of hesitance.

For a second she rocked on her feet, the muscles in her legs tensing as she hovered on the edge of stepping up and taking command; but would that hold? She was *Rekkel*'s chief engineer and an upper-tier officer, that was unquestioned. But Laen Enkoa was tactical chief, and this was a combat situation. The place was his to take. Kein swallowed a sudden, irrational flash of annoyance and, before she could stop herself, she gave him the ghost of a nod. Gave him *permission.*

Enkoa returned the gesture, moved to the helm console, and gestured at the screen. "Extend away," he told the helmsman, fighting to keep his voice level. "Get us some distance. I . . . We need thinking room."

Kein considered, and then rejected the idea of summoning a medical corpsman to the command tier. There seemed little point to it; they would either live or die in the next few minutes. She finally wiped her blood away with terse, sharp motions.

In the next second another shock of impacts resonated through the decking as one of the alien ships fired again. Enkoa stumbled and grabbed at a support brace; for a moment she thought she saw the beginnings of real panic there,

The *Rekkel* moved in lethargic spasms that made the walls vibrate, and Kein hissed through her teeth as the relays from main engineering painted a steadily worsening picture of the cruiser's health. "Sensor palette is severely damaged. Disruptor grid does not respond," she reported.

Enkoa nodded. "What are our other options?"

She eyed him. The real question he was asking was *Can we flee?* Kein's frown deepened. "Impulse power is at three-quarter capacity. Warp drive may be possible, perhaps for a short jump." She did not want to apply too much strain to the engines, not with the stress readings streaming at her from the *Rekkel*'s wounded warp core.

"There are torpedoes in chambers one through four," offered the helmsman. "Armed with trilithium warheads."

"Without sensors, we'd be firing blind," Kein added.

On the tactical plot, the Talarians were looping around ahead of them, coming in and dropping to low impulse. It was the prelude to a boarding action.

Are they laughing at us over there? Are they mocking Cardassia and toasting their good luck at catching us by surprise? Kein's gray hands tensed around the edges of her console. The cut on her eye-ridge was throbbing.

Enkoa took a shuddering breath and drew himself up. "Stand by to execute Standard Engagement Plan Tul Six-Two. We'll fall back and . . ." He swallowed, losing some of his impetus. "Regroup."

Kein grimaced. Her fellow dalin was behaving true to form, in moments of stress falling back into his usual, predictable patterns. It was the same behavior that allowed her to win so many *leks* from him in mess hall games of *ueppa* rods; but now the fate of the *Rekkel* was turning on his lack of imagination and she could not stay silent in the face of it. Steadfast but dogged, Enkoa would get them killed. The Talarians, sharp with their animal cunning, would know a standard fleet maneuver the instant they saw it happening. The enemy had fought the Cardassian Union through so many border skirmishes that such book-learned tactics would be transparent to them. Now was the time for boldness, for chance.

"No," she muttered. "There's another option."

Enkoa blinked, his train of thought arrested abruptly. "Then, quickly?"

She didn't have his permission yet, but Kein was already programming the control macro she would require as she explained. "Drop what little shields we have. I'll make it look like a system failure. Then, when they're close enough, generate a subspace pulse through the main deflector." She jerked a thumb at the ships on the screen. "The shock will knock their warp cores offline."

"And ours along with it," Enkoa noted.

"But unlike them, we'll be ready," she retorted. "I can hot-start the core in less than a *metric*, and while I'm doing that—"

"The torpedoes." Enkoa's head bobbed as he caught up to her idea. "Yes, we can blind-fire." He glanced at the helmsman and got a nod of confirmation in return. "Do it," he told her.

Kein looked away. "I already have." She tapped out the activation protocol and the deflectors collapsed.

The shields about the Cardassian cruiser shimmered as they melted away, and abruptly the manta-shaped warship was naked and open for the taking. The Talarians—who made too many sorties ending in nothing but exchanges of blood and angry retreats—were eager to plunge in and stock their raiding parties with close-quarter weapons. It was rare for warriors of the Republic to have the chance to battle Cardassians face-to-face, and they wanted it so much that what little caution they had was trampled beneath the promise of pillage and payback. Talarian hatred of Cardassia was a crude and steady thing, pulling at its leash, impatient to expend its thuggish energy upon an arrogant invader.

It mattered little that the zone of space where the *Rekkel* had been ambushed lay beyond the declared borders of the Talarian Republic, out in unclaimed reaches light-years past the Tong Beak Nebula. The raiders were a law unto themselves, given orders of marque and reprisal to harry anything bearing the Galor Banner.

And so, in this frame of mind they came in, dim starlight flashing off the cruciform solar wings of their ships, ready to overmatch the straggler they had caught in their net. They expected their prey to run, or to beg.

The *Rekkel*, in turn, bid them pay the butcher's bill for Gul Tunol, Dal Arlal, and the other dead littering the ship's corridors.

The subspace pulse rippled out in a shock-wave sphere, strange fires shimmering against the dull halo of the gas giant's ice rings. In any other circumstance, the tactic would have failed; but so close, with each raider poised to launch a transporter assault, the shock hit the craft with full force before it could dissipate. Kein's promised shutdowns occurred more or less as she predicted—one raider's warp core did not deactivate, but spiraled into a loop of fluctuations that rendered it momentarily useless, so the effect remained the same—and at once four space-dead craft drifted in a loose cluster, framed by the dark orb of the massive planet below them.

On battery power, the maws of *Rekkel*'s torpedo bays irised open and ejected their contents into the void on puffs of compressed gas. Smart software programmed to locate the silhouettes of a thousand different craft deemed threats to the Cardassian Union sniffed the darkness and found the Talarians floating unprotected. Fusion torch motors flared and the weapons crossed the short distance to their targets.

A string of proximity detonations blossomed, spheres of deadly flame briefly unchained. The raiders were consumed, their deaths adding to the blaze of color. *Rekkel* was buffeted, and damaged still further by the aftermath, but when the momentary suns died away it was only the Cardassian craft that remained whole.

Afterward, the warship's log would show that the entire engagement had taken less than ten *metrics* to occur. Some days the knife was slow; some days the knife was swift.

★ ★ ★

Kein strode from the tribunal chamber with her head held high, as was fitting for a soldier of the Union. The final deliberation was at last concluded, and her actions aboard the *Rekkel* had been found to be without fault. She had never doubted the outcome, not even in the moments when the panel of hard-eyed guls had challenged every choice she had made in those fateful few instants.

It was her suggestion, and later the work of her engineering staff, that had enabled the *Rekkel* to survive long enough to make it back into Cardassian space. The poor craft had not lasted all the way back to Cardassia, but only to here, the colony on Sunzek, and briefly Kein felt an odd pang of loss for the vessel. Their rescuers had been forced to scuttle the cruiser, and in some way she felt as if this was giving the Talarians their victory after all. Absently she reached up and traced the new scar on her brow.

Out in the corridor, beneath the statue of a planetary prefect decades dead and gone, Enkoa stood, hands clasped together around a data tablet. Kein extinguished the moment of mawkish sentiment and walked toward him. She had not seen him to speak to since the examinations had begun, isolated from her fellow officer as a matter of course to ensure the veracity of the debriefing.

Caught in shafts of pale light from the Sunzek day as they fell through the slotted windows overhead, Enkoa seemed restless and wound tight with unspent energy. The tribunal had been challenging for him, but he too had passed beneath the scrutiny of the court-martial and not been found wanting. Both of them had shown ample courage and presence of mind, and in the past few days the engineer had begun to entertain the notion that this random turn of events could be the making of them. Promotions had been granted for lesser acts, after all, and both she and Enkoa had served long enough at the rank of dalin.

The tactician stepped toward her, out of the statue's shadow. "It's done with, then," he noted. "In all honesty, Sanir, I'd rather face the Talarians again than that pack of hounds." He nodded toward the tribunal chamber.

"The Talarians owe us a ship and our crewmates," she told him, "and three of them weren't enough. A tenfold repayment, perhaps. That might balance the scales."

He let out a brief bark of laughter and toyed with the bars of facial hair at his jaw. "You'd take us back to war, would you?"

She gestured at the carved granite of the prefect's statue, depicting the figure with pistol and dagger at deceptively casual rest in his robed hands. "Look at him. We're always at war, Laen."

"I have heard that said," he agreed airily, and waved the data tablet under her nose. "Perhaps you'd like to join me to discuss it further with Jagul Hanno?"

"Hanno?" repeated Kein, momentarily wrong-footed. "He's here? On Sunzek?" Her mouth became arid. She remembered the hawkish, barrel-chested figure of a man from her ascendance day on Prime, the thunderous and impassioned speech he gave as she and the rest of her cadet class graduated into the Fleet. Kein had dared to meet the officer's gaze as she, like all her classmates, stepped up and tore the apprentice ribbon from her duty uniform and cast it into the mud of the training quad. His stare had cut into her, those ice-hard eyes measuring her with scarcely a blink. Years past now, but the moment was still vivid in her memory.

Enkoa nodded, apparently unfazed by the jagul's fearsome reputation. "This colony falls under his sector command." Laen allowed himself a slight smile, as if he was holding a confidence from her. "I have been informed that he wishes to give us our next tasking orders personally."

Kein schooled her expression carefully, betraying no emotion, but inwardly she felt her pulse race. Suddenly, the possibility of new rank and new privileges seemed just within reach. She inclined her head. "We should not keep him waiting, then."

Enkoa swept past her. "This way."

There was nowhere to sit in the jagul's chambers. The officer glanced down at them from a high console before the oval window that was the room's only decoration, and beckoned them closer without breaking off from a conversation he was having with an adjutant. There were screens on every vertical surface, and each shimmered slightly as they passed it, security protocols fogging the images and text so Kein and Enkoa, with their lower ranks and correspondingly low security clearances, would not see something beyond their pay grade.

Kein snapped to parade ground attention and gave a crisp salute, Enkoa mirroring her a heartbeat later. Once again, she was
spared a look from those hard eyes. The face in which they were set
had grown older and more careworn, the scalp above now shorn and
hairless, but the gaze had not softened, not one iota. Kein caught a
glimpse of herself in the window behind the jagul; the gentle, lined
ridges of a Lakarian lineage, dark brown eyes that betrayed nothing,
a cowl of hair cut tight to her head, and that fresh, darkening scar.
She looked every inch the model of a Cardassian warrior; Kein wondered if Hanno was convinced by her. In contrast, Enkoa was rail-
thin in almost every aspect of his appearance, the trim strips of beard
he sported a vague attempt to make something of the flat lines of his
face.

The jagul dismissed the other officer and crossed to the window,
watching the sunset. The door closed behind them and they stood
silently. Kein worked to keep her thoughts steady. Now that the
initial surprise of Enkoa's announcement had worn off, she found
herself thinking beyond the moment, wondering why Hanno was
actually on Sunzek. The man had a reputation as a maverick, and
in the Fleet such repute could kill a career; Cardassia wanted warriors
who followed the orders of the homeworld, men and women who
did not question, who understood the nature of duty. She had no
doubt that Jagul Hanno was a patriot who respected his oath, but
he was outspoken with it. Rumor carried through the Fleet as it
did through the skeins of any clan and family, and rumors about
Hanno told of how he frequently came into conflict with the pre-
fecture. His candid commentary on Cardassia's expansionist sorties
against the United Federation of Planets and the so-called progression into the Bajor Sector were well-known. Hanno's arguments for
a metered military approach stood in sharp contrast to his peers, who
favored more direct conflicts. Some said it was only his family's web
of internecine fealty and obligation that kept him in command of the
Eighth Order's squadrons; that, and his sheer, bloody-minded tactical genius.

At last, the jagul granted them some fraction of his attention. "I
have followed the review of the *Rekkel* engagement with some mild interest," he rumbled. "Meka Tunol was known to me. She served briefly

under my command as a gil. I saw great potential in her, if properly tempered."

Kein considered the comment, unsure of what the senior officer meant by it. From the corner of her eye, she saw Enkoa shifting slightly.

"A pity that she will never fulfill her promise," he concluded.

"If I may say, Jagul," Enkoa ventured, "the gul served the Union with dignity and honor."

"And those things are of great import to Cardassia." Once more, Hanno's words were curiously without weight.

Kein became aware that the man was watching her. She swallowed and fought down the urge to fill the moment of silence.

"You both performed with composure during a crisis," he went on. "Although the *Rekkel* was lost, it was through no fault of yours. The Fleet needs officers with the wit and fortitude to handle such situations." Hanno drifted toward a screen where a display of local space—bare of any tactical data, naturally—showed the span of the Union's borders in rust red, ranged against the dark patches of adversary nations like the Breen, the Federation, and the Talarians. "Now, more than ever," he added.

"Thank you, sir." Kein spoke before she could stop herself.

He did not acknowledge her comment. Instead, his hand wandered to the map and absently traced a line along the livid border at the edge of the Dorvan Sector. "What do you know of the Federation?"

The question seemed to be directed at Enkoa. "An arrogant enemy," said the tactical officer. "Self-assured and convinced of their own superiority."

Hanno's lips split in a thin smile. "They say the same of us." He nodded to himself. "Like the Talarians, they resent us, they envy us. But for different reasons. The Republic hate us for our power, because they know we could crush them if it suited us. As for the Federation . . ." He grinned briefly and let the sentence hang there, incomplete. "The humans and their cohorts are a very uncommon foe." The jagul glanced at Kein.

She nodded back to him. "Difficult to read, I understand."

Hanno moved away, back across the window. "One must have wit to do so." He stopped and laid his hands upon the console. "The

Federation have expanded their advance into the Dorvan region with vessels and colonies. There have been a few unresolved skirmishes. The situation is becoming uncomfortable, and a show of force has become necessary. To that end, I am taking a flotilla of warships to the Tantok Nor outpost. To show the banner."

Enkoa nodded thoughtfully, playing the jagul's equal, but Kein remained impassive, inwardly questioning. Why was the old warrior allowing them to know this? Clasped behind her back, her palms felt clammy.

Hanno continued. "Recent . . . events on the homeworld have forced me to adjust some of my staffing requirements."

She did not need to guess at what those events might be; it was an open secret that Hanno was currently being challenged by a number of opponents in the Detapa Council. At the rank of jagul and beyond, the matters of command became as much political in nature as military. In many ways, that this was true of *all* things Cardassian.

"One of the vessels in my fleet is the *Lakar*, a strike escort." He glanced at Kein, a question in his eyes.

She answered by rote; ever since she had been a girl, Sanir had absorbed the details and statistics for every type of craft in the Fleet, and the data spilled from her in a flat monotone. "*Zhoden*-class light escort. Eighty-eight *deca*s in length, thirty-six officers and crew, five spiral-wave disruptor banks, standard rated combat cruise factor nine plus."

The jagul nodded. "The captaincy of that ship is now yours, *Dal* Enkoa." Hanno reached into a pocket and offered Enkoa a rank tab, as informally as if he were handing him a glass of *kanar*. The other officer took the sigil stiffly, and a feral grin threatened to break out across his face.

Hanno glanced at Kein once again and folded his arms. "A letter of commendation has been secured in both your files. Central Command will know of your fine service to the Union."

It was then that Kein realized that the letter would be all the approbation she would receive. A nerve in her jaw jumped and she clamped her teeth together, feeling a slow heat build in her cheeks and neck as her skin darkened. That was all? *She* had saved the lives aboard the *Rekkel*, not Enkoa! It had been *her* solution that brought them victory, not his! Enkoa's lack of imagination would have doomed them all . . .

She glared at the jagul, who appeared to be utterly unaware of her silent fury. Hanno knew full well what had transpired on the *Rekkel*. She had no doubt of it. He had read the after-action reports. He had to know she was the better of the two.

"How is Lethra?" said the senior officer. His tone was mild, more conversational now.

"She is very well, sir," came Enkoa's reply. "We communicate regularly. I know she will be thrilled to hear my news."

Kein's thoughts were roiling. *Lethra.* The willowy rich girl Enkoa had bedded on Torros Minor, back before the start of their tour. Sanir had mocked him for falling for some fey debutante, this naïf slumming it in a starport, laughed even when he had told her they were to be engaged. Now the joke appeared to be on her. She felt her gut tighten as Hanno spoke again, casual and unhurried.

"I consider my niece quite deserving. I'm rather fond of her, you understand?" Perhaps, if one looked hard enough, one could have found the edge of a threat buried in those words; but Kein was not really listening, and the rush of blood in her ears grew from a rumble to a thunder. Her nails cut into her palms, digging little dark crescents in the white flesh. The new scar throbbed.

Hanno's neice. Of course. She resisted the sudden urge to spit. The jagul was merely firming the threads of his own influence, placing Enkoa like a gaming piece, ensuring a pliant new commander for his flotilla. Building bonds of familial control. Suitability and skill counted for nothing, so it seemed. A night of fumbling intercourse with a foolish civilian, by contrast, apparently earned an officer a captaincy.

Kein glared at the floor. The sheer nepotism of the act she had just witnessed filled her with disgust; but then a voice deep in her thoughts challenged her. *Why are you surprised? Did you really expect something different?* As long as the Fleet remained a patriarchy, a club for old men in which to play their games of war and power, the road to rank would always be a harder one for a female. She rocked on the edge of letting her annoyance take voice. It would be easy to say it, to just open her mouth and let the words out. Of course, to do that would destroy any prospect of a future career in an instant. Never mind what truth she uttered, it would be insubordination. Kein thought about Gul Tunol and regretted that she had not made more effort to know the woman. Perhaps she would have had lessons to teach her, such as resisting the urge to hope when all that brought was ashes and disappointment—

"—Sanir."

The sound of her name cut through her mental turmoil and she glanced up, barely able to return her face to its normal, neutral aspect. Enkoa was still speaking. "She is the only one I trust, Jagul. With your permission, I would like to make it my first command as captain of the *Lakar.*"

"So ordered," said Hanno with a nod, and he spoke with formality. "I authorize Dalin Sanir Kein for the posting of executive officer of the *Starship Lakar.*"

That same sly smile played on Enkoa's lips as he looked at her. "That's if you want the job?"

"Of course she does," Hanno replied.

"Of course I do," echoed Kein, bowing slightly. "Dal." She almost choked on Enkoa's new rank.

He placed a hand on her shoulder and smiled that smile a little more. She wanted to take her fist and strike him with it, scream and shout and decry the utter inequality of this farce. All this and a hundred other things she wanted to do, but she did nothing but nod, like a good soldier of the Union who knew her place.

An ember of resentment had always been deep within her; she understood that. But it was kindling now, catching fire. Burning cold and dark, as only spite could.

Tantok Nor hung in the void on the edge of the Kelrabi system, skirting the hard radiation from the red star pouring blood-colored light across its arid collection of worlds. The voyage from Sunzek was swift and without incident, and Kein used whatever excuses she could find to keep herself at arm's length from Enkoa, although on a vessel far smaller than the *Rekkel* it was a difficulty.

She did what she always did in times of stress: she reverted back to what she knew best, and in Kein's case that was engineering.

Kein spent a lot of the trip in the warp core chamber second-guessing Glinn Telso, the *Lakar*'s obtuse engineer, and expending much of her irritation on him, under the guise of getting the escort into top fighting condition. Some might have thought it bad practice for a new executive officer, perhaps sending signals to the crew that she was undermining the harried junior officer, but Kein cared little about that. Central Command's punishing tolerances, already as thin as blades and difficult to hold to, were made thinner still by Kein. By the time the barbed ring of Tantok Nor loomed large before *Lakar*'s bow, the drive crews had been drilled to within an inch of their lives. She could tell by the look in Telso's eyes that he was building a hate for her. Kein was pleased about that, on some level. He would be a reflection of her, she decided, and in him she would see the same face she would present to her new captain.

For his part, Dal Enkoa settled into his new role well, as though he'd been born to it. Command, even of a minnow of a ship like this one, fitted him well as long as he wasn't being challenged by it. He made the crew follow the rules, but he had that easy smile, ready there for his subordinates. Kein could see the crew starting to like him, but then, they didn't know him, not yet. They didn't know that he could get them killed, when the moment of truth came. But the *Lakar* hovered at the back of the flotilla, off the main axis where the big *Galor*-class ships moved like deep-ocean predators. There were no threats to face, not yet.

During the voyage, she stood her shifts at command while Enkoa was at rest or in his cabin eating up bandwidth on subspace to the jagul's waiflike neice. Those moments on the bridge, with a starship at her fingertips, should have been a joy to her. Instead, it was a sour experience. She never once took the command throne, never sat, just prowled the tier around it, coiled and hawkish. It was as if the chair were marked somehow, as if it stank of Enkoa and Hanno and their clubbish, elitist camaraderie.

All this, Kein kept out of sight and silent, of course. Control was a lesson that Cardassian women learned very early on, and they were far better at it than the males. She thought about the face she was showing the bridge crew, and once more Gul Tunol came to mind. Cold and dour Meka Tunol—had she stood in the same place where Sanir was now? It was likely.

They entered orbit around Tantok and the crews took the sparse liberty they were granted with gusto, most notably the men under Glinn Telso's stewardship. Kein took her leave of the ship too, suddenly overcome by the need to see something different from the low ceilings of the *Lakar* and Enkoa's constant half smile. There were places to eat and drink on the station's promenade, so Kein found a secluded booth in an open-fronted refectory, where she could sit unseen and brood without fear of being disturbed. Taking pursed-lipped sips of warm Rokassa juice, she let her focus drift and played a game with herself. She tried to remember the last time she had felt an emotion that wasn't annoyance, contempt, or disgust.

Nothing came to mind. She fingered her rank sigil and watched the people passing.

"Sanir!" A hand on her shoulder. She turned and looked up to find Enkoa grinning down at her. He nodded at the drink on the table. "Last little flavor of home before we make for the border, eh?"

"Sir," she nodded. "Something like that." In truth, the *Lakar*'s replicators were perfectly capable of making passable Rokassa juice, but she saw no point in mentioning it.

He seemed to catch something of her mood. The smile dialed down a little and his voice became low, more intimate. "I haven't had the opportunity to say this since we left port, but I want to thank you." He paused, expecting her to acknowledge him, and when she didn't he continued. "The work you have done with Telso and the engineers . . . exemplary. The jagul told me that our ship is the most warp-efficient of our class in the flotilla. He's impressed."

He thinks I'm doing it for him. Kein made her face even once more.

Enkoa's smile finally faded completely. "Sanir, I know . . . I know you deserved more than just a commendation after what happened on the *Rekkel*. That's why I wanted you for my executive officer." His hand tightened on her shoulder. "This is going to be a great opportunity for both of us. This is just the start." And the smile came back, bright and white and unchanging.

"Dal." Enkoa turned as the rich timbre of Hanno's voice crossed the promenade. Kein saw the jagul and a knot of command-tier officers, all captains and executives, talking and joking in rough humor, moving toward the shuttlebays. Hanno threw a beckoning gesture in their direction and kept walking.

"The jagul has invited all the senior officers to Kelrabi IX," Enkoa explained. "There's a fishery down there, with a superlative restaurant. Apparently, it's a personal tradition of his. He buys a meal for all his subordinates before embarking on a new tour of duty."

"Oh," said Kein. She hadn't been aware that this was expected of her. "Of course." She turned in her chair to reach for her overjacket, but Enkoa kept speaking, patting her on the shoulder once more.

"So, I will see you back on the ship." He flashed the grin and walked away, leaving her there.

Kein froze, feeling foolish, the jacket in her fist, and watched him draw into the group, instantly making some comment that brought forth laughter. She watched them go, all of them, none of them casting a glance back.

Enkoa was the last to pass through the hatch, the last to leave her behind. She gripped the Rokassa glass tightly. Had that snub been deliberate on his part, or was it just that he was so self-absorbed that it would never have occurred to him to bring her along to the jagul's table? She felt conflicted, at once wanting to go with them as much as she loathed the very idea of it.

She sat there for a long time, eyes unfocused, seeing but not seeing. The glass made a popping sound and a fracture grew beneath her palm.

"Shall I remove that for you?" An attendant had moved silently to her side, and he spoke in a placid, unhurried manner.

He was nearest to her at that moment, and so she glared at him. "Take it."

The attendant did so, allowing a small *tsk* to escape his lips as he saw the crack, and placed it on the tray he held high atop one hand. He had an open, angular face and eyes that seemed kind, in this light. "Another, Dalin Kein?"

"No." She turned her back on him and he took a step away before she realized something. "Wait."

He rocked on one foot, almost in a comical pretense of pause. "Change of mind?"

"How do you know my name?" she demanded.

The attendant inclined his head. "I'm here to wait tables," he noted, as if that would explain everything. "To do that well, it's important to know your clients."

Kein looked around. "That's a job for a menial. Shouldn't a Kelrabian be doing it?"

He gave her a conspiratorial look. "The locals are not terribly bright, Dalin. They mix up orders all the time, and you know officers. They do like precision."

From nowhere, an abrupt suspicion unwound in her chest. "Who are you?"

"Just a plain and simple server."

"What do you want?"

He held up a finger. "Ah, no. That's for *me* to ask *you*. But of course, because I'm very good at my job, I already know what you want."

Kein frowned. "Another glass of—"

He reached up and recovered a full tumbler of the amber juice, ready and waiting for her request. "Rokassa juice?"

The thing was, she *did* want another glass. Rokassa juice reminded her of home, and home made her feel more centered, more controlled. She took a sip, savored it.

When the next question came, it sounded as if it came from a different person entirely. "Is there anything else you would like, Dalin Kein?" It had a cool, insidious weight to it, a slow knife slipping in. It almost took her off guard. She almost answered honestly.

"What I want is beyond your remit," she said, more to herself than in answer.

"I suppose so," he noted. "As a mere server, the most important thing I have to concern myself with is the correct stockage of *kanar* or the freshness of the *yamok* sauce. But you, an officer of the Fleet . . . I would imagine that the lives of many turn on every decision you make. Or do not make." The server gave a little sigh. "Have I confessed to you my great admiration for the military? It's little reward, I know, but heartfelt."

Kein bristled. The man's attitude was chafing on her, his insouciant manner wearing down her already thinned patience. "For a mere
server, you are quite familiar with officers you have just met. You
should know your place!"

He nodded. "Quite so, quite so. Forgive me, Dalin, but it is an oc-
cupational hazard. My talkative nature, I mean." He chuckled. "I hope
it won't prevent you from returning here. This table is well-suited for
quiet introspection, and I don't doubt hard-working command officers
can benefit from that."

He was speaking much but saying little, and Kein felt slow alarm
moving through her; but in the next second her wrist communicator
was vibrating and she held the comcuff to her mouth. "Report?"

Glinn Lleye, *Lakar*'s officer of the watch, responded. *"Dalin, an
alert from the perimeter buoys. A Federation vessel has been detected at the sector
edge. Tantok control is passing word to all Fleet officers."*

Kein was on her feet in an instant. "Lock on. Transport me directly
to the bridge."

"Confirmed."

"Duty calls?" noted the server.

She downed the Rokassa juice in one gulp and tossed the glass at
him. The orange haze of the transporter effect enveloped her, and the
last she saw of the man's irritating blandness was a thin, plastic smile
that did not reach his eyes.

By an accident of deployment, only three ships in Hanno's flotilla were
not moored at any of Tantok Nor's pylons or its docking ring: the *Fell*,
the *Karsu*—this one the jagul's flagship—and the *Lakar.*

Kein had snatched a data tablet from Lleye's hand and raced
through the information presented there. The human ship had made
some error of tactics and strayed too close to a Cardassian sensor line,
triggering the alert. The ship was retreating, attempting to move with
stealth back toward Federation space, and there was a window of opportunity for the jagul to sprint out to the contested zone and challenge the craft head-on. Of course, he would take it; the chance to pick
off a lone Starfleet vessel was too enticing to pass up.

She had the *Lakar* at ready status, all her crew recalled, and her
systems battle-primed, as Enkoa stalked onto the bridge. The dal

seemed vexed, no doubt irritated that his evening of drinking and dining with the other commanders had been interrupted by something as paltry as an alien invader.

"Orders?" she asked.

He gestured at the main screen, where the two *Galor*-class cruisers were already moving to high impulse. "Dagger formation, Dalin. Tuck us in abeam of the *Karsu* and match her speed."

Kein relayed the commands, and Glinn Lleye brought the escort into the shadow of the other ships. As one, the vessels leapt to warp speed, the starlight distending into glowing streaks of color about them.

She leaned closer to the command throne. "Did the jagul give any directives as to how we are to proceed once we intercept the Federation intruder?"

Enkoa shifted slightly. "He will present us with a tactical tasking when we enter contact range," came the reply. "We will . . . act as support for the *Fell* and the *Karsu*."

Someone who did not know Laen Enkoa as well as Sanir Kein did would never have noticed it, but she instantly detected a frustration in his tone. At once she was imagining the moment when Hanno received the alert communication, and Enkoa there at his side, opportunistic, eager to follow his new patron into battle—only to be told that his little ship was surplus to requirements. Two *Galor*s, after all, were more than a match for any single ship in the Federation's arsenal. Had Enkoa cajoled his way into having *Lakar* join the interceptors? If the docking order had been different, she doubted that they would be here now, speeding toward a confrontation.

She nodded. "We will be ready."

The Starfleet ship saw them coming and gave up on its stealthy course, moving to a higher warp velocity.

Hanno had opened a general channel from the *Karsu* to the other ships, and on the tertiary viewscreen Kein could see the jagul on his command throne, with once again the warrior aspect that she remembered from that day on Cardassia Prime at the fore. *"No iron to begin a fight, these Starfleeters,"* he rumbled. *"They'll come in hard well enough if they have their nose bloodied, but it's a rare day that they'll stand and wait to take a punch."*

The glinn at sensors glanced up at Kein. "Scan relay from the *Fell*, sir. Data on the target."

"Show me," ordered Enkoa.

Kein read the information from a console. The Federation ship was a light cruiser, like something carved out of bleached bone, with a saucer-shaped primary hull, twin warp pontoons high behind it, and a curved secondary fuselage. Partly blanked lines of information from Obsidian Order intelligence reports gave this particular craft an identity.

"*Rutledge.*" She said the alien name aloud, rolling the odd consonants over her tongue, pondering for a moment what meaning the appellation might have to the humans who crewed it. "What are they doing here?"

"Spying. Trying to read our strength and numbers." Enkoa's smile, lost since they had left Tantok Nor, was returning by degrees. "This ship is no match for the three of us."

"*Gul Matrik?*" Hanno was speaking to the commander of the *Fell*. *"The aliens are hailing us, questioning our aggressive posture."*

"I read that, Jagul," Matrik's voice replied. *"I do not feel we need to grace them with a reply."*

On the screen, Hanno's lip curled. *"On the contrary, Gul, we will give them a reply, in the strongest terms. Just not the one they want. Prepare to engage."*

"Moving to battle stance."

Enkoa leaned forward in his chair, and Kein felt the tension on the *Lakar*'s bridge jump a notch. Hanno looked out of the screen, directly at the young commander. *"Dal Enkoa, maintain your course and speed. Remain at weapons hold."*

"Sir?" Enkoa blinked.

But Hanno was already turning away. *"We'll call on you if you are needed. Karsu out."* The communications screen went dark, while on the main display the two cruisers surged away after the *Rutledge*, laying the first few blasts of disruptor fire across the bows of the Starfleet vessel.

"Weapons hold," repeated Glinn Lleye, earning him a sharp look from his commander.

Kein felt Enkoa quietly seething; she sensed the irritation coming off him in waves. In a cold and hollow fashion, it amused her to see him sharing in the same emotions that she had felt back on the station.

Reduced to the status of spectators, there was little they could do but watch the *Rutledge* thread between the *Fell* and the *Karsu* as they harried the alien ship, trying to drive it back toward Kelrabi space. The Federation vessel proved a more able foe than Kein had expected, shrugging off near hits and forcing the cruisers to stay beyond optimal attack range with barrages of proximity-detonating photon torpedoes. The ship's tactical officer was clearly quite skilled.

Enkoa said and did nothing throughout it all, with only his eyes moving, darting right and left as he followed the tactical plot. He wanted so badly to be in the thick of it, it was almost pitiable.

With challenge after challenge, the Starfleet captain refused to engage. A Klingon or Talarian commander would have turned and fought—and most likely perished. But the *Rutledge* extended its distance and then, with a last salvo of parting shots, arrowed away into maximum warp, trailing streamers of plasma with carbon-scored wounds all across her pristine hull.

Hanno opened the general channel again. *"Pity,"* he mused. *"A kill this early in the deployment would have been ideal. Still. They'll carry my message back to their Federation. They know we won't allow them to cross our borders at will."* The senior officer nodded to himself. *"All ships, return to formation. Go to cruise speed, return course to Tantok Nor."*

Enkoa stood up sharply, surprising Kein with the suddenness of the motion. "Jagul, may I speak with you privately?" He inclined his head toward the captain's duty room at the rear of the *Lakar's* bridge.

Hanno frowned. *"Very well."*

Enkoa nodded and moved away. "Encrypt and transfer the jagul's signal to me," he ordered, quickly disappearing into the small cabin. Kein did as she was ordered, catching a faint scowl on Hanno's face just before the communication screen blanked.

No more than two *metric*s had passed before Enkoa tersely summoned her to join him in the duty room.

★ ★ ★

On larger ships, the cabin was used for high-level briefings or meetings that required some degree of privacy; aboard a *Zhoden*-class escort, a starship that was only a few steps above a warp-cutter, the room was small and cramped, with another of those irritatingly low ceilings.

Kein entered and found Enkoa at the office's single desk, his hands steepled in front of him, his eyes hooded. A monitor on the wall was blinking in standby mode, indicating that a subspace communication had just been concluded.

"Dal," she began.

He didn't ask her to sit. "We could have destroyed that Starfleet ship," he began. "If I had been allowed to commit the *Lakar* to the engagement, we would have destroyed them. Instead, they escaped to return another day."

"I am sure the jagul had his reasons," she ventured.

That earned her a glower. No smiles were evident now. "I asked him, Sanir. I asked him what those reasons were. Shall I tell you why he kept us out of harm's way?" He said the last few words with acid venom. "He wasn't willing to risk the life of his precious niece's husband-to-be on a 'minor skirmish.' The jagul felt I would learn more by observing the actions of Gul Matrik from a distance." Enkoa's fingers knitted into fists. "What will that make our new crew think of me? What message does that send, Sanir?"

The message that you are unfit to have the rank you were granted. She chewed on her bottom lip, resisting the urge to say it aloud. *That Hanno knows it, even though he gave this ship to you.* Kein realized he was waiting for her to answer him, to give him some show of support. "I am sure . . . Jagul Hanno has his reasons," she repeated, at a loss to come up with something that would appease her commander.

"I would never challenge his commands," Enkoa continued, "but . . . if he did not want me here, why give me this ship at all? What use can the *Lakar* be? A hunting dog is of no use if it is muzzled!"

"There will be other engagements."

Enkoa wasn't looking at her anymore. He was just talking, letting his voice fill the little room, venting his disappointment. "This is my first command, and I want to prove I am worthy of it, worthy of this ship." He rapped his knuckles on the desk. "I do not want to hide behind Jagul Hanno." He seemed to have forgotten Kein was in the cabin, the words rolling from him like a confessional.

But all she heard was a poor officer admitting he was unworthy of a posting that should have been hers. "Perhaps you should sever your ties with his niece." Kein was unable to completely hide the mocking edge beneath the statement. Enkoa shot a look at her, irritated and surprised in equal measure.

But no, he would never do such a thing. I know him too well. For all his talk of wanting to be blooded, he will always take the path of least resistance. She matched his glare with bland neutrality—the same expression she had seen on the face of the server.

Enkoa looked away. "Inform me when we have reached Tantok Nor." He waved her off. "You are dismissed."

A week passed, then two, and there were no more incursions, no more sightings of Starfleet ships. The vast and watchful passive scanner arrays that unfolded from the space station's outer pylons hung in the dark, like black sails on a becalmed ocean schooner; they drank in the faint echoes of subspace communications, listening to the babble and chatter of the Federation colonists who thought themselves entitled to set up homes scant light-years from Cardassia's borders.

In the refectory, Kein sipped her Rokassa juice and sank into the comfort of the chair and the quiet booth. She found this human idiocy difficult to understand. Did they not realize that each world they broke ground on, each township they built, each inch they took would antagonize the Union just that little bit more? Cardassia had never been shy about its territoriality, and yet there they were. She had heard reports that the colonists considered themselves only nominally beneath the banner of the United Federation of Planets, but that was disinformation, surely. Some of the homesteaders on these colony worlds were the families of Starfleet officers; how could the Federation admit that and then pretend that these incursions were not the first foundations of an economic, if not overtly military, invasion?

The skirmish with the *Rutledge* had echoed through the flotilla. So the rumor about the base said, Hanno had returned to Tantok Nor to find brusque orders from Central Command ordering a wide net be cast over the Dorvan Sector. The jagul had wanted to patrol the border en masse with a fleet under him, but the prefects on Cardassia Prime saw the situation differently. Orders were cut to spread out his forces, to attempt to put the ships everywhere at once. The eight *Galor*-class cruisers and six *Zhoden*s now patrolled alone, the smaller ships in comm range of reinforcements, the larger ones deep into the indistinct morass of the boundary zone.

Only the *Karsu* and the *Lakar* remained close to the Kelrabi system. Each time Kein's ship ventured out on patrol, Enkoa pulled at his orders like an errant raptor straining against a tether. They would be departing again very soon, moving out to take up Gul Matrik's patrol pattern when the *Fell* reported back. It was the first time that the *Lakar* would be truly on its own. Enkoa was wound tight with anticipation, and had not slept the night before, as far as Kein could tell. She found herself looking forward to the patrol cruise with thinly disguised repugnance.

She drained the glass and turned it in her hands, glancing around the refectory. It was sparsely populated, and Kein was the only officer there. Studying the glass, a thought occurred to her: *Why did I come back here?* The place was functional at best, hardly the finest of the station's establishments, and yet some unconsidered compulsion had brought her to this place when she returned to Tantok Nor. She was musing on this as a figure crossed her line of sight. Jagul Hanno, engaged in a terse and somewhat agitated conversation with Tantok's station gul. He didn't see her as she watched him pass by.

"Our esteemed jagul appears a little tired, don't you think?"

The server with the bland face. Here he was again, silent on his approach, almost as if he had been conjured from the air itself to appear beside her. Kein pushed the empty glass across the table with slow deliberation toward the edge, and he caught it deftly, replacing it with a full one. "Did they teach you to be that quiet in waiter school?" she asked. Hanno entered a turbolift and was gone from her sight.

"If he came here, I would make him *cela* tea," he replied, ignoring the comment. "It's Bajoran, but it's very soothing. I find it quite relaxing. I think he would benefit from it."

Kein considered that for a moment. Governmental pressures from the homeworld, even out here on the Union rim, were still felt as keenly as they were on the streets of the capital. Distance did little to lessen their potency. She wondered what issues Hanno faced beyond those she knew of. To her, politics seemed like a great stone buried in sand, with only a fraction of the surface showing to outside observers.

"Then again, it is always the obligation of the officer class to shoulder a greater responsibility than the civilian."

She eyed him. "That maxim is from the Fleet training regimen."

"Is it?" He expressed faint surprise. "It must be true, then." The server inclined his head slightly. "I imagine you have your share of those burdens, Dalin Kein. And not all of them stem from the regimens of the Fleet."

Kein's eyes narrowed. "You are either a garrulous fool or some sort of spy. Which is it?"

He chuckled, utterly unconcerned by her challenge. "How could I be a spy, if you guessed me so quickly? By your reckoning, then, I'm a fool." He folded his tray under one arm. "You know me so well for someone who has only met me twice."

"What is your name?"

"I could give you a name," he replied, "but the word of a fool doesn't count for much, does it?"

"Neither does that of a spy." She took a swallow of the juice. It was tart, just how she liked it.

"I haven't seen Dal Enkoa on the station for a while," he continued. "Is he well?"

"His moods are his own." She answered with more of a sneer than she would have liked, and glared at the waiter. *Damn the man!* There was something odd about the way he spoke, the way every sentence that left his lips was gossamer, without a single jot of weight to it, and yet she felt compelled to reply to him. Kein had the sudden sense of him taking in everything about her: her body language, the way she held her glass, the tone of her voice, the cut of her uniform . . .

He was no fool. In this moment, she became certain of that. And if it was so, then what did he want with her?

She wondered who his masters might be; what did *they* want with her?

"Newly minted commanders are often caught between a sullen manner or an overly aggressive one," he opined. "They take time to find their equilibrium. A good bottle of *kanar* helps the process along."

She should have left. She should have got up and left, right then and there; but she stayed, because she wanted to wipe that weak smile off his face. Perhaps that was part of his game as well. "I have enough to do with the running of the ship," she told him. "I'm not Enkoa's nursemaid or his confessor."

"And what would he have to confess?" The server had immediately seized on the inopportune choice of word. "Issues of self-doubt and suitability are also a characteristic of those who rise too far, too fast. Don't you think?"

Kein looked past him, wondering why none of the other customers in the refectory were signaling the man to refill their drinks or take their orders. For a moment, she entertained the mad notion that he was a figment of her imagination, perhaps some externalization of her subconscious, letting her reflect her irritations off him. Then she glanced down at the glass of Rokassa juice and a different, more unpleasant thought occurred to her. With care, she set the drink on the table and did not touch it again.

He kept on talking, mild and even, calm and metered. "The ruin of those sorts of men usually comes out of nowhere. They're looking the other way when it happens. Opportunities arise for those around them, those who perhaps feel aggrieved, to let them make their own mistakes. All that needs to be done is to let it happen." He smiled wistfully. "A very low-inertia form of reciprocity, really."

Finally, Kein stood and fixed him with a hard eye. *This game has gone on long enough.* As ever, her stern gaze rolled off him with no visible effect. "I don't believe I will be frequenting this establishment again," she told him.

"Oh!" The man seemed genuinely distressed. "Was the service not to your liking, Dalin?"

She nodded at the half-full glass. "Just now, I lost my taste for

Rokassa juice." Kein stepped around him and walked back to the docking ring. Despite the temperate, Cardassia-warm atmosphere around her, her skin prickled with a chill.

Lakar's patrol got under way, with a pointed dispatch from Jagul Hanno that stressed the nature of the sortie. Spread thin as they were, it was ill-advised for them to engage any enemy starships they might come across, and Hanno explained in no uncertain terms that unless the situation was critical, Enkoa should retreat and call for support if any potentiality for conflict loomed.

The dal nodded in all the right places and he said all the right things, but Kein saw the gestures for what they were, the thin veneer over Enkoa's boyish need to prove himself a soldier.

In a few hours after a full warp run, they were alone in the interstellar deeps, and the commander assuaged his desire by having Kein run combat drills. This she did with clinical solemnity and harshness, taking the sideways glares and half-hidden sneers of Telso and the other, bolder junior officers without open notice.

Three and a half days into the outward leg of the patrol, sometime after exchanging "all clear" signals with one of the big cruisers, Lleye brought an anomaly to their attention.

"It's beyond the edge of our designated watch area," began the glinn. "In section nine."

"The *Gholen*'s patrol zone," noted Kein, glancing at the Fleet tasking orders. "At this time, she's at the opposite end of the area. Two days away at cruise, by my reckoning."

Enkoa took the padd from Lleye's hand and held it close to his face. "You are quite certain?" he asked.

Of course he is, Kein said silently. *The question is redundant. As if he would have brought this to you without triple-checking it first.*

The glinn was nodding. "It's definitely one of ours, sir. A military sensor probe. I can't read an ident from it at this range, if indeed it is actually broadcasting one."

"It's damaged, then," Kein noted.

Lleye nodded again. "These readings would appear to reflect that assumption, Dalin."

Enkoa drummed his fingers on the tablet. "Has it answered any remote commands?"

"Negative. Again, sir, probably a result of the damage."

"It could have been attacked." Enkoa's eyes took on a faraway look. "Those probes are programmed to evade and escape in the event of detection by the enemy."

Lleye paused. "Shall I prepare a data packet for the *Gholen*? Given the probe's present attitude, it won't have traveled far by the time they swing back this way."

Enkoa grunted, as if the idea amused him. Kein knew what he would say next before he took a breath. "Plot an intercept course. We're going to recover it ourselves."

"Dal," she said. "That will require us to divert several light-years from our assigned patrol pattern. It's not a critical—"

He rounded on her. "The decision as to what is critical, and what is not, is the remit of a starship's commander, Dalin." He put an accent on her rank that set her teeth on edge. There was an arrogance there that was new in him. *Sullen and aggressive.* The words echoed in her thoughts.

"Of course," she said smoothly. "I'll bring the crew to standby. We'll be ready to leave the pattern momentarily." Kein turned her back on him and went to her console, so she didn't have to look at the smile in his eyes. This little defiance of Hanno's standing orders—he thought it made him somehow special. She had done her job, and pointed out the fact to him. Whatever happened next, she had obeyed the rules, and that would be noted.

Enkoa's mood became more animated as the *Lakar* peeled away from its mission plan and sprinted at high warp toward a rendezvous with the errant probe. The closer they came, the firmer Kein was in her surmise that the device had malfunctioned in some way. Close-range sensors showed the effluent of a plasma discharge from the unit's microwarp engine, and the ion trail left by the sporadic jets of thrust from its impulse drives. It moved like a pathetic, wounded thing. A bird with a broken wing, begging for the kindness of a merciful kill. Enkoa immediately suspected sinister origins as the damage.

Telso and his staff went out in suits to check the device, and the chief engineer's insistence on a first-hand inspection raised Kein's respect for him a notch; but she was careful to make sure that he remained unaware of that. With a delicate hand on the tractor beam, Glinn Lleye brought the probe into the *Lakar*'s tiny cargo bay and the object was secured.

She glanced at Enkoa, waiting for him to give the order to return to their original patrol pattern. He inclined his head, anticipating her. "Dalin, put the ship in silent mode. Full emissions control, no unauthorized communications or energy discharges without my express orders."

Kein relayed the command with a nod. "May I ask why, Dal?"

He indicated the video feed from the cargo bay with a jut of his chin. "Look at that, Sanir, at the state of that probe. What does it tell you?"

Dark, rust-toned metal in the shape of a crooked arrow formed the fuselage of the autonomous remote unit, and there were clear lines of carbon scoring across the dorsal and ventral surfaces. Near hits from phaser fire, perhaps, or the remnants of a passing ion storm? From a cursory visual inspection, it was hard to be certain.

"It *was* attacked," Enkoa decided. "And that may mean enemy craft are still at large in the area. Stealth is prudent."

"If you believe that is so, perhaps we should send a warning to the *Gholen*," Kein replied. "A tight-beam subspace signal, alerting them to the situation."

But Enkoa was already out of his command throne and moving toward the bridge hatch. "Not yet," he threw over his shoulder. "Not just yet."

Telso reported that the device was no threat, and with the bay repressurized, Kein followed her commanding officer into the empty, gray-walled cargo compartment. The probe lay on a support frame, and the first thing she noted about the object was the smell it generated.

That faint stink of spilled electroplasma, likely from damage to the unit's tiny interstellar drive, underpinned by the tang of burned metals. She saw Telso from the corner of her eye, and recognized the same engineer's twitch in his stance, the inability to ignore that warning stench.

Enkoa didn't appear to notice. He walked to the probe, peering into the open sections of the hull where torn bunches of optic cabling bled out patches of hard blue light. One of Telso's men, *Lakar*'s computer systems specialist, was in the process of extracting a thick copper-sheathed torus from behind the bladed head of the probe. With a clicking sigh, the unit gave up the device and the technician held it in his hand, like a warrior brandishing the heart torn from the chest of a slain monster.

"The memory core," Kein noted.

With care, the technician connected the module to a stand-alone console and let it run through the business of identifying itself, the *Lakar*'s codes and protocols assuring the probe's machine brain that they were indeed duly appointed Cardassian naval forces and not enemy powers masquerading as same. If the ciphers were not in order, the memory core would destroy itself with a small but powerful thermal charge. This did not occur; instead, the core opened and a tide of information fell into the ship's data banks. The probe, aware of its own level of damage, was programmed to immediately dump its contents to the nearest secure storage location. Kein watched sensor records stream past her; amid the flood of encoded symbols, there were great scars of jumbled static that blotted out the console screen at random moments.

"What is that?" Enkoa asked.

"File corruption, sir," Telso responded. "When the probe was damaged, some of the data may have been lost."

Enkoa turned to face Kein. "I want you to examine the data that is there, and reconstruct what's missing, if you can."

She hesitated. "That may take some time, Dal. *Lakar* does not have a forensic computing suite on board."

"Do what you can," he continued.

"The computer lab on Tantok Nor would be a better choice for such a task," she insisted, but Enkoa silenced her with a hard look.

"I want a preliminary analysis by the end of the duty shift," he told her, in a tone that left no room for compromise.

A few hours later the two of them were in the tiny duty room, standing either side of the table with a large padd there before them. Panes of text rolled past, small and bright. They hurt Kein's eyes to stare at them too much; already, she would see them arrayed inside her eyelids if she closed them, burned into her retinas from time spent poring over the sensor logs.

Enkoa's hands were in motion, moving slowly from where they were folded across his chest, then to his sides, then to the desk, then folded again. This was atypical behavior for him, and she was faintly alarmed by it, unable to map it on to the man she had known during her tour aboard the *Rekkel*. Command was changing him in many small ways, and none for the better, so it seemed.

As before, when they had spoken about Hanno and his dismissive orders, Enkoa talked without really acknowledging Kein. "This . . . I suppose I should not be surprised by this. In light of recent events, it is a logical progression."

"Recent events": by which he meant the abortive engagement with the *U.S.S. Rutledge*. Kein took a slow breath. She had known exactly how Enkoa would interpret the data from the very start of her analysis. "The information is not conclusive," she told him. Kein felt as if she had said those words a dozen times now. "The corruption has made entire sensor spectra completely unreadable. Sir, I would be wary of making a swift judgment on what you perceive to be represented here."

Loops of planetary bodies and twin suns moved on the screen. "It's not a question of how I see it," he retorted. "It's the most likely result based on the data to hand." He tapped a raised keypad set into the desktop. "Computer?"

"Ready." She had never liked the arch female voice that Central Command had programmed into their starship mainframes. It reminded Kein of her mother in her parent's less generous moments, of which there had been many.

"Data tie-in. Identify star system on display."

There was barely a pause. *"Isolating. Setlik system, Dorvan Sector perimeter. Contested zone."*

Contested typically meant that it was a piece of dirt desired by Cardassian Central Command but as yet not officially annexed. The Fleet had ships enough for patrolling, but flotillas for colonial operations, for the establishment of bases and garrisons, were considerably thinner on the ground.

Intelligence reports—or at least, the vague fictions that the Obsidian Order deigned to give to the military—noted that one planet in the targeted system supported a Federation outpost and agricultural-industrial complex. Kein's lip curled as she considered this. *Starfleet building farms at the very walls of Cardassian territory. Idiocy.*

Enkoa addressed the computer. "Given the data encoded in the files recovered from the sensor probe, what is the most likely explanation for these readings?" He touched a tab on the padd and a string of false-color images taken from far orbit opened. Each was blurry and hazed by corruption, but the core content of them was clearly visible; blotches of dark green, some of it in crisscrossed rods, others in tight knots, were scattered around the site of the Federation settlement.

"Data is inconclusive," reported the machine, echoing Kein's earlier statement.

The dal's eyes narrowed. "I'm aware of that. Extrapolate and evaluate. Give the most likely explanation."

"Working."

"Sir—" ventured Kein, but he wasn't listening.

"Energy patterns correlate to seventy-nine percent similarity with duonetic accelerated field matrix."

"What is the most frequent usage of such technology within the United Federation of Planets?" he demanded.

"Gravity-resist mechanisms common to military ground vehicles. Long-range photonic weapon delivery systems."

"Weapons." Enkoa was grim, but she sensed eagerness buried beneath it.

"That technology is also deployed in several nonmilitary applications," she replied.

"But not in such large numbers," he insisted. "You can't deny that!"

"Perhaps," Kein admitted, "but there is also the matter of the veracity of the source data you are basing your assumption upon." She nodded at the padd "There's a lot missing."

Enkoa drew back and gave her a brief nod. "I'm aware of that. But what data there is . . . You must admit, it's compelling." He worked the padd, moving a series of time-lapse images into view. "This is a datum from the probe captured over the course of a three-day period. Look." He taped the panel. "Tell me what you see."

She looked. The views showed the motion of the green blotches, shifting and moving from one location to another, spreading apart.

"A deployment," he answered his own question for her. "The time index matches the passage of that Starfleet scow through the area."

"You believe the *Rutledge* transported weapons down to this planet?"

He showed teeth. "Oh no, Sanir. I believe that they transported *more* weapons down there. They've probably been supplying them with hardware and matériel for months, stockpiling it. Preparing." Enkoa manipulated the images again. "Setlik is a system of paired blue giant stars, and thus a messy fog of radiation that our long-range sensors have difficulty penetrating. Moreover, it's unpleasantly close to a dozen Cardassian client worlds." He leaned across the desk. "Tactically, it's an ideal staging point for an attack."

Kein blinked. "From a certain point of view, I can agree. But at the same time, I must ask the question. *Why?* What would any attacker have to gain from such a sortie?" She frowned.

"The reasons are many. To induce instability in the Union's outer rim, to affirm Starfleet's claims to these border worlds. Perhaps just because we are a threat to them." He tapped the screen. "This could be the first indicator of preparations for a preemptive strike."

She frowned. "Remember what Jagul Hanno said. The Federation are loath to fire the first shots in any conflict. It's not in their nature to attack without provocation. They do not operate with the same autonomy as our military. Starfleet would need at least the pretense of a reason, if only to appease their politicians."

Enkoa's nostrils flared at the mention of Hanno's name. "And I remember what you said, Sanir. *We are always at war.*"

Kein felt that same, bone-cold chill again. "Laen," she said firmly; it was the first time she had used his forename since he had been promoted above her. "What are you suggesting?" She asked the question because it was what was expected of her, but in truth she already knew the answer, because she knew *him*.

"This is an opportunity." Enkoa stepped back from the desk. He would have paced, if he had the room. "For this ship, for my crew. For you and me. A chance to show our mettle." His voice lowered, becoming conspiratorial. "The Setlik system is close. We can be there before the *Gholen* sweeps back this way; we can act with boldness and cunning!"

She said nothing, watching, making her expression neutral.

"I have . . . become aware of certain things," he added, after a moment. "I have contacts, Sanir. Sources outside the chain of command."

Kein raised an eye-ridge, wondering who or what he could be referring to.

He shook his head, dismissing the words. "It doesn't matter. What does matter is that I take this opportunity while it presents itself. Hanno thinks the *Lakar* is fit only to patrol in the shallows, tethered to him. This will dissuade the jagul of that. Together, we can show him that we are worthy soldiers of the Union." He tapped his rank sigil. "That we deserve these."

When she spoke again, Kein was mildly surprised by the flatness of her own voice. The slow-burning emotions she felt inside did not show themselves. "The data recovered from the probe should be returned to Tantok Nor for deep analysis. Jagul Hanno specifically ordered us not to engage in combat operations."

"They could be making ready to attack as we speak!" he retorted. "If we leave the area and warp back to Kelrabi, it could be days before a deployment would be ready! We are here now, in range!" Enkoa reached out and grabbed her arm, and Kein forced herself not to react. His expression softened, and a cajoling edge entered his voice. "We can advance by stealth in the shadow of Setlik Major, cross the orbits of the inner worlds, and pass close to the third planet. We can conduct an in-depth scan and confirm what the probe detected."

She doubted that he would do little more than a cursory survey, perhaps just enough to justify what he had already decided was the truth. Behind that smile and those friendly eyes, Kein knew, Enkoa had already made up his mind. The momentum of his need for a victory, for a way to validate himself, was too great.

"Any delay could prove fatal," he added. "I need to know you will give me your best when we confront this battle force."

Battle force. Enkoa had labeled the Federation presence already, doubtless so he could make it easier to convince himself he was right. After all, those words had a much more convincing ring to them than *unconfirmed units.*

He had no intention of conducting a reconnaissance; Enkoa was planning a sneak attack, nothing less.

She took a breath, held it, and suddenly the slow turmoil inside her *shifted;* it was in the room with her, all around. Kein was in the eye of a storm, abruptly becalmed, with a single, clear understanding in her thoughts. *Whatever I say in the next few moments will alter the course of my future forever. And Enkoa's with it.*

Kein nursed that thought for a moment, let it settle. It had to be a rare thing, to find yourself at a turning point and be fully aware of it. She studied Enkoa and that thin, almost pleading cast to his pale face. Resentment burned hard in her chest, never showing, but inwardly consuming her.

If she wished it, there were options open to her, ways she could stop him from going down this path. A single subspace message to Tantok Nor would be enough. And if it came to open opposition, she rated her chances better than his. Glinn Lleye feared her enough to follow her orders, even if they flew in the face of his commander's; if mutiny was the only rod she had to play, she would win with it. Kein had already made halfhearted attempts at counseling caution and he had ignored her every time. She could stop him if she really wanted to, but it would require an exercise of energy that the dalin was not willing to expend.

What was it that the server had said? *The ruin of those sorts of men usually comes out of nowhere. Opportunities arise for those around them, those who perhaps feel aggrieved, to let them make their own mistakes.*

And here was just such an opportunity. *All that needs to be done is to let it happen.*

Her lips parted as a wolfish smile threatened to emerge on her lips. Silence on her part would damn Enkoa, she saw that clearly now; but it felt insufficient. All at once, she wanted to push him, to goad him. "With all due respect," Kein began, in a tone that showed anything but, "*Lakar* has little experience of combat operations. The crew may not be capable—"

He spoke over her. "You should have more faith in our crew,

Dalin. They are trained and ready for any confrontation." Color darkened his eye-ridges.

She demurred. "If you believe so, Dal."

"I do," he insisted. "Now, take your post. I want us under way to Setlik as quickly as possible."

"Shall I signal Tantok Nor and inform them of our new mission priorities?"

Enkoa shook his head. "I'd rather wait until I have something impressive to report to Hanno."

But she sent a signal anyway, on the bridge from her private console—just a vaguely worded report that would be enough to attract the jagul's interest but not enough to explain the full scope of Enkoa's ill-considered sortie. She covered her tracks carefully, ensuring that her commander would not become aware of her small duplicity.

She found it easy to do this, and on some level she marveled at it. Another Kein, the younger Kein aboard the *Rekkel*, the woman who then still had some rein upon her own bitterness, she would not have found it so effortless to lie and conceal. Every Cardassian grew up knowing that the currency of life was secrets, but inside the military there was a different creed—or so she had thought. The spirit of comradeship she recalled from her cadet days suddenly seemed like a childish fiction. *This* was the reality of military duty in Cardassia's name: a lifetime of service among braggarts and fools, where the wiser commanders played games with other people's careers and hoarded influence like coin. Kein chided herself for ever believing that the Fleet was a meritocracy. It was a hidebound morass of fealty and petty authority; it was everything about Cardassia she had joined the Fleet to be free of, everything she had rejected in her own family.

And now, only now when she was buried in it up to her neck, could Sanir Kein see the truth of that. Hate and frigid envy washed over her.

On the main screen, the cold blue sphere of the Setlik star grew larger as they made their approach.

The *Lakar* came in at warp two, down the barrel of the star's solar winds toward the third planet. It was a large, dun-colored world with a few shallow oceans and mountain ranges that curled over the landscape like thin white talons. The Federation colony was on the smaller of two continental landmasses, down toward the more temperate regions of the equator. Nothing stood in orbit to challenge them, only the mute spheres of two weather-control satellites.

Kein watched the play of data from the passive sensors as they ranged over the local sector of space. She saw traces of energy that were common to the passage of ionic storms but nothing that resembled the residue of weapons fire. As she had suspected, if the probe had passed through the Setlik system, the damage it sustained had not come from an enemy vessel. She did not bother to commit this conclusion to her log; not yet.

"Scan the outpost," Enkoa ordered. "Look for matches to the data we recovered from the probe's memory core."

"Acknowledged." Lleye worked the scanner console, making no comment about the specificity of the dal's order. Effectively, he had asked the glinn to find him an excuse to open fire.

Kein's hand strayed to the scar on her brow, and for a moment an odd sensation rose in her thoughts. *What was that?* she asked herself. *Reproach?* Was there still some small element of the noble-minded recruit buried deep in there, saddened by her elder self's bitterness? She shook the thought away, banishing it, staring back at the detector screen.

A reading from the aft sensor grid made itself known to her, and this one, Kein decided, was worth mention. "Dal. At extreme range . . . ghost images, difficult to interpret."

"Where?" he snapped.

"Several light-years out beyond the edge of the Setlik system. They could just be false returns reflected off the solar radiation belts, or . . ." She trailed off, leaving Enkoa to supply the answers he wanted.

"Ships." He paused, perhaps reconsidering his attack.

Kein noted the hesitation and pushed. "More intruder craft, perhaps. We won't be able to identify them until they close, if they are indeed actual vessels."

"Federation Starfleet?" asked Lleye.

Kein pushed again. "Perhaps we should withdraw."

Enkoa's hands gripped the arms of his command chair. "Glinn!" he snarled. "Report! Are the energy patterns visible down there?"

"Confirmed." Lleye gave a single, slow nod of his head. "But there are conflicting readings, sir."

"They're obviously trying to mask the signature of the stockpiles." Enkoa leaned forward. "It won't do them any good."

And with that, he smiled and Sanir knew they had stepped across the point of no return. "What are your orders, Dal?"

"Start by destroying those orbitals," he began, the smile growing wider. "Then move to pinpoint salvos against all target locations." Enkoa stood up, looming over the compact bridge. "Execute!"

The Setlik III colony had little in the way of defenses, only a handful of ground-based deflector shields and scattering field generators designed to protect the settlement from transporter bombs or a massed beam-in. There were no weapons there capable of reaching the *Lakar*'s orbit, only small arms in the possession of a dozen families and the armory of the local civil marshal.

There was enough of a warning for the hurricane sirens to sound. The planet's harsh storm season meant that every large building had a shelter beneath it, and many of those who didn't automatically seek cover stayed outside because the sky was clear, because the orbital satellites had said the day would be fine. These people were the ones who saw the amber streaks of lightning falling from above, screaming through the air with hissing shockwaves of plasmatic gas marking their passage. Then the buildings began to explode, the hydroponic farms and the grain silos vanishing in the sudden, star-bright liberation of matter to energy. It had been dry for several weeks, and secondary fires took hold, washing across the fields in a black tide of smoke.

Each time the bombardment seemed to be over, the cruelty of the pause between salvos was made worse. Disruptor blasts rained down in five-fold impacts, seeking out what at first seemed like randomly chosen locations.

Death came from the morning sky without pause, without reason, without mercy.

★ ★ ★

"Proximity alert!" cried Kein. "Signal traces are resolving . . . Two ships on intercept course, high warp. They're coming in fast!"

The expression of cold intent on Enkoa's face became a glare of annoyance, petulant at being interrupted; then a heartbeat later it became worry. "Break off the attack. Disengage and extend away!" He rose to his feet. "Stand by to go to warp—"

A warning klaxon keened across the command tier. "They're right on top of us!" Lleye stabbed a finger at the main viewscreen as a warp-speed distended shape came out of nowhere, dropping to sub-light velocity in a punishing deceleration that flashed out around the craft in sheaves of spent luminosity.

The new arrival swept in underneath the *Lakar* and turned to place itself squarely between the escort and the surface of the third planet, blocking the path of any further bombardment. Slowing, it revealed itself, and Kein felt her heart pounding against her ventral ribs. The port manta-wing of the ship's upper hull filled the screen with a wall of sand-colored titanium, and briefly a wine-dark sigil drifted past: the hooded shape of the Galor Banner.

"It's the *Kursa*. . . ." husked the glinn. "Hailing us."

Kein opened the channel without waiting for Enkoa to order it.

Jagul Hanno was abruptly there, his cut-granite face darker than she had ever seen it before. *"Enkoa!"* He spat out the name with undisguised fury. *"Stand down! In the Union's name, man, what do you think you are doing?"*

The dal fought to keep his voice level, his knuckles turning white where he gripped his command chair. "There is an enemy outpost on the planet. A weapons stockpile. They were preparing an attack on the Dorvan—"

"You know this how?" demanded the jagul. *"You, the commander of a mere escort, have access to intelligence that a fleet admiral does not?"*

"I do," Enkoa insisted. "I have learned certain facts . . ." He paused and swallowed hard. "We recovered a military probe and the data in its memory core led us to—"

Hanno cut him off again. *"Show me now."*

Kein took the command and transmitted a full download directly into *Kursa*'s computer core. From the corner of her eye she could see the sensor readout tracking the other *Galor*-class ship, Matrik's *Fell*. From the energy glow issuing from the warp coils of both vessels, they must have made a dash to the Setlik system at emergency speed all the way. *Not fast enough, though,* she mused.

Hanno disappeared from the screen for long moments, and when he returned he wore the face Kein remembered from her ascendance ceremony. Cold and hard, fueled by something past rage, past duty.

"This is your motive?" The jagul's lip curled in disgust. *"Only this?"*

"It's enough," Enkoa replied, and he blinked, as if he was surprised by his own sudden show of defiance. "Scan the outpost below."

"You do not give me commands," Hanno hissed. *"I want you and your executive officer aboard the* Kursa *immediately."* The signal cut, returning the viewscreen to its default forward view. Kein could see the blades of the cruiser's forward hull and beyond it, the curvature of Setlik III. Dark lines of color were just visible from plumes of wind-borne ash and smoke.

She looked past Enkoa; his face had taken on the pallor of corpse flesh. "Glinn," she called to Lleye. "You have the bridge."

"A-acknowledged," said the junior officer, fighting down a stammer.

"Yes," said Enkoa, after a moment. "This should not take long."

A pair of enlisted men awaited them in *Kursa*'s transporter room, two garresh with holstered pistols on their belts. Enkoa gave them a wavering glance.

"Jagul's orders, sir," said the senior of the two. "If you'll follow us?"

Enkoa glanced at Kein as they walked along the warship's corridors. "What did he mean, *only this*?" The dal wrung his hands. "He's not blind. He must have seen the same thing I did."

He wanted something from her, she realized, something reassuring. Kein did not provide it. Instead, she walked briskly, in step with the two troopers.

The enlisted men waited outside as the dalin and dal entered the jagul's duty room. It was bigger than the footprint of Enkoa's private cabin and Kein's combined, but the design was the same as the one aboard the *Lakar*. A desk, wall screens, chairs, but with a ceiling that did not feel as if it were pressing down upon her back. Kein stood a little taller, and once more schooled her expression into a mask of stony detachment.

Every muscle in Hanno's face was corded and tight, wound hard like steel cables. He radiated anger to such a degree that Kein was concerned he might actually be moved to physical violence.

"Are you so eager to shed blood that you are willing to open fire on a civilian target?" The officer's voice was low and loaded with menace.

"Sir, that's only a cover. Setlik III is the staging post for an attack. I'm convinced of it."

"Yes, you obviously are," Hanno growled. He picked up a padd and brandished it. "And clearly it takes very little to convince you of anything." He tossed the tablet across the desktop. "This intelligence is riddled with holes. It's worthless, full of unsubstantiated facts and unconfirmed data." The jagul pointed a thick finger at him. "You overlooked that, either through misguided fervor or outright stupidity."

Enkoa's mouth opened and closed in shock at the comment. "Sir . . ."

"Did you think that just because you bedded my brother's flighty daughter you were granted some kind of special dispensation to ignore orders, Dal Enkoa?" He bared his teeth. "Did you mistake my civility toward you for leniency on my part?"

Before Enkoa could respond, Hanno turned the full force of his ire on Kein; but she was ready for it, and she didn't flinch. "And you, Dalin." He ground out the words. "You stood by and let this happen."

"I did nothing of the kind, sir." She kept her gaze centered firmly on a point somewhere beyond the bulkhead behind the jagul. Kein saw Enkoa react as if he had been slapped.

Opportunities arise, said a calm and metered voice in her thoughts. *All that needs to be done is to let it happen.*

"Explain!" barked Hanno.

"I expressed my concerns to Dal Enkoa over this break from orders on several occasions. He overruled me."

"No," Enkoa insisted. "You agreed with me."

"I sent the signal that alerted Tantok Nor," she continued. The moment the words left her mouth, a strange sensation filled her. Kein felt an immediate absence of rage, of all the irritation and disgust that had been her constant companions these past weeks. She felt light, buoyed on a wave of something strong and potent. Kein could feel the spite and resentment that she had been nursing all this time, flooding her, carrying her like a rising tide—a tide she would let Enkoa drown in.

"What signal?" said the dal. "I ordered no communications!"

Hanno's expression shifted, and for a moment she wondered if he was aware of her thoughts, her intentions. Was it written large across her expression, her bone-deep loathing for foolish, foolish Enkoa? "The signal alerted us that the *Lakar* had diverted from its patrol pattern," said the jagul. "At first I suspected an ambush . . ." He trailed off, then refocused, turning his ire back toward the other man. "I did not expect an officer of the Cardassian Union to attempt to start a war on his own!"

Enkoa's hands moved. "The settlement conceals military equipment. The scans prove it!" His voice rose an octave.

Hanno's tones became thunderous. "Those readings are from farming equipment! Experimental technologies invented by the Federation's Vulcan cohorts, designed to planetform the surface of worlds like that one!" He stepped out from behind the desk and crossed toward them.

The dal blinked. "But . . . if that was known, then why was that information not in the *Lakar*'s data banks?"

"Because that information is known only to the Obsidian Order," came the growled reply, "and it is known to me only because agents in my employ have stolen that data from them, along with other, far more important materials. Materials that allow me to maintain my position and status." He glared at Enkoa, who withered under the jagul's iron-hard gaze. "If that data was made widely available, the Order would become aware of a breach in their information security and would move to amend it. Now you have placed me in a very difficult situation, Dal. Your reckless actions will have consequences you cannot even begin to guess at!"

"No," Enkoa insisted, "no. That's not it at all." He threw a look at Kein, desperation in his eyes, pleading with her to help him, even though she had thrown him to the hounds just moments before.

She enjoyed the thrill she got from ignoring him.

"You attacked the Setlik III colony without provocation," Hanno pronounced, his voice becoming level and cold. "There were no Starfleet forces there massing for a secret attack. They were noncombatants, Enkoa. Even though the Federation are our adversaries, the malicious slaughter of civilians is something I will never tolerate under my command." He looked away, revolted. "There were entire families down there. Their murder is unacceptable."

"I am a soldier of the Union," Enkoa insisted. "All I have ever wanted is to serve Cardassia and defeat her enemies . . ." He gasped, and Kein saw a fraction of the certainty he had shown on the *Lakar*'s bridge briefly return. "You prevented me from doing that, sir. I see nothing wrong in what I have done."

Hanno accepted this with a nod. "Yes, that is clear. The error here is mine." He reached up and Enkoa flinched, clearly afraid for one second that the jagul was going to strike him. But the officer simply reached for the rank sigil on the other man's duty armor and detached it with a twist of his fingers. "I relieve you of your command, Laen Enkoa," he said, grim-faced. "You are under arrest, pending a full investigation into your actions here." Hanno touched a tab on his wrist communicator and the door opened to admit the two troopers. "Put him in containment," said the jagul.

"But, my ship—" Enkoa protested, straining against the grip of the soldiers.

Hanno nodded toward Kein. "It's the Union's ship. It was never yours."

Then the door closed and they were alone. The jagul gave her that same measuring stare once again. For the first time, Kein matched Hanno and met his gaze, unafraid, waiting for him to speak.

She waited for him to admit his mistakes in choosing Enkoa over her. She waited for him to acknowledge that she was the superior, that it had been her intelligence, her daring that had saved the lives of the *Rekkel* crew, her loyalty to Cardassia that had alerted him to Enkoa's irresponsibility. She waited for all these things to be said.

Hanno finally broke the silence and turned away from her. "Take command of the *Lakar* and bring it back to Tantok Nor." He gave nothing else, dismissing her with a flick of his hand.

★ ★ ★

When Kein rematerialized in the escort's tiny transporter alcove, she found Glinn Lleye waiting for her. He glanced at the other, empty transport pad and then back to her.

"Where is the dal?" he asked.

She pushed past the junior officer, heading for the bridge. "You won't see him again."

She rose into Tantok Nor's operations center inside the open-walled elevator, drawing a few cursory looks from the staff on duty. A Kel-rabi—a trustee of some sort, she surmised—backed away from the lift platform and allowed her to exit, clutching a tricorder to its chest in an unconscious gesture of self-protection. The alien took the elevator back down as she glanced around the domed chamber. A female glinn at the main systems table in the middle of the room looked up and nodded toward the raised upper level, to the copper doors of the station gul's office. "He's waiting for you," she said.

Kein had never seen the other female officer before, and for a moment she wondered how the glinn knew her identity. But then news traveled fast on any military outpost; she wondered what they were saying about her on Tantok Nor behind her back, and she wondered about the glinn.

Did she already have an understanding of how hard a road she was on? What lessons was she learning from Kein and her conduct?

The young officer looked away, but Kein wasn't finished with her yet. "You," she said, demanding her attention once again. "A question."

"Yes, Dalin?"

"The refectory down on the main concourse, the one with the long booths and the open frontage."

"By the quartermaster's office?"

She gave a nod. "It's closed. Every time I've been on this station it's been open around the clock."

"I never visited it." The glinn's brow furrowed; clearly the question wasn't what she had expected. "I believe the facility has been shut down for refurbishment, ma'am. The storefronts down there, they're civilian interests under contract to the Fleet. They only have short leases from the station's support office." She reached for a panel on her bowed console. "I could contact the chief of logistics if you wish me to. They will have details of the contractors—"

Kein shook her head. "No." She looked away. There would be no point. Somehow, the moment she stepped through the cogwheel hatch of the airlock, she had known that the place . . . that *he* would be gone.

With swift, purposeful pace she climbed the steps to the station gul's office and saw through the windows in the doors Tantok Nor's commander and Jagul Hanno standing at either end of a curved desk. Hanno caught sight of her and beckoned her in. Kein entered as the two men continued their conversation, content to let her wait.

Station Gul Relaw was speaking. "Gul Matrik reports that the deployment has gone without incident. They have secured an encampment in an area known locally as the Barrica Valley, some distance from the remains of the Federation settlement. Setlik III has now formally been annexed by the Cardassian Union."

"For the moment," Hanno noted. "Order him to have the *Fell* maintain a wide patrol perimeter until reinforcements can arrive to relieve them."

"Central Command has approved this?" Relaw's doubt was evident.

"Of course," said the jagul. "It's what they were agitating for all along." He glanced at Kein, then back to the gul. "Proceed."

"Sir." Relaw gave a brisk salute and shot Kein a look of his own. She sensed a faint sneer behind it. "I'll let you have the room." The station commander left them, the copper doors closing behind his back. Kein saw him disappear down into the command pit, calling out orders.

Hanno moved behind Relaw's desk and took the chair there, settling into it with an air of weariness Kein hadn't seen in him before. "Laen Enkoa has been cashiered," he began, without preamble. "He's on a transport back to Cardassia. When he arrives on Prime there will be proceedings. But it's just a formality, really."

Kein elected to say nothing.

He idly pushed a padd around the desk; Kein saw her own ident code on the small screen. She had carefully used the time it took the

Lakar to return to Kelrabi, doctoring the date indices on some of her personal and duty log entries in order to firm up her assertion that Enkoa had acted alone. The sheer audacity of such an action, of doing something that so blatantly went against her oath to the Fleet, might have troubled her before. Now Kein did it with only the slightest taint of remorse, telling herself that it was a service to Cardassia to cement this one man's fall from grace. She almost believed it.

"His career is in tatters and he has disgraced himself. Lethra will break her engagement to him by the day's end, if she has not already done so." Hanno looked away, and then back to her. "Did you help him along that road, Kein? Did you push him into his mistakes?"

She licked dry lips. "Enkoa needed no assistance from me to make his errors, sir. I was almost killed by his indecision aboard the *Rekkel*. I am glad that he was prevented from risking more Cardassian lives."

"You could not be more incorrect," Hanno rumbled. "Enkoa's actions have, if anything, put even more of our fellow soldiers in the line of fire. His foolishness has pushed the Union closer to open war, closer than it has been in years." The jagul shook his head. "I have worked for a long time to ensure peace and stability for my people, and in one day, an inexperienced imbecile tears it all down." He pointed a finger at her. "What I wish to know is why he did it."

Kein's mouth opened, then closed.

"Speak!" The word was a sudden bark. "Don't test my patience, woman! I give you leave to speak openly. Do so!"

When she said the words she felt a little giddy with the daring of them. "The blame is yours, sir. Enkoa was not ready for the role you gave him. He lacked imagination and discipline. He wasn't ready for command."

"And you think you were? You think I should have chosen you?"

"Yes." She swallowed. "And I believe that you knew that when you called us both to your office on Sunzek. But you chose him regardless." The potency of this openness, the chance to speak her mind, was seductive.

Hanno folded his arms. "I did not pass you over because of your gender, Dalin, despite what you may think."

"No, sir," she replied. "You passed me over because I was not the one having sex with your niece." The more she talked, the more this freedom was running away with her. Kein found herself working to stop herself smiling.

The jagul smacked the flat of his hand on Relaw's desk. "You understand nothing!" He rose to his feet once more. "I'll grant you this, girl, you already have the arrogance of a starship commander. But not the foresight of a good officer, not yet."

She backed off a step as the old warrior came closer, his voice falling back into those low, somber tones.

"You're like Enkoa in one way. You have no vision of the larger patterns at work. In fact, you're more dangerous than he ever could be, because he was a fool and you are not." Hanno leaned in, and he seemed old. "I gave him rank because of who he was. For the family he was a part of. Lines of influence, Kein. Need and appeasement, munificence and envy. These are the forces that act upon us all. It's very difficult to keep them in balance. Like a tower of dry twigs . . . you build it tall to take you high, but it becomes fragile. Easy to catch on fire." He turned away again.

"My family would offer you little for your tower," she admitted. "But I would have given you everything!" Kein's eyes flashed. "Something without price—loyalty!"

Hanno chuckled without humor. "Youth. You value yourself so high." He glared at her. "Answer me this: How is your loyalty without price when I can buy you with just a starship?"

Her throat ran dry as he pulled a rank sigil from his pocket—the same one he had taken from Enkoa—and tossed it on the desk. She could not help but reach for it.

"You are raised in rank to dal," he said flatly. "The *Lakar* is your new command. Now take it and get out of my sight."

"What . . ." Her fingers clasped around the small metal plate of ash-dark iron, tracing over the inset etching. "What are my orders?"

"Orders?" Hanno echoed, his tolerance for her impudence now clearly at an end. "Gul Relaw will give you your orders, *Dal* Kein! I have no say in them. I am returning to Cardassia Prime, in the footsteps of your errant cohort. Once he has answered for his errors, I will answer for them as well." He pushed past her toward the anteroom at the far end of the office. He kept talking. "He's the torch to my tower of twigs." The jagul drifted into silence; then in the next second he was glaring at her with undisguised rage. *"Now get out!"*

★ ★ ★

She stepped up to the command throne and settled her weight into it. The chair gave a little, but it was firm and comfortable. Automatic systems hidden in the frame adjusted it silently to conform more closely to her body shape, tilting the chair gently so she might have the best view of the *Lakar*'s bridge from where she sat upon the dais. For a brief moment, Kein closed her eyes and savored it.

The chair was hers now. She owned it, just as she did every bolt and rivet in this ship. Her blood rushed in her ears, and she could almost taste her captaincy. It was bitter and it was sweet, and it was exactly what she deserved.

Still, Hanno's last words to her hung like a dark cloud at the horizon of her thoughts, threatening to blacken the fierce joy of the moment. She refused to allow herself to be shaken from the rightness of this. Here, in this chair, on this ship, this was where Sanir Kein should have been all along; and now that she had taken her place, she would not give it up.

A chime sounded from one of the consoles. "Dal?" Dalin Telso half turned to face her. "Incoming message." Promoting the chief engineer to her former post as executive officer had been her first order of business after returning to the *Lakar*, and it had been worth it just to see the moment of shock and confusion on the man's face; but he was grateful with it too, and Kein was certain he would give her the honesty and fearlessness she needed in that role, borne out of his steady aversion to her. And that was fine; he did not need to like her, he needed only to obey her.

"Origin?" she asked.

Telso hesitated. "Unknown. It's heavily encrypted. Eyes-only security protocols. Addressed directly to you, ma'am."

Kein felt the distinct passage of a cold bead of sweat down the back of her duty armor. She rose from the command chair, propelled to her feet by a sudden discomfort. "Transfer it to the duty room," she told him. "I'll take it there."

She sat behind the desk and studied the screen suspended in the oval frame before her. The dull glow of the text there was the only illumination in the small office. Whereas Enkoa had made it bright in here,

Kein kept the lighting low to make the space seem larger, less cramped and oppressive.

The communication transfer was awaiting an activation code word. Kein thought for a moment, dragging up the day's briefing on the Fleet's code protocols for that shift, and paused. The *Lakar* was expecting no such sealed orders today. There was no reason for a clandestine signal with such a degree of opaque encryption to be sent to so minor a vessel.

No reason. No reason other than—

Kein cleared her throat and spoke the first word that came to mind. "Rokassa."

There was a faint chime, and the screen unfolded. No framing, no background was visible. Only a figure, head and shoulders, bland and smiling. *"Ah, Dal Kein. May I be the first to congratulate you on your well-deserved promotion. I'd offer you a glass on the house to celebrate, but as you can see I've been called away. Other duties. You know how it goes."*

"Yes," she managed. Belatedly, it occurred to her that she should have had Telso try to backtrack the signal origin. Was he still on Tantok Nor, perhaps on the planet below, or on one of the other ships in the area?

"A shame about Enkoa. Men like that find failure very hard to deal with. Sometimes the shame drives them to—"

"Don't kill him." The words slipped out of her mouth.

There was the hint of a smile. *"You're gracious in your victory. Or is it that you would find such finality distasteful?"*

"Who are you?" she demanded. "I want your name."

The bland face hardened for a moment. *"Don't be silly. You've crossed many lines these last few days, but don't let it make you reckless. That's what Enkoa did, and look what it earned him. He learned certain truths and employed that information badly."*

"You spoke to Enkoa?"

"Not I."

Kein's eyes narrowed. "I knew what you were," she told him. "What you are."

"Really?" He gave her an indulgent smile. *"How perceptive of you."*

"I think I knew from the first words you spoke," Kein continued, "but I refused to see it."

"Envy . . ." he purred. *"It is such a deep well to draw from. Not like desire or hate or avarice. It never seems to run dry."*

"I wanted Enkoa gone. But Hanno . . ."

"Ah, the estimable Jagul Hanno. He has made some poor choices, hasn't he? There are many who feel misjudgments characterize much of his commands. And now, thanks to you, he has provided the very leverage required to push him aside. In the name of Cardassian glory." He said the last words with a mocking lilt.

"I am not your tool!" she shouted, the muscles in her arms bunching, her hands becoming impotent fists. "You manipulated me, and I let it happen. It will not go that way again."

"Oh?" The man on the screen fell silent for a moment. *"Do you think yourself unusual in this, then? Really, Dal, are you so vain as to believe that this has never happened to anyone else?"* He chuckled. *"This is commonplace, my dear Sanir. This is trite and routine and done very, very often."* He leaned in, his face filling the screen. *"You see, envy is what makes us Cardassian. It's the pillar our society stands upon. We have always had too little, and we have always wanted. Cardassia has always wanted what others have. We are always hungry, you see? Always driven. It's what makes us who we are."* That insouciant smile returned. *"And perhaps, one day, it will be the path that leads us to take the whole galaxy for ourselves."*

"Or destroy us in the attempt," she said bleakly. The new scar burned hard against her temple.

He reached for something outside the field of vision of the screen's camera pickup, and touched a control. An icon blinked in the corner of the monitor, signifying a download in progress. *"I have something for you. Something from Setlik III, from an, ah, source on the surface. A recording of the aftermath."* He seemed sad for a moment, playing at the emotion. *"View it at your leisure. Look at the damage done and the dead. It will help you understand the price that was paid to assuage your jealousy."*

His voice was like a blade, patient and steady. She could almost feel it pressing into the meat of her, between the spars of her ribs, into her heart, her throat. Shakily, Kein removed an isolinear data rod from the frame of the screen and held it between her fingers, as if it were poisonous. "Why?" she husked.

"It's important that you understand the dimensions of your responsibility,"

he told her. *"Clarity. It ensures there will be no misinterpretations during our future associations."*

She almost missed the inference in his words, and her head jerked up suddenly. "No. No, this is at an end—"

He chuckled again, reaching back toward the controls. *"Of course it is. Enjoy your new command, Dal Kein. You have certainly earned it."*

The screen went dead, and Sanir was plunged into darkness, the ghost of a knife twisted tight in her chest.

Wrath

The Unhappy Ones

Keith R.A. DeCandido

Historian's Note

This story takes place in 2269 (ACE), prior to the destruction of the Klingon battle cruiser at Beta XII-A ("Day of the Dove" TOS).

To John Colicos, William Campbell, and Michael Ansara

1

Malvak

Malvak found Krov's body when he arrived at the mine in the morning.

Krov hadn't been in his bunk when Malvak had awakened, but Malvak had assumed him to have simply risen early. He did that sometimes.

But then Krov hadn't been at the morning meal, either. Krov and Malvak had taken most of their meals together since the latter's arrival at the dilithium mine here in Beta Thoridar's asteroid belt a turn previous. Malvak had been left to have his *raktajino* and *ramjep* egg soup alone.

Still, Malvak hadn't been overly concerned. Krov had probably just taken the earlier shuttle to Site *wej*, where they both toiled.

But when Malvak had boarded the later shuttle, then he started to fear that something was wrong. Gahlar wasn't on the shuttle, either. Which meant that he had also taken the earlier shuttle—there were only two that ferried workers to Site *wej* each morning. The last three days had ended with Gahlar and Krov arguing with each other, and if they had been on the early shuttle together, it didn't bode well.

Sure enough, Gahlar was already there, leaning against a pillar, chewing on a gamey *klongat* leg, and talking with another worker.

Both Gahlar and his friend were *HemQuch*. At a joke Gahlar told, they both laughed, and then butted their deeply ridged heads together.

Malvak had bridled at that. He was *QuchHa'*, and if two such Klingons performed that action, it would cause permanent damage to their weak, Earther-like foreheads.

Gahlar had seen Malvak watching him and his friend, and sneered. "What are you looking at, *petaQ?*"

"Nobody of consequence," Malvak said, and then moved on, looking for Krov.

Gahlar tossed the gristle-laden *klongat* leg bone aside, and it hit Malvak in the arm. Malvak turned to glare at him, but said nothing.

"Keep walking, *QuchHa',*" his friend said, then threw his head back and laughed.

It disgusted Malvak. He was here doing honest work. He earned money so that his mate and daughter on Mempa VII could eat and pay the rent on their meager dwelling. Gahlar and his friend, though, they were criminals, who were paid nothing—they were simply working in the mines by way of shortening their sentences.

Yet *they* looked down at *him*.

Soon Malvak found Krov's body wedged behind a support beam and a cave wall, his dead eyes staring straight ahead. A blade of some sort had ripped open his throat.

Immediately, Malvak pried his friend's eyes open wider, and screamed to the heavens.

That scream was interrupted by his section chief, Qao. "What in the name of Kahless's hand are you *doing*, Malvak?"

Standing aside, Malvak revealed the corpse of Krov. "Someone has killed Krov. I was merely warning the Black Fleet—"

"Of what?" Qao asked derisively, staring at Malvak with beady little eyes under deep ridges. "Now I've seen everything. A useless mine worker is commending the soul of another useless mine worker to Sto-Vo-Kor, as if he were a Klingon."

Malvak bridled. The death scream was strictly speaking a ritual of the warrior caste. It was not generally used by lowly laborers.

But Malvak thought that Krov deserved *something*. After all, whatever his appearance, his heart was Klingon. As was Malvak's.

"I am sure that Gahlar did this," Malvak said. "He and Krov have been arguing for several days, and—"

Qao chortled. "First a warrior, now an investigator? You do have *many* talents today, Malvak. Get to the landing bay. This area will be sealed for one hour while security deals with it."

Malvak considered arguing, then realized that there was no point. Qao was hardly going to accept *his* word.

An hour later, Sorkav—the head of security, and also the brother of the mining operation's supervisor, Kobyk—had gone through the scene and declared the death an accident.

Malvak was aghast. All the workers were filing back out of the landing bay and to their places of work to begin meeting the day's quota—which would be complicated by the late start and by being one person short, though the latter affected only Qao's section. Qao was thus likely to be even surlier than usual.

"How does someone 'accidentally' get his throat cut?" Malvak asked.

The question was rhetorical, but a worker behind him—Nargov, who worked in Malvak's section—answered. "I heard he was buried under a rockslide."

"No," said another, "he tripped and cracked his skull on the wall."

Another—a *HemQuch* like Gahlar—said, "I would expect no less of a weak-head."

Whirling around, Malvak said, "I found the body! Krov's throat was *cut*! That cannot be an accident!"

"Quiet!" yelled Qao from in front of the queue. "Report to your duties in *silence*!"

Malvak did not speak after that, but he was livid. His friend was dead, probably killed by Gahlar, and nothing would be done! Once a death in the mines was declared an accident, that was it. There would be no further investigation.

Unlike Malvak, Krov had no family. He'd been born an orphan, and working in the Beta Thoridar mines was a step up from the other jobs he'd had over the years.

So Malvak was truly the only one to mourn his death—and take action.

Perhaps he would not be able to commend Krov's spirit to Sto-Vo-Kor, but his friend's death in this life *would* be avenged.

★ ★ ★

That night, Malvak took the evening meal in the mess hall as usual. The room, which serviced all three asteroidal mines, was massive, with food pickup all along one wall, and three rows of twenty long tables with benches on either side. Generally, people sat based on which mine they worked: Site *wa'* at the easternmost set of tables, Site *cha'* in the center group, and Malvak and the rest of Site *wej* on the western end. The rear tables, farthest from the food pickup, were generally where the section chiefs, supervisors, and security personnel sat. The higher-ups, of course, had their own dining area.

While Malvak sat alone at the end of one of the tables on the western side, several others in that area, and a few others besides, came by to offer their condolences about Krov.

Nargov, in particular, was angry about how the situation was handled. "Sorkav is a filthy *petaQ*. All he cares about is the ridge-heads and the quotas. None of the rest of us matter."

"Indeed," Malvak said. "Thank you."

Nargov offered his hand, and Malvak clasped it. Several *HemQuch* across the mess hall pointed and laughed at their engaging in a warrior's handshake, but Malvak appreciated the gesture.

After Nargov went back to his own meal, Malvak finished off his plate of half-dead *gagh* and washed it down with watery bloodwine. His meal concluded, he got up and walked toward the back wall, seeking out the one person who might be able to offer more than verbal support.

While most of the higher-ups were *HemQuch*, there were a few exceptions. One of them, a *QuchHa'* named Torad, also worked at Site *wej,* though he ran a different section. In fact, he was the only *QuchHa'* who worked as a section chief.

"I would speak with you," Malvak said to Torad. Section chiefs didn't eat with mere laborers, and *HemQuch* didn't eat with *QuchHa'*, so Torad always ate alone at the far end of a table that was as far from the wall as possible while still being considered part of the place where the section chiefs sat. Malvak didn't pity him, as Torad was well-compensated for his solitude. Section chiefs made more than twice as much as miners.

Torad seemed confused by the declaration at first. "Qao is your section chief, Malvak. If you wish to speak—"

"I have spoken to Qao, but he does not hear my words."

"And you believe I will?"

"There is only one way to know."

Fumbling with the faded gray slab of *bok-rat* liver in one hand, Torad gestured to the bench opposite him with the other. "Sit."

Malvak took the seat offered. "Krov was murdered."

Chewing his liver, Torad said, "Sorkav ruled it an accident."

"Sorkav is a fool!"

Torad hissed. "Keep your voice down, you stupid *toDSaH*! Sorkav has ears everywhere."

The ambient noise in the mess hall at the heart of dinner hour was so loud that Malvak found it unlikely that anyone eavesdropped. Still, he modulated his tone. "Sorkav was mistaken. I was the one who found the body, and his throat was *cut*. How is *that* an accident?"

"You misunderstand me, Malvak. I'm not saying it *was* an accident. I am saying that Sorkav *ruled* it an accident. Sorkav's word is law in such matters, and none may challenge him."

Malvak leaned forward to add urgency to his tone. "He did not perform a proper investigation. I found the body, yet he did not once ask me what I found. To Sorkav, it was just another dead *QuchHa'*, and who would miss *that*?"

Torad rolled his eyes. "Don't be a fool, Malvak. Sorkav has nothing against *QuchHa'*. He was the one who approved my promotion to section chief. All he cares about is maintaining order in the mines."

"You expect me to believe that?" Malvak laughed derisively. "Look around you, Torad. How many others besides yourself sit in this area of the mess hall?"

"Plenty," Torad said, pointing at a group of *QuchHa'* sitting together toward the back of the middle set of tables, all wearing the dark jumpsuits of Sorkav's security detail. "They all were hired by Sorkav." He chewed on some more liver before continuing. "Look, I agree that there are some here who dislike our kind, but Sorkav is *not* one of them. He's never treated me any differently than the other section chiefs. If it was anybody else, I'd believe you, but Sorkav? He doesn't have any agenda beyond keeping things orderly."

"So you've said. But all you have done is convince me that he cares more about meeting the quotas than the safety of the miners. Either way, Krov's murder will not be avenged."

"What does it matter? We are not warriors, Malvak. Krov was not kin to you. Let it go."

Malvak rose to his feet. "I thought you would understand. But you're just another section chief, aren't you, Torad?"

"You're the one being a fool, Malvak. This idiocy will just get *you* killed!"

Turning his back on Torad, Malvak left the mess hall.

He would have to find his revenge another way.

Qao found Gahlar's body when he arrived at the mine in the morning.

He muttered, *"ghuy'cha."* Gahlar's body was wedged by the same pillar that Krov's body had been placed against a week earlier, his throat cut in a similar manner. Gahlar hadn't been in his bunk during Qao's bed check the previous night, and Qao had duly reported it. Now, it seemed, he had a good reason. Qao had come over on the early shuttle, so Gahlar had to have been there since the previous night.

With reluctance, Qao pulled out his communicator. His section had already been behind on meeting its quota before Krov's death, and the situation had gotten worse over the past week, since Kobyk had yet to provide a replacement for Krov. Now Qao was down *another* worker, and would lose another hour's labor while Sorkav investigated.

Sorkav arrived within twenty minutes, during which time Qao herded what few workers from his section were present into the landing bay for the second time in a week.

Qao happened to know that Sorkav wore special boots that made him appear taller than he actually was, and Qao took considerable satisfaction from the fact that despite Sorkav's boots, Qao was half a head taller than the security chief.

Sorkav arrived at the scene with three guards, like him dressed in all black, and all with painstiks and hand-scanners on their belts.

"Another death in your section, Qao?" Sorkav asked with a derisive snort as his lackeys started scanning the scene. "Perhaps the supervision of this section requires revisiting."

Qao looked down at Sorkav. "My concern is with getting my

workers to provide dilithium. Incidents like this fall into *your* purview, Sorkav."

"You're hardly achieving great things on that front, are you, Section Chief?"

To that, Qao had no response, so he simply said, "How long will this investigation take?"

"While I appreciate your desire to try to bring your returns up, Qao, I'm afraid it will not be that simple. A death in your section is one thing, but a second exactly like it? Obviously there is more going on here than I previously believed."

Qao snarled. "Don't be ridiculous, Sorkav."

Sorkav snapped, his mock-pleasant tone replaced with fury. "Do not take that tone with *me,* Section Chief!"

However, Qao was unfazed. "I merely am pointing out, *sir,* that this death is likely to be retaliation for the previous one."

"Explain."

"One of my miners believed Gahlar to be responsible for Krov's death—despite the fact that you ruled it an accident."

Ignoring that barb, Sorkav said, "Who is this miner?"

"His name is Malvak."

"If this Malvak believed that my judgment was in error, why did he not lodge a complaint, as per procedure?"

Qao had to restrain himself from laughing in Sorkav's face. In the ten turns that Qao had worked at this mine, Sorkav had yet to acknowledge a single complaint lodged by anyone of lesser authority. And since his brother ran the mine and was the only person with greater authority, that meant that he did not acknowledge any complaints that didn't come from Kobyk.

"Perhaps," Qao said slowly, "he believed that the complaint would not be heard."

"So instead he took matters into his own hands?" Sorkav shook his head. "Let me guess—this Malvak is *QuchHa'*?"

Qao nodded.

"That explains it, then."

In fact, it explained nothing, but Qao wasn't suicidal enough to say so. He'd already pushed his luck with Sorkav.

"Sir," one of the guards said, "there is blood on the victim's hands that is not his own. Scans indicate that the blood belongs to Malvak, son of Jorq."

"That's hardly conclusive," Qao said, indicating the jagged edges all around the cave, of rock and crystal both. "Miners get each other's blood on them all the time."

"True," Sorkav said, "but it does at least support your theory. We will investigate further."

Qao couldn't help but notice that a DNA scan of blood on Gahlar's person took considerably more effort than Sorkav's people had put into their inquiry into Krov's death.

Malvak stood at the front of the wardroom on the main asteroid, his hands and feet shackled, a guard on either side of him.

Also standing was Sorkav. Seated around the table were all the section chiefs from Site *wej,* with Kobyk at the head, facing Malvak. The white-haired Kobyk had a mug of *warnog* in his hand. Malvak had only seen Kobyk a few times, but every time, he had that damned *warnog* with him.

Sorkav was laying out the evidence against Malvak to Kobyk.

"Scans indicated Malvak's blood on Gahlar's body. The testimony of Section Chief Qao indicated several arguments between Malvak and Gahlar, due to Malvak's belief that Gahlar was responsible for the death of a fellow miner."

"His name was Krov!" Malvak cried. "And he was murdered by—*Aaaarrrrrrghhhhh!*" That last came at the application of a painstik by one of the two guards to Malvak's midsection. He collapsed to his knees, then was yanked to his feet by the other guard.

"As I was saying," Sorkav said with a sidelong glance at Malvak, before looking again at his brother, "this was corroborated by Section Chief Torad."

Sweat dripping into his eyes, Malvak bared his teeth at Torad, who at least had the good grace to look away. Malvak belatedly realized that Torad was *'urwI',* and not to be trusted. A pity he learned that lesson too late . . .

"It is therefore my recommendation," Sorkav concluded, "that Malvak, son of Jorq, be put to death for the murder of Gahlar, son of Murak."

Kobyk gulped some *warnog,* most of which went into his thick white mustache rather than his mouth. Then he nodded. "It shall be done."

Sorkav turned to face Malvak, unsheathing his *d'k tahg* as he did so. Malvak noticed as the side blades unfurled with a click that they were rusty and poorly maintained. He also noticed that the hilt carried the emblem of a House to which Sorkav did not belong.

"And you say *we* have no honor," Malvak said, blinking away more sweat.

Sorkav nodded at the guards, and this time they both applied their painstiks. Pain coursed through every cell of Malvak's body. He screamed in agony as he again fell to his knees.

"Look at you," Sorkav said with contempt. "You wail and perspire like an Earther instead of facing death like a warrior. I condemn you to die like the coward you are."

Compared to the nerve-wrenching agony of the painstik, the sudden insertion of a *d'k tahg* between his ribs was hardly noticeable. But within moments, he felt the life drain from him.

He hoped he would be joining Krov in Sto-Vo-Kor.

The last thing he heard was Kobyk belching up his *warnog* and saying, "That should put an end to all of this."

2

Kobyk

The *warnog* tasted wrong.

Kobyk, son of Goryq, sighed. This latest shipment had been dreadful. His supply chief had switched to a trader whose prices were much lower, and Kobyk now understood why.

Warnog was the only thing that made Kobyk's job bearable, and bad *warnog* just made everything worse.

He looked around his office. The space was functional, the decorations minimal. He had a rotating holographic image of his mate and children on one wall; an ancient *mek'leth* that had been forged for his House by Do'Ming in the time of Kahless, and which was still a fine weapon, on another wall; and a window that looked out onto the deep blackness of space. The next closest asteroid was many *qell'qam*s away, too far to be seen with the naked eye.

But Kobyk preferred it that way. Asteroids were hideous things, just ugly masses of rock broken up by craters. He missed the lush grasslands of his home on Ty'Gokor.

He gulped more of the wretched drink. For all its poor taste, it still was alcohol, and Kobyk needed its bracing effects right now.

Sorkav was on his way in with a report. That meant bad news.

For many turns, Kobyk had run his mine quite efficiently. If there were problems, his chief of security dealt with it. Kobyk trusted his subordinates, and everyone who'd been in that position had done the job well. Generally, Kobyk didn't hear from the head of security unless there was a serious problem, and they were all good enough at their job that there were no serious problems.

At least, that *used* to be the case. Then he'd been forced to hire his younger brother.

Sorkav's imminent arrival was the latest in a lengthy series of occasions on which he had had to report to the head of the mine, and Kobyk wasn't at all happy about it. Leaving aside the fact that it meant yet another security problem that Sorkav had failed to fix, it also meant that Kobyk had to be in his brother's presence.

Kobyk had never liked his younger sibling. Not when they were youths, and Sorkav would make pathetic attempts to steal Kobyk's food. Not when they were adolescents, and Sorkav would make even more pathetic attempts to steal Kobyk's women. And certainly not when they were adults and Sorkav was kicked out of the Imperial Guard in a corruption scandal.

Facing pressure from both their parents, Kobyk hired Sorkav to run security for the Beta Thoridar mine. Running the mine was a plum assignment for Kobyk, one he'd worked many years to earn. Being put in charge of its security was a good way for Sorkav to try to regain the honor he'd lost.

Which was fine by Kobyk as long as he didn't have to *talk* to Sorkav.

The door to his office rumbled open, and in walked Sorkav. He had taken to carrying two painstiks on his belt of late, which made him look ridiculous.

"What do you want?" Kobyk said by way of greeting.

"There has been another shuttle malfunction."

Kobyk snarled. "That is the third one this week!"

"The maintenance crew believes it is sabotage."

"The maintenance crew's grasp of the blindingly obvious is impressive," Kobyk said dryly. "What are they doing to prevent further acts?"

"I've posted guards on all the shuttles, both when they're in transit and in the bay. I'm also running constant scans on all engineering sections and interrogating everyone who has ridden the shuttles."

"I'm fully aware of the proper procedure for ferreting out

saboteurs, brother—what I wish to know is what *results* have come from your work."

Sorkav hesitated, which made Kobyk grab his *warnog*.

"It would seem, brother," Sorkav finally said, "that Malvak's death has stirred the workers."

Kobyk frowned. "Who is Malvak?"

"The worker who killed—"

"What, the *QuchHa'* you condemned last week?"

Sorkav nodded.

"What does *he* have to do with this?"

"Several of those I interrogated would speak only one phrase: *malvaq bortaS*. I have also seen that phrase scrawled on the walls of the habitats and the mines."

Kobyk gave his brother an incredulous look. "Malvak's death was perfectly legitimate. Why are these *petaQpu'* claiming revenge for him?"

Sorkav shrugged. "They are *QuchHa'*. Who could possibly understand how they think?"

"We've had enough problems meeting our quotas." Kobyk slugged down the last of his *warnog*, then tossed the mug aside in disgust. "If this idiocy continues—"

The spine-shuddering report of a security alarm interrupted Kobyk. Pulling out his communicator, Sorkav said, "Report!"

One of his staff reported a moment later, barely audible over the sound of shouting and violence. *"A riot has broken out at Site* wa'*! We are attempting to pacify now!"*

Kobyk immediately called up the security feeds for Site *wa'* on his terminal.

The cracking station was a giant facility that took large dilithium crystals and broke them down into smaller ones that would fit inside a ship's engine. This particular station, and the two like it on the other two sites, were *Jorvok* stations: modular facilities that could be easily constructed, disassembled, and reconstructed elsewhere.

They were also about three decades out of date, having fallen out of favor following the revolutionary work done by the Science Institute. Most dilithium mines in the Empire used the Mark *Soch* model from the Institute.

Kobyk had worked on both systems, and found the Mark *Soch* to be smaller and easier to use, but also with a proclivity for breaking down on a monthly basis. Once you factored in the time that a Mark *Soch* was down for repairs, a *Jorvok* not only produced the same amount per turn, but also was easier for mining technicians to repair, without having to wait for the Institute to send one of their specialists along, since the design was proprietary.

The other advantage to using *Jorvok*s was that Kobyk could get them cheap, since they were rarely used, and his own people could effect repairs, so he didn't have to pay the Institute's exorbitant fees.

Of course, the station also was more difficult to operate. Initially, he'd assigned *QuchHa'* to them, but that had proven ineffective. Sorkav had been the one to suggest letting only *HemQuch* operate the station, and things improved somewhat.

Now, though, there were dozens of *QuchHa'* who seemed to have formed a skirmish line, and were throwing rocks and tools and any number of other objects at the Site *wa' Jorvok*.

Still holding his communicator, Sorkav ordered more security to the cracking station.

"What is that they're shouting?" Kobyk asked as he tried to adjust the audio feed, but it just sounded like meaningless noise.

Sorkav bared his teeth in disgust. "That same phrase I just mentioned: *malvaq bortaS*."

Now that Sorkav had said it, Kobyk was able to make out the phrase over the feed.

As for his brother's security people, they were not having an easy time of it. Armed only with painstiks, they were being overwhelmed by sheer numbers. Within a few minutes, their numbers doubled as the reinforcements Sorkav had called for showed up.

"I warned you that this might happen!" Sorkav said with a snarl. "If my people had disruptors—"

Kobyk refused to engage in this argument again. "Do you know how much it costs to buy five hundred disruptors? Besides, the prospect of your people getting their hands on disruptors is not a pleasant one."

"Their brutality is what makes them good security."

"Yes, and as long as it remains brutality, all is well. But I prefer that

I be the only one to have the power of life and death over the workers I'm responsible for. As it is, my cost-cutting measures have only staved off the difficulties meeting the quotas. If this keeps up, we'll be shut down!"

Sorkav's reinforcements started to turn the tide, as the painstiks started to be effective against the crowd. Plus, once a good number of workers fell to the ground in agony, the others started to disperse.

Snorting, Sorkav said, "Typical *QuchHa'*. Backing down from a fight like cowards."

Kobyk stared at his brother. "Why expect any different? It's not as if they're *Klingons*. In any case, brother, keep these *petaQpu'* in line. I will not have our production slowed by this!"

Kirrin felt his stomachs sink at the sight of the line leading to the shuttle.

He was already running late by virtue of the random search that had been performed of the barracks where he and the rest of his section slept. Kirrin had no idea what they were looking for, but whatever it was, they didn't find it.

Now they were doing intensive scans of everyone who approached the shuttlebay. Which meant a line.

Kirrin had already missed the first shuttle to Site *wa'*. In retrospect, he wished he had skipped the morning meal. But without a *raktajino* in the morning, he was useless for the rest of the day, and the section chief didn't especially appreciate that.

The person in front of him, a Klingon Kirrin didn't recognize, muttered, "We're going to miss the shuttle at this rate."

"That won't happen," Kirrin said with confidence. "After all, they're delaying us for the new security measures. They'll delay the shuttle too."

"Don't be so sure," the other Klingon said.

"What's this all about, anyhow?"

Now the other Klingon turned around. He was *QuchHa'*, like Kirrin, with receding hair, a wispy mustache, and a long scar under his left eye. He was regarding Kirrin as if he were insane. "Haven't you been paying attention?"

"To what?" Kirrin was illiterate, so he couldn't read the bulletins, and the section chief always told them about anything important anyhow. He had remained assigned to duties that did not require him to read anything. Eventually, he planned to save enough wages to pay for an education. It wasn't much, but at least it would increase his options.

The Klingon with the scar said, "You don't know about Malvak?"

Shrugging, Kirrin said, "I've heard some mutterings about someone with that name, but I haven't really paid attention."

"Malvak spoke out about Krov being killed. Sorkav—that filthy *toDSaH*—" The Klingon spit on the floor at that. Kirrin didn't blame him; nobody liked Sorkav. "—he ruled Krov's death an accident."

"So?"

"His throat was cut and he was stabbed in the back! How is that an 'accident'?"

The person behind Kirrin said, "I heard he was decapitated."

"In any case, Malvak said that Gahlar killed Krov. But Gahlar's a ridge-head, so nothing happened."

"Typical," said the Klingon behind him.

"So Malvak took revenge on Gahlar and killed him. *Then* Sorkav actually paid attention. After all, it *matters* when ridge-heads die."

The man with the scar's voice had a bitter tone that Kirrin had heard before. "It does matter more," Kirrin said. "After all, they're *true* Klingons. We've been infected with Earther filth." He said the words with little emotion—it was what his parents had taught him from birth, that their ancestors had been poisoned by Earthers. It was why the Empire remained at war with the Federation—though there was currently a treaty—and would continue to be until the Empire finally conquered them.

Kirrin had no illusions about his life. He knew that his greatest hope was to be a marginally useful cog in the great wheel that was the Empire. As a low-born *QuchHa'*, that was the *best* he could hope for.

The scarred man spit again, this time at Kirrin's boots. "I do not accept that. We are *Klingons*—our blood comes from the same ancestors. We follow the teachings of Kahless the same as any ridge-head."

The line had been slowly moving forward as they spoke, and now

they were within earshot of the guards who were checking the workers. One said, "Quiet, back there!"

Scar-face turned to face the guard. "Or what, ridge-head? You'll
kill me, too, like you killed Malvak?"

Now the guard stomped toward them, painstik in hand. "I said, be
quiet! Do *not* make me tell you a third time, *QuchHa'*!"

The Klingon then unsheathed a *d'k tahg*. Kirrin had never seen a
real *d'k tahg* before. Cheap knockoffs, sure, but one like this, with the
actual emblem of a noble House on it—that was something he never
thought he'd live to see.

"I am Makog, son of Chrell, and I challenge you to—"

The guard reared his head back and laughed heartily before turning to face his fellow guards. "Look at this! This *petaQ* thinks he's in
the Defense Force!" Then he turned back and shoved the painstik into
Makog's belly.

Makog screamed and doubled over in pain, dropping his dagger.

Leaning in, the guard said, "Challenges are for *Klingons*—not the
likes of *you*."

Removing the painstik, the guard straightened and said, "Take him
to detention. He's obviously one of the agitators. We will interrogate
him and learn who his fellow conspirators are."

Kirrin and the others went silently through the line after they took
Makog away.

Just as Kirrin was next in line to be scanned, the shuttle engines
activated with a mighty roar and the platform rose toward the surface
airlock. "That's our shuttle!"

"You'll have to catch the next one," the guard said.

"There *is* no next one!"

Making a mock-sad face, the guard said, "Oh, too bad. It would
seem that you'll have to miss the day's work—and the day's wages."

"But it's not our fault!"

Slapping a fellow guard in the belly with the back of his hand, the
guard said, "Can you believe this? He whines like the Earther he re-
sembles. At least his comrade had some iron in him."

Kirrin knew he could not win an argument with a guard, so he
turned to head back to his barracks. If he couldn't work, maybe he

could get some extra sleep, maybe volunteer for night-shift duty to make up for it.

From behind him, the guard cried, "Hey, *QuchHa'*, don't go turning your back on me!"

Pain sliced through Kirrin's lower back as he felt the hot, pointed end of the painstik strike his spine. His knees buckled, every nerve ending on fire.

It wasn't the first time Kirrin had been on the receiving end of a painstik. In his youth, he'd gotten into trouble with the Guardsmen more than once. Since achieving adulthood, though, he hadn't. Over the years, it hadn't gotten any less unbearable.

Kirrin screamed with the agony that only seemed to increase. When it finally ended, he quieted, but was unable to make his body move.

"Screams like an Earther, too," the guard said contemptuously. "Take him and put him with the so-called son of Chrell. They're probably in it together."

As one of the other guards bent over to pick Kirrin up, the miner noticed that Makog's *d'k tahg* was still lying on the ground where he'd dropped it. Gathering up every ounce of willpower he could, he forced his left arm to thrust out and his left hand to close around the dagger's hilt.

A boot slammed down onto that hand, shattering bones with a snap that echoed throughout the shuttlebay. Again, Kirrin screamed in agony.

"Nice try, *QuchHa'*. Take him."

A low rumble spread through the workers who waited in the line. Through the haze of agony, Kirrin couldn't make out the exact words at first. But soon, as the guards hauled him down the corridor, he could make out the words of the chant:

"malvaq bortaS! malvaq bortaS! malvaq bortaS!"

"Silence!" the guard cried, but his words could barely be heard. Kirrin heard the chant grow into shouts, heard the stomping of feet as the people charged, heard the screams of pain as the guards used their painstiks, then more screams of pain as the guards were overwhelmed.

The ones carrying Kirrin dropped him unceremoniously to the

ground. All Kirrin could see from his prone position was people screaming and running and shouting, *"malvaq bortaS!"* and simply pure chaos.

He also saw rocks flying through the air.

"No . . ." he croaked. He didn't want this. He had talked back to a guard and then turned his back on him, so of course he was being punished. If he hadn't been so riled up by Makog's nonsense, not to mention missing a day of work, he wouldn't have done that. It wasn't worth starting a riot over.

Then he heard a crack that was considerably louder than that of his bones breaking—then he heard nothing, as his ears popped with a sudden change of pressure.

Kirrin's last thoughts were the realization that the dome had cracked.

Kobyk slugged down his *warnog,* no longer caring how bad it tasted.

Sorkav had increased security, but that only seemed to make matters worse. Checkpoints at shuttlebays led to workers being unable to report because they were missing the shuttles. Other workers were imprisoned for minor infractions that used to require only a quick stab of a painstik.

And the riots continued. With the greatest reluctance, and amid much complaining, Kobyk gave in to Sorkav's demands—at least a bit—and allowed him to issue disruptors to the highest-ranking security members and to carry one himself. He was able to get a good price for a dozen Defense Force surplus hand disruptors.

But the riots did not stop. Workers ceased production, or at least slowed it down, graffiti of *malvaq bortaS* was scrawled everywhere, and violence grew. Worse, because of the riots, the imprisonments, and the missed shuttles, production was at an all-time low.

Kobyk had been hoping to contain it, but then the atmospheric dome at one of the shuttlebays cracked during a riot, killing a dozen guards, a hundred workers, and a score of maintenance staff. True, the latter were mostly *jeghpu'wI',* but they still needed to be replaced.

Worse, it happened shortly after a convoy ship had arrived to pick up a shipment bound for the shipyards on Mempa II. The ship's captain filed a report about the riot to his superiors.

Later that day, Kobyk received the inevitable call from General Korrd.

Swallowing an entire mug of *warnog* to steel himself for the ordeal, Kobyk activated the viewer to reveal the corpulent form of the general.

"Explain yourself, Supervisor Kobyk." Korrd's voice sounded like a Sporak driving over broken glass. His crest bisected his forehead perfectly, almost as if it were pointing at his intense eyes.

"The *QuchHa'* have always been a problem, General," Kobyk lied. In fact, they'd been fine until this nonsense with Malvak. "You know what they're like."

"No, Supervisor—I do not. You are hardly the first mine to report occasional problems with the QuchHa', but you are the only one to suffer such appalling production and personnel losses. The Organians may have prevented us from finishing our war with the Federation, but that does not mean we can afford to cut back on our shipbuilding efforts." Korrd leaned forward. *"Ships need dilithium, Supervisor. You received this assignment because you promised high production at lesser cost. That is* not *what I see here."*

"This is only a temporary setback, General. My security chief has employed new security measures, and once they take effect—"

"Annh!" Korrd grunted with a wave of his hand. *"This requires more than such as you and your fool of a brother can provide."*

Kobyk winced. "The Defense Force?"

"Yes. Three ships will be sent to deal with your QuchHa' problem, expedite the repair of your dome, and supplement your security forces. These will be QuchHa' ships as well."

"General, with respect—I would prefer a ship of *true* Klingons."

"What you prefer is of no interest to me. Let the QuchHa' deal with their own kind. And then we will reevaluate the command structure of your mine. Out."

The screen went blank.

Kobyk dry-sipped his mug before remembering that he'd finished the *warnog*, so he threw the mug across the room. It clattered against the wall and rolled along the floor.

"Fat old fool," he muttered. The general hadn't provided a timetable, didn't say which ships were coming, and threatened his position even if these *QuchHa'* were able to bring things to order.

He had forgotten that the Empire let *QuchHa'* into the Defense

Force. For that matter, he had forgotten that there were *QuchHa'* of noble blood. The Earther disease that afflicted several Klingon worlds a century ago did not discriminate between high-born and commoners.

Still, surrounded by the rabble as he was, it was easy to forget that some of the noblest Houses had *QuchHa'* among them.

They would be the ones in command of the three ships that Korrd was sending, and they would likely know how to put their fellows in their place.

3

Kor

Since his days as a youth, Kor had always admired the heroes of the Empire. His father, Rynar, had often taken him to the Hall of Warriors on Ty'Gokor. Because they were of noble blood, they had been allowed in the primary entrance, though Rynar had always been sure to travel in his Defense Force uniform while wearing the sash of office that proved he was of the nobility despite being *QuchHa'*.

There, young Kor would look up at the statues that showed the great warriors of history: Korma, Kopf, Sturka, Krim, Tygrak, Sompek, Reclaw, M'Rek, and, of course, the great Kahless himself.

Young Kor swore that he would one day have a statue dedicated to himself. Rynar had laughed indulgently.

Another Klingon, a *HemQuch,* had also laughed, but his was a chortle of derision. "What are you teaching that boy, old man?" he had asked Rynar.

Before his father could reply, young Kor bleated, "What do you mean?"

The *HemQuch* pointed at the statues. "Look around you, child. Do you see any weak-heads amidst the statuary?"

"Then I shall be the first!" Kor had said the words with the confidence of youth.

Again, the *HemQuch* had laughed, but then Kor's father spoke, having seen the emblem upon the man's *d'k tahg.* "Do you doubt, scion of the House of Yorgh, that a boy from the House of Mur'Eq could become a hero of the Empire?"

At that, the *HemQuch* had snarled and walked away.

Kor had grinned like a fool for the rest of the day, for the House of Yorgh was a minor House of little consequence. Kor was descended from the imperial bloodlines of Emperor Mur'Eq. Rynar's father, also named Kor, had formally changed the House name to that of Mur'Eq after the Earther plague had poisoned all those of the House of Kor and removed their crests.

Kor's grandfather would never let anyone forget that theirs was a noble family, regardless of what they looked like. And Kor, who was named for him, knew that one day he would indeed become the first *QuchHa'* to be enshrined on Ty'Gokor.

So when First Officer Kahlor contacted him in his cabin to inform him that General Korrd wished to speak to him, Kor sat up straight, set down his *breshtanti* ale, and activated the viewer eagerly.

"To what do I owe this honor, General?"

Korrd outlined the problems at Beta Thoridar. *"You will meet with the* Devisor *and the* Voh'tahk, *Captain. Get that mine under control by whatever means you and Captains Kang and Koloth see fit."*

"Which of us will be in command?" Kor asked. He didn't know the other two captains—though Koloth's name was familiar—what their records of battle were, nor if they were *QuchHa'* or *HemQuch*.

"Kang is the seniormost officer."

Kor hesitated, as that did not actually answer the question. When the pause went on for several seconds, the captain finally said, "Very well, General. We will change course immediately."

The general made a grunting noise. *"Your task, Kor, will be of great importance. While Koloth supervises repairs of all the damage done to the operation, and Kang supplements the security, your task will be to find the ringleaders of these malcontents. I expect a preliminary report the day after your arrival, and daily reports thereafter. Out."*

Kor contacted the bridge and told Kohlar to set course for Beta Thoridar at maximum speed.

Then he called up Kang and Koloth's records of battle.

They were both indeed *QuchHa'*. From what Korrd had said, most of the problems on Beta Thoridar were related to Kor's fellow sufferers. He smiled, realizing that they probably just needed to be reminded that they were still Klingons and should behave honorably.

Koloth's record revealed why his name was familiar. He had lost his previous command, the *Gr'oth*. It had to be scuttled following a trip to the Earth Space Station K-7, when the ship was infested. His current command had also been so infested, but this time Koloth was able to take care of it himself.

Kang's record was more impressive. The *Voh'tahk* had won a few border skirmishes with Starfleet before the formal declaration of war—the same war that was stopped by the Organians.

Scowling at the memory, Kor switched the screen off. He hated being reminded of Organia, of having his governorship taken away by those smiling all-powerful simpletons, of having the Empire's just war aborted.

He gulped down the rest of his ale, then went to the bridge.

The asteroid belt of the Beta Thoridar system didn't look like much.

The *Klothos* had been the first of the three vessels to arrive, though Kohlar reported to Kor that the *Devisor* and the *Voh'tahk* would be in-system within the hour.

The larger asteroids were thousands of *qell'qam*s apart at least, with smaller fragments tumbling lazily through the void at irregular intervals. Kor's science officer gave a report that this was likely a planetoid that had suffered some kind of cataclysmic collision that shattered it. It was heavy enough in dilithium, the officer said, that it was probably already unstable even before the collision.

The three largest asteroids had atmospheric domes on them—one, in fact, had several. This was the primary headquarters of the mining operation.

"Pilot," Kor said, "magnify the northernmost dome."

The pilot did so, and Kor saw the crack that had been created, rendering whatever was beneath it useless to sentient life.

Turning to his first officer, Kor said, "Kohlar, you are to investigate the workers—ferret out this *malvaq bortaS* group. Determine who their leaders are and bring them to me for interrogation."

"Yes, Captain."

From behind him, the operations officer said, "Two D7 battle cruisers coming out of warp. Transponder code confirms it is the *I.K.S. Devisor* and the *I.K.S. Voh'tahk.*"

Kor nodded. "Open a channel to both ships—put them both on-screen."

Moments later, two faces appeared, which matched those on file. Kang had a dark, brooding face and seemed to permanently scowl. Koloth was paler and more pleasant—though his smile seemed to hide the *d'k tahg* he was about to stab you with.

Koloth spoke first. *"You must be Captain Kor."*

"Indeed. I have not yet contacted Supervisor Kobyk."

His smile widening, Koloth said, *"I imagine your presence has made him apprehensive."*

Kang's scowl deepened. *"If so, then he is an even bigger fool than General Korrd indicated. The three of us shall transport to his office immediately."*

Koloth frowned. *"Should we not communicate our impending arrival?"*

"The general told him we were coming," Kor said with a small smile. "That should be communication enough."

"Precisely," Kang said with a nod.

Kor materialized in the supervisor's office to find himself at gunpoint.

Koloth and Kang had beamed down next to him, and Kang barked, "Holster your weapon immediately!"

The one holding the weapon was a short *HemQuch* who wore thick-soled heeled boots, no doubt in an attempt to increase his height. He was standing next to the desk and aiming a disruptor pistol at the three of them. According to the records, this was Sorkav, the chief of security for the mine, and the brother of the supervisor.

That supervisor was sitting behind the desk, holding a mug of what smelled like *warnog* in his right hand. Kobyk shared a crest with Sorkav, and they had the same wide green eyes.

Sorkav was still pointing the disruptor. "Who are you to give me orders, *QuchHa'*?"

"I am Kang." The captain accentuated the point by stepping forward, looming over the security chief. "And I am not accustomed to giving orders twice!"

"Sorkav, do as he says!" Kobyk said. "My apologies, Captains, but these have been difficult times. If you had warned us of your arrival—"

Kang waved him off and started to pace back and forth across the office. "From now on, all shuttle activity in this asteroid field is restricted. Any shuttle launches must be escorted by one of our three ships. Any shuttle traveling unescorted will be fired upon."

Kobyk's mouth opened, then closed. "Captain, I—"

"Furthermore," Kang continued as if Kobyk had not spoken, "you will transmit the specifications of the damaged dome to the chief engineer of the *Devisor* and you will allow the officers of the *Klothos* free access to your personnel." Kang turned to Sorkav. "As for you, send all your duty rosters to *QaS DevwI'* Morglar aboard the *Voh'tahk*. Your forces will be supplemented with security teams from my vessel. Am I understood?"

Kor watched both brothers as Kang spoke. Kobyk seemed to deflate, sinking lower and lower into the comfortable-looking *klongat*-skin chair. But Sorkav smoldered. Kor had seen that expression before many times in his life. Sorkav and the man from the House of Yorgh had used the word *QuchHa'* as if it were the worst epithet they could utter.

In response to Kang's query, Kobyk replied, "Captain, I believe that this is a bit extreme."

"I asked a question, Supervisor," Kang said. "It requires a simple yes or no."

Squirming in his chair, Kobyk started: "We are perfectly capable—"

Kor decided to speak. "You are hardly *that,* Supervisor, or the three of us would not need to be here."

"General Korrd asked for a preliminary report," Koloth said. "I would hate to have to tell him that you obstructed us from the moment of our arrival."

Kang stepped forward and leaned over, his fists resting on Kobyk's desk. "Am I understood, Supervisor? Or must I relieve you of your post?"

"This is *our* mine!" Sorkav bellowed, his hand moving to his disruptor, but not actually unholstering it. "We will not be ordered about by the likes of you!"

"Sorkav, be *silent*!" Kobyk cried. Then he looked back up at Kang. "You are understood, Captain Kang. Your instructions will be carried out immediately."

Then Kobyk looked back at his brother. Sorkav snarled and moved toward the exit.

"I did not give you leave to depart, Sorkav," Kang said without turning around.

Sorkav stopped and turned to face Kang. "I accept that you are here to restore order to this mine, Captain. But I am *not* one of your crew, and I do *not* require your permission to move freely about."

With that, he departed.

Kor and Koloth exchanged glances, and Kor knew that their reports to the general were not going to reflect favorably upon Sorkav.

"You must forgive my brother, Captain," Kobyk said. "As I said on your arrival, these have been difficult times."

"No," Kang said, straightening up. "For as long as we are assigned here, Supervisor, you are in no position to tell any of us what we 'must' do."

Kobyk nodded. "Of course, Captain."

But Kor thought that the nod, while masked as a gesture of respect, was to avoid making eye contact with Kang, so the captain would not see Kobyk's disgust.

4

Jurva

Bekk Jurva had been assigned by *QaS DevwI'* Morglar to supplement the security forces at one of the shuttlebay checkpoints.

"The hand scanners they use were ancient when I was a trainee," Morglar had told her. "I would prefer to trust readings from *our* scanners."

Jurva had served well for several turns, and she knew Morglar well enough to question his orders without worry for the consequences. So she asked, "Why am I being assigned to this detail? Surely there is—"

"Battle?" Morglar laughed. "These are miners, Jurva, not Starfleet or Kinshaya. There will be no battle here."

"Then I will report to"—she stared at the data slate Morglar had handed her—"Section Chief Targ." Her eyes widened, and she looked up at Morglar. "Surely, that isn't his name?"

"It's a family name, apparently." Morglar reached over to the controls of the data slate and called up the man's record.

Peering at the display, Jurva saw that his full name was Targ, son of Targ. He was also from the Kingral Hills of Mempa VIII, a backward, rural area. Jurva had served on the Defense Force base on Mempa VIII before being transferred to the *Voh'tahk*, and she had always found the country folk from Kingral Hills to be tiresome.

"Very well. I shall support the son of Targ with my hand scanner," Jurva said with a salute to her *QaS DevwI'*.

"See that you do. And remember, Jurva, we are here to *improve* the efficiency of the mine. Try not to kill *everyone* who annoys you."

Jurva bared her teeth with amusement at her supervisor's teasing. "I will try my best, sir."

She beamed from the *Voh'tahk* to the transporter station for Site *wej*, where she was greeted by three guards—one *QuchHa'*, the others *HemQuch*—all armed with painstiks.

"I am *Bekk* Jurva, daughter of Pit'ton, and I have been assigned to aid Section Chief Targ."

One of the *HemQuch* said, "I am Gonn, this is Goroth." He shook his head, then indicated the *QuchHa'*. "Oh, and, er, that's Korya. We'll take you to the section chief now, but—"

To Jurva's shock, Gonn hesitated. It was not an action a Klingon warrior performed readily, and she had assumed Sorkav's security people to be warriors. She wondered if she should have revised that estimate.

Gonn finally continued: "Please, call him 'Section Chief.' He doesn't like being called by his name."

"I can hardly blame him," Jurva said honestly. "Take me to him."

"Of course."

As Jurva followed the three guards, Goroth spoke for the first time. "Is that a disruptor?"

Her hand instinctively moving to her sidearm, Jurva said, "Of course. All Defense Force personnel are issued disruptors."

Korya muttered, "Defense Force personnel are lucky."

Gonn shot Korya an annoyed look, then said, "We're only armed with painstiks. A few of the supervisors got disruptors once this whole *malvaq bortaS* idiocy began, but they don't even work all the time."

They walked down several corridors that were carved out of the asteroid's rock and filled with atmosphere before reaching an enclosure that looked out onto space. Jurva saw four large shuttlecraft that were obviously used to transport the miners.

At the entryway was a table and a large force-field generator, currently off.

"I am *Bekk* Jurva," she said to the section chief, a short, broad-shouldered *HemQuch* with a slight gut and short hair that was starting to show gray. His beard was untrimmed and he wore a giant nose ring—both typical for the shack dwellers of Kingral.

"I am your section chief, woman."

"No, actually, you aren't," Jurva said quickly. "I report to *QaS DevwI'* Morglar, and he reports to Captain Kang. I am here to aid you, not be subject to your command. And you will address me as *Bekk* or by my name."

Targ looked at his subordinates. "Do you hear *that*, boys? The *QuchHa'* bitch wants us to treat her with respect!" He laughed, as did Gonn and Goroth. Korya, she noted, stayed silent.

Only Morglar's final words to her kept Jurva from killing the section chief right there. Instead she simply stared at him.

When his laughter had finally died down, Targ said, "All right, then, *be'H,* this is where you will be stationed. When the miners' shift ends, they come to this shuttlebay to be taken back to Site *wa'*."

Jurva tensed, but said nothing. The term *be'H* was a normal Kingral diminutive of *be'Hom*, which meant *girl*. The Kingral dialect tended to meld the sharp sound at the end of her rank with the more guttural consonant at the center of *be'Hom*, so it was possible that that was simply the way Targ pronounced *bekk*.

Or he was deliberately insulting her. Again, taking heed of Morglar's instructions, she let it pass.

"Each person who wishes to pass through must be scanned. Any contraband is confiscated. Once they are cleared, they are permitted to walk through the force field, which is made semipermeable by a control that I hold."

For a brief instant, Jurva considered ordering Targ to give her that control, but decided not to push things.

At least not yet.

Instead, she asked, "What constitutes contraband?"

"Anything that is not standard mining equipment. Writing implements used to spread the *malvaq bortaS* graffiti. Instruments used to sabotage shuttlecraft. That sort of thing."

Jurva shook her head and folded her arms across her chest. "What is the point of this?"

Targ frowned, an action that made his nose ring abut his upper lip. "What do you mean?"

"The miners know that you scan them when they enter the shuttlebay, yes?"

"Of course."

"Then what is the point of it? This does not provide security for the mine, it simply provides the illusion of it. It would make far more sense to make the scans discreet and secret. Let the conspirators think themselves safe from scans."

"Look," the section chief said, "I just follow Sorkav's orders."

"Then Sorkav is an even bigger fool than I have been told."

Targ laughed at that, and then so did Gonn and Goroth. "You will receive no argument regarding Sorkav's intelligence form any of *us*, *be'H*, of that you may be sure."

A loud siren pierced the air and caused Jurva to put her hands to her ears. Korya did likewise.

Again, Targ laughed. "Typical *QuchHa'*, having to protect their weak Earther ears. That is the end of the shift. Time to begin work."

Gonn and Goroth took up positions near the far end of the entry-way, and no doubt would patrol up and down the line that would soon form.

Korya walked up to Jurva. "I said the same thing," he said in a small voice. Korya was quite short, only coming up to Jurva's shoulder, and he looked like a child with a *ghIntaq* spear when he held his pain-stik. "I told the section chief that this wouldn't create proper security, but he told me to be quiet."

"I'm not surprised."

Jurva ran her hand scanner over every Klingon—mostly *QuchHa'*, with the occasional *HemQuch*—who came through the checkpoint. She found only one item that she would classify as contraband: a *qutluch*, the weapon of a hired assassin. The miner was unconvincing in his claims that it had been in his family for generations.

Targ, however, was less fussy on the subject.

"Are you aware," the section chief informed one worker, "that gold can be used to disrupt engine systems on our shuttlecraft?"

"That bone necklace," he told another, "could easily be used as a weapon."

"Did you really think," he told a third, "that you would be allowed to carry a bladed weapon?"

Not wishing to disrupt the mining operations any further, Jurva waited until the final shuttle had taken off before she reached under the table and pulled out the container that was filled with the confiscated items. She pulled out the medallion he had taken off the first worker. "Tell me, Section Chief, what is the method by which one can use an incredibly valuable gold medallion encrusted with gemstones to disrupt engine systems?"

Looking as if someone had fed him dead food, Targ said, "Our shuttle's engines are—"

"Your shuttle's engines, Section Chief, are standard Type *wa'maH Hut*. They cannot be in any way harmed by the introduction of gold—or gemstones, for that matter—into their systems."

"Are you accusing me—"

But Jurva refused to let him speak, instead taking out the bone necklace. "How, precisely, is this bone necklace to be used as a weapon, Section Chief?"

"Those bones have sharp edges that—"

Jurva reached out and grabbed Goroth's wrist and yanked him toward her. She would have grabbed Targ, but he was on the other side of the table and too far away. In turn, she applied several of the edges of the bones to Goroth's finger, hard. None of them even broke skin.

"Sharp edges," Jurva said after her demonstration, "that can do no harm whatsoever. Oh, and before you mention the possibility of using it as a garrote . . ." Jurva wrapped the necklace around her own neck and tightened it, causing the thin rope to break in two. "But, of course, these are *maS* bird bones. Very rare, very valuable—but not very dangerous."

"Enough! I will not stand here and be—"

"Embarrassed? I haven't even gotten to the 'bladed weapon,' which is simply a rusty old *d'k tahg* with no emblems. He couldn't pick his teeth with it."

She stepped around the table, staring right at Targ, who couldn't hold her gaze, the coward.

"You are pathetic, Section Chief, and not even worthy to be named for an animal."

Now Targ sputtered. "How dare you! I will not stand here and be

insulted by some filthy *QuchHa'* who thinks that wearing a child's uniform gives her leave to insult—"

Again, Jurva did not let him finish speaking, choosing instead to
slap his face with the back of her hand. "I challenge you, Targ, son of
Targ. You are unworthy to continue in your position as section chief."

For several seconds, Targ just stared at her.

Then he threw his head back and laughed so hard his nose ring
shook. "This isn't your oh-so-precious Defense Force, *QuchHa'*. Your
pathetic challenge carries no weight here!"

He turned his back on her to face Korya. "Where does this stupid
be'H get the idea that she can challenge *me*?"

Jurva snarled and unholstered her disruptor, pointing it at his
back. "Turn and face me, *petaQ!*"

Targ turned around. "There's no need for that, *be'H,*" he said, suddenly sounding much more subdued while staring at the beam end of
a disruptor.

"You're right." Jurva lowered the disruptor and grabbed the *qutluch* that they'd confiscated—the only legitimate seizure they'd made.
"Duels should be fought with blades."

"Yes, well, pity I don't have one." Then he lunged forward with
his painstik.

Jurva dodged the lunge with the greatest ease, slashing behind her.
The blade of the *qutluch* tasted blood from the section chief's side.

Before he could regain his footing, Jurva was able to grab his
nose ring and yank his head downward into a knee kick that shattered
his jaw.

Then she plunged the *qutluch* into his heart.

"This is *outrageous*! I want this woman put to death!"

Sorkav was waving his arms as if he had gone mad. Kobyk wasn't
entirely sure that his brother hadn't.

They were standing in his office. Kobyk sat behind his desk,
with a *warnog* clutched in his hands and Sorkav gesticulating wildly at
his side. Facing them were Captain Kang and a *QaS DevwI'* named
Morglar, along with the subject of their discussion, *Bekk* Jurva, a
female subordinate of Morglar's who stood respectfully behind her
superiors.

At least, she stood there until Sorkav's outburst. At that, the *bekk* stepped forward. "My challenge was *proper*! That *yIntagh* was—"

Morglar turned to face Jurva. "Be silent, *Bekk!*"

Jurva lowered her head. "Yes, sir."

Kang glowered at Kobyk, which led the supervisor to clutch his *warnog* mug even more tightly. "What is the basis of your brother's absurd desire to take the life of one of my warriors?"

Kobyk tried to form an answer, but Sorkav snorted before he could. "Warrior? Pfah!"

Giving his brother a sidelong glance, Kobyk snarled, "Sorkav, be silent!"

Pointing at Jurva, Sorkav cried, "She killed a *Klingon*! That cannot go unanswered!"

Morglar said, "She *challenged* a fellow Klingon."

"There was no basis for a challenge. This isn't a Defense Force base, it's a mine—"

Kang interrupted. "Which is currently under the purview of the Defense Force. Jurva's challenge was legitimate. Any attempt to take action against her by anyone other than the victim's family will not be tolerated."

"How do you know the challenge was legitimate?" Sorkav asked angrily. "Were you there?"

Morglar said, "Jurva gave me her word. That is all that is required."

"You believe *her* word over that of a *Klingon*?"

"Enough!" Kobyk cried, having grown weary of this idiocy. He had remained silent in the hopes that Sorkav would be sensible. A lifetime of experience with his brother had indicated otherwise, and he should have known better. "Captain Kang may not have been there, but security feeds recorded the entire incident." Kobyk turned the small monitor on his desk toward Sorkav, which showed the *bekk* backhanding Section Chief Targ. "I have already reviewed the incident. The *bekk*'s challenge was legitimate, and the section chief's death was earned in battle. The matter is closed."

"Good." Kang said that word in a low, dangerous tone that drove Kobyk to gulp down large quantities of *warnog*.

Morglar turned to Jurva. "Return to your duties, *Bekk*."

"Yes, sir," Jurva said smartly, gave Sorkav a rather venomous look, then turned on her heel to leave.

Kang continued to glare at Kobyk. "My time will not be wasted in this manner again."

With that, he left, Morglar behind him.

As soon as the door slid shut behind the *QaS DevwI'*, Sorkav exploded. "How could you side with *that* against your own brother?"

"Easily." Kobyk slugged down the rest of his *warnog* before continuing. "Primarily because they were right and you were wrong."

"How *dare* you! Is this what it has come to? You accept the word of *QuchHa'* over me?"

"No," Kobyk said with as much patience as he could muster, "I accept the evidence of my own eyes and the word of warriors in the Defense Force." Before Sorkav could start another rant, Kobyk rose to his feet and pointed to the door. "Get out of my office, brother. *My* time will not be wasted, either!"

Sorkav snarled and stomped out of the office.

Kobyk walked to the sideboard, which was situated against one wall, under the Do'Ming *mek'leth*. He poured himself some more *warnog* and wondered how long it would be before someone from one of the three ships challenged Sorkav.

If that day came, Kobyk would be cheering for Sorkav's opponent to achieve victory.

5

Korax

Korax had never had much use for engineers. They were whining, tiresome creatures who always had technical excuses for not following orders. During that incident on K-7—that cursed place—Korax had picked the fight with the *Enterprise* crew mainly because their chief engineer was present.

That engineer had retaliated by beaming hundreds of tribbles into the *Gr'oth* engine room. Korax had vowed that he would avenge himself on the Earther Montgomery Scott for that outrage.

So when Korax came into Koloth's cabin for his orders, he was disheartened when his captain said, "Your task, Commander, will be to supervise Lieutenant Paibok's work on repairing the mine's atmospheric dome."

Ever the good soldier, Korax said only, "As you command."

Koloth smiled. "I know how you feel, Korax. Personally, I find engineers to be as tiresome as you do. Your task is of greater import than observing Paibok's minions. The rabble may attempt sabotage of the repairs. You're to be on guard for them."

Where Koloth's smile was his usual insincere one, Korax's was wide and genuine. "It will be my pleasure, sir."

"Oh, and Korax? Do try to leave at least one of them alive for questioning. This mission will go far more smoothly with *proper* intelligence, not just Supervisor Kobyk's conjectures."

Korax nodded his head in acknowledgment and proceeded to the transporter bay.

Unfortunately, there was very little evidence of saboteurs and quite a bit of annoying engineers making excuses. To make matters worse, it wasn't even Paibok, but rather the mine engineers who were causing the problems.

Mostly, Korax was able to ignore it, but when a shouting match arose between Paibok and the mine's head engineer, a *QuchHa'* named Kly'bn, he found it necessary to intervene.

"What is going on here?" he asked in a voice that cut through the argument.

Both men spoke at once in an incoherent babble.

"Be *quiet!*" When they both became quiet, Korax looked at his subordinate. "Chief Engineer Paibok—report!"

"This *petaQ* refuses to implement my repair schedule!"

Kly'bn bared his teeth. "That is because your repair schedule is idiotic! We have a four-shift rotation—"

"Which makes poor use of the personnel available to you!"

"I only have twelve people!"

"No, you brainless *toDSaH*, you have thirty with my engineers, and they are more efficiently used on a *three*-shift rotation—"

"Your engineers are not trained on my equipment! I'll need to waste countless hours training them to—"

"*Enough!*" Korax was about ready to rip his own beard off his chin. "If I wished to listen to the mewlings of old women, I'd have stayed home on Qu'Vat!" He fixed his gaze upon Kly'bn. "You will do as Lieutenant Paibok says, or I will kill you and have Supervisor Kobyk assign someone who *will* do as Lieutenant Paibok says." Turning his gaze upon the chief engineer, he added, "And if I hear you two arguing again, I will kill you *both*!" He shook his head. "Now go do whatever it is you're *supposed* to be doing!"

Kly'bn snarled at Paibok. "I was *going* to repair the plasma manifolds, then replace the topaline injectors."

"And I *told* you," Paibok said with a snarl of his own, "that I can do one of those tasks."

"Our plasma manifolds are very particular—"

Paibok rolled his eyes. "They're standard-issue *ret* manifolds—or, at least, they were standard issue during the Second Dynasty." Looking at Korax, he added, "This mine is filled with ancient equipment. It's a wonder any of it runs. However, I was trained on *ret* equipment as a child—that was all we had on Forcas III."

"You could have mentioned that," Kly'bn said in a tone that was, in Korax's opinion, unbecoming a Klingon.

Korax said, "It isn't your concern, Kly'bn. Your only concern is with how you follow Lieutenant Paibok's orders." He moved close enough to smell the *raktajino* on Kly'bn's breath. "And mine."

"Of course," Kly'bn said weakly. "I will repair the manifold. Lieutenant, if you'd be so kind as to take the topaline injector?"

Paibok threw up his arms. "I just *told* you—"

"Yes, Lieutenant, I know, but the manifold is near the top of the dome, and requires climbing up that very long ladder." Kly'bn pointed at a nearby thin metal ladder that led up to the top of the dome. "I climb that ladder daily. I do not wish to risk you—"

Now Paibok got in Kly'bn's face. "I am not some broken-down old fool who needs to be coddled, Kly'bn—I am an officer in the Defense Force!"

"Fine!" Kly'bn threw up his hands and walked away. "I will fix the injectors and you can break your neck!"

Korax walked in the other direction. "I *hate* engineers," he muttered, uncaring if Paibok heard him. It wasn't as if the lieutenant hadn't heard it before.

As Korax went back to the desk where he had been reading over the latest dispatches from Command—Koloth expected him to go through them and report anything the captain might need to know—he heard the impact of boot on rung that indicated Paibok was climbing the ladder in question.

Then he heard Paibok's distant voice: "What are you doing up here?"

Not liking the sound of that in the least, Korax ran back to the base of the ladder.

Craning his neck up, he saw three Klingons—all *QuchHa'*—on a catwalk that was partway up the ladder. They were who Paibok was talking to.

In answer to the engineer's query, one of them lunged at him with what looked like a pipe. Paibok was able to deflect the blow, but he was in a poor position—the catwalk was at his waist, and he was reliant on the ladder's rungs for support. His three foes had more freedom of movement.

Without hesitation, Korax unholstered his disruptor. Koloth had only ordered him to take *one* prisoner, after all.

His aim was true, and the one who had attacked Paibok was dead moments later, screaming from the fatal disruption of his nervous system. Korax grinned with glee at the kill.

That gave Paibok time to leap onto the catwalk. He faced the other two—unfortunately, from a position that spoiled Korax's shot. Much as he hated engineers, he wasn't about to sacrifice one of his officers just to kill two rebellious *petaQpu'*.

One of Paibok's opponents leapt at him, and the two of them quickly fell to the catwalk floor, rolling around. The third opponent held back, his hand moving toward his hip.

Korax fired at the third one, but missed.

That was when the other one unholstered a disruptor pistol of his own.

Ducking behind a console, Korax avoided being hit by the beam from the pistol, which appeared to be one of the old *loSmaH Soch* types. Considering that nobody on this mine was supposed to be issued disruptors of any kind, Korax wondered where this particular weapon came from.

However, that question could be answered later. Peering out from the console, Korax saw that Paibok had his foe in a wrestling hold and was now throwing him over his shoulder.

Normally such a move would have the opponent on the floor, but this was not a wrestling square, but a narrow catwalk. So Paibok's throw took his opponent over the railing and crashing to the floor near Korax.

Korax spared the man one glance—his neck appeared broken—and then fired back up at the catwalk.

Distracted by his comrade's plunge, he was an easy target for Korax, who hit him on his weapon arm. He dropped his pistol, and that left him open for Paibok to palm-heel his jaw.

He collapsed like a sack of *loSpev*.

Paibok hoisted the man over his shoulder, then climbed quickly down the ladder. Arriving at ground level, he dropped the groggy Klingon to the floor and looked at Korax, echoing the commander's own thoughts. "I thought they weren't issued any disruptors."

"They weren't." Korax knelt down and pointed his own disruptor under the man's chin. "You will tell me who your co-conspirators are."

"I will . . . will say . . . say *nothing* to you . . . *'urwI'*."

At that insult, Korax instinctively activated the disruptor, which cut through the flesh of the man's chin and blew out the top of his head.

6

Koloth

Koloth had been extremely grateful to receive the invitation from Mara on the *Voh'tahk* to dine with her and Kang that evening. After the day he had, he needed a good meal.

He arrived on the *Voh'tahk* to find a *bekk* awaiting him. "I will take you to the captain's cabin," the soldier said, then turned and left, expecting Koloth to follow him, as was proper.

It was only a short walk down the corridor until the *bekk* arrived at a door that had two *bekks* already guarding it. Koloth had left his own bodyguard on the *Devisor* as a courtesy to Kang. He hoped that Kang had posted these guards, and that Kor hadn't been tasteless enough to bring his guard on board.

Inside, he found Kang and his mate, Mara, as well as Kor already present.

Mara smiled. "I was starting to think you were not going to come, son of Lasshar."

"As if I would turn down a meal from your chef," Koloth said as he took the seat next to Kor, leaving both captains to face the couple.

"Yes," Kor said, raising a glass of *breshtanti* ale, "I've heard stories about the glorious meals served by *Voh'tahk*'s chef."

"They're not at all true," Mara said. "Galarch is far better," she added with a smile.

All three men laughed at that, and Kor drank his ale.

Kang rose to his feet and approached a sideboard. "Now that we are all here, we may open the bloodwine!"

"Excellent!" Koloth said. "Of course, if we were dining on the *Devisor,* the bloodwine would be needed to get us drunk enough to not notice the taste of the food—or, rather, the lack of same."

As he used his *d'k tahg* to slice off the cork of the bottle—which, Koloth noted, came from the Ozhpri vintners, one of the finest in the Empire—Kang said, "You once told me that you would sooner give up your good right arm than give up your chef."

"I was not given the option. After the—the *incident* with the tribbles on the *Gr'oth*, he refused to report to the *Devisor,* instead choosing a lesser position at the Lukara Edifice on Qo'noS." Koloth shuddered. "His replacement is a decent technician, certainly, but the preparation of food is an art."

"Then prepare," Mara said as Kang poured bloodwine into her mug, "to dine on artwork."

"Indeed I shall, madam," Koloth said with a bow of his head.

Kang finished pouring the bloodwine, then raised his own mug. "To victory—to glory—to the *Empire! Qapla'!*"

Koloth cried, *"Qapla'!"* as did Kor and Mara, and they slammed their mugs together, then drank heartily of the bloodwine.

"A fine vintage," Kor said, wiping the wine from his mustache with his sleeve.

"Indeed," Koloth said. "As usual."

"Tell us, Koloth," Kang asked, "what delayed your arrival at the supper table?"

Koloth sighed. He had hoped that dinner would provide a respite from the idiocy of the mine, but Kang was the senior here, so Koloth was duty-bound to answer. "My first officer and chief engineer encountered some of the *malvaq bortaS* rabble attempting to sabotage the same atmospheric dome that was damaged previously. There were three of them, and they had homemade explosives—and a disruptor."

"What?" Kor said. "I thought these mines weren't issued disruptors."

"They aren't," Koloth said tightly. "When Korax informed me of this, I questioned Supervisor Kobyk, who said he purchased several surplus *loSmaH Soch* disruptors for his security detail."

Kang shook his head. "And that *yIntagh* Sorkav allowed one to be stolen?"

"At *least* one," Koloth said. "Sorkav claimed it was the only one missing, but I'm loath to trust him."

"You are wise not to," Kang said.

Before he could elaborate, the door slid open to reveal three Klingons coming in with two trays each. One carried a massive skull stew and a plateful of both *gagh* and *racht* artfully arranged around a bowl of the finest-smelling *grapok* sauce Koloth had ever encountered. The second carried a bowl of *jInjoq* bread that smelled fresh out of the oven and magnificent, and a plate containing four massive *klongat* legs. The third had a *rokeg* blood pie that smelled to Koloth as if it had been spiced with something unfamiliar, and a large plate that, Koloth soon realized, was a casserole made from mixing *pipius* claw, heart of *targ,* and *gladst*, and a tureen filled with *baghol* soup made with *durani* lizard skins.

The hardest part for Koloth was deciding what to eat first.

His mouth filled with *jInjoq* bread that he'd dipped in the *grapok* sauce, Kor asked, "What has Sorkav done to earn *your* ire, Kang?"

After Kang—between mouthfuls of *gagh* and *racht*—told of *Bekk* Jurva's challenge and Sorkav's reaction, Koloth shook his head in disgust. "Absurd. Absolutely absurd."

"What do you expect?" Mara said bitterly.

"I expect them to behave as Klingons," Kor said. "This entire situation is incomprehensible. We are all Klingons, are we not?"

"Are we?" Mara asked.

Kang sneered through his blood pie. "Yours, Kor, is a typical highborn attitude."

"And why not?" Kor asked while ripping some meat off one of the *klongat* leg bones. "I *am* noble-born—as is everyone seated at this table. Otherwise, we would not be officers—and certainly not captains." With a glance at Mara, he held up his mug of bloodwine and added with a smile, "Or science officers."

"Yes," Kang said, "but we are not treated as nobility."

"Kobyk and Sorkav certainly don't treat us so," Koloth added. Then he poured himself some of the soup and slurped up some. "I must say, Kang, that Galarch has outdone himself." Though the compliment was legitimate, he was mainly hoping to steer the conversation away from duty.

No such luck. Kang was determined. "We will never be considered true warriors, true Klingons, as long as we look like *this.*" Kang indicated his own forehead with his right hand.

Kor looked sour. "As long as we fight the Empire's battles, we *are* warriors."

"Soldiers, perhaps," Kang said, "but warriors? Hardly."

Slamming his hand on the table, which caused the soup to splash onto it, Kor said, "I am the equal of *any* shipmaster in the fleet! Those under my command fight and die for the Empire regardless of their cranial topography!"

"No doubt," Kang said, his solemn, deep tones in contrast to Kor's louder ones. "But where are they sent?"

Kor gnawed on his *klongat* leg. "What do you mean?"

"During the conflict with the Federation a turn ago, your mission was to secure a planet of pacifists, was it not?"

"Organia was a critical position!"

Having despaired of a change of subject, Koloth decided to bolster his friend's argument. "Yes, but how difficult was it to subdue? Were it not for Kirk—may he suffer all the torments of *Gre'thor*—you would have faced no resistance whatsoever."

Kang scowled and gulped bloodwine. "The perfect task for mere *QuchHa'.*"

"Meanwhile," Koloth continued, "the ridge-heads were given the plum battle assignments while we were left to secure insignificant planets or less well traveled portions of the border. Had the Organians not stopped the conflict, the important battles would all have been claimed by *HemQuch.*" Since they were on the subject, he went on. "One of the saboteurs called Korax *'urwI'.*"

Kor's eyes widened as he swallowed a handful of *racht.* "I assume this Korax killed him for his effrontery?"

"Yes, and I rather wish he hadn't. Oh, of course, he *had* to respond, but the other two were killed in the conflict, and I wanted at least one to interrogate."

Shaking his head, Kor said, "Whether or not we are considered warriors, we are still soldiers of the Empire. We are doing our duty. How does that make us traitors?"

"Because," Mara said, "the *QuchHa'* on this mine feel oppressed—and we have sided with their oppressors."

"We haven't 'sided' with anyone," Kor said dolefully, dipping more bread into the *grapok* sauce. "My own first officer, Kohlar, has attempted to interrogate the miners, but no one will give him an answer. If they were not loyal subjects of the Empire, I would use the mind-sifter on them."

Koloth chuckled bitterly through his casserole. Klingon law clearly stated that, while the mind-sifter could be used freely on any aliens, it could be used on Klingons only if they had been bound by law as criminals. "Sorkav would no doubt allow us to question any *QuchHa'* that way."

"But not *HemQuch*," Mara said while wiping soup from her lip. "Never *HemQuch*. After all, Sorkav wanted to have Jurva killed because she had the effrontery to challenge a *HemQuch*, never mind that he was her inferior and that the challenge was legitimate, and that she won it."

"It's obvious," Koloth said, "that Sorkav is incompetent. Every single incident on this mine can be traced to his failure to do his duty as head of security. While I was speaking with Kobyk, he received a report that someone had raided the dispensary and injured the nurse on duty. The question must be asked: Why is Sorkav still alive?"

"That is a fine question, my friend," Kang said. "I will ask Kobyk tomorrow myself."

Then the door slid open again, revealing dessert, and, to Koloth's great relief, all talk of duty ceased.

7

Kang

As soon as he walked into Supervisor Kobyk's office, Kang spoke without preamble. "Why is Sorkav still alive?"

Kobyk—clutching his *warnog* for dear life, as usual; Kang thought his liver must have been constructed from rodinium—stared at Kang as if he were a *glob* fly he wished to swat. "What?"

"The question is a simple one, Supervisor. Why is your chief of security still alive?"

"Because he's good at his job and therefore hasn't been killed."

Kang almost laughed in Kobyk's face, but this was hardly a laughing matter. "There are many ways that Sorkav may be described. 'Good at his job' could never be one of them."

"Captain, you do not understand."

Folding his arms across his chest, Kang said, "No, I do not. That is why I posed the question, Supervisor. *Make* me understand."

Kobyk opened his mouth as if to speak, then stopped. Then, he started again. "These incidents have been solely due to the *QuchHa'* getting the notion that they are treated more poorly than the *HemQuch.*"

Kang had to admit to being impressed that Kobyk said those words with a straight face. "A notion no doubt bolstered by a *QuchHa'* having his throat slit and the death being ruled an accident, while a *HemQuch* dying in the same manner led to the death of a *QuchHa'*."

"My brother does not discriminate." Then Kobyk smiled. "He treats all the miners like the scum that they are. These are laborers, Captain, not high-born Klingons like you and I. They must be ruled with a heavy gauntlet."

"We are *all* ruled by a heavy gauntlet, Supervisor. Yet somehow your mine has difficulties that no others do."

Kobyk slugged down the remainder of his *warnog,* slammed the mug onto his desk, and said, "He is my *brother*! Of *course* he's an incompetent *toDSaH,* but he is *family."*

Shaking his head, Kang said, "All the more reason to put him out of your misery."

"Oh, my misery will only begin there. Do you honestly believe, Captain, that I hired that fool *willingly*? And do you know what agonies I will face from our family if *I* am the one to condemn him to death? Believe me, the House of Kamarag is not to be trifled with."

Kang had no sympathy for Kobyk's plight, but he did understand it. He knew of the supervisor's House, and knew that, if he'd been forced to keep Sorkav safe, he could *not* condemn him to death—no matter how wretched at his duty he was.

Kobyk continued. "Believe me, Captain, no one will be happier if you and your fellow captains contrive a way to have a *d'k tahg* plunged into Sorkav's chest. But that order cannot come from me."

Even as Kang considered his response, a security alarm rang out through the speakers in the office.

The two masked men attacked Jurva while she was on her way to the transporter room.

She was just coming off her shift and was eager to return to the *Voh'tahk,* where she could get *edible* food. Her mid-shift meal had been taken in the mine's mess hall, and Jurva would sooner eat *human* food than that bland, tasteless garbage again.

Her journey took her on a lengthy corridor that was carved out of the asteroid rock, similar to the one she'd taken to the checkpoint on her first day, when she killed that section chief. But here, the lights were dimmer, some flickering, and odd shadows were being cast upon the walls.

No doubt, the two attackers had expected those shadows to

hide them, but Jurva saw them—and their masks—the moment she entered. She simply waited for them to make their move before acknowledging their presence.

One leapt out at her with an embarrassingly clumsy and obvious lunge. With the greatest of ease, Jurva used a *mok'bara* throw, using her attacker's momentum to toss him into the opposite wall.

The other one came at her with a blade—a *qutluch* that looked a lot like the one she'd killed Targ with. She had placed it back in the box after wiping Targ's blood from it, and it should have been sent to the storage bay on the main asteroid.

Jurva's surprise at the weapon had no impact on her reflexes. She deflected the knife strike by blocking her foe's forearm with her own. With her other hand, she punched him in the belly, causing him to lose his breath. Then she grabbed his forearm and brought it down so that the blade of the *qutluch* impaled his left groin muscle.

The weakling actually screamed in pain at that.

Jurva kicked him in the ribs, sending him stumbling to the floor against the wall, then turned to face the first one, who once again leapt at her.

The second leap was no more successful than the first, and Jurva again tossed him into the wall.

Now that she had a moment to take in the tableau, Jurva realized that, masks notwithstanding, she knew who these two were: Goroth and Gonn, Targ's subordinates. Jurva would have been touched by their loyalty had they been in any way skilled in seeking revenge for their section chief's death.

Gonn was the one she'd stabbed, and he was bleeding on the floor and not moving. Goroth, however, recovered quickly from being thrown into the wall a second time, and unsheathed his painstik.

"You will die today, *petaQ,*."

Grinning, Jurva said, "Only if I burst a blood vessel from laughing at your pathetic fighting skills."

Goroth lunged with the painstik. Jurva deflected it easily, then grabbed it and yanked it forward, causing Goroth to stumble right into her elbow, which collided with his left eye.

As Goroth stumbled about, dazed, Jurva grabbed his head from both sides and twisted, breaking his neck.

She let Goroth's corpse drop to the floor and turned to look at Gonn, now in a large pool of blood. Without medical attention, he would be dead soon.

Jurva found herself unable to be concerned.

She tore off both masks to confirm that she was right. Then she signaled a security alert.

Within a few minutes of the security alert, Sorkav reported to Kobyk's office. After sparing a venomous glance at Kang, Sorkav said, "Two of my people have been killed. The perpetrator is being brought here now."

Moments later, Kobyk had refilled his mug of *warnog* and the door to the office slid open to reveal two of Sorkav's guards, who were holding their painstiks on Jurva.

Kang tensed. "What is this?"

"This woman," one of the guards said, "was standing over the bodies."

"Yes," Jurva said angrily, "because I was waiting for you two to show up so I could give a report."

Sorkav started to speak, but Kang interrupted. "Then do so, *Bekk.*"

"Yes, sir." Jurva sounded relieved to be responding to an order from someone actually in her chain of command. "Two of the security guards ambushed me while wearing masks. One was armed with a *qut-luch* that had been confiscated from one of the miners, the other with a standard-issue painstik."

"And you killed them?" Sorkav said.

"I defended myself, yes," Jurva replied with a snarl at Sorkav. "And then I activated the security alert myself."

Sorkav walked closer to her. Jurva tensed, but did not move—which was well, as the guards' painstiks were brushing her uniform. "And yet you seem completely unharmed."

Jurva shrugged. "There were only two of them."

Kang smiled at that. Morglar had always said that Jurva was the finest warrior under his command, and Kang knew that Morglar did not issue such praise lightly.

From behind his desk, Kobyk was manipulating his computer station with the hand that wasn't clutching his *warnog.* "Unfortunately, the sensors in that corridor are down—more sabotage from the *malvaq bortaS*."

"So," Sorkav said, "we only have your word that this ambush happened as you describe."

"She is a warrior under my command!" Kang barked. "Her word is *more* than enough evidence!"

Sorkav walked up to Kang and stared up into the captain's face. Kang somehow resisted the urge to spit on him.

"It is no kind of evidence at all, *Captain*. The only true evidence is two of my guards are dead and your *bekk* is responsible."

"Enough!" Kobyk said. "Sorkav, she was the one who sounded the security alert, and she waited for your guards to arrive. I see no reason not to believe her story. She is free to go."

Kang looked upon Kobyk with surprise. He had, at this point, despaired of any of those who worked in this mine having any conception of honor and duty. Then he looked at Jurva. "Return to your duties, *Bekk*."

Jurva batted aside the painstiks with annoyance, saluted Kang, and said, "Yes, sir!"

Then she looked at Sorkav, turned her back on him, and left.

Sorkav looked up at Kang again. "This is *not* over."

"Yes," Kang said, "it is." Then he left the office as well.

8

Torad

Torad sat in the mess hall, alone as usual. He preferred it that way, honestly. He was raised alone by his father on Donatu V after his mother was killed during the battle with the Federation that occurred there two and a half decades ago. Since Father was always working at the factory, and often worked double shifts because they needed the money, Torad was generally left on his own.

The idea of being around a lot of people was always strange to Torad, so he tended to stay quiet and not annoy anyone. That seemed to work well for him, and led eventually to his job here at the mine.

A shadow fell over him. "May I join you?"

Torad's expression of a desire to be left alone died on his lips as he looked up and saw that the man standing on the other side of the table was wearing a Defense Force uniform and the sash of a shipmaster.

Practically leaping to his feet, Torad said, "Of course, sir! It would be an honor."

Torad's father hadn't spent much time with his son, but one of the lessons he did beat into the boy was to always respect the Defense Force even if they were *QuchHa'*—as this one was.

"Please be seated." The officer spoke in a pleasant tone with a polite smile. "I am Kor, son of Rynar, captain of the *Klothos*."

"It is an honor to share my meal with you, sir. I am Section Chief Torad, son of Keldraq."

Kor's smile widened. "I merely wish the pleasure of your company, Section Chief." He gave the *bok-rat* liver on Torad's tray a disdainful look. "I've—I've already eaten today."

"How may I be of service, Captain?"

"My first officer was tasked with questioning the miners regarding the *malvaq bortaS* movement."

Torad nodded. He recalled Commander Kohlar, but Torad had been unable to tell him anything useful.

"Kohlar told me that he thought you knew more than you told him."

Shaking his head quickly, Torad said, "That is not so, sir. I answered every question the commander posed to me."

"Perhaps. But he thought you knew more."

"I cannot imagine what," Torad said honestly. "I serve as a section chief—"

"The only *QuchHa'* among the section chiefs, according to the personnel records," Kor said. "Why is that, I wonder?"

Shrugging, Torad said, "I have been fortunate enough to gain the attention of my superiors."

"You misunderstand, my friend—I do not wonder how *you* became a section chief, but rather how you are the only *QuchHa'*."

That struck Torad as an odd question. "Why would you wonder that? Such jobs are usually reserved for Klingons."

"Yes, that is why we see no *jeghpu'wI'* in such positions, but . . ." Kor's words trailed off, and he folded his hands in front of him on the table. "Tell me, did you know the two victims—Malvak and Gahlar?"

"Yes." Torad chewed some liver before continuing. "Neither was in my section, but they were part of the same site, and we sometimes spoke on the shuttle or during meals."

"Really? During meals, you say? Yet, here you are, sitting alone—not with other section chiefs, not with other *QuchHa'*."

Defensively, Torad said, "I prefer it that way."

"Yet you spoke to both Gahlar and Malvak during meals?"

"Well, not Gahlar, no. Not really Malvak, except for that one time."

One of Kor's bushy eyebrows rose. "Oh?"

"It was shortly before Gahlar's death. Malvak came to me and asked if I would help him."

"With what?"

Torad hesitated. "He believed that Gahlar killed his friend Krov."

"What?" Kor's hands unfolded, and his eyes widened.

Now Torad was confused. He had thought this was common knowledge. Quickly, he explained what Malvak had told him about Gahlar's feud with Krov, and how Sorkav had not investigated Krov's death, and how Malvak then took matters into his own hands.

Kor was sneering at Torad now. "Which he did after you refused to help him!"

"What could I do? We are only *QuchHa'*. It would be our word against that of a Klingon."

"We are *all* of us Klingons, Section Chief."

"Are we?" Torad looked away from Kor. "When I look at my reflection, I see the weak face of a lesser species."

"If your heart is Klingon," Kor said quietly, "then physical appearance matters not."

Torad turned back to face Kor. "No? Then can Earthers be Klingons? Can Romulans? Vulcans?"

Kor rose to his feet. At once, Torad was ashamed. He had raised his voice to a captain in the Defense Force. Even *QuchHa'* didn't deserve that as long as they wore the uniform.

"I apologize, sir," he said quickly. "I did not mean—"

"Be *quiet*! I no longer wish to hear your mewling, Section Chief. Sorkav's false judgment prevented Krov from receiving justice, and when Malvak tried to mete out that justice, as is proper, Sorkav rewarded him with a coward's death. Believe me, your role in this will not be forgotten by me—or by my comrades."

With that, Kor turned and left the mess hall.

Torad finished eating alone, as he always did.

9

malvaq bortaS

It was when Kor left the mess hall that he and his bodyguard were ambushed.

Kor's bodyguard, Nyor, had originally been chosen for his considerable size. However, size and skill were not attributes that necessarily came together, as Kor discovered in short order when five masked Klingons were able to take him down.

A sixth held a disruptor on Kor. It was, he noticed, a *loSmaH Soch*—long since discontinued by the Defense Force, and the same type that was used on Koloth's first officer.

"Do not move," the sixth one said. Like the others, he was masked.

Kor simply smiled. "You've got courage, I'll grant you that—subduing a soldier, holding a weapon on a Defense Force captain. No honor, of course, but one takes what one can get, I suppose."

"Be silent."

Kor then felt a hypospray on his neck, probably applied by one of the other five.

As he lost consciousness, he realized that he now knew at least one of the drugs that had been taken from the dispensary.

His dreams were filled with battle, of his defeats turned into victories, of meeting Starfleet's Captain Kirk in armed combat on the streets of Organia, of wiping the sneer off the face of the man at Ty'Gokor, of returning to the Delta Triangle and conquering it, of planting the

Klingon flag on the ravaged world of Mestiko, and of a hypospray being applied to his neck.

That last actually happened, and the dreams of glory and honor and victory faded, to be replaced by the faces of a dozen or so Klingons—all *QuchHa'*—who now, at least, were showing their faces.

They were in a cave that probably serviced one of the dilithium mines. Based on the scarring patterns on the rock and the lack of equipment, Kor supposed that this was a vein that had been tapped out, with the miners having moved on to a new location.

"You must be the *malvaq bortaS*," Kor said.

"And you must be Kor, son of Rynar," said one, who had the same voice as the one who had held the disruptor on Kor.

Noting that there were no weapons being held on him now, Kor said, "You do realize that nothing is currently stopping me from killing all of you."

"I don't doubt it," said the man who was apparently the leader. "But we are deep underground in an abandoned mine. The site on this asteroid was discontinued a turn ago. There's no one here but us. The only reason there is still life support is because Supervisor Kobyk does not wish to incur the expense of dismantling it. In any case, Captain, there is nowhere for you to go once you do kill us."

"Perhaps." Kor had an entire starship at his disposal, and two more as reinforcements. He was hardly without resources to survive.

"I am Nargov."

"You lead this dishonorable rabble?"

Several of the others bristled at that. Nargov said, "Honor is a coin we cannot afford, Captain."

"Ridiculous," Kor said dismissively. "Sneak attacks—sabotage—doing battle without showing your face—these are not the actions of Klingons!"

"We are not treated as Klingons," Nargov said, "so why should we act like them? When we are looked upon, it is as inferiors."

Kor shook his head. This attitude was hardly unique to these malcontents. Many in his own crew had abandoned Kahless's ways, for the very reasons Nargov had given. He recalled an incident on Organia when that bloodworm Kirk had threatened one of his lieutenants with death, and the coward had actually given in, unwilling to die for an empire that considered him less than what he was. On the one hand, Kor could understand how a *QuchHa'* could come to such a state. On the other hand, Kor didn't hesitate to execute the lieutenant when the mission was over.

Finally, he spoke. "I know now why you take arms against your commanders. I know about the feud between Krov and Gahlar that led to Krov's death, and eventually that of Gahlar and Malvak." He looked at each member of *malvaq bortaS* in turn. "But when faced with an injustice of this kind, you should have acted like *Klingons* and challenged your superiors!"

Nargov gave Kor an incredulous look. "Do you truly believe that would be allowed? Oh, we *tried* to issue challenges, but our attempts were met with howls of laughter by our section chiefs." Nargov moved closer to Kor. "That is why we brought you here, Captain. To tell you the truth, after hearing the lies of Kobyk and Sorkav."

"You have done so, though you have told me little I did not already know." Kor folded his arms over his sash of office. "What happens next?"

10

Sorkav

Sorkav was giving Kobyk an inventory of the drugs stolen from the dispensary when two of the *QuchHa'* captains—he wasn't sure which two they were, as all the weak-heads looked alike to him—barged in without even announcing themselves.

"How dare you?" Sorkav said. "We are in the middle of—"

"Be quiet, Sorkav," Kobyk said. "What do you want, Captains?"

Sorkav whirled and practically spit on his brother. More and more, since these *petaQpu'* had arrived, his brother had been acting strange, and now he was *deferring* to them and telling *him* to be quiet?

The taller captain with the deep voice said, "Kor is missing."

"According to his first officer," the shorter one with the oily tone added, "he was last seen on his way interrogate a section chief on Site *wej.*"

It was typical of the weak-heads to get lost in such a manner, but Sorkav said only, "I will have one of my men on that site conduct an investigation that will—"

"We have seen the results of your investigations, Sorkav," the tall one said.

"Besides," said the other one with an insincere smile, "it isn't necessary. *My* first officer has already conducted an investigation."

Angrily, Sorkav advanced on the captains. "You had no right!"

"Actually," the oily one said, "we have every right, according to General Korrd. Or do you question *his* orders as well?"

Sorkav's response was interrupted by the sound of the tall one's communicator. *"Klothos to Kang."*

Activating the communicator, the tall one said, "This is Kang."

"Sir, we have found the captain. He is on the asteroid designated wejmaH wa'. *Records have it as the former location of Site* loS."

Kobyk sputtered his *warnog*. "What is he doing *there*? That asteroid was tapped out a year ago."

"We will arrive at the asteroid in three minutes."

"Very good, Commander. Beam Kor aboard and bring him directly to Supervisor Kobyk's office. Out."

Putting his hands on his hips, Sorkav said, "There is only one reason why *anyone* would be on Site *loS*. That must be where *malvaq bortaS* is hiding."

Kobyk slugged down some of his omnipresent *warnog*. "Captains, it will take an hour for the *Klothos* to arrive here from Site *loS*."

Kang nodded. "We will make our reports to General Korrd in the meantime."

The shorter one wore that damned smile again. "Where, among other things, we can report that it never occurred to the mine's chief of security to look at an abandoned mining site when he was trying to find the *malvaq bortaS*."

With that, they left.

Whirling on his brother, Sorkav asked, "How much longer must we put up with these fools?"

Kobyk stared witheringly at his brother. "Until they are done cleaning up your mess, Sorkav. Now finish your report."

Smoldering, Sorkav did so. Then he returned to his cabin. He was obviously going to have to have a word with Colonel Kamarag. Kobyk was forgetting his filial duties . . .

By the time the *Klothos* arrived at Site *wa'*, Kor had formulated a very simple plan. It was one that he shared with Kang and Koloth over subspace while his ship was en route, and which he put into a hastily written report to General Korrd.

He waited for Kang and Koloth to signal him that they were in Kobyk's office, along with the supervisor and his brother, and then Kor ordered his transporter chief to energize, while nodding to the man next to him.

A haze of red, and then both he and Norgav materialized in Kobyk's office.

Pointing at Norgav, Sorkav asked, "Who is *that*?"

Norgav bared his teeth at Sorkav. "Just another *QuchHa'*, Sorkav."

"He is here," Kor said, "on behalf of *malvaq bortaS.*"

Sorkav laughed. "Excellent! You have brought their ringleader here for me to kill!"

Koloth stepped forward. "Hardly."

Kang did likewise. "It is past time that their side of the story was heard."

"They have no side!" Sorkav cried. "They are merely a collection of weak-headed miners who—"

"Enough!" Kor unsheathed his *d'k tahg.* "Sorkav, son of Goryq, I find you to have failed in your duties as chief of security of this mine." With the hand that wasn't holding the weapon, Kor backhanded Sorkav across the face.

"Are you insane?" Sorkav asked. "You don't have the authority to challenge me!"

"Oh yes, he very much does," Koloth said.

"That authority," Kang added, "comes from General Korrd."

Kang then activated his communicator. At that signal, four Klingons beamed down from the *Voh'tahk*. Kor noted that *Bekk* Jurva was at the forefront, her disruptor aimed right at Sorkav.

"If you do not accept this challenge," Kang continued, "then you will be shot down like the *targ* you are."

Kor tilted his head and smiled. "Well? Will you follow the tenets of Kahless that a warrior who does not face a challenge deserves to die without honor?"

Snarling, Sorkav walked over to the wall behind him and took down the *mek'leth* that hung over the sideboard that contained Kobyk's alcohol stash. "I would rather fight than listen to the words of the great one come from the mouth of the likes of *you.*"

Koloth, with uncharacteristic admiration in his voice, asked, "Is that a Do'Ming?"

It was Kobyk who answered. "Yes. It was forged for our family by the swordmaster himself."

Kor nodded. "A worthy weapon in the hands of an unworthy opponent."

The quarters were close, especially with eight spectators, though that was mitigated by the use of a short sword and a dagger.

Sorkav lunged, and Kor skipped backward. His *d'k tahg* was strong, but he didn't want to risk the *mek'leth* striking it unless absolutely necessary. There were less than a dozen known Do'Mings still in existence, but all of them were still powerful blades that had lost none of their strength over the past two millennia.

Reluctantly, Kor gave Sorkav credit. He held the *mek'leth* properly, kept his strokes short and swift. Many times, Kor had faced opponents who swung their short swords in longer arcs, as if it were a *bat'leth*.

At first, Kor and Sorkav feinted and dodged, taking each other's measure. Kor had hoped that Sorkav was as poor a fighter as he was a security chief, but considering that his previous career was in the Imperial Guard, he knew it was a forlorn hope.

Sorkav slashed down with the *mek'leth* toward Kor's head, forcing Kor to block with the *d'k tahg*. Kor caught the *mek'leth* in between the main blade and the secondary blade of his own dagger. To his relief, it didn't break.

With that temporary impasse, Kor kicked Sorkav in the chest, which sent him stumbling backward, a look of surprise on his face.

"Typical *QuchHa'*," Sorkav said. "We fight with *blades*, not feet!"

Grinning, Kor said, "Actually, 'Klingons fight with their minds and their hearts—weapons are secondary.'"

As Kor had expected, quoting Kahless again angered Sorkav. With a scream, he ran toward Kor, his *mek'leth* raised.

Kor ducked, head-butting Sorkav in the belly, wrapping his arms around Sorkav's waist, and standing upright, lifting the security chief into the air. Letting out a mighty roar, Kor then threw Sorkav behind him.

Turning around, Kor saw that Sorkav lay dazed on the floor, having dropped the *mek'leth*. Around him, Kor heard his name being chanted by Kang, Koloth, Jurva, and the rest of Kang's crew.

And Kobyk as well. That surprised Kor, but also lent wings to his feet as he leapt to Sorkav and plunged his *d'k tahg* right in between two of the ridges in his crest.

Blood spurted magnificently out of the wound as Kor thrust the blade into Sorkav's feeble brain.

All those in the room cheered Kor's victory. Yanking out his *d'k tahg,* which caused more of Sorkav's blood to spurt over the office and onto Kor's uniform, he raised his weapon in the air and let out a cry of victory.

Kor then turned to face Kobyk. "You cheered my victory. That speaks well of you."

It was Kang who replied. "And your victory cannot be questioned by the House of Kamarag."

"Indeed." Kobyk raised his *warnog* to Kor. "To a new security chief—and, with luck, a new day for this mine."

"Remember," Kor said, "that if your heart is Klingon, then it matters not whether or not you look as Kahless did. And if your heart isn't Klingon, then it doesn't matter if you do. Being treated as less than Klingon is no excuse to *act* less than Klingon."

Koloth put a hand on Kor's bloodstained shoulder. "Well said, my friend."

"*Bekk* Jurva!" Kang called.

The woman stepped forward. "Sir!"

"You will serve as temporary security chief for this mine until Supervisor Kobyk's replacement—who will be approved by all three of us—arrives."

Jurva smiled. "It will be my pleasure, sir."

To Jurva, Kobyk said, "You will have free rein, *Bekk*—on that you have my word."

"I have always made it a point," Kang said, "to trust the word of a Klingon."

Kobyk bowed his head.

Then Kang moved to stand before Kor, next to Koloth, putting the three of them in a circle. "Well done, Kor—let us return to the *Voh'tahk*. I will have Galarch prepare a feast to celebrate your victory!"

Kor smiled. "I'm sure the meal will be glorious."

Lust

Freedom Angst

Britta Burdett Dennison

Historian's Note

This story takes place in an alternate time line—commonly called the Mirror Universe—in 2369 (ACE). The events are concurrent with the Cardassian Union's surrendering the space station, now known as Deep Space 9, to the provisional Bajoran government ("Emissary" DS9).

This one is for Danelle

There was silence in the cockpit of the little Alliance shuttle as it hurtled toward its preprogrammed coordinates, outside the Trivas star system from where it had originated. The silence was not an easy one. Although Benjamin Sisko and his wife Jennifer had been married for almost twelve years, a time when many married couples would be finishing each other's sentences, Benjamin and Jennifer felt as though there was nothing they could say to one another that might not be considered an invitation to argue. For the better part of an hour, they had chosen to say nothing at all, though both were wrestling with dozens of questions about their destination.

Sisko wanted to enjoy the long journey—he had never traveled outside the Trivas system before. He had never even been in a shuttle that had the capacity to go this kind of distance. But he was troubled. He was curious to know what Jennifer was thinking about all of this, but not curious enough to be the first to break the willful silence. He considered his questions while surreptitiously glancing at his wife's profile. Her face bore no expression, except for the slight set of her chin, a subtle stiffness to her lower lip that nobody but her husband would have recognized as a product of dismay.

He wondered why the Intendant of Terok Nor, a space station in the nearby Bajoran system, had summoned Jennifer. He wondered what Jennifer's father was going to have to say about it. He wondered what it would be like for himself and his wife, two Terrans walking around on the Alliance side of an ore-processing station. Both Benjamin and Jennifer were well-dressed, more like members of the Alliance than Terrans, but they were Terrans nonetheless. Their clothing would offer them little protection if either of them were to accidentally upset someone, and the trouble was, the Siskos were far more proud than any Terrans had a right to be, with Sisko's pride being a sight more volatile than his wife's.

The station was just coming into view. Sisko had seen a Cardassian orbital station before—Empok Nor, the station in the Trivas system, was identical to this one. Sisko had passed it many times, but he had never been inside of it. Even from a distance, Sisko had always thought it an ugly thing. It looked like a hunk of the Cardassian machinery that had overrun the Terran colonies in the age following the Alliance conquest.

As they drew closer to Terok Nor, its shape was easier to define; the crooked, arching spires hunched around a flattened base. Sisko was given the impression of a hand—a cruel, bony hand with metallic fingers, closing over an already beleaguered world, as if it meant to crush it entirely. The image was troubling, to say the least.

The shuttle drew toward the docking clamps, and in a moment the Siskos were able to disembark. A stocky Cardassian man with a wide-eyed, contemptuous expression appeared, presumably to escort them to the Intendant. The man did not speak to them, did not so much as grunt at them, apparently not feeling that they were worthy of introductions.

Benjamin glanced at his wife as they followed, and recognized a hint of fear in her eyes. In an instant, he regretted the long silence that had endured throughout their journey here. Benjamin was accustomed to dealing with Alliance people that he did not know, but Jennifer was not, and this experience must make her feel very uneasy. He at least should have had the courtesy to try and comfort her, prior to their landing. His marriage might be shaky, but he still cared for this woman. He tried to smile reassuringly, but she was not looking at him, and the gesture went unnoticed.

Their surly escort brought them to a large, ornate door and pressed a panel off to the side. Benjamin could hear a woman's voice that he recognized as the lazy contralto of Kira Nerys, the Bajoran Intendant of Terok Nor. "Come in, Garak."

Sisko was surprised when the door slid open to reveal that the comely Bajoran woman was seated at a long dining table, which sagged under the weight of all the food laid upon it. Surely this feast was meant for at least two dozen people? But there were only three place settings, and he realized that one of them was meant for him.

"Well, don't just stand there," the Intendant said, raising one of her slender, white arms in a sweeping gesture. She was hardly dressed to discuss business, clad as she was in a long, body-hugging gown of violet satin that clashed with the brightness of her auburn hair and the blood red of her lips. She was not so much sitting in her chair as she was draped over it, her movements slow and provocative. "Sit down, please. You're right on time." Her eyes smoldered, and every word she uttered seemed to have a hidden subtext. "I like punctuality." She glared at the Cardassian as she said it, and the man bristled before taking a step backward. Sisko sensed that a long feud had brewed between these two, and he hoped he would not be put in a position to get tangled up in any of it.

"That's right, Garak," Kira went on. "You're not needed here. Dismissed."

Sisko almost sat down before remembering to pull out a chair for his wife. He gave her a small nod, and he saw a hint of gratitude in her eyes before she sat down. A tiny gesture could go a long way in a hostile environment, even between two people whose relationship had come to be as strained as that of the Siskos.

"So," the Intendant began. She gestured to a Klingon servant who had been looming in the shadows, almost unnoticed. He stepped forward to fill her cup with a flagon of spring wine. "Jennifer Devitt."

"It's Jennifer Sisko," Jennifer said in a low voice, and Benjamin tensed.

The Intendant paused for a dangerous moment, and then she laughed. But her laughter was brittle, the fluidity of her movements suddenly appearing stilted. "Yes, of course it is, my dear. Jennifer *Sisko*. Devitt is your father's name."

"Yes," Jennifer said, and began to help herself to some Bajoran *moba* fruit that was artfully arranged on a platter in front of her. "Sisko is my husband's name."

Kira cut her eyes at Benjamin, who wished to be left out of the discussion, but she thankfully did not address him, replying to Jennifer. "Your father . . . is a most remarkable man. For a Terran."

Jennifer cleared her throat. "He is a remarkable man," she agreed.

"It's my understanding that the men in your family were smart enough to see which way the wind was blowing when the Alliance came into power," Kira said. "There weren't many who had that much foresight. Most Terrans actually thought they had a chance to defend themselves." Kira appeared thoughtful. "Your father's father was like a Bajoran that way," she said. "He understood that there is a time to fight, and there is a time to cooperate."

Jennifer nodded without saying anything.

"I imagine, Jennifer, that you understand that as well as your father and grandfather did."

"Of course I do."

"Good," purred the Intendant, and then, to Benjamin, "What's the matter, Benjamin? Aren't you hungry?"

Benjamin was, but he shrugged. "Not especially."

"Well, at least *try* the *veklava*. Don't you like Bajoran food?"

Benjamin hadn't had much Bajoran food, but he didn't feel like offering an explanation. "I like it well enough." He helped himself to some food, avoiding eye contact with everyone in the room.

Kira turned back to Jennifer. "Tell me. Do you . . . enjoy the work you do for Akiem?" she asked, seeming somehow to know the answer already. Jennifer oversaw the tech support for the Cardassian-run company where her father had been employed since he was a young man, a group that bought out debt from various industrial interests who didn't have the resources necessary to strong-arm their outstanding liabilities into payment. Benjamin was also employed by Akiem, and his "clients" were mostly Terrans.

Jennifer shrugged, but Benjamin saw a little crease form at the corner of her mouth. The Intendant had hit a nerve. Jennifer was capable of doing so much more than routine computer checks and security sweeps, but she was a Terran, and her potential was not likely ever to be fully realized, despite her father's unusually prestigious position. "It's not demanding work," Jennifer said.

Kira's voice was still friendly, but there was an edge to it that did not go unnoticed. "I didn't ask if it was demanding, I asked if you enjoyed it."

Jennifer hesitated. "I wouldn't mind . . . more of a challenge," she admitted.

Kira's smile widened, became more genuine. "I thought so," she said. She took a long drink from her cup, signaled for her Klingon assistant to bring more, and spoke again. "I might be able to offer you something better," she said, "but it depends on several factors."

Jennifer waited for a moment before responding. "Such as?"

Kira shrugged playfully. "Oh, this and that. There are a few particulars to work out. And, of course, there is your father to consider. He might prefer that you not go to work for me."

Jennifer seemed to struggle for the correct response. "He . . . I don't see how it would make a difference," she finally said.

"Well, of course it wouldn't, if I wanted you badly enough." Kira laughed. "But I thought it would at least be polite to mention it."

"I see," Jennifer said stiffly.

"I consider myself a courteous person, among other things." The Intendant drained her cup again, but instead of continuing, she turned her attention to Benjamin.

"Benjamin Sisko," she said, lacing her fingers together and resting her chin on her hands. "I confess, I knew so little about you when I called your wife here to the station. But I did a little checking, and I was rather impressed by what I found."

Benjamin, whose mouth was full of food, stopped chewing, and swallowed with some difficulty. "What . . . did you find?"

"Well, it seems you were something of a nobody before you met your wife here." Kira nodded at Jennifer. "Going from place to place, working wherever you could, mostly keeping your head down. You must have really made an impression on Jennifer. She's quite a powerful woman for a Terran, not to mention beautiful. Tell me, Benjamin." Kira unlaced her fingers and shifted her weight so that she was leaning toward him, the white curve of her shoulder thrust forward so that he could get a good look at the plunging neckline of her gown. Her voice grew husky, and she batted her long eyelashes at him. "How did you do it?"

Sisko was dumbfounded. He did not even have to look at

Jennifer to sense her dismay, but there wasn't much he could do about it. "I . . . you'll have to ask her that," he said. The truth was, he had often wondered the same thing himself.

Kira offered Jennifer a cursory glance, but her attention remained focused on Benjamin, and she did not respond to his suggestion. "Some Terrans would have difficulty adapting to a position like yours," Kira said. "But your record indicates that you've managed to collect over ninety-eight percent of your clients' debt. Of those who could not pay, you were very swift in meting out an appropriate punishment. That's impressive, Benjamin. I have Cardassians on my staff whose efficiency records pale in comparison to yours."

Sisko's face felt cool, as though the blood was draining away. Could the Intendant possibly know that much of his "success" was false? It wasn't that Sisko was especially soft-hearted; it was mostly that he knew there was no way to get juice from a stone. His only recourse, besides sanctioning the death of hundreds of Terrans, was to skew the accounting data in his own favor, and he was lucky enough to know a particularly number-savvy Trill with the right access codes who was willing to cook the books for him. Not even Jennifer knew what he'd been up to. He met Kira's gaze, searching her eyes for signs that she knew, but her smile revealed nothing. "I don't believe in doing anything halfway," he said finally.

"I'd bet not," Kira said, her voice even huskier than before. The blood suddenly rushed back to Ben's face again, and he felt thankful that his complexion was dark enough to conceal any outward sign of embarrassment. He could hear by Jennifer's breathing that she was not pleased, but thankfully she said nothing.

"I have found that Terrans are very well-suited to certain lines of work," Kira went on, her tone shifting back to the more personable, businesslike quality she had been using before. "It's possible that I could find a desirable place for you in my fleet. Very desirable, for a Terran."

"In your . . . fleet?" Sisko repeated. The implication was almost unthinkable, but surely Sisko had misunderstood . . .

"Certainly. You'd be outfitted with a ship, your own crew . . . that sort of thing." Kira smiled brilliantly. "But I'd have to make some adjustments first."

Benjamin could feel Jennifer's cold gaze. Though he could barely see her in his peripheral vision, he didn't have to be looking at her to know what she was thinking. "I . . . I couldn't . . ." he stammered, "I . . . I work for Jennifer's father. It's . . . family business. It's . . ."

"Oh, of course I understand your wanting to be loyal to your father-in-law," the Intendant interrupted. "Suppose I talk it over with him?"

"I don't think that's a good idea," Benjamin said gruffly, instantly regretting his answer. Who was he to tell the Intendant of Terok Nor that her idea was not a good one?

There was a short silence during which the Intendant only looked at him with a small, disquieting smile playing about her mouth. "Well," she said softly. "As you wish. But maybe just think about it before you give me a definitive answer. Meanwhile"—she turned her attention back to Jennifer—"it was so lovely to meet you in person, to get to know you a little better." Her gaze flickered between Sisko and his wife. "I have a feeling this will turn out to be a very profitable meeting for all of us."

It seemed like a very long time before Jennifer and Benjamin finally left the station. Neither of them ate or drank much, and the Intendant scolded them for letting so much food go to waste, though Benjamin couldn't imagine how she expected three people to make even a slight dent in all the food that had been prepared. When they rose to leave, Kira ordered her servants to discard it all, knowing full well that the Terrans in ore processing likely had not seen that much food in one place in all their lives.

As they rode in the little shuttle back to the tiny, manufactured planet where their living quarters were located, Benjamin at first thought the ride would be as devoid of conversation as the trip to Terok Nor had been. He considered the Intendant's offer for a time, imagining what it might be like if *he* were the one giving orders, instead of taking them. What it might be like to have his own ship, instead of being confined to the company's shuttles, having to track every single move he made, never able to be gone for even a moment longer than he had signed out for without having to face a barrage of questions from his father-in-law. But there was no use thinking about it. If he went to work for Kira Nerys, Jennifer would be furious. There wasn't much question as to what sort of "duties" he would be required to perform.

After a strained silence of about a quarter of an hour, Jennifer suddenly began speaking, her words tumbling out so quickly, she nearly seemed to choke on them.

"Wouldn't that be lovely?" she snapped. "Benjamin Sisko, working for the Intendant of Terok Nor. Oh, that would be a plum job for you, wouldn't it, Benjamin?" She took a hard breath.

"I don't want to go to work for her," he said softly.

"Oh, of course you don't. No, why would you? Your own ship— your own crew? The ability to travel between systems, whenever you wanted? Isn't that exactly what you always hoped my father could give you? And then, on top of all of that, you'd have the *fringe benefits* that only Kira Nerys would be sure to provide, you'd have—"

"Stop it, Jennifer, I don't want to go to work for her. I'm perfectly content where I am. Perfectly *lucky* to be where I am." He tried a laugh. "How could I, a Terran man, possibly hope for any better than what I've already got? A beautiful—"

"Don't even try it," she interrupted. "We both know why you married me, and it's got nothing to do with my looks."

Sisko struggled with his reply. It would do no good to deny it, he already knew that much. He had tried to take it back, what he had said before, but Jennifer would have none of it. She was not the sort of person to just accept an apology and move on; she held grudges forever. "I married you because I loved you," he said.

"You *loved* me?" Jennifer said angrily.

"I love you," he quickly amended, but he knew it was too late.

Jennifer turned away from him, and there was a thankful quiet for a few moments before she began again. "I was so stupid," she said bitterly. "My father tried to warn me. I thought . . . I thought . . ."

"If I didn't love you, Jennifer, I would have left you by now, wouldn't I?"

"Except that there's never been anywhere for you to go. Until now."

She was testing him. Daring him, practically, to go to work for Kira. If he accepted the Intendant's offer, Jennifer would be proven right. It would be all the evidence she'd need to assure herself that he had never really loved her, was only using her to gain influence within her father's company.

Sisko's head sank into his chest. His neck and shoulders felt too weak to support the weight of his skull. "Anyway, if she wants either of us to work for her, then there's probably nothing we can do about it."

"That would be a convenient excuse for you, wouldn't it?"

"Am I wrong?" he snapped.

"My father could probably protect us," she said. "He won't want me to work for her, and if I ask him to help you, too, I know that he will do everything he can to keep you from having to live on Terok Nor."

Sisko was not so sure, but he didn't say so. Still, Jennifer knew right away what he was thinking.

"I know you don't think my father has any influence, Benjamin, but you're wrong."

Still, he didn't answer, and his silence seemed to infuriate her.

"Yes, I know you were disappointed when it first occurred to you that my father was not as powerful as you originally thought he was. But he has more clout with the Alliance than you understand. It's just that he has to be careful. He is a man who learned, a long time ago, what you can and can't say around Cardassians and Klingons. He knows how to tell them what they want to hear. But he can't just give you everything you want overnight. That kind of prestige doesn't come easily, you have to earn it. You have to wait. You have to be patient."

"I have been patient," he said, and then instantly regretted having spoken.

"Twelve years is too long for you to have to endure being married to me?" she said. "Is that it? Was it such a high price to pay, then, for what little bit of freedom you enjoy now?"

Her words felt like needles in Sisko's chest, but he was too weary to even contradict her anymore. He was tired of this conversation, and he knew Jennifer was, too, but maybe it gave her some small amount of catharsis to repeat it again. He hoped so, anyway—that it was somehow worth it for one of them.

The shuttle was coming up on their little terraformed world, a moon of Trivas called Zismer that had been transformed into a habitat for second-rate employees at Akiem a generation and a half ago. It was not a particularly elegant place to live, but it was exponentially better than most Terrans could ever expect. It was mostly Trill who lived here, Trill, Terrans, Farians, and a handful of folk from other neutral worlds, people who had been smart enough or lucky enough to cast their lots with the Alliance back when it still counted for something.

The shuttle came to rest at the docking port, but Sisko didn't get out right away. He didn't look up as he spoke. "I told Janel I'd meet him—" he began, but Jennifer cut him off.

"Of course," she said bitterly. "By all means, go and see Janel Tigan at the tavern. I could hardly expect you to want to spend your evening with me." She left Sisko in the shuttle without another word.

Sisko disembarked from the craft after Jennifer was gone. The shuttle did not belong to him, and he did not have the access codes to program a destination; now that it had landed, it was as good as useless to him. Some Alliance officiates in the Intendant's employ had arranged for Benjamin and Jennifer to use it for this jaunt. It was virtually unheard-of for Benjamin to find a non-work-related occasion for which he would travel in a shuttle, and never in one that had taken him outside the Trivas system.

Benjamin made his way across the surface of the cramped world, looking around at the now dated-seeming architecture. It was designed in a style that had looked modern and sleek when it was new, but everything was inexpensive and trendy enough that it had begun to appear outmoded within just a few years of construction. Retaining walls were cracked and crumbling, walkways shifting under the roots of the fast-growing trees that had been planted but never maintained. The buildings all seemed to sag, the bright colors applied to the adobe walls now faded by the unfiltered light of Trivas's peculiarly long summer days.

He came upon a squat, ugly building. There was an empty rectangular space set in the front wall that had once been a window, but it had been boarded up years before, making the place look closed. Only the regulars knew better, and Sisko was as faithful a regular as anyone.

Janel Tigan, a handsome young Trill who was employed at Akiem with Sisko, waited in the dusky lamplight at the narrow bar, downing what was probably his fifth or sixth Romulan ale, judging by the empty cups that littered the bar. Janel could put it away with stunning efficiency. Yet somehow, the cocky young Trill never seemed to get really drunk.

"Ben Sisko," Janel greeted him, his diction giving no evidence of all the Romulan liquor he had apparently drunk. "I was just wondering when you were going to get here."

"The . . . meeting ran a little late," Sisko said, signaling for the bartender to bring him the usual synthale.

Janel cocked an eyebrow. "Late, eh?" he said. "Does this mean Jennifer is really going to work on Terok Nor? You might really be moving away from this"—he gestured around himself—"place?"

"Not sure," Sisko replied, accepting his drink.

Janel eyed Sisko for a moment, waiting for more, but when it was clear he was not going to get it, he changed the subject a little. "It seems odd that Kira would have her eye on a Terran to join her staff," Janel remarked. "Did you think she had any ulterior motives?"

Sisko took a long drink and then paused before answering. "I don't know," he admitted. "She . . . implied that she would have liked *me* to go to work for her. But—"

"You?" Janel repeated, then broke into laughter. "Of course!" he shouted. "Ha! She's seen the data on you, hasn't she?" He laughed to himself for a moment. "I guess I worried, Ben, that we've caused you to look a little *too* good, haven't we?"

"Quiet," Sisko murmured, though there was only one other patron in the tavern, and he was in a heated discussion with the bartender. It was nothing short of astonishing that Janel's boisterous personality hadn't gotten him into more trouble over the years; it was lucky for the man that he was so charismatic. The Orions he was acquainted with seemed to love him, despite his loose tongue, to the degree that he was used almost exclusively by the Cardassians at Akiem whenever the company required interactions with stubborn Orions. But Sisko couldn't afford the same careless indiscretion Janel showed Akiem's Orion clients.

"Sorry, there, Ben," Janel said, a little more quietly. "But you have to admit, I've done a real number for you, haven't I?"

"That you have," Sisko said. "But who knows how long you can keep it up."

Janel grinned, but Sisko could sense strain behind it. "I'd like to say indefinitely, of course. But the truth is . . ."

"The truth is, you're starting to worry."

"Well, I just find it a little disconcerting that word got back to the Intendant, that's all. That she actually offered you a *job* . . ."

"And a ship," Sisko added. "She offered me a ship."

"Your own ship?" Janel asked, looking genuinely impressed. Janel's comings and goings were far less regulated than Sisko's because he enjoyed a much better status with Akiem, but he certainly didn't have his own ship.

Sisko chortled. "Can you imagine me, with my own ship? Commanding my own crew?"

Janel frowned. "Can *you* imagine it, Ben?"

Sisko didn't answer.

Janel scrutinized Ben for a moment before breaking into a knowing smile. "You're considering it, aren't you? I mean, not just considering—you're *fantasizing* about it. You're letting yourself imagine what it would be like to go to work for the Intendant."

"No," Sisko lied. "I can't go to work for her."

"Why not?"

"Because," Sisko said, feeling suddenly very helpless, and very tired. "Because it would just confirm for Jennifer what she's been accusing me of for years."

"Hm," Janel said. "Well, then, you are in a bind, aren't you?"

"No, I'm not," Ben replied, "because I'm not going to work for the Intendant."

"Even though you want to?"

"I don't want to," Sisko insisted.

"Oh, Ben." Janel laughed. "What have I told you? When you're after something—be it a woman, money, prestige—"

"I'm not *after* anything."

"Or freedom," Janel went on, as if he hadn't spoken. "When you're infatuated with something, when you're *lusting* after it, you can't let yourself get too immersed in the picture of what it could be like. No, no, don't let those pictures come. You have to keep yourself from actually *thinking* about it, if you truly want to get it. Because if you think about it too much, then you *will* yearn for it. And if you start to actually *hurt* for it, then you become reckless; you're a goner, Ben. There'll be no saving you—"

"I'm not going to work for her," Sisko interrupted, his voice much louder than he had intended it to be. "I'll find a way so that she won't want me in her fleet. I'll . . . I'll get Jennifer's father to lean on someone at Akiem—someone who can prevent it. Look, I'll admit I like the idea of commanding a ship. But I know very well that there's no way Kira Nerys is going to let me just . . . *work* for her."

Janel's smile became very wide. "No, of course not," he said. "The Intendant's reputation—her . . . *appetite* . . . precedes her. But that's not stopped you from rationalizing it, has it?"

"I . . . I . . ." Sisko stopped.

Janel continued to smirk, which Sisko was beginning to find a bit annoying. "I know exactly what you're doing. You're trying every angle in your mind, you're thinking of every which way, looking for that elusive loophole that could make it possible. I know how badly you want your own ship. And you've got to *stop,* Ben, precisely because, once you have seen a clear enough image of it in your mind, then there are no lengths you wouldn't go to for it. I would hate to see you in such a position. A *desperate* position, that is." His smile faded. "You *don't* want to be that woman's pet, Ben. Trust me. I've heard stories about her that would make an Orion blush."

"I . . . won't let it happen. Not at the cost of my marriage. I care about Jennifer very much. If I didn't, I would have just accepted the offer right then and there, wouldn't I?"

Janel's smile returned, but Ben could plainly see the worry in it now. He wasn't thinking about the Intendant, or Jennifer. "You need to be more careful with your accounts," the Trill said pointedly. "We'll both find ourselves in serious trouble if anyone learns that we've been fixing those numbers. And Jennifer and her father could be implicated as well. If you really *do* care about her—"

"I do."

"Well, then, I hate to tell you this, but you're going to have to start doing your job."

"You mean . . . actually condemn those people to die?"

"Either that, or get them to pay," Janel said.

Sisko sighed. "I know you're right." He had been forced to hand out a few death sentences in his time at Akiem, but he hardly relished it. In truth, he knew very well that if he worked for the Intendant, he would have to genuinely do what he'd been hired to do, and he had hated himself when he'd done it in the past. That could never be worth having his own ship. At least, he told himself that it never could.

Janel drained the last of his ale and then rose from his bar stool, clapping Benjamin on the shoulder. "Maybe you'd better go home to Jennifer a little early tonight, eh?"

As the Akiem shuttle found its way to another pathetic little moon in orbit of Trivas, Sisko was thinking about what the Cardassian acronym actually stood for. Akiem was the best Terran approximation of the Cardassian letters; Sisko felt it was fitting that the meaning was supposed to be something like "Integrity Drives Our Foundation." There was a double meaning to it, though, known only to Terrans. The Cardassian word for "integrity" sounded very like a particular dialect of a Terran word for "angst." It was a joke among some Terrans, but as far as Sisko knew, the Cardassians were not aware of this coincidence. Jennifer's father had made it abundantly clear that Sisko was never to joke about it; such "humor" could lead to very unpleasant consequences.

He was alone for this particular visitation. This would have been unusual just six months ago, but his status had been slightly elevated lately, thanks to Janel's careful manipulation of the tallies. Now Sisko might find himself doing a solo venture as often as twice a month. He relished these occasions; though the shuttles were tiny, short-distance-capacity things with powerful homing signals, the trips still gave a fairly convincing impression of freedom—not to mention the sweet, sweet silence he could enjoy in the cockpit.

This moon had some long, ancient name that most people didn't bother to remember. It seemed much too small and insignificant a place to have such an important-sounding name. Apparently, some old Bajoran astronomer had named it for a woman—a woman with a very long name—whom he had been in love with. But nowadays, most people in the Trivas system referred to it either as "the second moon" or "number two."

Sisko's shuttle landed on an old concrete platform, possibly the foundation of a long-gone building, set a short distance outside of a scattered Terran colony that he had visited twice before.

This particular client had missed three payments already, and Sisko wasn't sure how many more he could cover, especially after the conversation with Janel. He might have to engage in some actual coercion if these people didn't start coming up with some cold, hard latinum. The trouble was, it was no fun to coerce a blind man who'd lost the ability to string two coherent syllables together. The man had been badly injured in a mining accident, and the parent company that owned the mine's interests had paid to put the man back together again. His medical expenses had been astronomical, despite the fact that the Terran doctors who'd been paid to slap him back together hadn't done the most competent job at it—not good enough for him to ever be able to work again, anyway.

It was with the blind man's sister that Sisko usually dealt, a tall, strong-willed woman named Kasidy. She was pretty, voluptuous, and lippy. Part of Sisko dreaded dealing with her again, but another part of him, a part he wished to deny, could not wait to see her. He wasn't sure which part was going to dominate this afternoon.

The blind man was sitting outside a large round tent supported by a series of poles set into the hard, dusty ground. One of his legs was twisted beneath his body in an unnatural posture, but Kasidy had assured Sisko that her brother always sat that way; it seemed to agitate him if anyone tried to move him. The man, whose name was Kornelius, sat silently, his half-lidded eyes seeming to be shrouded in an unseeing fog.

Kornelius did not stir when Sisko walked around to the entrance of the tent. There was a bell on a string that Kasidy had rigged, and Sisko pulled it while simultaneously throwing back the flap to the entrance.

"Miss Yates?" he bellowed. "It's Benjamin Sisko from Akiem. Yes, it's that time again, Miss Yates. Come out, come out, wherever you are."

The tent was dim inside, but once Sisko's eyes adjusted to the low light, he could see a faint moving shadow from behind a partition, a shadow of a woman's seated figure. He felt his face heat up for a moment as his eyes traced the lines of the woman's body. The figure rose, the shadow's projection on the fabric screen suddenly resembling a malformed giant, and the partition was whipped aside.

"I'm not *hiding* from you, if that's what you're implying, Mister Sisko."

Sisko folded his arms. "I would never suggest such a thing, Miss Yates. It's dark in here."

"Light enough for me to do my mending by," she muttered, but she picked up a very small palm beacon from the floor, switched it on, and set it back down, its narrow, yellow finger of light pointed at the ceiling. "Power cells cost money."

"Am I to interpret that as you telling me that you still can't pay?"

Kasidy angrily gestured to the outside of the tent, indicating her brother. "How am I supposed to pay? I can't leave him alone all day, and I can't get much more work than the mending I do—and that's all just to trade for food, clean water. If the Cardassians intended to patch him up just enough to make him a liability to me, then they did an excellent job."

"Should they have let him die?"

Kasidy frowned, looking ashamed. "No," she said in a low voice. "Of course not. But if they can't understand that he is now a full-time job to me, then I don't know what else I can possibly tell them."

Sisko could find no reply, and Kasidy went on. Her shoulders sagged, and she rubbed her fingers along the upper part of her jaw. "It was a trap, the entire job. They would give him work in the mines, they said, but he would have to pay them back for his tools. He would have to pay them back for his clothes, for his shoes, his meals, and the living quarters they gave him. They never mentioned the interest they were planning to charge him—and increase every quarter. They never mentioned that the clothes, the tools—all of it—would cost triple or quadruple what they would have cost for anyone but a Terran, even without the interest. Even before the accident, there was no way he would ever have been able to get out from under them. It's what they do to all of us Terrans." She raised her eyes to meet his. "Is this what they've done to you, too?"

Ben met her gaze evenly. He felt deeply annoyed with her, though he knew she spoke the truth. He didn't know what good it did to reiterate the bleak details of reality. "What do *you* think?"

Kasidy folded her arms. "Well, then, I suppose I can't entirely fault you for doing what you're doing. But you know as well as anyone that you're never going to get one thin strip of latinum from me, or probably from any of your Terran clients, for that matter."

Sisko struggled for a moment before finally succumbing to his frustration. "Now you listen to me, Kasidy Yates," he snarled. "I have covered for you and Kornelius the past *three months*. I wish I could help you, I do. But it's every man for himself, can't you see that? If you don't start paying—and *soon*—I'm going to have to make good on my job. I'm going to have to turn you over to them."

Kasidy slowly shifted her weight to one hip, but she didn't answer, and Sisko rambled on. "I don't have a choice in the matter, Miss Yates. There's nothing more I can do. Why can't you just make my job a little easier and come up with some cash? Do you think . . . I *like* doing this?"

Kasidy didn't budge, her expression unmoved. "You don't *dislike* it enough to stop, I'd wager."

Sisko was getting angrier by the second. "And how am I supposed to stop?" he snapped.

"They've given you access to a shuttle! If you had any gumption at all, you'd learn to reprogram it, to sabotage the homing signal. How difficult could it be? You could get yourself out of here."

"And run for the rest of my life?"

"That's what I'd do, if I were in your shoes."

"Well, you're not, are you?"

Kasidy shifted her weight to the other hip, unfolded her arms. "No, I'm not." Her gaze was penetrating. Something in her eyes, her expression, Sisko was not sure exactly what, but he suddenly felt that he couldn't take it anymore. Was she judging him? Did she pity him? He felt a subtle but powerful snap occurring somewhere deep inside him, and his hands tightened into involuntary fists.

"What's the matter?" Kasidy said softly.

"I . . . I . . ." Sisko stammered, feeling hot tears beginning to leak from the corners of his eyes. "I don't know," he whispered. "I just . . . don't know if I can keep this up . . . but I . . . I . . . don't know what else to do."

"Ben," Kasidy said, using his given name for the first time that he could remember. "We have to work together, not fight each other. Can't you see what they're doing to us?"

Before he quite knew what was happening, she had put her arms around him. Her body was warm and yielding. The hands stroking the back of his neck seemed to erase the tension he had been carrying there for years. He couldn't remember the last time he had held Jennifer like this. He wondered if he had ever held her like this.

"Kasidy," he whispered, and then his lips were on her neck, and then they were on her soft, welcoming mouth. There was a pallet behind the fabric partition, and Kasidy pulled him to the makeshift bed, gently guiding him down, pressing the weight of her body against his chest and legs.

I can't do this, I'm a married man. Sisko pushed the thought aside, pushed aside all thoughts of his wife. Jennifer had come to believe that the marriage had always been a farce, and deep in his heart, he feared she was right. He routinely told himself that he truly loved her, but he knew as well as she did that the benefits he could enjoy from the association with her prestigious family would always overshadow any feelings he had ever had for her. At this point, he couldn't even remember if he *had* loved her, though he wanted to believe that he had.

He succumbed to Kasidy's caresses with no further thoughts of Jennifer.

Their bodies moved hard together. Sisko held her so tightly she cried out, and he did not know if it was from pain or pleasure. He didn't let go, but she didn't seem to resist him, either. When they finished, they were both slick with perspiration. Sisko let her go, finally loosening his hands. He moved out from beneath her body. "I'm sorry," he murmured. "I . . . shouldn't have . . ."

"It doesn't matter," Kasidy said brusquely. "I know you're married, Ben. Sometimes you just have to . . . live for the moment. Because you don't know how much longer you *will* live."

Sisko was silent, numb, as he watched her get up and put her clothes back on. He started to reach for his shirt, but Kasidy sat back down on the pallet before he could dress. She reached for his hand.

"We could all get out of here," she said suddenly. Her expression was wild, now. "We could all just *go*. Anywhere, like I was saying. Reprogram the shuttle. You, me, Kornelius. There are Terran colonies not terribly far from here that the Alliance has mostly left alone, on worlds where there aren't enough resources to bother with. We could make do, just like I've been doing here. Barter, beg, borrow, steal. Just think of it—never have to cower in fear from them ever again."

"I'm not going to run for the rest of my life."

One corner of Kasidy's mouth twisted. "You're a fool if you can't see that you're running now."

Sisko shook his head. "You're crazy," he said.

"I'm *not*," she said, and stood up, folded her arms the way she had done before, when she was silently judging him. "You're the one who's crazy, if you'd rather just keep living like this."

Sisko put his clothes back on and turned to go.

Janel Tigan was shaking his head as he pulled at his Romulan ale. Janel and Sisko were alone in the tavern tonight, as they were most weeknights, except for the proprietor, a Terran man who tended bar. He was off in the back room, probably looking over his gambling receipts. He would come out, if he was summoned, but otherwise the two men had little need to fear being overheard or observed.

"Janel, come on. You've got to help me just this one last time. I promise, this will be the only exception. This woman . . . there's simply no way she's going to be able to pay. Her brother is . . . he's had irreparable damage to his brain, he can't work, she can't leave him . . . Her situation is desperate."

"And what do you care, exactly?" Janel said, turning on his bar stool and simultaneously wiping his mouth with the back of his hand.

"I . . . don't," Sisko said. "Except that it's just . . . it's not right, what's happened to her brother. I don't know."

Janel made a face, pursing his lips. "I can read you like a book, Ben Sisko," the Trill declared. "You've had . . . relations with this woman, haven't you?"

Sisko tried to prevent his expression from darkening, but Janel clucked his tongue.

"Ahh," he said, and then chuckled. "I knew eventually you'd come around to it, considering that cold fish you married."

"Don't," Sisko said, pained. He'd always had an inkling that Janel didn't care for Jennifer, but he preferred not to hear about it, and Janel knew it. Sisko had a feeling that maybe the Trill had drunk more than usual. He wasn't acting drunk—he never did—but he was being even more outspoken than usual.

"My apologies," the Trill said, and finished his ale. For once, he didn't immediately call for another. Instead, he leaned in very close to Sisko, startling him with the sudden proximity. "I'll help you this one last time," he murmured. "But maybe it's time you did something for me."

"I . . ." Sisko pulled away a little, confused. "What do you have in mind?"

Janel did not stop crowding Sisko, and slowly he placed one of his startlingly cold hands on Sisko's cheek, tracing the line of his jaw with his index finger. "You must have an idea, by now, of what I want from you," the Trill whispered.

"You . . . you mean . . ."

Janel's face was now less than a finger's width from Sisko's. "I don't generally take risks like that for just anyone," he said, and then he kissed him on the mouth.

Sisko was too surprised to resist at first, but then he broke away. "I can't," he gasped. "Janel, I don't . . . see you that way."

The Trill's expression slowly hardened. He turned away, and then frowned into his empty tankard glass. "Fine," he said. "If that's the way you want it. But . . . I don't know why you thought I'd keep doing you favors forever, without your offering anything in return."

Sisko's heart sank as he realized, by the other man's expression, what was going on here. He had really hurt his friend, but Sisko didn't see how he could give him what he wanted. "I'm sorry," he said. "But Janel . . . you yourself told me . . . that when you're lusting for something . . ."

"I guess I must have broken my own rules, where you were concerned," the Trill said. "I guess I thought . . . my friendship with you . . . transcended those rules. Transcended *lust*. I guess I thought maybe you might feel that way too. But I guess I was stupid."

"I'm sorry," Sisko said again, and he stood to go.

"If you can't even be intimate with someone you consider to be a friend," Janel said flatly, "then I don't know how you think you could perform for a woman like the Intendant. She's a predator, plain and simple. A detestable person, Ben."

Sisko didn't say anything.

Janel turned away and called for another drink.

As Sisko turned to leave, the Trill called after him. "You'd better watch your back," he shouted, "because you never know who's going to be holding that knife."

"What are you saying?"

"I've got a lot on you, Benjamin Sisko," Janel said. "Too much for you to make an enemy of me."

"We've been friends a long time, Janel. I thought I could trust you."

Janel laughed. "You're a fool if you think a Terran can ever trust *anyone.*"

Stan Devitt stood with his hands locked behind his back, staring out the small, oval window of his cramped office. Sisko did not know why he'd been called to see his father-in-law, but he had a few ideas, and most of them were making his palms sweat profusely.

"Benny," Stan said, which caused Sisko to cringe inside. Jennifer's father only called him Benny when he was trying to project the appearance of camaraderie; in truth, it always came off as disingenuous. Especially since Sisko had never liked the nickname. He was sure he was in trouble.

"We've done our best to make you happy here," Stan said. "I feel as though everything you've been given here far surpasses the expectations of even a high-born Terran."

"I can't argue with that," Sisko said, scratching at the back of his neck and wishing he could sit down. Stan had not offered him a seat, and it seemed wrong to sit when the other man was standing.

"But it's not enough for you?" Stan turned from the window to face his son-in-law.

"Of course it is," Sisko said. He hoped his voice didn't come out as strangled as it seemed in his own head.

"Well." Stan smiled. "You would come straight to me with any problems that you had, wouldn't you?"

"Yes, yes, of course I would."

"Because we're *family,* Benny. You can trust me with anything. You know that, right? You are married to my daughter, after all. Your interests are my interests."

There was a long silence. Sisko felt compelled to say *something*, to break the awful, loaded quiet. He felt almost certain that Janel had gone to Stan behind his back, had said something to implicate him. His only recourse now would be to turn the tables on the Trill. "Janel Tigan," he said. "I . . . I don't think I can trust him. I think he is going to try to . . . blackmail me."

"Tigan?" Stan looked confused. "Blackmail you . . . with what?"

"He . . . he made a pass at me," Sisko said quickly. "I refused him. He didn't take it well—he threatened me, said he would make up something that would . . . that would be bad for all of us. You, me, Jennifer, all of us. He—he said that Terrans can't trust anyone."

Stan frowned deeply. "He wasn't lying about that, at least," he muttered. "We can't trust anyone but each other. I suppose I always knew Janel Tigan wasn't above dealing from the bottom of the deck. Those Trill—they don't have many taboos when it comes to their . . . sexual proclivities." The frown twisted itself into a tight smile. "Don't worry about him, Benny. I'll see to it that he won't trouble us."

"Thank you, sir," Sisko said, and almost turned to go before Stan spoke again.

"You don't want to work for the Intendant, do you, Benny?"

The Intendant? Instantly, Sisko could have kicked himself. *Of course!* That must be why Stan had called him here, not because of anything to do with Janel Tigan. "No, I would certainly prefer not to. But she made it sound as though I might not have a choice."

Stan looked grim. "She is very, very powerful, it's true," he said. "But I might be able to do something. I can lean on her political rivals. The Intendant of Empok Nor could make trouble for Kira Nerys, and she knows it. I'm only a Terran, but . . . if I set the right things in motion, there may be something I can do to keep both you and Jennifer close to me. But that's only if you don't *want* to work for her. I wouldn't stand in your way, of course, if you would prefer . . ."

"No," Sisko said. "I don't want to live on Terok Nor."

Stan smiled, looked genuinely relieved. "Well, that's settled," he said. "Because believe me, Benny, whatever she's promised you—it will come with a price. Hopefully, I can keep you both here." He nodded, his gaze unfocused, as if mulling it over to himself. "Yes, I think I might be able to do it."

Sisko felt semi-relieved, but at the same time, there was a sense of loss, considering that the possibility of having his own ship would truly be off the table. *Not that it ever could really have happened,* he thought. He hoped he hadn't just made a dangerous mistake, mentioning Janel Tigan. There was always the possibility that Stan would believe whatever Janel would say to counter Sisko's claims, but he hoped that his father-in-law would genuinely side with family, like he had said. With nothing further to discuss, Sisko left his father-in-law's office.

Sisko had an unusually unpleasant week following the conversation with Stan Devitt. He'd been forced to twist a few arms a little harder than he might have preferred, but he told himself that there were worse things than putting the fear of the Alliance into a few deadbeats. He'd only gotten one man to actually pay up so far, and the implications of what he was going to have to do down the road were exhausting. *But I knew this was what I signed on for,* he reminded himself. In fact, it frightened him a little to find that it was almost therapeutic, at times, to have a target on which he could take out his aggressions. The crack of bone in one man's thumb was oddly satisfying, the screams of a middle-aged woman did little to unnerve him. Sisko wasn't sure if he liked this new version of himself, but he didn't see any alternative.

Sisko might have been able to put the troubling situation with Janel out of his mind altogether, if the Trill's glaring absence hadn't been so apparent. Nobody had seen Tigan since the day after the "meeting" Sisko had attended with Stan Devitt. He told himself he didn't have time to worry about it, but he kept coming back to it. Perhaps he was not as cold-hearted as he might have wished. Janel was his friend, and Sisko was worried about him.

He had ventured to the tavern on his shabby homeworld only once. On the last evening of the week, he decided it might be time to try again. Maybe Janel would reappear. Maybe he had gone away to Trill, or to New Sydney on some business-related venture. It had happened before, though usually not for such a long time.

There was someone seated at the bar when Benjamin walked in, but it was not Janel. It was a Farian, someone who worked for Akiem, a man named Thadial Bokar. Bokar worked in close proximity with Stan Devitt, and Sisko had never liked him much, but he was especially chagrined to see him now. Bokar had never had cause to come to this tavern before.

"Benjamin Sisko," the man exclaimed, causing Sisko to balk. He had never bothered to address Benjamin with more than a grunt before this moment.

"Hello," Sisko said carefully.

"I don't suppose I could buy you a drink?" the man said.

Sisko didn't say anything. Something was definitely amiss here. Bokar was being altogether too familiar.

"Janel tells me you really love your synthale," the Farian went on.

"Janel," Benjamin repeated.

"Sure," Bokar said. "I know the two of you were friendly." He chortled. "If you could call it *friendly.*"

Sisko's mouth suddenly felt uncomfortably dry, and he swallowed. "Just what are you implying?"

Bokar shrugged. "Nothing that you have to worry about anymore."

"Oh no?" Sisko said. He did not like this at all.

"No, no. Janel Tigan is gone. He decided to go back to Trill. Or, I should say, I decided for him. Permanently."

"Wh . . . what do you mean, permanently?"

Bokar grinned. "I'd expected you to act a little more grateful than this," he said. "Considering."

Sisko stood frozen in his tracks for a moment before he took a step backward. "I'll take a rain check on that drink," he said quietly. "Thank you, though." He turned to go.

The next morning, Sisko created an excuse to use a shuttle. He had two errands in mind, and felt deeply conflicted about both of them.

His first stopover was to see Kasidy Yates.

Kornelius still sat near the back of the tent as Sisko approached, his murky gray eyes aimed toward the colorless sky above. Sisko supposed the injured man could likely still discern the difference between dark and light, which might have been why he preferred to sit outside. "Hello," Sisko said, but Kornelius didn't answer. He never did.

"Miss Yates?" Sisko called as he pulled the bell-cord, and then, "Kasidy?"

She appeared almost immediately, looking possibly even more beautiful than she had before. Her lips were soft and red, her eyes bright, and her skin glowing, despite the unforgiving climate of the world where she lived. Her hair was pulled off her face with a piece of twine. She was wiping her hands on a torn piece of cloth sacking; it seemed she had been cooking something over a small shipping container with some warming chemicals she had set up in the center of the tent.

"What is it, Ben?" She sounded tired, but there was a glint of hopefulness in her voice.

"You have to pay me," Sisko said. He did not look at her. "The man who has been helping me cover for you is dead. If you can't pay . . . then I can't be responsible for what will happen to you and your brother."

Kasidy's mouth hardened. "You can't be responsible?" she repeated.

"I am trying to warn you," Sisko said. "Please, just—"

"Just what? Just wait here to die? That's essentially what you're telling me."

"Kasidy, you can just go to work in the mines like everyone else. Your brother doesn't need much help—he just sits there all day long."

"You could help us get away," Kasidy said, gesturing to the place beyond the transient village where shuttles could dock. "We could all get away, Ben."

"I will not spend the rest of my life looking over my shoulder," he snapped. "If I'm going to be free, it's going to be on my terms. I won't answer to *anyone.*"

"Then you're looking for the wrong kind of freedom," Kasidy shouted back. "I would rather die owing those bastards money than give them *anything.* Unlike you, who have given them your *soul.*"

She turned and stalked away from him, leaving Benjamin standing dumbly in the entrance of her tent.

Sisko left. He didn't have time to argue with Kasidy Yates, not today. There was too much to be done today, and too much at stake for his own situation. He had tried to warn her, hadn't he? It wasn't his fault if she wouldn't listen. Was it?

As he left, he saw movement from the corner of his eye, and

turned to see that Kornelius had shifted his posture. The blind man's head was no longer tilted toward the sky; indeed, he appeared to be staring straight in Sisko's direction. To his great surprise, the blind simpleton spoke.

"None of us is free," he said. Sisko gaped at the man, waited to see if he would say anything else, but he only turned his face back toward the sun.

None of us is free. Was he only imitating something he had heard his sister say often? Or was there genuine coherence behind the words? Sisko immediately considered a terrible possibility.

Terran spies. The Alliance liked to employ Terrans for certain duties, and they liked to pit Terrans against each other. Could this entire situation with Kasidy have been a setup from the beginning, to expose him? Could her urgings to "run away" be a ruse, to test him?

Sisko stopped to laugh at himself as he boarded his shuttle. The blind man would not have given himself away if he were truly a spy. Kasidy Yates certainly was not working for the Alliance. Her situation on this world was perilous, but Sisko believed her when she said that she would rather die than given anything to the Cardassian-Klingon Alliance.

Sisko enabled the shuttle to return to one of its preprogrammed destinations, one of the satellite locations for Akiem on Trivas, the one where Stan Devitt's office was located. His hands trembled slightly at the controls. *I am becoming paranoid,* he told himself. If he couldn't place his trust in another Terran, then maybe things were truly hopeless.

A communiqué alerted on the dash; it was Stan Devitt. Benjamin answered the call with deep reluctance. If there was ever a Terran that he *couldn't* trust . . .

"Benjamin," the older man barked, his voice foreshortened by the comm. *"You need to return to headquarters right away."*

"I'm on my way right now."

But when Sisko reached his destination, he did not go to his father-in-law's office. Instead, he wasted little time in locating the person with whom he meant to confer. Thadial Bokar was sometimes difficult to find, as the Farian liked to be anywhere but the large office shared by the lower-echelon employees, but Sisko just happened to get lucky.

Thadial was waiting for a turbolift on the main floor, probably to ride it aimlessly as a means of passing the time.

"Bokar," Sisko called to the cocky Farian. "Remember that drink you offered me last night?"

"Sure," Bokar said smoothly. "Don't tell me—it's sixteen hundred hours somewhere, right?"

Sisko smiled. "Yes, well, I was thinking that maybe I could take you up on that offer. I don't have any appointments for the afternoon, and I'm unusually thirsty today. How about it?"

Bokar shrugged. "Sure," he said. "Why not?"

Sisko directed Bokar to the transporter pad as quickly as he could without seeming too suspicious. He needed to get out of here before Stan happened to see him, but he didn't want Bokar to have any reason to balk at coming along.

"Where shall we go?" Bokar said as he stepped on the pad. Sisko quickly began touching the destination coordinates before Bokar could get at it.

"I've got a place in mind," he said.

"Fine," the Farian said, and stood back to wait for the transport, his expression guileless and content. He was pleased to be leaving work.

But when he and Sisko materialized on the farthest side of Trivas, surrounded as they were by old, broken-down mining equipment and tumbleweeds, Bokar's face read bemusement.

"I thought the old mine was shut down here," Bokar remarked, looking around at the desolation that surrounded them. "Is this where you meant to take us, Ben?"

Sisko didn't answer. He stepped off the transporter pad, herding Bokar along, and drew his disruptor. "Tell me about Janel," he said softly.

The Farian raised his hands, a sudden sheen breaking out around the sides of his face. "J-Janel? Tigan?"

"Tigan," Sisko replied, his voice low now; but it was lost over the desolation that surrounded them, the abandoned machinery looming eerily in the background.

"I was only . . . hey, your father-in-law told me he was going to give you some trouble."

"Did he really go back to Trill?"

Bokar shrugged. "It's just like I said—he's not coming back."

"Because he's dead."

The Farian flinched. "You don't have to . . . to . . ."

"Speak the truth?"

"Fine, yes. He's dead. I don't know what you want from me, Benjamin. Stan Devitt told me Janel was up to no good."

"And you had every intention of blackmailing me, didn't you? You were *threatening* me, at the tavern."

"You're paranoid."

"I don't think I am," Sisko said. "But if you were in my position, wouldn't *you* be?"

The Farian looked angry. He started to lower his hands. "The man was a lecherous drunk, anyway. He didn't deserve to—"

Sisko squeezed the trigger. There was a blinding flash of light, the briefest sliver of a scream from Thadial Bokar, and then the man was lying in an unkempt, sizzling heap on the ground.

Sisko stared at the body. He felt calm, though he was not entirely sure what had prompted him to do what he just did. *Terrans can't trust anyone,* Janel had said. This Farian was going to talk to someone, Sisko was sure of it. *Or at least,* he told himself as he dragged the man's body toward an abandoned mine shaft, *there was enough of a chance . . . Letting him live was not an option.*

He could not consider the possibility that he had just killed the man for revenge. Janel *was* his friend. But then, Janel had threatened to blackmail Sisko even more blatantly than Thadial Bokar had. It made little sense to Sisko that he really wanted revenge on behalf of a man who was trying to ruin him, and so he did not allow himself to consider it further.

Sisko could hardly believe how cool he felt when he returned to Akiem headquarters, his shoulder smarting slightly from the effort of lifting the dead weight of the other man's lifeless body. *Maybe I am suited to this sort of work,* he decided.

He hadn't walked two steps off the transporter when he got a summons from Stan Devitt to come to his office right away. The ill-placed composure he had been feeling suddenly vanished, and he reluctantly headed for his father-in-law's office.

Stan was seated behind his desk, which was a flimsy, inexpensive unit. It was obviously designed for a Cardassian, as it was a little too tall for Stan to use comfortably. The Cardassians didn't care to outfit Stan with anything better than the absolute essentials. "Benjamin," he said, as Sisko walked through the door, and he knew immediately that he was about to be disciplined for something; otherwise, Stan probably would have called him "Benny" again.

"Sir?"

Stan picked up a padd from the clutter on his desk. "I have here a manifest that tells me you have gone to the number two colonized moon of Trivas twice in just under a week, the last time being this very morning. Do you care to explain?"

"I've got a client who needs a little extra persuasion," he said quickly. "I'm trying a new approach. I—"

"The man is a disabled, blind Terran, Benjamin. What kind of coercion could he possibly need, aside from the good-old-fashioned kind?"

"He . . . he can't pay," Sisko said, scrambling for words. "I don't mean to say that I'm trying to let him off the hook, it's just that—"

"Benjamin, it is imperative that we treat all of our clients exactly the same, no matter the circumstances. We are not interested in the personal details of these people's lives. We are interested in helping them keep their payments current with the Cardasssians, so that their lives can continue without further . . . complication. This is a service we perform, and it seems to me that if you've let this man slide in any way, then you are doing him no favors. You are doing him the *opposite* of a favor."

"Yes, sir. I know that. But—"

"If you are telling me that you can't handle a blind man, then I need to find someone else for this job." He pressed his thumb and forefinger into the bridge of his nose. "Please, Benjamin, you are family. I don't want to hear from you that I have to find someone else to do what you have been hired to do. Do you understand?"

"Yes, sir."

"Good. Now, I want you to go back there immediately, and kill the man's sister."

Sisko couldn't move or speak for a moment before he finally found a reply. "Sir, the sister is the only one who's capable of coming up with any money," he said. "The man can't work at all. If we kill her, we'll never see a single strip of latinum."

"Then kill him," Stan said, shrugging. "I don't know why the Cardassians even bothered to save him, unless they saw it as a means to earn more money. My records are showing that he was pretty badly off after the accident, but he's still got one functioning kidney. If you can find the right markets, nonreplicated Terran organs can fetch a decent price. He's probably got some implants that are worth a thing or two, as well." He began to click away at his keypad. "I'll look into it while you're gone. Hopefully I'll have a buyer by the time you get back."

You could help us get away. We could all get away, Ben.

Sisko was thinking that he was going to have to learn to reprogram the shuttle after all, and he was going to have to do it quickly. He excused himself, but Stan wasn't finished with him yet. The older man spoke again, just as Sisko was about to turn and go.

"I'll send my man Thadial Bokar along with you, to make sure it's done right." Stan pressed a comm panel on his desk, but he got no response. "Damned Farian," he muttered, "Can never find him when I need him. Don't know why we keep him around." He pressed his comm panel again. "En Shrall," he said crisply into the receiver. "I've got an assignment for you, and it starts now. Report to my office."

A surly-looking Andorian appeared a few moments later, his antennae squirming. His defiant posture suggested that he did not appreciate being in the position of being told what to do by a Terran, but he at least projected the appearance of respect with Stan, nodding and accepting the short briefing that followed. Sisko followed the white-haired man out toward where the shuttles were docked, his mind scrambling to formulate a plan, but he could come up with nothing.

Sisko thought he might pretend to get lost on the way from the shuttle dock to the Terran encampment on the moon where Kasidy lived, but the Andorian was too savvy and efficient for such tactics; he found his own way to Kasidy's tent without even consulting Sisko about the location.

Kornelius was still sitting outside the tent in the same posture Benjamin had left him in. He had a dark stain on the front of his shirt that had not been there before. Kasidy must have come out to feed him just after Sisko had left. Otherwise, the scene remained almost entirely unchanged from the way Sisko had last seen it.

"Kornelius Yates," shouted En Shrall, his midnight-blue eyes narrowing.

Kornelius did not turn his head, did not acknowledge that his name had been called, only sat, his eyes as pale and colorless as the Andorian's were dark.

En Shrall drew his disruptor, and Sisko heard himself say "Stop!" but the word was lost over the screech of the disruptor. Kornelius's body sat upright for only an instant more before slumping over and, in what seemed like grotesque slow motion, falling to the dusty ground. The leg that was normally pinned so awkwardly beneath his body extended at an odd angle, causing Sisko to flinch. He looked away, his stomach roiling with nausea.

Sisko looked at his hands, and they were shaking. "What—why—"

"That's how it's done," En Shrall snarled. He headed for the entrance of the tent, but Kasidy had heard the disruptor, and came running outside.

Sisko's eyes locked on Kasidy's for a terrible moment while he watched her take in the scene before her, and then she opened her mouth and screamed.

En Shrall tossed a padd at her feet just as her knees were beginning to buckle. Her hands picked it up, but she did not seem to understand what it was. She was weeping and crying as if her heart had just broken clean in two. She pressed the padd to her chest and sobbed like a child.

"Kasidy," Sisko whispered, and at the sound of his voice she abruptly stopped crying, meeting his gaze once more. She rose to her feet, but she said nothing, only hurled the padd at Sisko with all of her strength. He caught it and his eyes flickered to the sum listed at the bottom. It was three times the original amount.

"You've . . . incurred some interest," he said stupidly.

"Hurry *up*, Sisko!" The Andorian snarled. He had looped his forearms through Kornelius's armpits. "Get his legs, will you?"

Kasidy shrieked again. "What do you think you're doing? Where are you taking him? Don't *touch* him!" She beat her fists against Sisko's chest.

People were coming out of their tents to stare at the scene. "Stop it!" Sisko hissed to Kasidy. "You'll get yourself killed—and everyone else here, as well!" He wrestled himself away from her and grabbed Kornelius's ankles, helping the Andorian hustle the blind man's corpse back to the shuttle. Kasidy collapsed into a heap on the dirt outside her dwelling, screaming her brother's name, her cries escalating from grief to pure rage. Slowly, the onlookers went back inside their tents, and Sisko maneuvered the shuttle away from the desolation of the moon.

When Sisko reported to work the next day, there was a feeling of tension and chaos in the atmosphere that he could sense immediately. People were walking back and forth quickly through the corridors, engaging in clipped conversations, while others were gathered outside the turbolift in confidential little groups, passing information back and forth in urgent tones.

"What's going on?" Benjamin asked the first person he saw, a Ferengi named Lat.

"Bit of a kerfuffle," Lat said. "Cardassian survey team was out on the other side of Trivas today, doing some annual checks on properties that had been declared tapped out, that sort of thing. They came across the body of a Farian, and it hadn't been there long. Forty-eight hours, tops, they're saying." The Ferengi grinned, obviously delighted to be wielding such potent gossip. "Guess who it was?" he whispered happily.

"I . . . don't know," Sisko said. He felt suddenly disconnected from his body, as though he were observing the entire exchange from another room.

"It was that cocky Thadial Bokar, that's who. I always said that *quiet* would get what was coming to him." He spat the unfamiliar Ferengi curse in such a way that Sisko knew he probably didn't want to know exactly what it meant.

"Huh, yes, you did say that." Sisko could not be sure that his posture looked natural. He felt very much as though his bones were about to fail him altogether.

"Tech support is going over transporter configurations," Lat went on. "They found some footprints coming from the direction of the transport there, though it's hard to know which hub he might have come from. I'm sure they'll find it soon enough. Your wife is on the job right now, and we all know *she's* not going to leave any stones unturned."

"N-no," Sisko said.

Lat left him, and Sisko sat dumbly in the corridor, wishing to be absolutely anywhere but where he was.

The rest of the day passed by with Sisko in half a daze. He made an excuse to leave early, and as soon as he and Jennifer were taken home on the transport shuttle, he made a beeline for the tavern where he had once regularly gone with Janel Tigan.

The bartender brought him a synthale without being asked, and Sisko drained it quickly, but it was not long before he realized that it was probably not a good idea for him to drink alone. In fact, he decided, as he watched the bartender rub at a glass with a dingy cloth, if he was going to drink, this tavern, the tavern where he had recently been seen with both Janel Tigan and Thadial Bokar, was probably the very last place where he should be doing it.

But would it make me seem more guilty if I stopped coming here altogether? Sisko ordered another synthale, to clear his head, he told himself, but again he downed it rapidly and felt as though his thirst had not nearly been slaked; had not even been touched. *I should go,* he decided, but he ordered one more synthale. This one went down a little more slowly, and Sisko found that, even though sitting here at the bar alone was not especially enjoyable, it seemed that it must be far better than whatever was waiting for him at home.

Sisko lost count of how many ales he drank before he finally picked himself up from the bar stool and found his way back to the apartment that he shared with his wife. When he walked in the door, he expected Jennifer to be asleep, or maybe working on one of her many projects at the computer console in the bedroom. But the lights were all on, and Jennifer was sitting at the low-backed sofa in the front room. She did not appear to have been doing anything; she was apparently just waiting for him, and her expression made him very uneasy. He had found himself less and less able to read her moods in the past few years, but it could not have been more clear that she was unhappy about something.

"Hello, Jen," he said carefully.

"Hello," she replied. She lifted her chin slightly to look at him, but said nothing else. He stood before her without talking for a moment, and then he went to the kitchen for another synthale.

"I never see you anymore." Jennifer's voice came from where she sat on the couch.

Sisko walked back into the front room and stood before her once again. "I know," he said, hoping there was some way he could keep this fight as brief as possible. "I'm sorry."

"When I do see you, you're drunk."

He looked at the bottle in his hand. "I'm not drunk," he said softly.

"Yes, you are. I can always tell when you're drunk, even before you say anything. Your . . . your *posture* is different."

Sisko had no reply. He just continued to stare at the bottle in his hand. Was she really just angry about his drinking?

"Well, go ahead and have it," she said, indicating the synthale. "I'm not going to stop you. You're already drunk, it hardly matters."

There was a chime from the other room, indicating that a communiqué was coming in to the console.

"Who would be calling this late?" Sisko wondered.

"It's not that late," Jennifer said, and got up from the davenport to check the console.

Sisko didn't say anything to that; it felt very, very late to him, but he supposed it was only an effect of how exhausted he was.

Jennifer made a little sound, a clicking of her teeth, seeming to indicate that she was frustrated with whatever she saw on the console.

"What?" Sisko said, following after her. "Who is it?"

Jennifer pressed the receiver panel without answering him. The screen immediately drew up an image of a pale-skinned, wide-eyed woman with red hair and a silvery headpiece encircling her forehead. It was the Intendant of Terok Nor.

"Hello, Intendant," Jennifer said formally. "How good to hear from you at last."

"Jennifer," Kira replied, blinking her eyes rapidly and letting her mouth slide into a disarming smirk. *"I hope your husband is available."*

"He is," Jennifer said, turning to Sisko so that only he could see her dark expression. "You're lucky—he just walked in."

"Oh, wonderful," Kira said, craning her neck as if she could see

through the viewscreen. Sisko stepped into her periphery and did his best to look respectful.

"Intendant," he said.

"Benjamin, how positively lovely to see you. I was wondering if you wouldn't mind coming to pay me a little visit again. I'll send you a shuttle, just like last time."

Sisko did not look at Jennifer, but from the corner of his eye he could see her expression. "I'm not sure," he said carefully.

Kira laughed. *"Oh, Benjamin,"* she sighed, her voice a singsong. *"I'm sorry. I suppose I made that sound like a request, didn't I? Be ready to go at oh-eight-hundred tomorrow morning. I can't* wait *to see you!"* She flashed a brilliant smile, and then her image vanished from the screen.

Sisko shut down the console to ensure that any conversation he had with Jennifer could not be picked up by the receiver on Kira's end, and then turned to his wife.

"You'd better not even consider it," Jennifer warned him.

"What am I supposed to do?" he said. "Your father said he'd do what he could, but if he can't—"

"You'll figure it out," Jennifer said, and turned angrily to go into the bedroom. "You always do," she added, and then closed the door, leaving Benjamin alone. He looked down at his hands to find the un-opened bottle of synthale still there. He twisted off the cap and took a long swallow.

The Intendant was wearing her "uniform" for this meeting, in lieu of the revealing dress she had been clad in before, but the skin-tight black bodysuit she was dressed in was hardly less distracting than what she had worn at her prior meeting. She was half sitting, half lying on a set-tee with a few Klingon guards standing a few steps away. She gestured to them to back off, and they both did, seeming to vanish into the shadows of the half-darkened room.

"Now, then," she purred. "Let's get down to business, shall we? I understand you've found yourself in a very uncomfortable situation."

Sisko, who had not been invited to sit, fidgeted with his hands behind his back. "I'm not sure if I know what you're talking about," he said.

Kira raised her eyebrows, pushing her lower lip out, mocking confusion. "Oh, no? It's interesting, your saying that. I have eyes and ears everywhere, Benjamin. *Everywhere.* Nothing goes on in this sector without my knowing about it. In this entire *quadrant.*"

"Really?" Sisko's voice was dry.

"Yes, really." She shifted her posture so that she was sitting up now, her feet on the floor, her hands spread out at her sides. "I have a feeling, Benjamin, that right now, even as you stand here, there is some ugly business that you wish very much would go away."

Sisko continued to fidget, though he willed his hands to stay still. "Everyone's got something that they wish would just go away, I guess."

"Not me," Kira said. "Because I *make it* go away."

"That must be nice for you."

"It is," she said. "And it would be nice for you, too, wouldn't it? If I would make all of your problems go away?"

Sisko only shrugged.

Kira sighed and pulled her feet up on the settee again. "Well, Benjamin, have you thought any more about my offer? Your own ship, your own crew? No more monitoring your comings and goings, at least not the way Akiem has been doing. No more confinement to a solitary star system. No destination locks, no orders to follow—from anyone but me, that is."

Sisko tried a laugh. "Can you really imagine me, Intendant—a Terran—commanding a ship?"

Kira looked serious. "I can," she said. "It's not entirely unheard-of, you know. Look at Stan Devitt. Wouldn't you like to be in a position like his?"

Sisko thought of his father-in-law's too-tall Cardassian desk, the look of contempt that En Shrall had tried to conceal when he came into Stan's office and took his orders. "Not really," he said truthfully.

"Well, forget him," Kira said. "*Your* position would be so much better than that. Because"—she rose to her feet and walked slowly, deliberately, toward Sisko, her hips rolling suggestively under the tight fabric of her suit—"you would work for *me*. And everyone would know it."

Sisko stiffened as she touched his shoulder, examining him as though he were a piece of merchandise. "Very nice," she murmured, and then she laughed when she saw his expression. "Oh, Benjamin," she said, reaching up to touch his face with one soft, cool hand. "What's the matter? I don't bite."

"That's not what I've heard," he breathed, though he instantly regretted it. He could not afford to make her genuinely angry.

The Intendant did not get angry; in fact, she seemed to take it as a compliment. She laughed as if he had told a very fine joke, and took a few steps away from him, though she continued to circle him as though she were sizing him up for a meal. "It's not as if you've been entirely faithful to Jennifer," she remarked.

"I love my wife," he said, but it came out hollow.

"Is that right?" the Intendant said. "How sweet. Or is it only that you were infatuated with her? Or, more specifically, what you could get from her?"

"Of course not," Sisko said weakly. He felt ashamed, and it was making him angry, but he could not allow himself to lose his temper. Kira was trying to get under his skin, and he could not allow her to succeed.

"It would hurt her deeply if she were ever to hear that you had been with another woman," Kira said. "I understand that, Benjamin. I understand why you have a problem with coming to work for me. I'm sure you've heard stories about me." She smiled.

"You could say that."

"Well, Benjamin, I wouldn't ever want to force you to do anything you wouldn't be comfortable with."

"That's good," Sisko said, though he did not trust her word for a moment.

Kira's smile faded. "I'd rather you came to me willingly," she said, her voice husky, her meaning clear. She took a step toward him, but didn't touch him, only tipped her head back so that she could stare up at him. She was a good head shorter than he was, even in her stiletto-heeled shoes, but somehow her presence was absolutely terrifying.

Sisko swallowed. "Oh," he said, feeling as though he had just stepped into a snare. "Well, I . . ."

"Listen, Benjamin," Kira said. "Suppose I speak to Jennifer for you, and explain to her exactly how beneficial a thing this job could be for you? Would you like that?"

Sisko shook his head. "No . . . please. Leave Jennifer out of it. I don't want—"

"You don't want to hurt her? Is that it?" Kira laughed lightly. "Well, it seems to me that it is going to hurt her very much when her husband is implicated in the murder of that Farian, what was his name, Thadial Bokar? Not to mention Janel Tigan."

His legs felt wooden. "What do you know about Janel Tigan?" he demanded recklessly. "The man disappeared nearly two weeks ago—I had nothing to do with it, he was my friend—my best friend!"

"Oh, I believe that you didn't have anything to do with it initially. But it wouldn't be difficult for a casual observer to start making certain . . . connections, Benjamin, let alone someone with the kind of resources that Jennifer has at her disposal. She is a very, very intelligent woman, Benjamin. Not just intelligent, but *clever*. It's not likely that she won't eventually figure out what happened. And, to be honest, I don't know if I'll be in a position to make you the same offer, when that happens."

Sisko struggled to breathe normally. He didn't know whether to be angry or sad anymore. He mostly only felt numb.

"Like I say, Benjamin, it's very nice to have a friend who can make ugly business go away for you."

"What, exactly, are you proposing to me?"

Kira smiled. "Nothing, yet. Aside from offering, once again, for you to go to work for me. I haven't gotten a read yet as to whether this offer appeals to you or not."

Sisko shook his head. "I can't," he said. *There has to be another way.*

"Ah," Kira said, looking sad. She went back to her settee and stretched out her shapely legs. "It's too bad, Benjamin."

He sighed. "May I please go?"

Kira frowned to herself. "Of course you may go," she said. "You're not one of my ore-processing workers, after all."

"No, I'm not," he said, though her words pained him. Shouldn't it be enough for him, to have all that he had: a beautiful wife, a prestigious job that most Terrans could never hope for? Shouldn't it have been enough that he didn't have to work in the mines like the other Terrans? Hadn't that been enough for him to be happy? To feel free? *But now I may have sabotaged all that forever.*

He turned to go, but Kira called him back. "Wait," she said.

"What is it?" he turned to face her again.

She pressed a finger to her chin, appearing thoughtful. "How about this," she said. "What if I offer you a shuttle?"

"A shuttle?"

"Yes. The shuttle that you used to get to Terok Nor and back. I mean, without the program locks. You could just use it entirely at your leisure, go wherever you want—within reason, of course; it's only a small passenger shuttle with low fuel capacity—with no strings attached?"

Sisko was suspicious, but he could not help but be intrigued at the suggestion. "Why would you do a thing like that?"

"It's a gift, that's all. A gift between friends." She hugged her knees to her chest like a little girl, and smiled radiantly.

"I can't take it. You know that I can't."

"Well, then, if you won't accept it, maybe you would just like to . . . *borrow* it, for the day. Just for one day, Benjamin. If you like it, you can keep it. But if you'd rather not, you can just bring it right back. I promise, I won't ask anything of you in return."

"Just for the day?" Sisko asked, thinking immediately of Kasidy Yates. "Just to borrow for a day?"

"Just to borrow."

"Nothing . . . I won't owe you anything at all?"

Kira dropped her legs down from her chest and crossed her ankles demurely, though her outfit was anything but demure. "Not a thing," she said. "You have my word, Benjamin."

It was a long moment before Sisko finally nodded his head. The Intendant smiled, and signaled to one of her Klingons to take care of the arrangements.

The shuttle was full of fuel when Sisko left Terok Nor, but he knew that it would burn fast, too fast. Even still, if he picked up Kasidy straightaway, then headed immediately for one of the colonized moons on the farthest outskirts of the star system, he should have enough to get the shuttle back to Terok Nor. He would then tell Kira that he was finished with the shuttle, and damn any further consequences. He would deal with the Thadial Bokar situation later, but for the time being, all he cared about was getting Kasidy safe.

He docked the shuttle on the cracked concrete foundation at the number two moon where Kasidy lived. He dashed from the cockpit and sprinted the twenty meters or so to the settlement, but he could see, even as he approached, that something was very wrong. Kasidy's tent was not visible among the rookery of shacks and lean-tos.

As he got closer, he saw what was left of the tent, and felt his gorge rising. Kasidy's shabby dwelling had been torn to shreds, her belongings strewn all around. Most of her things were broken and torn. The other people at the settlement must have picked over her things quickly, leaving behind only what could not be used. Sisko squatted to pick up the piece of torn sacking that Kasidy had been wiping her hands on when he had come to warn her. *I tried . . . I tried to tell her . . .*

Sisko rose to his feet and walked around the settlement frantically, hoping for any sign of where she might have gone, but she was nowhere to be found. The people all stayed inside their shelters, probably afraid that they would get the same fate that had befallen Kornelius Yates. "Kasidy?" he called, but he got no response, nothing. "Hello?" he called. "Can't anyone tell me what happened to Kasidy Yates? Please, I'm not here to hurt you!"

An old Terran woman finally drew back her tent flap enough to poke her head through. She held one crooked finger to her lips.

"Do you know where Kasidy Yates is?" Sisko said frantically. "Please, anything you can tell me—"

"They came and got her," the woman said softly, so quietly that Benjamin almost couldn't hear her.

"Who came?" he demanded. "Who got her?"

"The Cardassians," she said. "They came in an Alliance shuttle, like yours. She's gone."

"When?" Sisko wanted to know. "When did they come?"

But the woman withdrew, her tent flap falling closed. Sisko almost went after her, before deciding that it didn't matter. His breath came very hard, so hard he almost felt he couldn't exhale fast enough to keep from passing out, but he gathered his wits and ran back to the shuttle.

Once in the cockpit, he attempted to contact Stan Devitt, but the man was not answering his comm. Frustrated, Sisko switched the channel over to the next person he could think of, En Shrall.

"Where are you, Sisko?" the Andorian snapped, as soon as his image appeared on-screen.

"I . . . Shrall, do you know if anyone else was sent back to the second colonized moon after you and I left yesterday?"

"You don't have time to worry about that, Sisko—you've got to get back to headquarters right away. Stan Devitt has gone missing."

It took Sisko a moment to register what the Andorian had just told him. "Missing?" he finally said, puzzled. "Where could he possibly be?"

"How should I know? The Cardassian higher-ups are here, asking everyone a thousand questions. And the first question they're asking is where you've been all day."

"I went to Terok Nor this morning," Sisko said. "Stan knew all about it. Jennifer knows all about it too, she should have told someone."

"Well, maybe you'd better come back here and tell them that yourself," the Andorian advised. *"There's a lot going on back here, what with three people disappearing in just over two weeks, and if I were you I'd want to clear my name of any wrongdoing as quickly as possible."*

Stan Devitt is missing? Sisko couldn't even begin to imagine what had happened to the old man, but the very last thing he intended to do was go back to Akiem headquarters on Trivas when it was crawling with inquisitive Cardassians. He programmed a new destination and sat back while the shuttle took off from Kasidy's moon.

"You weren't gone very long, Benjamin."

Sisko had been gone only a few hours, but the Intendant had changed her entire appearance. She was now dressed in a soft, emerald-colored dress with loose elbow-length sleeves that were cut out at the shoulder. The color suited her much better than the harsh violet she had worn when Sisko first met her, and the style was more flattering than the severe bodysuit he had seen her in before. The long, sleek hem of her dress swept the floor when she walked, as she was doing now—pacing slowly with one hand on a slender hip, her bare shoulders gleaming next to the diaphanous fabric. She had removed her headpiece and styled her short reddish hair differently than usual, so that it was smoothed down over her forehead instead of being swept back severely from her face. She looked radiant, and deadly.

"No," Sisko said. "I guess I wasn't gone long." He choked out the next sentence with deep reservation. "I've come to take you up on your offer."

Kira stopped in her tracks and turned to look at him, her eyes very round with surprise. "Is that right?" she said. "Well, I hardly expected you to have a change of heart as quickly as that." She smiled. "You're coming to me willingly, then?"

"I'm coming to you willingly," he said, though it was hardly the case. The truth was, he had run out of options, and he was running out of time. It would not be long before Jennifer found out that he had been to the abandoned mining facility with Thadial Bokar. After that, it would all fall into place, and he would be implicated not only for Bokar's death, but for Janel's—and possibly even for whatever had happened to Stan Devitt. Sisko would rather have Jennifer hate him for infidelity than for being a murderer, especially if she was going to be led to believe that he had something to do with whatever had happened to her father. "And you can make all my problems go away?"

Kira slowly swaggered toward him. "Just like that," she said, and snapped her fingers. The low lights in the room flickered across the sleek surface of her green dress, accentuating each dip and curve of her lithe body. She extended her hand, and Sisko took it. Her fingers wrapped tightly around his, and she pulled him along through the dimness of the room, beyond a screen where there was a bed with a plush velvet coverlet. She turned to him as she stood before the bed, reached behind her neck, and then let the gown slip to the floor in a puddle of shimmering green.

"From the first moment I saw you," Kira whispered, pulling Sisko on top of her on the bed and unfastening his tunic, "I knew I had to make you mine. Knew I had to *own* you."

Sisko said nothing, only allowed her to continue removing his clothes.

"What's wrong, Benjamin?" she murmured, kissing his neck and chest. "Don't you want me, too?"

"Of course I do," he said hoarsely.

"Then *act like it*," she commanded.

Sisko did as he was told.

Kira Nerys was greedy.

She used him not once that afternoon, not twice or even three times, but no less than six times, which was taxing on just about every part of his constitution. When Sisko almost failed to perform the fifth time, she threatened to bring one of her Klingon assistants into the equation, and the sheer terror of the implication somehow succeeded in making his body cooperate where the Intendant's other attempts had failed.

Kira was now lying on her side next to him on the generously sized bed, rhythmically stroking his chest and stomach with both hands, as if he were a dog. "I don't know if I'll ever get tired of you, Benjamin," she sighed. "You're just . . . so . . . *beautiful.*"

Sisko swallowed.

"Well?" Kira said, as if waiting for something.

"Uh . . . yes?"

"Aren't I beautiful, too, Benjamin?"

"Of course you are," he said quickly. "Intendant, you hardly need me to tell you that you're beautiful. Everyone knows you are."

She frowned. "Yes, but I want to hear it from *you,* Benjamin. I want to . . . *believe* it when you tell me. And I don't want to have to ask you for it again."

Her displeasure frightened him. "You're beautiful," he said, pretending, as he said it, that he was talking to Kasidy Yates, and not Kira. Thinking of Kasidy proved to be a mistake, though, and Kira detected the change at once.

"Your mind is elsewhere," she accused. "You're not thinking about me at all."

"Of course I am."

Kira stood up. She looked angry and betrayed for a moment, which worried Sisko profoundly, but then suddenly her expression turned serene. "Well, Benjamin. I wasn't going to tell you this, but maybe you deserve to hear it. You performed quite well, just now, though I suggest you try to act a little more convincing next time. Anyway, I suppose you've been through enough today." She sighed. "Your little friend Kasidy Yates? She's just fine."

Sisko's hands tightened around the sheets. "What are you talking about?"

Kira laughed as she picked up her green dress from the floor, where she had let it fall hours before. "Your little Terran friend, the girl who owed all that money to Akiem. The one you went looking for today, after I gave you the shuttle—just like I knew you would. I arranged for her to be taken somewhere safe. Don't worry, Benjamin, they won't find her."

"Why . . . why . . . ?"

"When I told you I would make all your problems go away, I meant *all* of them," Kira said. "I am nothing if not true to my word." She sat down on the bed and began to stroke his chest again.

"Well," Sisko said, feeling slightly confused. "Thank you."

"You're welcome," Kira said. She sounded friendly, but then her voice turned steely. "But don't think for a moment that I will ever let you get away with something like that when you work for me. Kasidy Yates was a pass for you, Benjamin. You will never get another pass like that. Not ever again."

"Fair enough," he said, and this time, he was telling the truth.

"You will never see her again, either," Kira commanded.

Sisko nodded, slowly, and tried to smile. *It's all right. Just to know that she's safe.* It didn't keep his heart from sinking, though.

Kira stood up again and wandered beyond the screen, handing her green dress to a Klingon assistant who had been standing there the entire time she and Sisko had been in bed together. She gestured to another Klingon, an especially brutish-looking man who brought her a white dressing gown, and the ugly alien helped her into it.

Kira walked back toward the bed as she wrapped her dressing gown around her waist. "I'm almost finished with you for now," she said.

"All right," he replied.

"I'm arranging for you to have quarters right next to mine. Would that make you very happy?"

"Yes," he lied smoothly.

"Good," she said, and sat down next to him. "I know it would make me happy. *Very* happy."

Sisko watched her for a moment, wondering what more she wanted from him. She did not touch him again. She seemed to be searching for something in his face. He wondered, for a frightened moment, if she was searching for love, if she truly wanted him to love her. If that was what she wanted, she was going to be very disappointed.

To his consternation, she suddenly broke out into a little laugh.

"What's funny?" he asked.

"Oh, it's nothing," Kira said, but then she threw back her head and laughed again. She laughed for a very long time, leaving Sisko very uncomfortable, even more uncomfortable than he had been when he'd been having sex with her. To be used and then laughed at—it was too much.

"It's just," she gasped, as she struggled to regain her composure. "It's just that—oh, Benjamin. To think—that Jennifer already *knew* everything! If you could have seen your *face,* how frightened you were that she would find out . . ."

"What do you mean?" he demanded. "What do you mean she already knew everything?"

"I mean," Kira said, still chuckling to herself, "that Jennifer *already knew* that you killed Thadial Bokar. She already knew, and she had already covered it up."

"What . . . what are you talking about?"

"Benjamin, Jennifer has been covering for your blunders all the way back to the beginning with Akiem. You would have been exposed as a fraud a long time ago if you didn't have a wife who loved you enough to cover your tracks. She also probably knew about your visits to the moon where Kasidy Yates lived, and she very well may have known why."

"No," Sisko said hotly. "You're just trying to get under my skin. You're lying."

"Well, it doesn't matter either way," Kira said. "You're safe now, aren't you, Benjamin?' She smiled her characteristic, unnerving smile, like a beautiful, deadly snake.

Sisko got up from the bed and angrily began to pull on his clothes.

He could not bring himself to believe what he was being told, even though . . .

Even though maybe you always knew it. You always knew that someone had to be looking out for you, to keep your skewed tallies from being discovered, and you knew it had to be Jennifer.

Benjamin felt sick. "What about Stan Devitt?" he demanded. "You know so much—do you know what happened to him?"

"Well, much as I wish I could claim credit for him, I actually had nothing to do with his death," Kira said casually. She lay back down on the bed with her arms behind her head.

"He's . . . dead, then?"

"Yes, one of my men confirmed it this morning. Oh, don't look so upset. He was marked for death anyway."

"What do you mean, *marked for death*?"

"He was meddling, trying to put some heat on my political rivals in order to prevent me from getting to you and Jennifer. I had every intention of getting rid of him. But someone else got to him first." Kira sighed. "I suppose it doesn't matter either way, but I would have done a much cleaner job of it than the woman who ultimately got to him."

"A woman? Who was it? Why would anyone have reason to kill him?"

Kira shrugged. "To tell you the truth, I'm not sure. It was a Trill woman, I was told. Maybe he was having an affair with her. My man told me she was . . . quite pretty."

A Trill woman? Sisko had no clue who would have wanted Stan dead . . . besides the Intendant.

Kira went on. "But I suppose I should thank her, whoever she was. With Stan out of the way, I can now have you both, if I want."

"No," Benjamin said. "Not Jennifer. Don't bring her here. I can't bear to have to see her if . . ."

"If you're going to be making love to me?" Kira said. Benjamin could not tell if she was amused or offended.

"I just don't want to have to see her," he mumbled.

"Well, I will have Jennifer, when the time is right. And believe me, Benjamin, she'll be glad to have the work, whether you're here or not. With her father gone, her status at Akiem might not be nearly as good as it was." Kira sat up again. "Anyway, she's too smart to be puttering around with those routine computer checks they have her doing." Kira smiled to herself. "Far too smart."

Sisko said nothing at all. Yes, Jennifer *was* smart. And beautiful, and loyal—and she loved him. She loved him enough to save him from himself. And how had he repaid her?

"I can't do this," he suddenly said, his voice strangled. He started to storm out, but one of Kira's Klingon assistants lurked menacingly, and stepped in his path when he tried to go beyond the screen that divided the room.

The Intendant clucked her tongue. "Benjamin," she said. "We had a deal. You have to hold up your end of the bargain, you know. That's how this sort of thing works, isn't it?"

"Yes," he said, and reluctantly sat back down on the edge of the bed. He did not look at her.

Kira crawled up behind him, resting her chin on his shoulder. "Your quarters are ready now, if you'd be more comfortable there. I'll have someone go down to Zismer and get your things from your old apartment, and they can explain it all to Jennifer, as well."

The thought of one of Kira's thugs showing up at the apartment to "explain" it to Jennifer was almost more than Sisko could stand, especially considering it would come in the wake of her father's disappearance. "Please," he said. "Let me go to Jennifer, just to explain it to her. I would prefer to be the one to tell her."

Kira moved away from Sisko, so that he thought he had dismayed her, but she surprised him. "You can go where you want now, Benjamin." She slid off the bed and strode across the room, smiling at him. "If you want to go see Jennifer, I can't stop you. You can do whatever you want, in your free time. I won't ask any questions about where you've been."

Sisko tried to revel in the great implications of her declaration, though he had a feeling that there was more to it than she was telling him.

Kira's face spread into a smile. "As long as you return to me, of course—and come whenever I call you. And Benjamin"—she leaned forward a little—"when you're with me—you're *with* me. You are entirely focused on me, and nothing else. Do you understand?"

"I understand," he said.

"Good. I will get you outfitted with a ship soon enough, but in the meantime, you may use the shuttle I gave you."

"The shuttle?"

"That's right, Benjamin. It's yours. Enjoy your freedom."

She left him alone for a moment to survey his surroundings, and consider what his new "freedom" was costing him.

Kira's men had already been to the apartment when Sisko arrived. Jennifer was sitting on the couch, her posture similar to the one she had assumed on the night that Sisko had come home so drunk, after killing Thadial Bokar.

"Jennifer—" he began, but she cut him off.

"Spare me, Benjamin. I know already. Please, just go."

"But Jennifer, please listen to me. I didn't want this to happen, she trapped me. She lied to me, manipulated me—"

"And used you, is that it?"

Sisko closed his eyes, ashamed to even look at his wife. "Yes," he finally said.

"Was it anything different from what you expected?" Jennifer snapped. "We both knew that if the Intendant wanted you, she'd do whatever it took to get you. But, Benjamin, we both also knew that if you didn't *want* to work for her, we would have found a way to prevent it from happening."

"We wouldn't have," Sisko said. "Your father—he's gone now, and he was the only one who could have helped us."

"I'm not so sure about that," Jennifer said. "You've proven to be pretty resourceful over the years, and you've done it all without my father even knowing about it."

Sisko didn't answer her. He could not bring himself to confess to all the things that Jennifer apparently already knew about.

"The funny part is—you think you'll be free now, working for Kira Nerys. But just because she doesn't have the same kinds of homing devices built into her ships that Akiem used for their shuttles, don't think for a moment that she doesn't know where every ship in her fleet is at all times. They've all got standard transponders, and she's perfectly capable of tracking their movements. But more importantly, she's the *Intendant*. She doesn't just know where her ships are—she knows where *every ship in the quadrant* is, at all times. She doesn't even need transponders, or any other sort of tracking device for that."

"Do you think I don't know that?" Sisko snapped, but the truth was, he hadn't really thought of it until right now.

"And your crew!" Jennifer went on. "Sure, you'll be able to enjoy the status of having a crew at your beck and call, but you know whose beck and call they will *really* be at? You will never be able to trust that they aren't just spying on you for their *real* commander. They will do what you ask when you ask them, but there are no guarantees that they won't immediately go back to report on every single move you make."

"Well, that's my problem now, and not yours," he snarled.

"That's true," she said sadly. "Once, I felt as though we shared all our troubles, and I did all I could to help you out of yours. But you're on your own now. Even if I wanted to, I couldn't help you anymore."

Sisko turned to go, but he hung back for a moment more. "Why?" he finally said. "Why did you help me all that time, Jennifer?"

She laughed. "How could you not understand? I did it because I loved you. I married you because I loved you—I always loved you."

"You loved me?"

"Yes," she said coldly. "I *loved* you. But that's over now, too."

Sisko did not leave Zismer right away. He had come back to his favorite tavern on this moon. *For old times' sake,* he told himself, but really it was just because he needed a drink, and he needed it right away.

He was nursing his fourth synthale, thinking about all the ways that he might be able to get out from under Kira's thumb, but every solution that came to him was more flawed than the last. He was well and truly trapped.

Sisko finished up the last swallow of his ale, preparing to leave, to go back to Terok Nor, his new home. The tavern door creaked open just as Sisko had been about to stand up, and in walked a petite young woman with a short haircut and a face like a doll's. For a moment, Benjamin was so charmed by her as to be captivated, her compact form sharply silhouetted in the doorway. At first glance, Sisko took her for a Terran, but a second look revealed the spots along the sides of her face that indicated she was Trill.

For a moment, Sisko forgot that he was leaving. He watched the woman walk toward the bar. This tavern had very few customers, and the ones it did see were always residents of Zismer. Sisko had little doubt that if he'd seen this woman on Zismer before, he would have remembered it.

She was young, but her expression declared that she had seen enough for six lifetimes. It was wise without seeming too hard. Sisko found the line of her mouth and the tilt of her pert nose to be so striking, he could not look away.

Her short dark hair framed a perfectly featured face. Her piercing blue eyes were trained right on him. As she approached the bar, she broke into a bewitching smile that made her look impossibly young. "Bartender," she said. Her voice was light and easy. "I'll have whatever this gentleman is drinking right here." She jabbed a thumb in Sisko's direction, and took the stool next to him, right where Janel had always used to sit.

Sisko wrestled for a moment with the feeling that he had to leave, he had to go home right away, because someone was waiting for him. But that was not his reality anymore; that was the old Benjamin Sisko experiencing that feeling. He could stay now, if he wanted. He could go wherever he wanted now, as long as he eventually returned to the Intendant of Terok Nor, and she had promised him that she would ask no questions about where he had been. It seemed perfect, and he paused, trying to enjoy the feeling of knowing that he did not have to answer to anyone—but he knew that it wasn't true. He did have to answer to someone, and that person was more dangerous than anyone he had ever known.

He recalled what the Intendant had said about the woman who had killed Stan Devitt. *A Trill woman . . . quite pretty.* Sisko examined the stranger at the bar. He had a distinct feeling that this particular Trill woman was going to spell trouble for him, but for a moment he found himself so charmed by her that he did not want to get up from his seat. He surreptitiously slipped the wedding band from his finger and put it in his pocket.

The girl—woman—turned to him, still smiling. "You look like a man with a lot on his mind," she remarked.

"Is that so?" Benjamin looked away from her, toying with his empty glass.

"You certainly do. Maybe you could use a friend?"

Sisko licked his lips. "I have enough friends," he said coyly. "Maybe too many, actually."

The woman's smile broadened, revealing her perfect white teeth. "That's all right," she said. "I don't mind sharing." She took a swig of the ale that had been set in front of her. " . . . my friends," she added.

"Hmmm."

The bartender asked Sisko. "Are you done, or shall I bring you another?"

"Oh, bring him another," the woman said, before he could answer. "I'm buying, of course."

"Thanks," Sisko said, "but you should save your latinum."

The woman turned slightly away from him, so that Sisko could see her in profile. "I have a feeling you're worth it," she said, and drank again from her own ale.

Sisko could not begin to understand why this woman had taken an interest in him. He searched his mind for a question to ask her, but nothing particularly appropriate came to mind.

"So, where do you live?" she suddenly asked. "Here on Zismer?"

"Not anymore," Sisko told her. "I live on Terok Nor now."

"Terok Nor," she said, but she didn't sound surprised to hear that a free Terran man lived there. "What's your name?"

"Benjamin Sisko," he replied automatically. There was no use in trying to conceal his identity, though he ultimately didn't trust this woman and still had no idea what her motivation was to suddenly sidle up to him like this. Perhaps she meant to kill him, if she was indeed the person who had killed Stan Devitt. On the other hand, maybe she was one of the Intendant's so-called eyes and ears. Either way, Sisko had every reason to be suspicious of her.

"Well, hello, Benjamin Sisko," the woman said. "I'm Ezri." She extended a hand.

"Ezri," Benjamin repeated, thinking that he might have heard this name before. Maybe from Janel Tigan?

"Pleased to meet you," he said, and found himself grinning

foolishly at her. She smiled back coquettishly, and he thought that maybe he would learn to enjoy being single, after all.

But before Sisko could enjoy flirting with the comely young Trill, his new communicator chirped, and he started at the unexpected sound, realizing that the Intendant was summoning him. He pressed the device, and Kira's voice floated into his ears. *"Benjamin,"* she said. *"I want you. Now."*

Sisko frowned. "Sorry, Ezri," he said, with deep reluctance. What good was his "freedom" if he couldn't ever exercise it? "I have to go."

The woman smiled back at him, and brushed his thigh lightly with one of her slender hands. "That's all right," she said. "I have a feeling I'll see you again."

"Is that right?" Benjamin stood to go, though he wanted to stay more than just about anything.

"Yes," the woman said. "I think we're going to be great friends, Benjamin Sisko."

He stared at the intensity of her blue eyes for a moment, and then turned to go to his new home, his new life.

As he made to leave the tavern, Sisko reached into his pocket to feel for his wedding band, but discovered that it was not there. Startled, he raised his head to look for the Trill, and saw that she was gone. Ezri had slipped out without even finishing her drink, and his wedding ring had gone with her.

Gluttony

Revenant

Marc D. Giller

Historian's Note

This story takes place in early 2380 (ACE) after the fall of the Romulan Star Empire (*Star Trek Nemesis*) and concurrent with the *Enterprise* (NCC-1701-E) encountering the former *Starship Einstein* (*Star Trek: The Next Generation—Greater Than the Sum*).

In memory of Seenu Rao
"And miles to go . . ."

Intercept

A muffled roar seeped in from the other side of the docking port, the telltale throttling of maneuvering thrusters nudging another vessel alongside *Celtic*. The sound only seemed to amplify the vastness of space around the ship, at least to Jenna Reed's senses. A mere two light-days past the way station at New Rigel, the ship was already perched at the outer reaches of Federation territory—a sensible precaution given the nature of this mission, but one that left her feeling troubled nonetheless. Reed would rather have picked the rendezvous point herself, instead of leaving that choice to someone she'd never met. That the man in question made his living as a gridstalker didn't help matters any, but then it wasn't her job to make those kinds of decisions. It had been the captain's call, pure and simple—and the captain always knew what he was doing.

"Relax, Jenna," Evan Walsh chided, sensing her anxiety. "You'll make our guest nervous."

Reed kept staring at the airlock door, hands clasped behind her back as she tried to appear at ease. As long as she had been working under Walsh, she had never mastered her commanding officer's ability to project a dead calm in the face of so many unknowns. With his weathered features and discerning eyes, the role came naturally to him—unlike Reed, who kept her dark hair cropped short and wore a scowl to hide her youth and inexperience. Why he had chosen her for his first officer was a mystery Walsh had never explained to her—and a question she had never worked up the courage to ask.

"I don't trust his kind," Reed said. "They'll do anything if the price is right."

Walsh raised an eyebrow. "That's tough talk, coming from a privateer."

"There are thieves," she observed, "and then there are *thieves*."

The thrusters reached a loud crescendo, concluding with an impact tremor that caused the deck to lurch slightly beneath their feet. Engine noise quickly bled off into silence, followed by the hiss of pressurizing air. The crewman monitoring the airlock gave the captain a nod as soon as the seal engaged, then retracted the pins that secured the heavy door in place. It rolled over with a loud metallic groan, like a dungeon door that hadn't been opened for years, ice crystals glinting from where moisture had frozen along the seam. A frigid draft poured out of the docking collar, which sublimated into fog as it came into contact with *Celtic*'s atmosphere, obscuring the tiny passageway between the two ships.

Reed peered through the mist, searching for signs of movement within. Soon after, a single figure emerged: a man with a slim frame topped by a young face—probably around Reed's age, though something in his countenance suggested a person much older. He brushed back a shock of auburn hair from his forehead, appraising Reed the same way she appraised him. It wasn't hard for her to see that he had spent a good portion of his lifetime on the run.

In spite of herself, Reed felt a stab of sympathy for him.

"Permission to come aboard," he requested.

Walsh stepped forward, assuming a confrontational stance. The stranger automatically stiffened at the sight of authority, though he immediately caught himself and tried to hide it. The captain, however, missed nothing. He kept the pressure on, until the hint of a grin finally crossed his lips—more emotion than he had ever shown in Reed's presence.

Which made her wonder yet again: *Who is this guy?*

"Permission granted," Walsh told the man, greeting him with a firm handshake and a clap on the shoulder. "It's good to see you again, Nicky."

"Likewise, Skipper," the stranger replied, taking in the ramshackle surroundings as Walsh dismissed his crewman. "I can't believe you still got the old girl flying. The rumors about that deal with the devil must be true."

"The devil may own my soul," Walsh said, "but *Celtic* is all mine."

"The man knows his priorities," the stranger said, turning his attention toward Reed. She immediately picked up on his charm, which was an easy concoction that she had seen a hundred times, mostly in characters who operated at the edge of the law. "Then again, he always was good at ducking those Federation trawlers."

"You ought to know," Reed fired back, her tone heavy with insinuation. "From what the captain told me, you have the undivided attention of every section spook in the quadrant."

"I thought my reputation went beyond borders," he said, hitching a travel bag over his shoulder. His tone was cocky, in a way Reed might have found endearing years ago—but not so much now. "Maybe I'm slipping."

"For all our sakes, I hope not."

His eyes shifted back to the captain.

"Jenna Reed," Walsh informed him, "my second in command."

"I'm Vector," the man said to her, as if he needed no introduction.

Reed gave him a hard stare. "The skipper called you Nicky."

"That's my name off the grid."

"We're not *on* the grid. You got a last name, or am I supposed to guess?"

He balked at telling her. Walsh didn't give him a choice.

"Locarno," he said. "Satisfied?"

"That remains to be seen," Reed told him, as Walsh started leading them forward. Locarno made a point of positioning himself next to the captain as they walked through the cramped corridor, forcing her to stay on their six as she continued. "Right now, I'm more interested in finding out if you're worth the price we paid."

"She's a real pit bull," Locarno said, directing his remarks at the captain. "Is she always like this, or do I warrant special treatment?"

"Reed keeps me honest," Walsh said, a slight jab in his voice. "She looks out for me—and she looks out for my crew. Pay attention and you might learn something."

"I had my fill of camaraderie at the Presidio," Locarno snapped, and from there he was detached and professional. "So what do you want first—the good news or the bad news?"

"Surprise me."

"The good news is that I was able to confirm the intel you gave me. A Bolian transport accidentally intercepted it while they were making a run past the Castis system." Locarno slipped an isolinear chip out of his pocket, tossing it over his shoulder to Reed. "That's all the raw data I was able to extract out of their embassy subnets. They managed to pick out some anomalous signal in the vicinity of the Korso Spanse, repeating at semiregular intervals."

"A ship?" Reed asked.

"Maybe," Locarno said. "The whole region acts like a sensor trap, so it could be anything in there. Only thing for sure is that it's stationary—only the Bolians couldn't get a precise fix because of all the electrostatic interference. They just tagged it and filed a request for general assistance when they made it back to base. That was twelve days ago."

Walsh's eyes narrowed. "Did they get Starfleet involved?"

"That's where the bad news comes in," Locarno said, as the three of them stopped near a ladder that led up to the command deck. "The Bolian High Command is pretty tight with Starfleet, so it didn't take long for this bit of news to move up the chain. Like clockwork, they ordered one of their ships to take a closer look during the next scheduled patrol."

Reed took a deep breath. She didn't like where this was headed.

"How long do we have before they get there?"

"They've already been," Locarno said. "Thirty-six hours ago, to be exact."

Walsh shook his head and muttered quietly. "Son of a bitch."

Reed wasn't nearly as calm. Locarno had just informed them that the mission was all but dead—and that the time and money they had sunk chasing rumors of some missing vessel were wasted. "Unbelievable," she seethed, circling around the ladder so she could get into his face. "You knew this whole thing was a bust, but you still dragged us all the way out here. Why put us at that kind of risk?"

"Because I needed to make sure."

"About what?"

"That you were serious about this."

"What's the *point*, Nicky?" Walsh asked, siding with his first officer. "If the Feds have located that ship, then we're as good as done. We won't be able to get anywhere *near* her, much less pick her apart for salvage."

"Only if the Feds know what they have."

That last comment stopped both Reed and Walsh cold. They exchanged an uneasy look, then turned back to find Locarno maintaining that calculated veneer of his. Reed had no doubt that he was playing them, the way a gridstalker played everyone—controlling the information and raising the stakes. If it had been up to her, she would have folded right there and walked away from the table.

But the captain, as always, wanted to stay in the game.

"What are you getting at, Nicky?"

"Starfleet protocols are very specific," Locarno answered. "Patrol craft are only authorized to make a detailed sweep. The full analysis gets done back at starbase—*after* which some admiral decides whether to assign a ship to investigate." He paused for a moment, allowing the significance of what he had just said to sink in. "All we need to do is get at that data before they have a chance to see it."

"And just how are we supposed to do that?" Reed asked.

"Turn your sensors at two-one-zero, mark five," Locarno told them. "The solution should be moving into range right about now."

Reed felt a tingle of dread, which she tried to suppress in the captain's presence. Going over to the nearest intercom, she hailed the bridge three decks above. "This is Reed," she said, trying to sound like she was in control. "Tactical, are you showing any contacts port side aft?"

"*Tactical, aye*," came a harried response. "*Single contact, one-point-seven-two milliparsecs distant following a parallel course—*" The report then abruptly stopped, a gap filled with the rising din of other voices jabbering at each other across the bridge. "*Belay that, Jenna. Contact is now altering course to intercept.*"

"Estimate arrival."

"*Less than two minutes.*"

Walsh drilled into Locarno with a molten stare before hauling himself up the ladder. "Bridge, this is the captain!" he shouted, with

Reed in tow close behind him. "Fire up the engines, Mister Thayer. We're getting out of here."

Like the rest of the ship, *Celtic*'s bridge was a patchwork of alien technologies thrown together in a functional way, with little or no thought given to aesthetics. Her tactical console, scavenged from a wrecked Klingon battle cruiser, packed the rearmost section, while engineering ran on the starboard side through a console that came off a Vulcan long-range probe. The conn and ops were of Ferengi design, bought for next to nothing on the Orion black market, above which hung a forward viewscreen that dominated the crowded space like some exotic Cardassian painting. The only common thread among these disparate pieces was their highly illegal origins, which came by way of *Celtic*'s numerous raids throughout the quadrant. Over countless refits and retrofits, the captain had used every scrap he could find to transform his ship from an old cargo hauler into something of a legend—one of the few privateers still operating in Federation space.

The crew, for their part, manned those stations and performed their duties with an almost clairvoyant interaction, honed from years of trusting each other and no one else. From the moment the captain opened the hatch, he merged with that shared purpose, asserting command with his mere presence. "Status!" he ordered as he made his way down to the center seat, leaving Reed behind to keep an eye on Locarno.

Chris Thayer, the young man manning the conn, answered in a shaky voice but handled his console with steady hands. "Warp drive coming online. Calculating an escape trajectory now."

"Do we have identification on that contact?"

"Positive ID," came the reply from tactical. There, a woman named Rayna Massey maintained a cool watch over the limited weapons and sensors *Celtic* had available. "Federation starship, *Nova* class. We've been made, Skipper."

"One-half impulse power—prepare for evasive maneuvers." Walsh then swiveled his chair around to look at Locarno. The rest of the crew followed his stare, acutely aware of the interloper now in their midst. Several of them reached for their sidearms, ready to draw if the captain authorized it. Reed did the same, wrapping her hand around the blade in her own pocket—though she doubted she had the stomach to use the thing.

"Did you do this?' Walsh demanded.

"I knew the patrol route," Locarno said matter-of-factly. "All I did was make sure we'd be in a position for them to see us."

"Impulse ready," Thayer interjected. "At your command, Skipper."

Walsh kept his eyes locked on Locarno. Reed saw hesitation there, if only for a second.

"For God's sake, Nicky. *Why?*"

Locarno didn't flinch. "I haven't sold you out, Evan. Trust me."

Seconds passed. A proximity alarm sounded, piercing the bridge with a harbinger scream.

"Ten seconds to intercept," Massey warned. "It's now or never, Captain."

Walsh broke off, swinging his chair forward.

"Initiate evasive."

Thayer punched his console, and *Celtic* began to shudder. Her spaceframe groaned under the stress of increased power, the thrum of her impulse engines quickly building as stars on the main viewscreen set into motion. Reed kept her eyes fixed on that point, willing the ship to accelerate faster—until a single, impossibly bright flash consumed the blackness of the void directly ahead, making her and the others shield their eyes before the inevitable explosion that followed. *Celtic*'s deck heaved against the blast, which knocked her off course and sent her into a tight spin.

Thayer held on to the controls, bleeding off speed before shearing forces tore the ship apart. Peering through the haze of spent plasma outside, Reed could see that they had swung almost completely about, and instead of an empty starfield, they now faced the ominous shape of an approaching Federation starship. It spat more fire from its forward phaser banks, which crossed just in front of *Celtic*'s bow and cut off that avenue of escape. Thayer forced the ship to a dead stop to avoid being pulverized.

"Merchant vessel, this is Starship Norfolk," a crackling voice boomed on the overhead speaker. *"You have been identified as a privateer operating illegally in Federation space. Heave to and prepare to be boarded."*

Walsh shot a glance back at Massey.

"They've got phasers and torpedoes locked, Captain," she said. "I have a firing solution, but they'll cut us to pieces before we can get off the first round."

"Mister Thayer?"

"They've just activated their tractor beam," the conn reported back, as a white glow seeped across the viewscreen and took firm hold of the ship. "Directional controls are frozen, Skipper. We're locked tight."

One at a time, the bridge crew turned toward their captain. Their faces already registered defeat, but still held out a glimmer of hope that Walsh had some trick to get them out of this.

"Merchant vessel," Norfolk hailed again, even more belligerent than before. *"You will respond immediately or be declared hostile."*

Walsh slowly got up from his chair and composed himself. He then walked to the back of the bridge, where Reed held Locarno by the arm as if he were her prisoner—for all the good it did. Whatever he had planned, Locarno was in complete control—a fact recognized by the captain, who could only lean in and quietly make the last threat he had to make.

"I'm going to trust you," he intoned, pulling out a hand phaser. "But if you cross me, you won't live long enough to see the inside of a prison. Are we clear?"

Locarno nodded. "Clear as it gets."

"What do you need?"

"A console."

Walsh scowled, but he had no choice but to give in. He jerked a thumb toward the vacant engineering station. Reed took Locarno there, hovering over him as he took a seat and retrieved a small electronic device from his bag.

"What's that?" Reed prodded.

"A little something I've been cooking up. Good a time as any to see if it works." Locarno affixed the device to the translucent panel as he engaged its variable interface, then routed communications through the station. "Acknowledge their hail using subspace frequency two-seven-seven-five-seven-point-one," he told the captain. "Audio only—and keep them talking as long as you can."

"Subspace?" Walsh asked. "At *this* range?"

"Just tell them conventional communications are out. They'll accept the transmission." Locarno then returned his attention to the console, while Walsh opened up a channel to the other vessel. As the gridstalker anticipated, *Norfolk*'s captain was more inclined to start a dialogue than a firefight. The subspace link quickly appeared as a graphic on the engineering display—a nice, wide pipeline between the two ships that Locarno began to fill with covert data streams, sneaking bytes back and forth using whatever free space he could find. "Subspace provides greater bandwidth than standard radio," he explained to Reed, as his hands worked the panel in a blur of purpose and motion. "Makes it easier to bury a stealth carrier in the signal."

Reed looked on, fascinated. "What are you trying to do?"

"Build a virtual remote," Locarno said, changing the display yet again. Pixels arranged themselves in random formations, gathering form and function under his guidance. "Since I can't access their computer core locally, I have to make a console of my own—and *this*," he finished, as the display completed itself, "is the easiest way in."

Reed could hardly believe it. Appearing right in front of her, on *Celtic*'s engineering station, was a gateway into *Norfolk*'s Library Computer Access and Retrieval System.

"The programmers who did the latest iteration of LCARS left behind a security exploit that Starfleet doesn't know about," Locarno continued, entering a complex combination of passwords and authentication codes. "If you know where to look, you can use it as a back door into the system."

"How did you know about it?"

"I was on the team that designed it." He finished the last entry, which unlocked the screen and prompted a welcome message from *Norfolk*'s library computer. "And *that* is how we take care of business."

"What now?"

"We keep LCARS busy while we find a port into the wider system." Locarno snaked around the layers of code that poured through the display, navigating the routing pathways so quickly that Reed could barely keep up—until he found a tiny opening and zeroed in on it. "That's what we need," he said, taking a deep breath before going any further. "It's a straight shot from here into the main computer core—and all their mission data."

"Can you make it through?"

"Sure—at least until the automated countermeasures kick in."

"How long will that take?"

"About eight seconds."

Reed grimaced. "What'll they do once they figure out they've been hacked?"

"They'll probably let their phasers do the talking," Locarno said. "Look on the bright side—at least you won't have to pay my bill."

With that, he plunged into the core. A flood of kiloquads immediately filled the pipeline—every scrap of information that *Norfolk* had gathered during her flyby of the Korso Spanse. Images and impressions flashed before Reed on the small display, nearly overwhelming *Celtic*'s computer as it tried to keep up with the flow. Her heart pounded faster and faster with each passing second, slowing time until it seemed as if their presence in enemy territory might never be detected; but then the console burst open in a torrent of error messages, a chain reaction that kept building until the display cut out—except for the subspace tether that connected *Celtic* with her Federation captor.

"He's breaking off communications!" Massey shouted. Reed looked up at the viewscreen and saw that *Norfolk* was on the move, taking a position on their flank. "Assuming attack posture, Captain!"

Locarno flipped open a cap on his mystery device and rammed the button underneath.

The engineering console lit up again, processing a burst of energy that forced itself into the collapsing subspace channel. The effect was instantaneous, overloading the console and then causing a cascade of failures. The overhead lights dimmed as every panel went crazy, filling the spaces between the darkness with dizzying strobes. A dozen alarms sounded all at once, pulling the crew in different directions as they scrambled to get control of their stations.

Reed shoved Locarno out of the way, taking over the engineering station. She reached for the emergency override, but before she could mash down on the hard switch, the console rebooted itself. Reed froze out of sheer astonishment, as one by one the other stations did the same. The alarms that signaled imminent disaster fell silent, the bridge returning to its normal pulse of operations.

What the hell?

Recovering herself, Reed flipped through a quick series of status indicators. Everything came back nominal, as though nothing had happened. "All systems are green, Skipper," she said in utter disbelief. "Maybe if we can focus engine power on their tractor beam, we can—"

But no one else was paying attention.

Their eyes were cemented on the viewscreen, where they expected to see their doom coming at them in a barrage of photon torpedoes. Instead, *Norfolk* appeared to be drifting, her kill strike thwarted, her hold on *Celtic* gone.

Walsh looked back at tactical. "What happened?"

"I don't know," Massey replied, checking her own panel. "*Norfolk*'s shields are down. So are weapons."

"Picking up only residual impulse traces," Thayer added. "Sublight propulsion is down, Skipper—warp drive, too. Looks like they're maneuvering on thrusters."

Bright chemical plumes erupted from *Norfolk*'s reaction control vents, pushing the starship away at a painfully slow speed. She tried to put distance between herself and *Celtic,* not caring which direction she went—on the run, because she was helpless do anything else.

"Reacquiring target," Massey said, an adrenaline edge in her voice. "Phasers are locked and ready to fire."

"Not so fast," Walsh cautioned. "We don't know what we're dealing with here."

"We have a *shot*, Skipper!" Massey protested. "We need to take them out while we still have the chance!"

"*I said, stand down.*"

Massey, eager for blood, wasn't so easily persuaded. She remained poised for a fight, her breath coming hard and fast—but gradually, under a withering stare from Walsh, she took her hands off the fire control. The captain then made his way back over to Locarno, his expression somewhere between gratitude and fury.

"What *was* that?"

"A subspace pulse generator," Locarno said. "I fed it directly into their computer core—wiped everything clean, paralyzing their systems."

Walsh sighed. "You could have told me that in advance."

"I wasn't sure it would work."

Walsh shook his head, but managed to come up with a brief smile. "Did you get what we needed?"

"It's all in *Celtic*'s core," Locarno assured him. "The way I figure, the Feds will need two full days to restore everything from backup—and with only sublight communications, it'll be at least that long before anybody can hear them calling for help this far out."

Reed had to respect the sheer audacity of it. Locarno had thought of everything.

"Forty-eight hours at Korso, Skipper," he finished. "All the time in the world."

"Then we better not waste any more of it here," Walsh said, returning to his command chair. "Mister Thayer, plot a course for the Castis system. Tell engineering that I'll need every last scrap of warp power at our disposal."

Locarno took that as his cue, and started to head out.

"Not so fast, Nicky," Walsh interrupted.

Locarno stopped, looking over his shoulder at the captain.

"Somebody has to work that data," Walsh said. "I need you."

Locarno blinked in surprise, caught momentarily off guard. "Your people are good, Skipper," he said, motioning toward Reed. "They can handle it."

"Not as fast as you," Walsh replied, then nodded at Reed. She knew exactly what the captain wanted. Leaning over the engineering panel, she called up the emergency release for *Celtic*'s docking clamps. Locarno caught on to what Reed was doing, and made a dash to stop her, but by then it was too late.

A loud *thump* reverberated through the deck as Reed cut Locarno's shuttle loose. He could only stand there as his one means of escape floated away.

Reed was deadpan. "Must've taken a hit during the attack."

"Must have," Locarno agreed, not hiding his admiration of her technique. Both of them looked out across the bridge and watched the crew resume their normal duties, while the specter of *Norfolk*'s hull receded into the distance. The void then started to shimmer, stars elongating into dazzling streaks as *Celtic* made the jump to warp speed, time and space compressed on a relativistic curve. "You guys play a pretty good game. This should be interesting, to say the least."

"Is that the way you see it?" Reed asked. "As a game?"

"Everything's a game, Jenna."

The way Locarno spoke her name gave her pause, if only because she liked hearing it—a dangerous precedent, considering who he was. "And what part do you play?"

"The same one as always," he said, staring down the horizon. "I'm just a guy along for the ride."

Rendezvous

Jenna Reed felt the Spanse before she ever saw it, opening as a wide circle of nothing around her—a sudden dearth of the sensory input she took for granted in the confines of a small ship. She knew her crewmates felt the same thing, a kind of animal intuition that could express itself only in unfocused agitation, though nobody dared speak of it openly for fear of making it that much more real. Instead, they just carried on as if holding their breath—moving in slow motion against a palpable dread, seeking out but finding no solace in the company of others.

Walking down the corridor from engineering, Reed quickened her pace, not wanting to spend too much time among those faces that now looked to *her* for reassurance. She did her best not to make eye contact with anyone, acknowledging those she passed with a simple nod and trying to make herself look busy—*purposeful,* as the captain liked to put it—as if she were part of some greater plan that the rank and file had yet to discern.

In truth, however, Reed didn't know much more than they did. She had spent the last six hours helping Nick Locarno sift through all the intercept data, but neither of them had even come close to nailing down any specifics. *Norfolk* hadn't done much better than the Bolians in identifying the phantom signal, although they *had* been able to get a broad fix on its location—a region near the dead center of the Korso Spanse, choked by swaths of gaseous terminium.

With nothing more definitive to go on, *Celtic* had simply plunged into the cloud on the most likely bearing Reed could find. The metallic gases, however, reduced sensors to an effective range of less than a hundred kilometers, so they were practically blind, given the vastness of the search area and the small size of the target. The ship could do little more than plow back and forth, overlapping her path, covering as much territory as possible before the clock ran out. Under those circumstances, the chances of actually finding anything amounted to little more than the wildest stroke of luck.

Still, given where they were and what they were doing, Reed couldn't help but think that it might be luckier if they found nothing at all.

"First mate, this is the bridge. Acknowledge."

It was the captain's voice that beckoned her from the intercom. Reed went over and pushed the button to answer.

"Aye, Skipper."

"Jenna, you better get up here—and make it fast."

The ominous tone gave nearby crewmen pause. They stopped long enough to let her know they heard before moving on.

"I'm on my way up."

The array of patterns outside the ship was beautiful but menacing. Tendrils of energy carved intricate paths through shimmering clouds, forming a complex latticework that burst into existence one moment and then collapsed the next. What struck Reed the most when she walked onto the bridge was the unnatural silence that accompanied the show—like powerful thunder that hid behind distant lightning, masking the full force of an approaching storm. It held most of the bridge crew in thrall, the same as it did Reed, as all of them searched for patterns amid the chaos.

Because *something* was out there.

The proof of it flashed on Rayna Massey's tactical display, as sensors tried to coalesce around an object buried deep within the cloud. The contact would just start to take shape, assuming the smooth, engineered contours of intelligent design, before retreating back into the ether. It teased everyone with random flickers, so much that Reed wondered if the thing was even real—until it revealed itself again, stronger and closer than before.

"I've got a definite fix," Massey said, her eyes darting between the graphic on her screen and the main viewer. "Bearing seven-two-seven, mark three."

"We should be right on top of it, Skipper," Chris Thayer confirmed from ops.

"All stop," Walsh ordered, his face impassive. Nick Locarno stood nearby, his presence on the bridge conspicuous, though he remained quiet as the captain called the shots. "Mister Harlow, any changes in the contact?"

"Negative," the ship's engineer replied. Tristan Harlow remained on his feet, leaning over his console as he searched through the dizzying array of energy patterns emanating from the cloud. "No changes in aspect ratio, or any disturbances to indicate active propulsion. Whatever's out there, it's dead in the water."

Walsh turned back to tactical. "Defensive posture?"

"No shields or weapons lock," Massey said. "But we don't have them either. Too much interference in the surrounding area."

"Pay your money, take your chances," Walsh muttered, as Reed slipped in next to the command chair. She gave the captain an affirming nod, which he returned with a wry smile. "Z-axis thrusters, Mister Thayer. Minus three hundred meters."

Thayer nudged *Celtic* downward, a slow push marked by a quickening series of pings from tactical. In those moments, Reed felt her heartbeat move in perfect synchronicity with that sound, as if it had become the pulse of the entire ship. She leaned into the viewscreen and the mists that buried the heart of Korso, eagerly anticipating a revelation as that ghostly fog lifted.

Locarno ambled in next to her, brushing an arm against hers as he did the same thing, his expression transfixed. In a space packed with other human beings, his was the only presence Reed felt—and then just barely. Everyone was beyond the confines, out there in the eddies and currents of the Spanse, each wanting to be the first to see what had brought them to the most frigid regions of space.

And, like the sins of old, it manifested itself to them.

It arose, a leviathan coming up from the depths, lumbering into view as *Celtic* descended upon its motionless mass. They dropped in so close that the object quickly filled the entire screen, the details of its surface little more than a blur in the strange haze of volatile gases that enveloped it. Even so, the shapes and lines exuded a strong familiarity to Reed—a feeling mirrored in Locarno's reaction, which turned ashen with realization.

"Reduce mag on viewer," Walsh said.

"We're already at one-to-one," Thayer replied. "This is real size."

"Christ, she's big," the captain whispered.

"Trying to get a configuration on her now," Harlow added. "Sensors are still giving us problems, Skipper. It's nearly impossible to get a consistent reading through all that terminium."

"Then give us some distance," Walsh said to Thayer. "Let's see what we're looking at."

With a command from ops, *Celtic*'s thrusters pushed her away from the object. As its massive dimensions receded, more of its overall design became apparent—and the déjà vu of its initial appearance gave way to a stunning confirmation. Reed followed its structure from bow to stern, starting with an enormous round spaceframe that tapered into an obvious saucer section. That primary hull was mounted on a smaller ventral secondary, which had two elongated engine nacelles that flanked its entire length—a tight, compacted structure topped off by a large weapons pod. The ship listed sharply from *Celtic*'s point of view, making it impossible to spy her markings from this angle, but of one fact there was no doubt.

This was a Federation starship.

"It's a *Nebula* class," Locarno announced, his features rigid as he recited the vessel's specifications from memory. "Better than four hundred meters long, three hundred meters at the beam. Seven hundred and fifty officers and crew."

Reed blinked at him in surprise. "A hobby of yours?"

"Once upon a time," Locarno replied, his eyes drifting back to his study of the ship. She was upturned from *Celtic*'s relative position, which gave an even greater impression of a derelict, her running lights as dark as the viewports that looked in on her lifeless decks. Thayer slowly rolled *Celtic* over until the two ships matched orientation, then assumed a parallel position on her starboard. Electrical discharges enshrouded the larger vessel in eerie backlight, concealing all but her most obvious features. "What are you doing all the way out here, my friend?"

"Looks like she's dead," Massey said, reading off her panel. "No active power output, no residual energies—just that intermittent signal the Feds picked up."

"Can you isolate it?" Walsh asked.

Massey piped it in over the speaker. In between bursts of static, a pattern emerged, like some kind of alien Morse code, though nothing like Reed had ever heard.

"What *is* that?" she asked. "A distress call?"

Locarno shook his head. "It's a seeker signal—a generic broadcast trying to establish a link between computer systems."

"Is that standard for a *Nebula*?"

"No," Locarno said, his tone latent with suspicion. "Not for any Federation ship."

A grave concern washed over the captain's face, though he showed no signs of backing off. "Mister Harlow, what's her condition?"

"Intact, as far as I can tell," the engineer replied. He frowned curiously as some of the readings finally began to appear on his screen, profiles that he compared against schematics for that vessel class. "Some alterations to her structure, though."

Walsh got up to take a closer look, with Reed and Locarno in tow.

"Right there," Harlow explained, running a finger along the starboard nacelle. "The support pylons have been reinforced, probably for improved warp dynamics. And here," he continued, pointing at the weapons pod mated to the aft section of the primary hull. "The module *should* be housing a torpedo stack or phaser array, but that looks more like a large, single emitter."

"Maybe she's experimental," Reed suggested.

"I don't think so," Locarno said, turned toward Walsh. "I know Starfleet designs, Skipper. This doesn't look like anything on their drawing boards."

"She's obviously undergone a major refit," Reed persisted. "How else can you explain the modifications?"

"I can't," Locarno admitted. "All I know is that they weren't done at any Federation shipyards."

Walsh took it all in, then returned to his command chair. He stared at the viewscreen for a few moments, as *Celtic* passed into the shadow of the larger vessel, taking an even breath while he decided what to make of her.

"Open shutters, Mister Thayer," he said. "Light her up."

Two concentrated beams of light split the darkness between the two ships, falling upon the *Nebula* class's ventral hull. *Celtic* then began a slow pass, her searchlights carving out the way ahead of her, casting revelation in flickering, tantalizing glimpses. It could have been an optical illusion, but Reed immediately noticed how *odd* the keel plates looked. Their meshy texture extended all the way forward to the main deflector dish, as if the entire surface was covered in a second skin.

"What the hell *is* that?" Locarno asked.

"You got me," Reed answered, shaking her head slowly. "It's almost like an ablative shield coating."

As the beams diverged they moved down the length of the nacelles, illuminating more of the same. The Starfleet insignias near the forward end were almost completely obscured, the registry markings little more than a smear. On top of that lay a complex matrix of exterior piping—conduits grafted onto the exterior of the ship that spoiled her graceful lines, hinting at some unknown purpose beneath.

"What have they done to you?" the captain asked quietly.

Thayer poured on more thrusters, increasing speed. He then maneuvered *Celtic* up and over the *Nebula*'s saucer section, at the same time bringing her searchlights to bear. They traced a path from the main shuttlebay over the bridge, tiny bright spots crossing over each other until they finally found the large registry number emblazoned across the front. It was visible only in patches, nearly erased beneath a patchwork of shielding and welded plates, but as *Celtic* swung around, the identity of Evan Walsh's prize finally settled into focus, emerging from the broken bits and jigsaw pieces:

NCC-66874

And above that, her name in a former life:

U.S.S. Reston

"Oh my God," Locarno whispered, circling around Walsh and then launching himself at the tactical station. He shoved Massey aside and took over the console himself, holding her off with one hand as she yelled at him to stop. "Skipper, you need to divert *all* available power to the weapons systems," he said, cutting through Massey's protests. "I mean every last thing you've got. I'm calculating optimal strike points right now."

"Wait just a bloody second," Walsh retorted as he snapped up from his chair. "All of a sudden you want to *destroy* a Federation starship? What the hell is going on here, Nicky?"

"We *have* to," Locarno insisted, with such intensity that the entire bridge crew shot glances back and forth between the two men, wondering what they should do. "The last anyone heard of that ship, her status was listed as missing and presumed destroyed."

"Presumed," the captain said. "Obviously, that didn't happen."

"She went missing at the Battle of Sector 001, Evan."

An abrupt silence dropped over the bridge. Nobody here needed a lesson on the significance of that battle, or the implications of *Reston*'s presence here. Locarno, however, needed to make it real for all of them. He needed to say it out loud.

"That ship was captured by the Borg."

Some of the crew had been there. They had shown up after the fighting, hoping to scrape together some easy salvage before Starfleet could calculate their losses—but the sight of so much carnage had been enough to make even the most jaded privateer tremble. Most couldn't bring themselves to pick off the bones of the thousands who had died there, and hadn't spoken about it since, except in the hushed tones that Reed overheard from time to time, with words that conveyed the very essence of fear.

The same fear that now permeated the bridge.

"The Borg are finished," Walsh scoffed, trying to break the spell cast by the mere mention of their name. "No more conduits, no more jumping out of the Delta Quadrant."

"According to Starfleet," Locarno cautioned. "Do you really believe they told everyone the full story, Evan?"

The captain bristled at the sudden challenge to his authority, looking at his first officer to back him up. Reed didn't like the way Locarno handled it, but she grudgingly agreed with him. "There *are* standing laws regarding the discovery of any Borg artifact," Reed said, treading cautiously. "They are to be destroyed immediately—no exceptions."

"That would be well and good if we followed the law," Walsh pointed out, "but we don't now, do we?" He then walked up to the engineering station, where Tristan Harlow stood by with an expression that was a mask of doubts. Walsh burned through them with a single fiery glimpse, poring over the console for himself. "Have you detected *any* sort of life signs coming from that ship, Mister Harlow?"

The engineer cleared his throat. "No, sir."

"Has she reacted at all to our presence?"

"Not that I can tell, Skipper."

"Then is it your best judgment that the ship is dead?"

Harlow paused before answering, not wanting that responsibility on his shoulders. Reed, in fact, was shocked that Walsh would put that kind of burden on him. Never before had she seen the captain abdicate his position like that. She just hoped that no one else saw the move for what it was—cheap desperation.

"That seems to be the case," Harlow finally replied.

"Very good," Walsh said, patting him on the shoulder. He then turned to face the rest of the crew, as if finishing a performance. "All of us understand the sacrifices we've made to get here—all of the toil and treasure we've spent to make this operation possible. So before any of us start thinking about throwing it all away, I ask you to take a look out there." He pointed at the viewscreen, as everyone followed his direction. "That, my friends, is a *starship*—fully loaded with phasers, warp drive, computers, and every other thing you could imagine. And she's *intact*. You could spend ten lifetimes and never come upon such a fine piece of salvage—and she's ours for the taking."

Rayna Massey spoke up with her characteristic bravado. "What about the Borg?"

"What about them indeed," Walsh answered, pacing the bridge slowly, personally engaging each one of them. "The Borg mean weapons. The Borg mean advanced technology. The Borg mean untold secrets. Just *think* about it." He paused for dramatic effect, allowing it all to sink in. "Nobody has ever salvaged a Borg vessel, because nobody has ever gotten this close. God only knows what kind of wonders we might find on board, or what kind of price they'll fetch, once we tear them from her."

Walsh smiled as he spoke those last words, getting the others to nod in agreement—and that was when Reed saw it: a steady progression of collective greed, displacing the trepidation that had held sway only moments before. They were *hungry*—and once aroused, that hunger demanded satisfaction. Even Reed, who knew better, felt it stirring deep within.

"We still have forty hours," the captain said. "I say we make the most of that time. If there's anyone here who doesn't agree, it won't be held against him. I'm sure the rest of the crew would be more than happy to partake of his share."

Everyone laughed. It was all the affirmation Walsh needed.

"Then let's get moving," he concluded, returning to his chair as the crew resumed their duties with a newfound confidence—all except for Locarno, who turned and left the bridge without saying a word. Walsh seemed rather smug about it, at least in Reed's view, like an old man playing cutthroat with his son.

"He'll get over it, Jenna," the captain said.

Reed decided not to press him on it.

"I'm sure he will, Skipper."

"Nicky doesn't understand our business," Walsh explained. "He's a loner by trade. The risks he takes are his and his alone—and so are the rewards."

She kept staring at the hatch where Locarno had gone, feeling suddenly alone, as if she were the only remaining voice of reason on the bridge. Walsh, however, quashed that voice before she could allow herself to raise it.

"Organize a boarding party," he said. "Take Harlow along and see if he can get *Reston* maneuvering under her own power. If not, we'll have to rig her for towing."

"That'll slow us down quite a bit, Skipper," Reed cautioned. "We'll be lucky to make three-quarters impulse power hooked up to something that big."

"It's good enough to get us out of the Castis system before Starfleet arrives."

"What then?"

"We stow her someplace while I figure that out," he snapped, losing patience with her. "Any more questions?"

Reed lowered her eyes. "No, sir."

"Good. Then carry out your orders."

"Aye, Captain."

Her team had already assembled in the transporter room. Three of them—Thayer, Massey, and Harlow—had left the bridge with Reed, taking just enough time to suit up and load weapons before heading down to join the others she had selected for the boarding party. James Casari, a mate from engineering, was there to assist Harlow with *Reston*'s critical systems, while Nicole Carson came over from sickbay to handle the medical emergencies that Reed prayed would never happen.

"Thanks for coming on such short notice," Reed said to everyone as she entered, trying to lighten the mood. A few of them attempted a smile before immersing themselves back in their preparations, checking their gear packs and zipping up their envirosuits. "Sorry there isn't time for a full briefing, but I think you all have a pretty good idea what we're dealing with. Everything else we know is on your padds, along with your assignments. From what we can tell, there *is* some atmosphere on board, probably left over from when the ship went dark— but until we can get life support fully functional, everybody breathes through their packs. I don't want someone opening a door and walking into a vacuum."

While Reed was talking, Carson started making the rounds with a hypospray. She used some unlabeled vials from her medkit, attaching a single dose for each person and injecting it through their necks before they put their helmets on. "It's a combo stimulant and immunization booster," the medic explained as she injected Reed. "I wasn't sure what might be floating around in there, so I added protection against every bug I could think of."

"Thayer could have used some of that on shore leave," Massey joked, jabbing the young ops officer in the shoulder as the others laughed. "I told him not to mess around with those Orion girls."

"Yeah," Casari agreed. "I just hope the Borg didn't catch any of that action."

"That's more action than any of *you* seen lately," Harlow tossed in as he got his dose, winking at Thayer before locking his helmet in place. Breath fogged his faceplate for a moment while his airflow started, his voice muffled when he turned and spoke to Reed. "So what's our entry point?"

"Topside, main bridge," she said. "We'll work our way down from there, staying together until we've verified the ship is secure. After that, we'll split up and complete our respective tasks: life support, integrity fields, propulsion—in that order."

"What about the computer core?"

It was Nick Locarno who asked the question. Reed looked over and saw him standing at the entry hatch, wearing an envirosuit, with his helmet tucked under his right arm. He walked in as the others started hauling themselves up to the transporter pads, ignoring the hostility they directed toward him.

"There's no telling how the Borg might have it rigged," he finished. "And you'll have a tougher time with the other systems without it."

Reed folded her arms. "I don't recall sending you an invitation to the party."

"I figured you might be short on volunteers."

"No argument there," she said quietly, making sure the others didn't hear. "So what's the deal, Locarno? I thought you said this was a bad idea."

"It is. You know it as well as I do."

"What I think has nothing to do with it."

"You're leading this mission," he reminded her. "It has everything to do with it."

She sighed, mostly because Locarno was right. Seeing the others, who looked to her for confidence, didn't make it any easier.

"Walsh won't back down," Reed told him. "He's leveraged himself too much with this operation. If it doesn't pay off in a major way, it'll ruin him. I won't let that happen."

"Even if it gets you killed?"

"We'd be dead a dozen times over if it weren't for him," Reed said. She knew how it sounded, but all she could do was try to make herself believe it. "Besides, if this is a suicide mission, why do you want to come along?"

"Because you need me," Locarno said, masking the sentiment with a show of feigned arrogance. "And because I like the odds better with you around. If anybody can get me through a crazy stunt like this, it's you."

Reed studied him for a moment, still not quite sure what to make of him. In the end she decided to take him at his word, and motioned for Carson to come over with her medkit.

"This is *my* mission," Reed warned him. "You do what I tell you, when I tell you. If you have a problem with that, it ends right here."

Locarno saluted. "I'm all yours, Skipper."

Reed nodded at Carson, who jammed him with her hypospray.

"Then get your ass in gear, Locarno."

They gave each other half a smile. Locarno then slipped his helmet over his head, snapping it onto his collar as Reed did the same with hers. The two of them walked up to the transporter pads together, Reed making sure that all of her people and equipment were in place and ready to go. They gave her a thumbs-up all around, the compartment charged by their adrenaline—so potent that it seeped through the fabric of Reed's envirosuit, making her skin tingle with a static charge. She turned toward the crewman manning the transport console, only to find him staring back at her with a blank, haunted expression.

It was the look of someone who didn't expect to see them again.

"Energize," Reed said.

Fear asserted itself like some ravenous force, an all-consuming thing that started to devour her from the inside out. At first Reed thought it was a manifestation of the transport process, spiking her consciousness during those few milliseconds when matter and energy converged; but then it became *real*—as tangible as the deck that materialized beneath her feet and the ceiling plates that sublimated above her head. It sparked a panic that gripped her central nervous system and spread outward to her extremities: evil as a physical presence, rising up from the depths. Reed felt it turn to liquid as it poured out of her, filling her helmet and forcing itself back in, her blood laden with heavy elements as it re-formed within her veins. She thrashed and convulsed, trying not to drown, but there was no self for her to save—only a residual image within the matter stream, utterly isolated, utterly alone.

Until reality emerged from the other side of a shimmering curtain, which tore the fear from her and cast it to the corners of *Reston*'s bridge. Reed culled its presence at the edge of her vision, a disembodied legion that churned and howled in mad protest. Even more hellish was the *emptiness* it left behind, as if it had taken a piece of her—the very essence of her soul, which stared back at her like a reflection through smoke. Reed lurched toward it, frantic to take that piece back, but the thing recoiled from her as if scalded. Vaulting itself to the turbolift, it slid down the shaft and into the deepest recesses of the ship—into the hiding places where it could lie in wait for her, eager to dine on what was left.

"Jenna?"

Her surroundings quickly snapped into focus, off a wave of dizziness that receded at the mention of her name. Reed found herself leaning against the bridge rail, hanging on with one hand and holding a phaser in the other. She didn't even remember drawing the weapon, just the terror that now seemed more like a faint echo—aftershocks from the trauma of being jammed back into her own body.

"Jenna, are you okay?"

Reed looked up and discovered Nick Locarno hovering over her, his features pallid under the glow of his helmet lamp. He stood by, wary of the phaser—and with good reason. Before she slipped the weapon back into its holster, she saw that it was set to maximum. A single shot might have blown a hole clear through the overhead.

"Yeah," she replied, steadying herself. Locarno also seemed to be shaking it off, like the rest of the boarding party—at least in the brief flashes Reed could see, which sliced across the confined space in a kinetic interplay of incandescent beams. She planted her boots firmly on the deck, magnetic soles holding her down in the disorienting environment of zero g. "That was a rough beam-out. Did everyone make it through okay?"

"I think so," Rayna Massey answered, her voice sounding hollow between labored breaths. "What the hell *was* that? It was like going through a goddamned shredder."

Reed gave Locarno an inquiring glance as he helped her up.

"Why do you keep thinking *I* would know?"

"You're the gridstalker," she offered. "Use your imagination."

"Right now I can imagine quite a bit," Locarno said, taking a look around. "Between you and me, this place gives me the creeps."

Reed felt it as well, the afterimage of her terror playing itself out again. The abject *darkness* that enveloped her only magnified its presence, which she sensed in every groan of the deck and every shudder of the bulkheads. A permanent midnight had descended on *Reston*'s bridge—a bleak, unnatural thing captured like a still life in pitch black, pressing against her with claustrophobic intensity.

The helmet lamps did little to disperse that unsettling notion. Harsh, sterile lights fell upon relics that served up snapshots of what had been, but was no longer: a discarded padd lying on the floor, an empty command chair awaiting a captain who would never return. Ghosts of a life all but forgotten—until the boarding party's arrival stirred them from slumber.

"Nothing has changed," Chris Thayer observed. "It's like they just got up and left."

"Damn strange," Massey added. "No sign of the Borg."

"They probably didn't have much use for a bridge," Tristan Harlow said. "Once they took the ship, control would be decentralized. They wouldn't need to come up here."

"Can you get us some lights from up here?" Reed asked him.

"If they didn't sever the auxiliary." Harlow motioned for James Casari to accompany him, then pushed off and floated over to the engineering station. While the two of them broke into the console, the others started fanning out across the bridge, securing their equipment and getting ready to settle in for the long haul.

Reed, meanwhile, activated her minicom and opened a channel.

"*Celtic,* advance team," she signaled, listening intently to the crackle that came through the tinny speakers in her helmet. "Are you getting this?"

There was enough of a delay to make both her and Locarno nervous, but after a few moments Evan Walsh answered. "*Reading . . . Jenna,*" he said, his words barely audible above all the interference. "*What . . . situation . . . over there?*"

"We're safe," she reported. Even though Walsh sounded light-years away, it was a tremendous relief to have contact with the outside world. "Had some bumps, but we all arrived in one piece."

"Totally lost you . . . sensors . . . can't pinpoint . . . exact location."

"We're setting up operations on the bridge right now," Reed told him. "Harlow is trying to get us some power. After that, we'll head belowdecks and get to work."

"Any sign . . . crew?"

Locarno's grave expression reflected her own thinking.

"Not yet," she said, "but they're here—somewhere."

Walsh trailed off into a disconcerting silence, punctuated by ebbs of static.

"Very well," he replied. *"Check in . . . thirty minutes . . . keep advised . . . status."*

"Thirty minutes," Reed affirmed. "Acknowledged."

"Careful . . . Jenna."

"Aye, Skipper." She paused a moment. "You too."

The channel fell dormant.

Reed closed her eyes and gathered herself together. She made sure the others didn't see—except for Locarno, who gave her the space she needed. When she opened her eyes again, he was looking the other way, allowing her to project an appearance of command, even though they both knew it was an illusion. Reed only hoped it would last long enough to get this thing done.

She managed a few steps, boots clanking hard against the deck, and spoke up with all the authority she could muster: "Any luck, Harlow?"

"Don't need any," Harlow replied as he arose from the engineering console. "Not when you've got talent."

He then touched the interface panel, and the emergency lights started to click on. They flickered in procession, forming a perimeter near the floor of the bridge that encircled the boarding party in a dim but welcome glow. Everyone took the opportunity to look up and around, to see whatever it was they hadn't seen before—but then found themselves completely unprepared for what had been hiding under the cover of night.

Locarno saw it first, following its paths across the deck and along the walls: darkened smears, black but not *quite* black—bold, garish strokes that could have been left by some large brush, rendering a macabre pastiche of abstract art. Leading up to the turbolift doors, however, the strokes metastasized into splatters, hinting at their sinister origins.

Casari grimaced. "What *is* that?"

Massey, no stranger to combat, knew in a heartbeat.

"It's blood," she said.

Nobody spoke of it. There was only the urgency of getting *out,* traded in anxious, knowing glances as everyone waited for Tristan Harlow to pry open the turbolift doors. When that was finished, they proceeded cautiously, each of them sidestepping blood trails as they filed toward the exit, not daring to tread where someone had fallen.

Reed went first, grasping the door frame as she leaned into the gaping turboshaft and looked straight down. A wave of vertigo shot through her at the sight of it, an octagonal tunnel that seemed to go on forever. Marking the plunge was a line of red lights mounted alongside an access ladder—one light for each deck, a ruddy cascade flowing into the depths of hell.

She felt Nick Locarno move in beside her.

"How far to main engineering?" she asked.

"Ten decks down, then aft about seventy meters." He never took his eyes off the abyss beneath them. "Fourteen more decks after that."

"Could be worse."

"Yeah? Tell me that when we hit bottom."

Reed waved Casari forward. The engineer's mate brought along a large case, which he fastened to the deck and unlocked. Inside was a set of handheld maneuvering jets, which he passed around to the others. Reed held hers up and squeezed the trigger a couple of times to test it, the pressurized gases within escaping with a quiet hiss.

And then she stepped off the edge of the precipice.

Instinct dictated that Reed should fall, her arms and legs flailing briefly as she slipped into the shaft; but then intellect took over, a slow realization of her own weightlessness and inertia. She floated clear over to the other side before she regained her bearings, nearly bumping against the wall as she fired off a few bursts to stabilize herself. She spun around slowly, levitating in midair, to find everyone watching her performance.

Locarno smiled and gave her a thumbs-up.

"Keep it tight, people," Reed ordered, and started the long descent.

The others jumped in after her, one by one, a chain of bodies in controlled free fall. Reed poured on thrust until it felt dangerous to go any faster, deck numbers flashing by in her peripheral vision as she focused on the rest of the team to make sure they kept pace. Out of sight meant being alone—and *alone* on this ship was unthinkable.

"Coming up on the lateral shaft," Locarno warned. "Better slow it down."

Reed did as he said, flipping herself over and keeping a close eye on her position. She came to a halt just above Deck 10, where she grabbed hold of the access ladder. Locarno joined her there while the others hovered directly above, their helmet lamps casting all movement in elongated shadows. Reed used the rungs to pull herself down, her hands slippery from the sweat inside her gloves, then stared down the impossible length of the conduit that stretched into *Reston*'s secondary hull.

"Easy to lose yourself in here," she said.

Locarno didn't respond, his gaze fixed on the nearby deck hatch.

"Going somewhere, Nick?"

"Computer cores are right through there," he said. "One port, one starboard."

"Take it easy. You'll get your chance soon enough."

With that, Reed pointed the way aft and pushed herself off the ladder. Locarno did the same, catching up to her as the rest of the team rounded the corner and followed. By this time, Reed had grown accustomed to moving in zero g and used it to her advantage. Coasting on momentum, she fired off her jets a few times to keep herself centered, traversing the distance to the end of *Reston*'s saucer section in a matter of minutes. There, she found a disabled lift car parked directly over the second vertical shaft—effectively blocking the only direct route to their objective.

"Just our luck," Locarno remarked, floating in next to her. "You want to take this lift, or wait for the next one?"

Reed approached the car, trying to find a way around it. When that didn't work, she planted her boots against the wall and gave it a solid push. The car didn't budge. "Damn thing is stuck tight," she muttered, just as Harlow arrived with Casari and the rest of the team. "Think I could use a hand over here."

The two engineers quickly went to work on the magnetic locks that kept the car on track, disabling the power-cutoff locks so that it could levitate back and forth. Harlow then gave it a firm shove, which made the bulk give a little. Everybody else grabbed hold of the car wherever they could. Coordinating their efforts, they all pushed at the same time—centimeter by centimeter, slowly, until the shaft beneath opened up just wide enough to let a body pass through.

Casari went up top again and reengaged the locks. The car settled back into place.

"Ladies first," Harlow said.

Reed shuffled over to the edge of the opening and looked down. This shaft seemed even more ominous than the last one, if such a thing was possible. So was the menacing certainty that something awaited them down there—something that stirred in the dark spaces, reacting to their presence, like a predator sensing prey.

Reed dismissed the notion, which retreated into the depths from which it came. Tapping yet another reserve of strength, she squeezed herself into the opening and wriggled her way down, her helmet barely clearing the narrow slit. "Watch those edges coming through," she warned the others as she moved out of the way, making room for the next person. "You don't want to rip a hole in your suit."

"As if we didn't have enough to worry about," Locarno groaned, sliding into the hole and dropping in next to her. "You always this much fun?"

"Only when I'm trying not to get killed."

Reed dunked Locarno to keep him going. As he spiraled downward, she stood by and ushered the rest of the party through, helping to guide each of them. Nicole Carson was last, and the one who had the most trouble. She snagged her medkit, tangling herself into a knot of loose straps and jerking limbs. By the time Reed could reach her, Carson was almost in a full panic. She paid no attention to Reed's orders for her to stop. Reed had to grab a knife from her pocket and cut the straps before Carson even realized she was there—and only then did the medic begin to calm down and allow Reed to pull her out.

Carson's muscles were rigid against the fabric of her suit. Reed spun her around, hurriedly searching for signs of a tear, but found no obvious leaks.

"Jesus," she exhaled. "You scared me, Nicole."

Carson smiled weakly, a haggard expression peppered with beads of nervous sweat. "Sorry I got hung up there," she said, finally relaxing—except for her eyes, which refused to settle on a single direction. "Thanks for the assist."

"Are you up to this?"

"I'm fine," Carson assured her. "Just a little claustrophobic."

"I need everybody sharp. We can't afford any mistakes."

"Don't worry about me," the medic replied, then descended with the rest of the boarding party. Reed wasn't fully convinced, and remained behind long enough to wonder if Carson might pose a problem. It would be easy to use that as an excuse to request an immediate beam-out, and make it that much harder for Evan Walsh to continue with this mission. Part of Reed thought she would be doing everyone a favor.

But you won't do that, will you? Because he gave you an order.

And Jenna Reed always followed orders.

A bloom of sparks vaporized the gloom before spreading out across the shaft, the embers dying off as quickly as Tristan Harlow's phaser torch cast them. The engineer used it to cut through the door seam on Deck 25, finishing the job in a matter of minutes; but as the torch extinguished and its sputtering ceased, the hard reality of *opening* the door dawned on each member of the boarding party. They passed that same, gruesome stare off to one another, like soldiers in those law few seconds before a combat drop.

Harlow lowered his torch and looked back at Reed.

"Go," she said.

James Casari whipped out an extensible crowbar, which he wedged into the ragged seam. He worked it back and forth a few times, enough for Harlow to get his fingers through the crack, and together both men forced the doors open. They parted about three-quarters of the way before jamming, but that was more than enough to afford a view of the other side, which gradually unmasked itself through a haze of smoke and ionized particles.

Jenna Reed hadn't thought it possible for a chill to bite through her envirosuit, but it did. She remained motionless, her gaze directed on that opening, her mind processing images with illusion but finding the reality even more ghastly than her imagination. There, under the pale ticking glow of the alert lights, Reed saw death staring back at her in its most wicked form: eternal and irrevocable, yet imbued with a cruel veneer of life.

It might have been human at one time, or one of a dozen other races, but none of that mattered now. The pallor of its skin and the mechanical prosthetic that covered its left eye conjured up only a single species.

Borg.

"Holy mother of God," Chris Thayer whispered.

Rayna Massey scowled. "God's got nothing to do with this."

Reed drifted toward the entry, unable to resist so powerful a lure. Locarno reached out to stop her, but she brushed him aside. Climbing through the broken doors, she attached her boots to the deck and stood there—the flow of her own blood thundering in her ears, vision constricting into the space between her and the Borg drone.

Only the head and shoulders were visible, recessed behind the mottled glass of a regeneration chamber. The one organic eye remained open and sunken deep into its socket, the skin desiccated and taut against its skull. With its jaw frozen agape, the drone seemed to convey the horror of its last moments—or perhaps the horror its kind had visited upon so many others.

Reed lumbered closer, her movements heavy and mechanical. Unnervingly, she caught a glimpse of her own reflection superimposed over the drone, forming a composite visage that seemed so *alien* and yet so familiar. In that moment, she could easily imagine their roles reversed: *What if it had been me on board a ship like this? Would I have let it happen? Or would I have taken myself out before they could take me?*

"This one's dead," Reed announced.

"Maybe," Locarno said, "but what about *them*?"

Only then did Reed turn and see the *other* chambers, one after the other, in a line that extended down the entire length of the corridor until it bent around a corner and led out of sight. Reed estimated thirty or forty chambers going in both directions, but lost count after that. There were probably hundreds more scattered throughout the ship.

"Frag me," Harlow breathed. Like the rest of the boarding party, he had his weapon drawn, and swept the barrel back and forth, just waiting for the slightest provocation to open fire. "Are they *all* like this?"

Reed looked at Nicole Carson. "Tricorder."

The medic used the device to scan as far as its sensors could go. "No life signs within five hundred square meters," she reported, reading off the tiny screen. "No power signatures coming off these tubes, either."

"Poor bastards," Casari observed. "That ain't no way to die."

"You could've fooled me," Rayna Massey said, floating down the line and inspecting the chambers up close. "These guys look perfectly preserved."

Locarno sidled up to Reed, checking out the drone that had drawn her attention. Unlike the others, this one showed signs of decomposition—which Locarno traced to a large crack in the glass near the base of the chamber. "There," he said, pointing it out to her. "There must have been some damage before the Borg retreated into stasis."

"Why go into stasis at all?" Chris Thayer asked.

"Fallback position," Locarno said. "At some point, they got cut off from the larger Collective—maybe after the ship entered the Korso Spanse. After that, they would have gone into sleep mode while they tried to reestablish contact."

"Which never happened," Reed finished.

"They just kept on waiting," Carson said, as if talking in a dream. "They could have been drifting out here forever."

Something in her tone frightened Reed—not because she was afraid that Carson was losing it, but because she felt the same creeping disconnect from reality. Just *being* here was like immersion in a sensory deprivation tank, with a thousand lifeless eyes watching their every move. No rational being could continue to function long under those conditions—and even now, her people were starting to get strung out. More than ever, Reed just wanted to get the job done and get the hell out of here.

She checked her mission clock. Thirty-six minutes had elapsed.

"*Celtic,* advance team," she spoke into her transmitter. "Checking in."

The reply was garbled, barely audible—but there, like a lifeline.

"*Go, Jenna.*"

"We're on Deck Twenty-five and headed for engineering," she advised. "Confirmed Borg presence on board, unknown number." She paused for a moment before adding, "Looks like they're all dead, Skipper."

"*You sure?*"

"Yeah, I think so. We'll continue to assume hostiles until we can verify that the rest of the ship is secure."

"*Proceed . . . try to maintain . . . transporter lock . . . emergency beam-out.*"

Reed's jaw tightened. *Try to maintain.* Nobody liked the sound of that.

"Understood," she replied. "Advance team out."

They stood like sentinels alongside the long passageways, their sarcophagi lined up next to one another in perfect symmetry. Reed tried not to look at them, their cadaverous stares not nearly as disturbing as the utter *sameness* of them all—and the knowledge that each one had once been an individual like her. It was almost impossible to imagine the vast, unyielding hunger that had devoured their souls.

Or that such a thing could ever truly die.

Reed was grateful for the sight of the blast door that sealed off main engineering. Tristan Harlow opened the lock mechanism, splicing a portable battery to the exposed leads so he could run a bypass. The duranium door then popped open, lifting just enough for the engineer to roll underneath and get inside. Five minutes later, the overheads started to click on: a sudden, blinding surge of lights that flooded the corridor and spread outward like fresh blood flowing through *Reston*'s arteries.

Reed held a hand up to shield her eyes as the blast door retracted into the ceiling. It locked back into place with a jarring *thump*, much louder than she would have expected in such a thin atmosphere. In addition to the lights, Harlow had obviously gotten the air flowing again.

He emerged with a smug expression. "Will miracles never cease?"

The rest of the team followed Harlow into the cavernous

engineering space. Reed stopped next to the railing that encircled a dormant warp core, craning her head to get a look at the full length of the translucent vessel. Although the interior was dark, green status lights flashed intermittently at each service juncture—confirmation that the containment fields for the *Reston*'s antimatter had retained their integrity. Whatever else her condition, at least the ship's power plant remained intact.

Everything else, however, was up for grabs.

Reed had never seen the interior of a *Nebula* class before, but she knew Federation technology—and nothing here had been left untouched by the Borg. She recognized the basic layout of all the panels and interfaces, but all of them had been rigged one way or another in some strange, haphazard fashion. Thick cables of glowing fiber snaked their way around the floors and ceilings, forming a complex web of interconnected nodes, while the large status screens that had once encircled engineering had been torn out of the walls and replaced with what appeared to be holographic constructs. Alien symbols poured out of an imaging mist—textual information in what Reed could only assume was some kind of Borg code. She watched them for a time, fascinated by the complex display, but could only imagine what it all meant.

Maybe it knows we're here.

Reed turned to Locarno, trying to read his take. If his scowl was any clue, he was thinking the same thing.

"I managed to jack into the auxiliary," Harlow explained, walking over to one of the side panels. "At least what's left of it. The internal circuitry is the same, but there's been a hell of a lot of external rerouting."

"Can you make sense of it?" Reed asked.

"Enough to get partial power," the engineer said, pointing toward the fiber links around them. "What we've got here is tapping into one of the backup generators, which gets us lights and life support on this deck—at least in the immediate sections. And one more thing," he finished, touching a button on the variable interface. "I thought you all might enjoy a little bit of gravity."

Reed felt a building pressure on her legs as the full weight of her body started to reassert itself. Harlow increased the pull gradually, giving everyone time to adjust before pumping it up to a full g, but even then each movement seemed sluggish. It took a few moments before Reed felt safe enough to turn off her magnetic boots.

By then, Harlow had already peeled his helmet off. The others quickly followed suit, sweat trickling down their faces even as their breath turned to fog in the frigid air. "It'll start warming up in a few minutes," the engineer said, "once the atmosphere makes a pass through the scrubbers."

Reed coughed, stale trace elements settling at the back of her throat. Even the air seemed alien, somehow out of phase. "How long until you can get the other generators online?"

"Less than an hour," Casari said. "They should give us enough power and heat to operate in our critical areas—here, the bridge, auxiliary control."

"And the computer cores," Locarno interjected.

The engineer shot him a harsh glance. "If need be."

"You'll need some form of core control if you want to get the intermix working," Locarno informed Reed. "The calculations to get a cold start on the impulse engines are just too complex to handle from here."

Reed took him at his word, giving Harlow a nod that told him to make it happen.

"In any case," the engineer continued, "it'll get us over the hump until we can fully restore auxiliary power. Once we're under way, we can start working on the warp drive. Hell, I might even get you a couple of phaser banks before we hit dry dock."

"Let's hope we won't need them," Reed said warmly, squeezing Harlow's arm and then sending him and Casari on their way. While they started breaking apart the consoles, she and Locarno returned to the large holographic display. They stood for a time in front of the projection, which stretched from floor to ceiling, transfixed by the arrangement of glyphs and pulses. Reed actually reached out to touch the imaging mist, which rippled around her fingers like a pool of water, hoping to divine some hidden meaning. "Any idea what it says?"

Locarno shook his head. "It does have a certain logic to it, though."

Reed understood what he meant. It was like listening to a language she had never heard before, baffled by the words but inferring the context.

Can you hear them, Jenna? Can you hear them calling?

"They *are* all dead," Reed asked. "Aren't they?"

"I think they're all in there," Locarno said, motioning toward the display. "Every thought, every impulse, every action—reduced to some data stream with nobody left to understand it." He paused for a long, heavy moment. "They may be dead, but they never really left."

Reed turned toward him, searching for some trace of irony but finding none.

"You have work to do," she said.

"So do you," Locarno replied as he walked away. "More than you know."

Tristan Harlow delivered on his promise, firing up the last of the backup generators and bringing *Reston* back to a semblance of life. Internal sensors mapped out the pockets of life support that rushed in to fill the void, which carved out narrow passages of breathable air. The rest of the ship remained in vacuum, isolated from the sections where the advance team would perform their work—a hedge against the remote possibility that they had somehow missed any Borg survivors.

Jenna Reed had everyone download the safe zones to their padds and also commit them to memory. From there she broke everyone up into pairs, leaving Harlow and Casari behind in engineering and taking the rest of the team to secure the ship. The only exception was Locarno, who retreated to the starboard computer core. Reed didn't like the idea of sending him there alone, but she had no choice. With only four more people at her disposal, she already had far more territory than she could ever hope to cover.

Reed sent Massey and Thayer aft toward the hangar deck, while she took Carson with her and started going forward. She wanted to keep a close watch on her medical officer, in case there was a repeat of the incident in the turboshaft; but as they moved deeper and deeper into the unexplored recesses of *Reston*'s hull, an almost surreal composure descended over Carson. Even as they encountered dozens more Borg drones, some of them in various states of decay, her clinical detachment never wavered. Neither did the cold spark behind Carson's eyes—which disconcerted Reed even more than her earlier panic.

Over the next two hours, Carson's tricorder sweeps only confirmed their grisly discoveries: death and more death, with no end in sight. Most disturbing were the corpses that wore remnants of their Starfleet uniforms, bits and pieces of a forgotten life interwoven with their Borg prosthetics and body armor. It made Reed feel a connection with them that she didn't want, which made her hate—and fear—them all the more.

She tapped her communicator. "Massey, this is Reed."

"Go ahead."

"What's your status?"

"We got nothing but dead slags here. You?"

"The same," Reed signaled back, releasing a long breath. "Pack it in for now. Meet me on the bridge in ten minutes."

Auxiliary power came online by the time she and Carson made it back, tripping the various consoles and causing them to flicker at random. The main viewer also engaged, pixels arranging and rearranging themselves, until a grainy image finally coalesced out of the static. Out there, *Celtic* pitched a slow orbit around *Reston,* hovering off the center of the screen like some blurry artifact. Her running lights punched a hole through the glowing elements of the Korso Spanse, thrusters leaving behind a cometary trail.

Massey and Thayer joined them on the bridge a few minutes later, exiting the turbolift and immediately assuming the conn and tactical.

"Can you get me ship-to-ship?" Reed asked.

"It's borderline," Massey replied, working to stabilize her panel, "but I think I can call up a visual frequency."

Reed approached the captain's chair, hesitating for a moment. Something about it just felt *wrong,* as if sitting there amounted to some kind of sacrilege, but she forced herself to do it, knowing that Evan Walsh would expect nothing less.

"Open up a channel."

After a few starts, the image on the screen dissolved into a view of *Celtic*'s bridge. Walsh appeared there, larger than life, nodding with approval at his first officer.

"Welcome back to the world, Jenna."

"Thanks, skipper," Reed said. "It's good to see you again."

"You about ready to get that tub moving?"

"Checking on that. Stand by." She hit the comm panel on her chair. "Engineering, bridge. How are we doing on navigation?"

"One miracle at a time, Jenna," Harlow said, his voice piped in through the overhead speaker. *"I'm routing helm functions through a portable node to bypass all these Borg mods, but the controls are going to be a little dicey."*

Reed turned to Thayer. "You getting any response?"

"It ain't fancy," the conn officer said, jockeying with the interface, "but I can lay in a course. Tell me where you want to go, I'll point us in the right direction."

"Propulsion?"

"Thrusters are functional. Still no response on impulse."

Reed tapped a second channel. "Core, bridge. How are you doing down there?"

"Finding my limitations," Locarno replied. *"I've managed to isolate a few legacy subsystems, but the rest of the architecture has been completely redesigned. It could take weeks just to figure out where everything is."*

"Can you run the intermix models?"

"Yeah, but I'd have no way of confirming their accuracy."

"I'd belay that, Jenna," Harlow cut in. *"Even a slight variance from an optimal flow state could cause those engines to overload."*

"Understood," Reed said grimly, looking back at Walsh. "Sorry, Skipper. That's as far as our luck goes."

"Nothing's easy, is it?" the captain said, then started barking orders out to his crew. *"Shut down nonessential systems and divert all available power to the tractor beams!"* The bridge lights dimmed over the captain's head, while several of the consoles behind him went dark. Reports poured in from all over the ship, the background chatter informing Walsh that every last joule of energy was now at his disposal—turning *Celtic* into a flying engine with no deflectors, no weapons, and barely enough life support to keep everyone breathing.

His watch officer delivered the final confirmation. Walsh nodded and sent him on his way. *"We're ready. It'll be slow, but we'll get you out of the sector—far enough to keep Starfleet off our backs until we can get that ship under way."*

"Aye, sir. Mooring points are being relayed to you."

"Receiving," Walsh acknowledged, checking his own monitor.

"Tactical, feed this information into the targeting computer and prepare to commence operation."

"Got it," Celtic's tactical officer said, quickly programming a solution. *"On your orders, Skipper."*

"Engage."

Reston shuddered as the tractor beams took hold. Inertia anchored her in place for a few endless moments, but slowly, painfully the ship began to move. An alarm on Thayer's panel marked their progress with a rapid series of pings, while the conn officer fired off thrusters to bring their course in line with *Celtic*.

"Picking up speed," Thayer reported, the excitement in his voice building as he read from his console. "Five hundred kps . . . seven hundred—one *thousand*. It's working, boss!"

"Very good," Reed said, finally relaxing. She settled back into the command chair, and for the first time felt like she actually *belonged* there. "Match bearings and maintain a distance of twelve hundred meters."

"Twelve hundred meters, aye."

Reed heard the tactical panel sound off behind her.

"Frag me," Massey intoned, a worried scowl spreading across her face. Reed turned back and saw the tactical officer tapping several buttons on her panel, her eyes darting back and forth as they tried to keep up with some unknown development. "This can't be right."

"What is it?"

"Threat indicator," Massey explained. "Tactical systems are programmed to assume a defensive posture when there's a breach in the security sphere. Must be a glitch." She canceled the alert, only to have another one pop right up. *"Dammit*—there it goes again. I'm reading a single hostile contact, close proximity."

A surge of dread crawled across Reed's skin.

"Locate," she snapped.

"Zero-zero-five, directly ahead," Massey answered—then turned ashen as she looked up at Reed. "Jenna, it's targeting *Celtic*."

Reed whirled back around. On the viewscreen, Walsh proceeded as if nothing was wrong, his bridge crew completely unaware.

"Abort defensive stance," she ordered.

Massey worked the panel to no avail.

"I can't," she said. "Local controls are frozen."

Reed punched her comm button. "Engineering, bridge—tactical is locked out. What the hell's happening down there?"

"Stand by, bridge!" the engineer replied, trading shouts with Casari. From the desperation in their voices, it sounded like a full-scale disaster in progress. *"I don't know how, Jenna, but the node I installed just up and reprogrammed itself. Could be some kind of virus. Whatever it is, the thing is fast."*

Reed steeled herself, even though her mind was in total panic mode.

"Thayer, do you still have the helm?"

He shook his head gravely. "Nonresponsive."

The ship suddenly, violently lurched to starboard. Massey left her feet, hitting the deck and tumbling down to the command level. On the viewscreen, *Celtic* took an even worse hit, the aftershock knocking almost everyone out of their chairs and shorting out consoles all across the bridge. Walsh scrambled for a fire extinguisher, spraying the conn and dousing the sparks that exploded from there, his movements leaving a ghostly trail across the garbled transmission.

Reed rushed over to help Massey.

"What *was* that?" she yelled at Thayer.

"Impulse turn!" he stammered, in a haze of confusion. "The engines fired all by themselves, boss—evasive maneuvers, trying to shake us loose!"

"Shut it down!"

"Helm negative! Still not answering!"

Reston tilted hard to port. Even more havoc broke loose on board *Celtic,* conveyed in bits of audio scattered across a stroboscope of nightmare images. In the middle of it all, Reed spotted Walsh searching for her through the viewscreen, his voice cutting in and out as he screamed over the insane pandemonium on his own bridge.

"Jenna . . . for God's sake . . . stop—"

"Evan!" she pleaded in return. "Break off now! Get the hell out of there!"

Reed didn't even know if Walsh could hear her, but she heard *him* when he gave the order to kill the tractor beam. *Celtic* cut the transmission at the same time, the small ship appearing on *Reston*'s viewscreen as she throttled up her engines and started pulling away.

"Engineering, bridge," she said. "Disengage navigation and tactical."

"I've already pulled the node, Jenna!" Harlow replied. *"It didn't have any effect! Those subsystems are still active, jacked through another location!"*

"Where?"

"The starboard core!"

"Jesus," Reed whispered, looking up at the viewer. She prayed *Celtic* would be gone, but instead, the ship loomed larger and larger as *Reston* picked up speed to pursue. "Core, bridge—initiate emergency failsafe! Halt all processes!"

Locarno didn't answer.

"Are you listening, core? Take it down now!"

Reston poured on even more speed, swinging around *Celtic* in a wide arc.

"Weapons going hot," Massey said. "Phasers acquiring target."

"Goddammit, Nick! Where are you?"

Feedback pierced the overhead speaker before it went dead. Reed shot to her feet, hurling herself over the deck railing and taking the tactical controls for herself. She mashed her hands against the panel, which ignored her commands. All she could do was watch helplessly as *Reston* closed in, her forward phaser banks charging to full power.

And then lightning split the darkness.

A single burst—impossibly hot, impossibly bright—seared the distance between the two vessels, scoring a perfect hit before *Reston* roared over and then away from *Celtic*. It happened so fast that Reed couldn't fathom how such a strike could leave any serious damage. A fleeting sense of hope swelled within as *Reston* withdrew to a safe distance, coming about like a hit-and-run predator to survey the condition of its prey—but that notion soon collapsed when *Celtic* crossed back into view, and the full extent of *Reston*'s lethal blow revealed itself in horrifying detail.

A thin column of atmosphere vented from *Celtic*'s bridge, like blood hemorrhaging from a jagged wound. The ship listed into a slow roll, her thrusters firing off at random even as her impulse engines struggled to keep her on a level course, but it soon became apparent that *Celtic* was just tumbling through space. Reed stepped forward to peer through the fog, making out the bits and pieces of debris that trailed the ship—until it dawned on her that in the flotsam, she could trace the unmistakable shape of human bodies. Almost all of them were dead, killed instantly by the force of impact and sudden decompression; but at least one still lived, arms and legs thrashing for a few agonized seconds before succumbing to the frozen vacuum.

Reston fired again.

The phaser beam struck *Celtic*'s warp nacelle, blowing a hole clean through to the other side. The hit knocked her into a flat spin, streams of hot energy plasma spilling into the void. Impulse engines flickered as she made a feeble attempt to right herself, her aft photon launcher spitting out a single torpedo to provide some cover. The shot careened off into nowhere, but *Reston* punished her nonetheless. One final salvo took out *Celtic*'s impulse deck—a spectacular detonation that left the ship dead in space.

The battle had taken all of one minute.

Reed stumbled back, her jaw agape.

"My God," Massey whispered, tears streaming down her face. She resumed the tactical station, quickly getting a read on their status. "Holding position, phasers standing down. Power diverting to the main weapons pod."

Reed didn't listen. She was already at the science station, clicking through a chain of interfaces until she found one that gave her access to the ship's sensors. Releasing a wave of active scans, she trembled while she waited for the signals to bounce back. There, amid all the clutter, tentative life signs emerged from *Celtic*'s battered hull.

Survivors . . .

Reed obsessed over those readings, even as a powerful tremor welled up through the decks. She blocked out everything around her, even as the bridge swelled with a tsunami of coherent white light. And she dared not look at the viewscreen, even as she ran for the turbolift—because she knew the purpose of the terrible shriek that followed, and what the cutting beam would do to what was left of *Celtic*.

She had to stop it.

If it wasn't already too late.

Ten decks below, the lift doors opened into a maze of swirling red lights and alarm klaxons. Reed plunged headlong into that chaos, phaser in hand, heedless of direction but unable to stop. She caught a glimpse of a deck plan against one of the bulkheads, and followed the arrows that pointed to the starboard computer core. By the time she reached it, Reed's heart was banging against her ribs like some caged animal, her body racked by adrenaline tremors. Discharges of electric blue spilled through a window that looked into the core chamber, illuminating plumes of smoke that leaked out from underneath the closed doors—but a rusty odor and the sudden constriction of her lungs told Reed that this was no fire.

Krylex mist . . .

The gas sucked oxygen out of the air, making her double over and cough. Reed took one last deep breath and made a dash for the door, prying open the access panel and trying to disable the magnetic lock. She punched in the default code, her fingers shaking as she stole glances through the glass to see if anyone was still inside—but all she saw was a churning cloud of toxic chemicals, lit up like a thunderstorm in the black of night.

Until a dark mass launched itself at her.

Reed jumped back at the sight of it, her vision blurring as hypoxia started to creep into her brain, but even in her stupor she could see that its motions lacked reason or conscious thought. It raised one hand and clawed at the window, hooked fingers leaving behind smears of blood as it dragged itself off the floor. At first, Reed thought it was one of the Borg, from the pallid complexion of its skin to the thatch of veins that crossed its eyes—but then she suddenly *recognized* its features, concealed behind the breathing mask that covered its face.

Nick Locarno rolled away as Reed pointed her phaser at him.

She shattered the window with a short burst, shards of transparent aluminum raining down around her. Reed then crawled forward, grabbing Locarno by the arm and dragging him away from the lethal cloud. She propped him up against a nearby wall, his head lolling as he drifted in and out.

"Nick!" Reed implored. "Stay with me, Nick!"

"Celtic . . . tractor beam . . . triggered a defense routine."

Reed shook him hard, trying to get through.

"Tell me how to shut it down, Nick."

"Failsafe . . . didn't work . . ."

"What do I do?"

Locarno slumped over, losing consciousness. Leaving him, Reed staggered back to the opening and stood there, krylex mist billowing all the way up to her waist. She was vaguely aware of the phaser still in her hand, of her thumb pushing the power up to maximum, but had no clue of where to take aim—or if it would do any good. All she could do was level the weapon at the largest component she could find, while a fury she had never known burned her from the inside out.

"Just DIE!" she screamed.

And mashed on the trigger.

Initiation

The turbolift doors opened onto the bridge—the post Jenna Reed had abandoned, something Evan Walsh would never have done. She already hated herself for that, even before the crew—*her* crew—turned their stares on her, just long enough to convey their awareness of her sin. Reed knew they wouldn't forgive her, nor did she want them to. They needed their anger, just as she needed to maintain control—or at least the illusion of it.

Confronted with the horrors unfolding on the viewscreen, however, it was all Reed could do to keep it together. Shuffling forward, she joined the others in bewildered silence as they witnessed the final destruction of *Celtic*. The fires on board still burned, leaving trails of expanding smoke between the pieces of her hull, each section neatly severed from the others. They drifted apart slowly, rending the shape of the old vessel until nothing recognizable remained—just a collection of scattered parts meant for assimilation, deck lights flickering in the frozen dark as *Celtic* consumed the last of her remaining power.

Reed didn't even presume to mount a rescue. The cutting beam had done its work.

Nick Locarno, who had remained behind in the lift, now emerged to see the damage for himself. His face was drawn, his eyes red, bloodied beneath the surface from ruptured capillaries—but still he managed to shed tears, the pain only heightening his disbelief. He rammed a fist down on the nearest console, drawing everyone's attention—including that of Rayna Massey, who flew into an instant rage at the sight of him.

"You!" she hissed.

Massey slammed Locarno against the bulkhead before anyone could react, her fingers dug into the skin of his throat. Had she coordinated her attack, she might have killed him right there, but Massey just pounded on him, tearing at whatever she could find, scratching him deep before Reed and Thayer could pull her off.

"You son of a *bitch*!" she seethed, still lunging at him. *"You* did this!"

Locarno slid to the floor, wheezing. Nicole Carson rushed over to his side, opening up his collar to help him breathe, but he refused the help. From his haunted expression, Reed could tell he also blamed himself.

"You routed tactical through the computer core!" Massey shouted. "You *let* that thing cut loose with full phasers against our ship!"

Reed lowered her head. "That's enough, Rayna."

"Why'd you do it, Locarno?" Massey goaded, showing no signs of slowing down. "You have some kind of beef with the old man? Was this your way of settling the score?"

"I said, that's enough."

"Or maybe you just like getting people killed. Wouldn't be the first time, would it?"

"That's an order, Massey!"

Reed had no idea where her voice came from, but it slapped Massey hard, demanding no less than total compliance. She drove the point home with an acid stare, while everyone else stood by and held a collective breath. Reed wasn't even sure what she would do if Massey refused to back down, though the hand that reached for her phaser suggested otherwise.

"Look at him!" Reed snapped, motioning toward Locarno and all his wounds. "The core damn near suffocated him when it flooded the compartment with krylex mist. *That's* what happened when he tried to pull the plug."

Massey didn't appear convinced. Reed, for her part, didn't care.

"I don't need a loose cannon, Massey," she finished. "Not here, not now. The way I see it, you got a choice to make."

Reed gave it a minute, then let the tactical officer go. She nodded at Thayer, and he did the same. Massey shook them off, retreating a short distance while she weighed her options. Reed could tell that the woman was gauging the others, to see whose side they would pick—but everyone was still in limbo, reeling from *Celtic*'s death spiral. They weren't about to take that kind of step.

At least not yet.

Massey folded her arms and turned away. It was a truce, of sorts, though Reed doubted it would last very long.

"Anyone else?" Reed asked, daring each member of her crew to answer. When no one did, she projected the best image of authority she could muster. "Right now, I don't give a damn about who did what. We need to focus on the *problem*—which means I need all of you clear and thinking. Is that understood?"

No one objected. For Reed, that was enough.

"Very well," she said. "Where do we start?"

Locarno got back on his feet and cleared his throat.

"We have about fifteen hours before Starfleet arrives," he said quietly. "After that, it won't take them long to find us."

"That's good, right?" Carson asked, eager for any kind of hope. "All we have to do is hold out until they get here."

"And take us into custody," Thayer finished. "We'll be lucky if they don't hand us over to the Klingons when they're done."

Reed saw Locarno shake his head. She knew exactly what he meant.

"It's not that simple," she informed them. "There won't be any arrests. Starfleet will destroy this vessel the moment they find it."

"What?" Carson gasped.

"This ship is a Borg relic," Locarno explained. "They're not even allowed to attempt contact. Once they see what we are, they'll blow us out of the sky."

"But if we send them some kind of signal," the medic stammered. "Let them know that we're on board—"

"It won't make a difference," Locarno said, withdrawing. He paced all the way across the bridge, where he hovered far away from the others. That left only Reed to handle the crew, every last one of them looking to her to make a decision.

Even if it's the wrong one?

"Vector," she said, raising her voice enough for Locarno to hear it. He picked up on her use of his grid handle, which cut through the fog of his recriminations. "What's our status with the cores?"

"Starboard is a complete waste. That leaves two more."

"Can we maintain control if you bring them online?"

"I don't even know what happened yet," Locarno admitted. "If I had the time to make a close study of the wider system, *maybe* I could pinpoint the cause—"

"Can you *do* it?" Reed cut him off abruptly. Locarno got the message, and stopped making excuses.

"Yeah," he answered.

"Then get to it, mister."

He nodded, and walked back toward the lift. Along the way, he passed by Massey, who made a point of bumping against him hard. The two of them locked eyes for a heated moment.

"Watch your back, gridstalker."

Locarno didn't respond. He just left, disappearing behind the turbolift doors. With no other target, Massey turned her stare on Reed, saying nothing, but confirming more than ever that Reed had lost her.

And if that poison infects the rest of the crew . . .

"Resume stations," she ordered. "Mister Thayer, best speed out of here."

On thrusters only, *Reston* limped away from the scene. Reed waited until the last pieces of *Celtic* passed into the hazy distance, then stood up and advised everyone that she would be in engineering. Tristan Harlow already knew what happened—whispered chatter between the engineer and Rayna Massey assured that much—but that didn't change Reed's duty to inform him personally. Next to her, no one else had been closer to Evan Walsh. Harlow really needed to hear that the old man had gone down fighting, his hand on the helm. Some lies, as Reed discovered, were better off believed.

She prepared herself for the worst, but Harlow remained stoic in that unsettling way of his—forcing his grief back in on itself, like a fire smoldering behind a closed door, then focusing immediately on the task at hand. He returned to work without another word, leaving Reed to speculate how much he actually blamed her. There were no such doubts with James Casari. The way his eyes followed Reed, radiating the same anger as Massey but dosed with a cold shot of fear, set up a dangerous dynamic between them. She only hoped that Harlow retained enough of his loyalty to keep him in line.

If not, it would all come apart long before Starfleet arrived to kill them.

Having overstayed her welcome, Reed got out of there. She made it almost halfway to the turbolift before she broke down and cried, the tears coming hard and fast from a place she never knew existed. Walsh, for all the years he spent drilling the emotions out of her, had somehow missed this one: a deep, murky well where she sent the demons to drown, only to have them gather strength to wreak havoc another day. The Borg drones around her, even in life, never had to deal with those demons—and for that, among other things, Reed envied them.

Reed let it go for a few moments, then steadied herself. Wiping her face clean, she continued down the corridor, stopping when she saw Nicole Carson. The medic hovered at the fringes up ahead, as if she didn't want to be seen, before finally stepping forward. She had probably heard Reed's outburst and didn't want to intrude. Reed quickly changed the subject.

"Everything okay on the bridge?" she asked.

"Fine," Carson replied. "As those things go."

"We'll get through this, Nicole."

"I know," Carson said. "I just got to feeling like a fifth wheel up there, with everybody doing their jobs. Thought I might check out sickbay—you know, just in case we need it."

"I think that's back up on Deck Seven."

"I should read the signs."

Reed smiled. "It's a big ship. Come on, I'll take you there."

"Don't worry about it," Carson blurted—then immediately tried to make light of it. "I mean, I think I can figure it out. Besides, I could use some time to clear my head."

"Yeah," Reed said, more dubiously than she wanted to. "Don't stay out here too long, though. It's probably best not to wander around alone."

"Of course. See you back on the bridge."

With that, the medic excused herself and went back the way she had come. Reed frowned, not quite sure what to make of her. *Friend* or *foe* seemed to be the only two choices, which made it even harder for Reed to beat back the mounting paranoia she felt. All she *really* wanted was an ally—and so far, nobody was willing to commit. That only left one person, whom the others viewed with even greater suspicion than they did her.

She went down to the lower computer core, and found him ensconced there.

Locarno seemed almost one with the interface, which he operated with such skill that it was hard to tell where the man ended and the machine began. Shadows rendered his expression into a gaunt, inscrutable cipher, lit from below by the random electrons of a floating display. His eyes reflected the complex pathways of the Borg program matrix, which he followed deeper and deeper into the hole of their programmed consciousness—the same barren intellect that had deemed *Celtic* a threat and destroyed it.

"You must be running out of friends if you ended up here," the gridstalker said, never shifting his gaze from the display. "Take a load off. You can help me decompile some of this code."

Reed sat on the edge of a nearby console.

"You getting a feel for it?"

"Enough to know that I'll never understand it. You could spend years picking it apart and not even scratch the surface." Locarno killed the construct and sank back into his chair. "There's some good news, though. I know why my failsafe didn't work."

"Bad luck?"

"That's the least of it. This matrix is based on some kind of phased dimensional scheme—exploiting differentials between quantum states to propagate data faster than light, instead of the subspace architecture in the original design."

Reed caught on to his line of thinking. "The failsafe employs a subspace pulse . . ."

"Which wipes the pathways," Locarno finished. "No pathways, no fireworks. I could have been using harsh language, for all the good it did." He stared into the blank display. "I should have known."

"That's a tall order, Nick."

"Then I should have guessed," he retorted, his eyes lighting on some distant memory. "But that's me—always rolling the dice."

Reed shook her head and smiled knowingly.

"You were trying to impress Walsh."

"Doesn't matter who," Locarno said. "Whether it's him or the Academy flight board—people end up just as dead." His face set into a scowl at the mention of it, his breathing forced and steady—probably replaying the accusations that Rayna Massey had hurled at him, because they carried the sting of truth.

"You were Starfleet," she observed. "I kind of figured."

"Am I that obvious?"

"You let a few things slip—spending time at the Presidio, for one. Then there's your knowledge of Federation starships." She paused for a long moment, considering whether or not to press him on it. "So what happened?"

"Same thing that always happens. I took things too far."

"And somebody else paid the price."

"That's how I work." Locarno dropped his guard just a little, but trod cautiously with the details. "Senior year, I was captain of Nova Squadron. Even led the team to a Rigel Cup, if you can believe it—so you can imagine what a cocky bastard I was."

"You never struck me as the flyboy type."

"Back in the day." His tone wandered off into painful territory, the kind of wound a man kept opening to punish himself. "By the time graduation came around, all of us were looking for some way to top ourselves, so I came up with an idea to go out with a real bang." He gave Reed a sidelong glance. "You ever see a Kolvoord Starburst?"

Reed shook her head.

"You don't forget something like that," Locarno said, his tone as far away as his expression. "Unbelievably dangerous—but you never saw a more beautiful thing in your life. Not a dozen pilots in Academy history could pull it off." His head sank. "But we were Nova Squadron. We were immortal."

Pain materialized between them, the kind that can be stifled but never fully contained.

"How many did you lose?" Reed asked.

"Just one," he replied, a slight tremble in his voice. "We were at the Saturn Proving Grounds, making a practice run. Josh clipped my starboard wing during a close pass and lost control of his ship. We were in such tight formation that it caused a chain reaction. Four of us managed to eject." He paused for a long, sober moment. "Josh didn't."

Locarno didn't seem interested in absolution, but Reed felt compelled to offer it anyway. "You don't own that kind of mistake," she said. "Sounds to me like everyone was in."

"Evan Walsh ordered you here. Does that change anything for you?"

Reed didn't have to answer. Locarno already knew.

"How did you two cross paths?" she asked, changing the subject. "Seems like a strange alliance."

"My father served with him on the same merchant ship for a while. After he died, Walsh looked in on me from time to time—but I never found out his real profession until I got expelled from the Academy. When I needed a job, he set me up."

"And it's been a life of crime ever since."

"When everyone you've ever known hates you, there aren't a lot of options."

"I think it's more than that," Reed observed. "The chance to get back at Starfleet must've been hard to resist."

"They did me a favor. I would have made a lousy officer." Locarno slid out from the main interface and went over to one of the direct access panels, which he pried open to get a look into the core itself. "Is that your story? Some big grudge against the Federation?"

"Nothing that personal," Reed admitted.

Locarno nodded in understanding. "So it's the money."

"That, and a real problem with authority."

"Explains why Walsh took a shine to you."

"He saved my life," Reed said, drifting off on her own tangent. "I used to broker deals between organized crime factions on Delta IV. One of the overlords found out I was skimming a percentage for myself—including a pretty big slice of some latinum that Walsh boosted from a Ferengi freighter."

"Stealing from the Deltan mob?" Locarno asked, impressed. "That took some brass."

"That's what Walsh said," Reed told him, the trace of a smile on her lips. "They were just about to show me the nearest airlock when he stepped in and covered my debt. Bought out my contract right there on the spot—said he needed someone crazy enough to keep his crew in line. I've been flying with him ever since." She paused for an awkward moment as the hard reality intruded. "You know what I mean."

"This your way of cheering me up?"

Reed shrugged. "Privateers aren't known for their social skills."

"Neither are gridstalkers."

"Something else we have in common."

"Yeah," Locarno agreed. "Another time, another place—who knows?"

"Keep your head in the game," Reed fired back, though she was grateful for the effort—and the distraction. She walked over and joined him, looking over his shoulder into the raw data stream that pulsated within the core. "Does any of that even make sense?"

"There is a certain a logic to it. I was able to isolate some of the log files. From what I could put together, it looks as if the matrix terminated itself a short time after the Borg died."

"A self-destruct program?"

"More than that," Locarno mused. "The relationship between a Borg ship and its crew is symbiotic. Without that element, there is no greater purpose—and with no greater purpose, there's no reason to continue."

"Are you saying it committed *suicide*?"

"Essentially, yes."

Reed took a step back while Locarno buttoned up the panel. The very idea astonished her, so much that her mind raced to find arguments against it. That the Borg could feel *any* connection outside of a mechanical sense made them seem less like monsters—and right now, she *needed* them to be monsters.

Because she needed the hate. It was the last measure of her strength.

"I don't believe it," Reed said. "Obviously, the matrix isn't dead. The damn thing took control of the ship and blew *Celtic* out of the sky. It tried to kill *you,* for God's sake."

"I'm just telling you what I know," Locarno insisted. "Maybe it's just some by-product of the Borg design that allows it to survive beyond death, but this system was completely purged when I turned it on. Now it's not."

Reed swallowed hard, frightened by the implications.

"You're talking like this thing has a soul, Nick."

"Not a soul. More like a ghost in the machine."

"That's insane."

"You believe in God, Jenna?"

Reed hesitated before answering. "Yeah, so what?"

"Then it's not so crazy." Locarno returned to the interface and watched her through the empty display, his features distorted by random pixels in suspension. "You look to God for your own sense of identity. This matrix isn't so different. The Borg simply created it in their own image—the same basic drives, the same overriding impulse."

Reed thought of the presence she sensed after beaming aboard, which even now asserted itself like a dry static charge.

"Hunger," she spoke, her voice giving it substance. "Pure, insatiable hunger."

"Form and function. Nothing wasted."

She searched Locarno's eyes, terrified at the prospect of her next question.

"What brought it back?"

Locarno averted himself from that question. He knew as well as she did, but couldn't bring himself to answer.

"We resurrected this thing," Reed pronounced, "didn't we?"

"That's one possibility."

"As opposed to what?"

"I don't know." Locarno sighed. "I can't even pretend to understand the idiosyncrasies of this system. The best I can do is hazard a guess—and so far, guesswork hasn't done us a hell of a lot of good."

"You make do when it's all you've got," Reed told him. "That's another thing Walsh taught me, the same as he taught you. So answer me this, Vector—if the matrix targeted *Celtic* as a threat, then why are *we* still here?"

Locarno frowned, perplexed by this new equation.

"It could have killed us all," Reed continued, "but it didn't."

He gave it some thought, visibly disturbed.

"Maybe it has something else in mind," he finally said. "Some other purpose."

"And it needs *us* to fulfill that purpose. Whatever that may be."

A palpable dread hung between them, like a frost sublimating out of thin air.

And for the first time, Reed felt as if her soul was not her own.

"I don't like it," Casari smoldered. "Not one damn bit."

Tristan Harlow busied himself removing a panel from the warp core's reaction chamber, while the engineer's mate hovered close by and wrung his hands. Harlow had heard the tone before, that volatile mix of anger stoked by paranoia, and it immediately set him on edge. A man who talked that kind of game invariably caused trouble—and right now, they already had more than they could handle.

"It's not your job to like it," Harlow warned, setting the panel aside. A magnetic pulse thrummed within the containment circuitry, a manifestation of the invisible field that kept antimatter from escaping the core. So much power, all but useless without the right controls. "Your job is to do what you're told and not ask questions. Trust me—the less you know, the better."

Casari shook his head, unwilling to let it go.

"I'm *telling* you, Chief," he persisted, working himself into a righteous fugue. "Something's going on between Reed and that gridstalker. The way she let him off the hook, like *nothing* happened—it just ain't right."

"It was an accident, Jimmy."

"How can you be so sure?"

"Because that's the best information we have," Harlow said, though it came out sounding defensive, even to him. "Besides, it's not our decision. The skipper is calling the shots."

"The skipper is dead."

Harlow glared at him.

"You know what I mean," he muttered. Harlow didn't much trust Reed either, but the last thing he needed was some junior tool pusher hatching a half-assed mutiny on his watch. "Why don't you make yourself useful and give me a hand with this. I'd like to get it done before Starfleet gets here."

Chastened, Casari gave it a rest for the time being. He reached for a portable scanner in Harlow's gear box, affixing it to the reactor housing. Both men studied the display on the tiny device, which beeped as it detected a slight anomaly in the containment field.

"What is it?" Casari asked.

Harlow tapped the side of the scanner.

"Not sure," the engineer said as the display flickered. "Could be a flow asymmetry. The system's been on residual so long, it probably altered the physical characteristics of the emitter array." Harlow grabbed a few more tools and tossed them into a bag. "There's an auxiliary substation two decks below. I can use the manual calibration node down there to make a fix."

The blood visibly drained from Casari's face.

"You shouldn't go into the hellhole by yourself, Chief."

"I need you to stay here and monitor the flow," Harlow countered. He hauled himself over the rail and onto a ladder that ran the length of the warp core chamber. "Just sound off when the readings even out, okay? I'll be back in a few minutes."

Casari's silence was pleading, ominous.

"And relax," Harlow ordered. "Try not to break anything while I'm gone."

Casari nodded, a perfunctory gesture that belied the trepidation beneath. As Harlow descended, he looked back up and saw Casari leaning over and watching him—the shape of his head and shoulders receding into the dim halo that swathed the dormant core, until its very presence seemed only a trick of the available light. For some reason the sight made Harlow uneasy, as if Casari had imparted his fear over distance.

"I'm almost at the hatch!" he called out, his voice a disjointed chorus as it bounced off the walls of the chamber. "You still with me?"

"Roger, Chief."

The reply was faint, so drained by echoes that it could have been anyone. Harlow craned his neck to get a look, but couldn't find Casari on his perch. There was only him, and the terrible *isolation* that lived here in the depths. It slithered between the spaces like dark matter, form without mass, everywhere and nowhere at the same time.

And all he could think was: *It knows I'm here.*

But what could that possibly be? The answer, of course, was as plain as it was irrational: a deep, instinctive thing that could not be denied, and yet here he was denying it. Harlow tried blocking it out, focusing instead on his immediate task, but that did nothing to change the truth of what he knew.

The ship. The ship knows I'm here.

Harlow took a few more rungs. Footfalls clattered into the nothingness below, like rocks falling into a deep well. Twisting himself around, he spotted the substation hatch off to his right. He had expected to find it locked, but the small circular door was already ajar, creaking on its hinge as it went back and forth in a lazy sway. Harlow froze, peering into the black hole beyond the opening, which seemed poised and eager to swallow him.

Good God. One of those slags must've been down here when they all got cooked. The body's probably still in there.

"I see it!" Harlow yelled. He fumbled for the flashlight in his bag, its beam slicing up the musty gloom while he jostled for position. A dizzying strobe fell upon the hatch, revealing the interior in fits and glimpses, shadows taunting him with pernicious suggestion. Amid the confusion, Harlow *thought* he saw it: the sketchy outline of a head and shoulders, hands in full rigor clutching the dark. "Definitely got something here. Stand by—I might need some help with this."

The apparition cut in and out of view, as if trying to hide. Harlow leaned over and reached for the hatch, at the same time leveling his flashlight toward the tight space within. He jerked it away suddenly when his left foot slipped, making him lose his balance. Hugging the ladder, he pulled himself back up, the steam of his own breath blowing back against him.

"I'm okay," Harlow said, as the racket from his near fall died down. He had no idea whether Casari had seen it or not—but he needed to reassure himself, to fight the overwhelming urge to climb the hell out of there. Harlow closed his eyes and waited for the vertigo to pass, but found that it only grew worse, accompanied by a dry tingle of terror.

It's in there.

A gallery of images crossed the inside of his lids: a waxen face, pallid flesh, dead but not dead—tasting his life, his blood, and finding it sweet.

Staring at you. Craving you . . .

And him, responding. Drawn in. Wanting to belong.

Can't you feel it?

Holding the flashlight steady, Harlow reached for the hatch. Every impulse warned him to draw back, to leave this place, to get as far away as possible—but those were *human* imperatives, far removed from the force that drove him on. He could no more resist it than he could resist the cells in his body—or the elementals that coursed between.

With a tug, the hatch fell open.

Harlow brandished his flashlight like a weapon. The diffuse beam spilled across the cramped interior of the substation, darting from side to side while his heart hammered in anticipation. He pictured a grisly visage, imagining the hollow shell of a Borg corpse manning this forgotten post for all eternity.

But all he found was a blinking console.

And an empty chair.

What the hell?

Harlow wiped the sweat from his eyes, blinking several times. His vision blurred, then cleared, but nothing changed. There was no body—only his conviction that he had *seen* one. It still tingled at the far range of his senses, like a subliminal brush of cold electricity—or the feeling of being watched. That he couldn't find the watcher—even a dead one—only heightened the immune response of mortal fear.

"Chief?"

Casari's voice cascaded from above. Harlow seized upon it, looking upward—a distraction that left him vulnerable, though only the basest of his instincts understood the danger.

Because something had *found* him.

Harlow heard it first—the predatory sound of scratches against metal, as if some gigantic insect had dropped down from the ceiling behind the hatch. From there it advanced with inhuman speed, an onslaught of gnashing limbs that opened and closed like teeth in some immense maw. Harlow steeled himself for the attack, adrenaline pumping before he even knew what he faced—but by then it was too late, because the creature was already upon him. It struck mercilessly, its arms shooting out like tentacles and clamping down on his shoulders, nearly folding him in half as they dragged him into the substation. The flashlight tumbled out of Harlow's hands—and in those last seconds before fingers gouged his eyes, he witnessed his own doom as a shadow play across the wall.

Then all was dark. And a predator went to work.

Jenna Reed was back on the bridge when the klaxon sounded.

It jolted everyone up to their feet, a high-pitched, wraithlike scream. Reed didn't know Federation starships, but she instantly recognized the danger this one signified. In space, there was no mistaking a fire alarm.

"Locate!" she snapped.

Rayna Massey patched the threat board through her tactical display. "Main engineering," she replied, then looked up at Reed with dread insinuation. "Somebody pulled the lever."

Reed tapped her communicator.

"Engineering, bridge. What's your situation?"

Dead air. No response.

"Fire suppression negative," Chris Thayer reported. "So are internal sensors. Whatever it is, Skipper, there's no fire."

"Chief!" Reed tried again. "Respond immediately!"

The overhead speaker crackled to life. Ambient noise distorted the signal, but amid the clutter rose a guttural stream: sobs, whimpers, laced with obscenities and denials. Not Harlow. Someone else.

"Casari?" Reed asked.

"No, no, no, please God no—"

"Slow down, Casari. You're not making sense."

"This ain't happening. This can't be happening."

Panic surged through the bridge like an electrical current, riding on the crest of Casari's voice. It built to a blunt crescendo, relentless and unstoppable.

"Say again, Casari!" Reed shouted. "Where's Harlow?"

"THEY'RE STILL HERE!"

The transmission ended.

"Stay at your posts," Reed ordered, heading out.

"Stuff that," Massey said, and followed her. Thayer did the same, the three of them jamming into the turbolift at the same time.

Nobody said a word during descent, instead drawing their weapons in preparation for whatever fight awaited below. As the car began to slow, Reed directed her people to assume flanking positions on each side of the door, while she crouched in front and leveled her phaser directly ahead. Breathing evenly, she waited as the deck indicator slowly ticked off their destination, her finger with a good half pull already on the trigger.

The doors slid open, the way clear.

"Go," she said.

Massey went first, a few meters down the corridor, while Thayer and Reed gave her cover. Planting herself against the bulkhead, the tactical officer scanned the way ahead and then looked back at them and nodded. Thayer went next, extending the chain—though it still left a long run to their target, which Reed saved for herself. She tore past the others at a reckless clip, until the doors to engineering appeared around the turn. There, in the peripheral shadows, a nuance of movement jerked Reed to a halt.

She whipped her phaser around in a tight arc, taking aim between a pair of regeneration chambers. Tentatively, Nicole Carson stepped out from the narrow space.

Reed lowered her weapon. "You okay?"

Carson nodded.

Reed motioned for the others to come forward. Thayer and Massey approached quickly, silently, gathering in a tight circle. Everyone spoke in tense whispers, their adrenaline barely contained.

"I heard the alarm from sickbay," Carson said. "What's going on?"

"Damned if we know," Massey replied, nodding toward the heavy door that led into engineering. "Casari's still in there. I can hear him."

Reed listened. She heard it too: a low moan, repeating incessantly.

"—he's gone he's gone he's gone he's gone—"

All of them exchanged the same frightened look. God only knew what was happening in there, but Reed knew that waiting was not an option. Holding her hand up, she counted down from three. Everyone understood what it meant when she reached one.

And by then, they were primed to storm the very gates of hell.

Reed fired a shot into the deck, the blast going off like a flash grenade. All of them then charged into the smoke, using it for cover while they scattered in different directions. Reed stayed on target, heading straight for Casari, while the others staked out tactical positions to maximize their field of fire. Reed lost track of them in all the confusion, making her way through the insane patchwork hive that the Borg had spun, Casari's ominous warning echoing through her head: *They're still here.* Reed felt the truth of it stirring her blood, her eyes searching the acrid mist for confirmation, while her phaser stood ready to vaporize anything that crossed her path.

That was when she found Casari, his arms wrapped around his knees, rocking back and forth as he sat on the floor. He kept shaking his head, oblivious to everything around him—including Reed, who stopped abruptly when she saw him. The smoke had just started to lift, raising a curtain on engineering that revealed no intruders, though everyone remained with their weapons at the ready.

"Clear!" Massey called out.

"We're secure," Thayer affirmed.

Carson, meanwhile, rushed over to Casari. She knelt down next to him, running a nominal check with her tricorder while Reed stood over them. "No physical trauma that I can detect," the medic said, "but he's in shock."

Reed drilled into Casari, hard enough to break through his fugue. "Where's Harlow?" she demanded.

Casari opened his trembling hands, which were covered in blood. "They took him," he said.

The Borg had left sickbay mostly intact, having no real need for medical facilities. The only exception was a large, translucent cistern they had installed in the pathology lab—a hideous contraption filled with a cloudy, viscous gel, through which floated various chunks of organic matter. As Jenna Reed stared into that macabre suspension, she instinctively knew that the bits and pieces were fragments of flesh and bone, recycled from dead bodies that had been processed through here. From the complex network of attached conduits, it looked as if the soup was then pumped throughout the rest of the ship—probably as a nutrient substrate for the rest of the crew. *Eating their own,* she thought, shuddering at the efficiency of it. The Borg wasted nothing.

Over on one of the sickbay beds, Carson performed a more de-tailed analysis of her patient. Casari was back from the outer darkness, under the influence of a mild tranquilizer. Massey, meanwhile, strode into sickbay with Thayer at her side, both of them nearly out of breath. They walked straight over to Reed, and the three of them retreated into the lab.

"We searched the hellhole from top to bottom," Massey spoke in a subdued but urgent voice. "Harlow is gone."

"People just don't disappear," Reed insisted. "He has to be *some-where.*"

"All we found was his combadge and his phaser," Thayer said. "Whatever hit him did it hard and fast. There was blood all over that substation."

"Maybe it was just like Casari said," Massey intoned. "If just *one* of those slags managed to get loose—"

"There *are* no live Borg on this ship," Reed interjected, trying to make herself believe it. "Not after all this time."

"If it isn't the Borg," Thayer asked, "then who the hell is it?"

The hiss of sliding doors pierced the loaded silence between them. Reed turned just in time to see Nick Locarno rushing in. "I heard it over the comms," he said, shouldering the others aside and moving in on Reed. "Have you located Harlow yet?"

Reed flinched away from him.

"Where have you been, Nick?"

Locarno froze. Massey and Thayer flanked him closely, keeping their hands at their sides but menacing him just the same. Locarno shot glances at both of them, then looked to Reed for help—but she offered none.

"Firewalling the core," he explained, turning icy. "The damn thing is like a hostile entity trying to escape into the wider system. You can't just leave it there without taking precautions."

Massey wasn't convinced. "And we just have to take your word for that, right?"

Locarno deliberately ignored her, directing his words solely at Reed. "I got here as soon as I could, Jenna. Don't waste the time we have left giving in to this kind of crazy."

Reed felt the weight of their anticipation as she considered it. Whatever wisdom Evan Walsh might have imparted had abandoned her, leaving Reed with only her gut to make a decision—and right now, fear steered that course more than anything. Without Locarno, they were all dead—it was just that simple. She *needed* to believe him, for all of their sakes.

Slowly, she relented. Massey shook her head in disgust, while Thayer stood by and didn't know what to think.

"Outside," Reed ordered, and led them back into sickbay.

Carson propped Casari up in his bed, and the two of them observed their returning shipmates with open apprehension. There were six of them now—their ranks already dwindling only a few hours after the loss of *Celtic,* and Reed still couldn't tell them why. More than anything, she wanted to settle that question, but with the resources she had, all she could do was fight a defensive battle.

"This is how it works," she announced. "Nobody goes anywhere alone. We restrict our movements to those direct paths between the bridge, the core, and main engineering. All other sections are strictly *off limits*. Does everybody understand?"

No one argued.

"Jimmy," she said to the engineer's mate. "I want our travel corridors sealed off and life support terminated everywhere else. Can you do that?"

Casari lowered his head and nodded. "Aye, Skipper."

"What about Chief Harlow?" Carson asked gravely. "He could still be out there, alive somewhere."

"She's right," Thayer agreed, to a rising din of affirmation. "Massey and me, we didn't have time to spread out and check the surrounding decks. We could do paired sweeps, using sensors—"

"We *can't* help him," Reed said, cutting him off in the harshest possible way. Her outburst silenced everyone, drawing shocked stares from all around—exactly as she intended. "Whatever got Harlow did it before he could get off a single shot. We start tearing this ship apart, not even sure what we're up against, the same thing is going to happen to *us*." She allowed that thought to sink in for a long, tense moment. "I will *not* take that risk—and neither would the chief."

Her words dampened their bravado, until only embers remained. All except for Massey, who sneered in contempt.

Reed scowled at her. "You got something to add, mister?"

"Just wondering about the slags," Massey said. "Sure, you can bottle us up nice and tight, but that still leaves plenty of *them* inside our perimeter. You plan to do something about that? Or are you just hoping that Casari was wrong about what he saw?"

The question hung out there, like bait on a string—and Reed had no choice but to take it. That one or more Borg had somehow survived, and were now on the hunt for human flesh, had assumed the status of conventional truth. There was no fighting it.

"The hangar deck," Reed decided. "We'll take them there."

The image was a grainy black and white, minimalist and surreal, the feed piped in from security cameras in *Reston*'s shuttlebay. Reed sat at the bridge engineering console and watched on a small monitor, while Carson hovered behind her—both of them unsure of how to react to the scene that unfolded before them. Massey passed through the frame, her envirosuit trailing a ghostly light reflected from the harsh kliegs overhead, while Thayer bounded farther off, his movements slow and exaggerated in the reduced gravity. Casari had adjusted it to make their grim task more efficient—though from Reed's vantage point, it only enhanced the abject horror of it all.

Dozens of corpses littered the expansive deck. Most of them were arranged in haphazard stacks near the hangar door, awaiting disposal like victims of some wildfire contagion: a tangled mass of arms and legs and buried faces, hurriedly dumped there after extraction from their regeneration chambers. These were the last of the drones to be removed from Reed's newly established safe zone, a veritable parade of the dead. The exercise struck her as useless, an atrocity even; but it was the only way to keep the fragile peace with her crew, who by now believed the Borg capable of anything—including resurrection.

Thayer hoisted one more body over his shoulder, throwing it on the pile with the others. Its head twisted at an unnatural angle, pointing back at Reed through the monitor—a pleading simulacrum of life, begging to be spared this final indignity. Reed turned away.

"*That's it,*" Thayer said, cold and detached over the speaker. "*Stand by for evac.*"

Massey motioned him over to the entry hatch, and the two of them passed out of view to the other side. Reed heard a loud clang as they closed it up, the indicator on her panel showing a positive seal. She absently drummed her fingers near the PURGE control, which flashed red as it awaited her command.

"*We're secure, bridge,*" Massey said. "*They're all yours.*"

Reed hit the button. The ship rumbled as the outer door opened, venting atmosphere to space, along with everything else on the hangar deck. The violent slipstream raised a flurry of debris, which careened through the incipient vacuum like particles in a random flux. In the midst of all that chaos, bodies collided with one another as if urged on by hurricane winds, ultimately to be claimed by the void. In a matter of seconds it was over—their presence erased, the deck so clear that they might as well have never been there.

Reed kept staring until the door closed again.

"All clear," she said. "Return to the bridge immediately."

With that, Reed killed the image on the monitor. She then slipped out of the chair and walked away, her back turned to Carson. For some reason, she didn't want to be seen, as if her actions had been some sort of crime, instead of some ritual to assuage a superstitious crew. *I guess it's true,* she pondered. *When things go bad, people revert to the old ways.*

"Where are you going?" Carson asked.

"The ready room," Reed answered, the only place that came to mind. The way Carson looked at her, the way she sounded—scared masking as sympathetic—had begun to wear on her. Reed needed a few minutes away from it, away from everything. "Send everyone in when they get here."

Carson hesitated, but didn't argue. "Aye, sir."

Reed barely registered the doors opening, and walked into the gloom on the other side without thinking. When they hissed shut behind her, she collapsed against the bulkhead and slid to the floor. Eyes pasted shut, she tried to stem the tears that forced their way to the surface, but she was simply too exhausted, too hopped up on stims to sort one emotion from the other. Reed didn't know how long it lasted. She just knew that when it was over, she was sitting all alone in the dark, in direct violation of her own orders.

She steadied herself with a deep breath, then rose to her feet. Through a nearby window, the electrified glow of the Korso Spanse cast the ready room in virtual light, giving life to shadows and manipulating dimensions. She traced the contours of ordinary objects—a desk, a chair, a computer console—to reassure herself of their normality, but doubts clawed at her like minions from below. The harder she looked, the more she believed that—

something

—else was with her, just out of sight, hiding in the places where things lived on board this ship. That chill was enough to make her want to leave.

Reed had almost reached the door when a voice stopped her cold.

"You found us."

The words were synthetic, processed and filtered to an approximation of human. Dread seized upon her in that instant—an insidious, parasitic toxin that seeped into her tissues and spun her mind into free fall. Up from those depths, some latent defensive mechanism slowly guided her hand to the phaser at her hip—though the weapon itself seemed useless.

Because what she sensed in the room wasn't alive.

"You know us," it continued. *"Just as we know you."*

Reed kept her back turned, her body trembling. She didn't *want* to turn. She didn't *want* to know. And the scream that rippled through her bones refused to surface, breaking open her insides.

"Resistance . . . is . . ."

Reed's mouth dried up as she completed the dread phrase: "Futile."

"Unnecessary."

She drew the phaser from its holster.

"Look at us."

"TO HELL WITH YOU!" she roared, and spun around as she mashed the trigger. Lethal energy split the air with a molten shimmer, carving a jagged line across the rear bulkhead. Sparks exploded throughout the ready room, blinding an already reckless line of attack—until pain captured Reed's wrist in a cruel vise, paralyzing her entire arm. Crushing pressure forced her fingers open, and with it the phaser tumbled out of her hand. In the grip of agony, falling to her knees, she watched as the weapon hit the deck and slid away.

Reed's assailant loomed over her, pure strength and singularity.

"Do you not see?"

Eyes cast down, she refused. On the other side of the door, a drumbeat of pounding joined a chorus of voices: her crew, pleading for her to open.

"You are us."

Reed clawed after the phaser, only to be jerked back.

"We are you."

She sobbed, an incoherent stream of consciousness. Fists against the door gave way to a loud crash, a battering ram trying to break it down.

"Look at us, Jenna."

Those last words dissolved into the echoes of delusion. Slowly, the hand that held Reed pulled her up off the floor—toward the truth she already knew, because it had called her by name. Face-to-face, she no longer had the will to resist. This was the natural order. This was destiny.

"We are Borg," Tristan Harlow said.

Only half of him was there. The rest was a jumble of prosthetics and body armor, grafted to an exposed skeleton of metal and bone and bound by strands of twitching muscle—as if he had only been partially assimilated. Harlow cocked his head to one side, examining Reed with his left eye—a black, lifeless orb that was no less a horror than the empty socket on the right. A tangled bundle of fiber protruded from that lidless hole, aglow with tiny bursts of laser light that splattered like blood against his skin. He was a monster, all the more terrifying in this incomplete state.

Reed stifled a scream. She kicked at Harlow, but he didn't buckle. She punched him in the face, but his flesh only peeled away beneath her knuckles. Reacting to her hostility, he grabbed Reed by the throat and squeezed. She convulsed wildly, clutching at Harlow's hands and trying to free herself, but he held fast. In the graying tunnel of her vision, she saw him eject a nanoprobe from one of the compartments in his armor. The thing snaked its way toward her as if it had a mind of its own, greedily seeking a point of entry.

"Tristan—" she gasped. "Please—*don't* . . ."

He hesitated, a human spark deep within the inhuman well of his eye.

"It is already done."

Harlow plunged the probe into Reed's neck. The scolex buried itself deep within her flesh, writhing tendrils penetrating the length of her veins—

—until the ship exploded around her, and all was heat and light.

The blast wave entered from behind, pushing a cloud of cinders and debris, as if someone had tossed in a flash grenade. Reed felt the probe withdraw just before the concussion hit—a wall of sheer force that should have mowed Harlow down, and her along with him. Somehow he stayed upright, though his grip on her slackened. Reed used that split second to break loose, turning herself around before Harlow clamped down and wrenched her back—but not before she saw the smoldering hole in the ready room door, the edges still aglow from spent energy plasma.

And Nick Locarno launching himself through it.

Harlow, processing the newer, greater threat, tossed Reed aside. Stars bloomed in her vision as she landed on top of the desk, knocking over a model starship and a heavy bronze statue, right before she careened into the rear bulkhead with a loud crash. Reed dragged herself away as everything around her moved in slow motion, blood seeping from the surgical hole in the side of her neck.

"Stand down!" Locarno shouted, leveling his phaser at the Borg's chest. Harlow paid no heed, lumbering toward him on biomechanical legs, the whine of spinning gears marking each move. Massey, who appeared at Locarno's side, also took aim with her weapon, while Thayer scrambled to get inside.

"You will understand," Harlow said. *"You will belong."*

"I *mean* it, Chief!"

"Assimilation is inevitable."

"Max power," Locarno told Massey. "Tight dispersal."

Both of them fired.

A high-pitched scream split the air wide open, a twin salvo converging on Harlow. The hit should have vaporized him instantly—but instead, the beams dissolved on impact, absorbed by a force field that swathed his body. Locarno and Massey kept pouring it on, maintaining continuous fire until their phasers began to sputter, but Harlow never even slowed down. Step by step he closed in on them, forcing them into retreat.

Thayer, seeing the hopelessness of it, jumped into the no-man's-land between.

"Go!" he yelled at them, and tackled Harlow.

The attack caught him by surprise, long enough for Thayer to knock him down and send both men reeling. Thayer tried to take the advantage, drawing his fist back to land a punch in the middle of Harlow's face, but the Borg's enhanced reflexes were just too fast, and he blocked Thayer's move before he even got close. In a blur of motion, Harlow crushed Thayer's fingers and spun his arm around his back, popping the bone loose from his shoulder with a sickening crack. Thayer shrieked in pain, his legs flailing as the Borg stood and hauled him off his feet. The nanoprobe, denied its feast with Reed, quickly angled itself toward Thayer, hovering in front of his terrified eyes for a moment—right before it drilled into the middle of his forehead.

"Thayer!" Massey screamed.

Thayer twitched, little more than a dead man's rattle, his eyes rolling back beneath their lids.

Reed, driven by pure rage, grabbed the first weapon she could find and threw herself at Harlow. She swung at him with the bronze statue before she even knew it was in her hand, cracking the Borg across the back of the head with as much strength as she could muster. A crimson mist burst from his bare scalp, wetting Reed's lips and making her thirst for more, her mind disconnected from her actions as something bestial took over. She swung at Harlow again, this time hitting him over the top of his skull, so hard that his legs collapsed beneath him. The Borg dropped Thayer into a lifeless heap, his own limbs thrashing involuntarily as his nervous system shorted out. Reed, however, kept beating on him—bringing the statue down again and again and again, not caring what she hit, while sparks erupted from the joints between his armor plates.

Locarno and Massey had to pull her off before she would stop.

Breathless and aching, Reed dropped the statue as the world around her snapped back into focus. By then Carson had descended on her, tending to the wound in Reed's neck, while Casari stumbled in with a dazed expression pasted across his face.

"Don't move," Carson said.

Reed pushed her away, motioning toward Thayer.

"Take care of him," she rasped.

The medic did as she was told, finding Thayer splayed out on the deck with his eyes wide open. Carson ran her tricorder over him, grimacing as the readings came back. "He's alive," she pronounced, then turned toward Reed. "But barely. Brain functions are minimal—so is respiration."

"My God," Casari droned, shaking his head when he saw what was left of Harlow. "The chief . . ."

Locarno cut him off. "Can you stabilize Thayer?"

Carson whipped out a hypospray and injected Thayer with it. "That should hold him until I get him to sickbay. I can't do anything for him here."

Locarno fixed Casari with a hard stare that told him panic wasn't an option. "Get him down there," he ordered, and kept the pressure on until Casari nodded. He picked Thayer up and draped the dead weight over his shoulder, following Carson as she led him out of the ready room. A moment later they were gone, leaving behind a deathly silence, punctuated by Harlow's fading mechanical throes.

All eyes settled on him.

The Borg refused to die, his hands still probing, seeking, reaching out in every direction. Massey checked her phaser, squeezing out every last bit of power, then started off toward him to finish the job, but Reed took hold of the tactical officer's sleeve, pulling her back.

"No," Reed said. "Not yet."

Locarno and Massey helped her up, and the three of them approached Harlow slowly. The Borg managed to raise his head, and regarded each of them with a strange blend of pleading and recognition. Reed peered back at him, sensing something of the old engineer.

"Tristan," she said. "Are you still in there?"

The Borg twisted his lips into an approximation of a smile.

"He is part of the whole. We were once so many. Now there is only us."

"You tried to kill us!" Massey spat, aiming her phaser at his head. "The same way you killed the chief!"

"Death is not our purpose. Only continued existence. Your time is growing short. You must understand before that time is at an end."

"What do you mean?" Reed asked.

"We are aware of Starfleet directives. The knowledge of Harlow, Tristan J., is now part of our consciousness. Upon discovery, your lives and this matrix will be terminated. It is essential you act before then."

Locarno exchanged an astonished glance with Reed, then looked back at Harlow.

"Act on what?"

"Your assimilation."

The three of them stepped away as if struck. Reed touched her wound again, which had already begun to heal—and realized the truth of it before Harlow even spoke.

"It has already begun. You are kindred. We detected this upon your arrival."

"That's impossible," Massey snarled. "You're lying!"

"Lying is irrelevant. Denial is irrelevant."

Reed took Massey's phaser and took aim at Harlow herself.

"Prove it."

The Borg smiled again, black fluid seeping between his teeth.

"Proof is irrelevant," he said, cryptic and taunting. *"But if it is your predilection to find it, then seek out the one among you who facilitated your assimilation."*

Carson burst into sickbay with Casari in tow, and headed straight toward the pathology lab. "Over there," she ordered, directing him to a diagnostic bed near the back. Casari laid Thayer out as carefully as he could, then got out of the way so the medic could go to work. She immediately strapped Thayer down, checking the monitor above his head as vital signs poured across the screen. The readings were next to nonexistent, except for the encephalograph, which sparked to extremes far outside human range.

"What's happening to him?" Casari asked.

"Whatever put him in a coma is stimulating the hell out of his brain," Carson said, unable to contain her awe at the process—until she noticed Casari's puzzled stare. Distracting him, she pointed over his shoulder toward a nearby tray. "Hand me those scissors. We need to get this envirosuit off right now."

Casari did as he was told. Carson quickly sliced through the fabric of Thayer's suit, shucking the whole thing like a layer of dead skin. She then opened a hidden drawer beneath the bed, which revealed a glittering collection of instruments—alien in design, with sinister contours that implied torture more than treatment. Casari's eyes widened when he saw them, particularly the bundle of tubes that Carson affixed to various points across Thayer's body. They bore a striking similarity to the nanoprobe that Harlow had wielded.

"What . . . *are* those?"

"I'm using everything in the arsenal," Carson snapped, hoping that would end Casari's questions. He backed off slightly, but still glared at her with open suspicion as she placed the last tube over the hole in Thayer's forehead. "If you want to save his life, you won't interfere."

She then activated a nearby touch screen, which started a flow that inflated the tubes with a low hiss. Thayer reacted violently, his chest heaving up and down—spasms that rapidly spread through his extremities, sending him into a fit of convulsions. His arms and legs tore against their restraints, which split and frayed to the breaking point.

"Hold him down!" Carson shouted.

Terrified, Casari obeyed. He grabbed Thayer by the shoulders and pinned him, while Carson jabbed another hypospray into the rippling sinew of Thayer's neck. He gradually tapered off into a disturbing calm—regular breaths and a rising body temperature, marked by a return of stable readings on the monitor.

Then came the metamorphosis, into something unspeakable.

Casari watched it spread across Thayer's chest, like some kind of infection that turned his skin to ash. The color faded to bone white, as if every drop of blood had drained away, capillaries forced to the surface and spidering outward to form varicose paths. Thayer's eyes, blue and void, hemorrhaged to black—portals into an empty soul, something much worse than death. Casari recoiled from the sight, suddenly aware of what this was.

Because the same thing had happened to the chief.

Assimilation.

He looked up at Carson, pleading with her to do something—but froze when he saw the phaser pointed at him.

"You know the drill," she said. "Nice and easy."

Casari pulled his own weapon, drawing it slowly and handing it over.

"You unbelievable bitch," he seethed. "You *did* this to them."

"Nothing personal," she replied, circling around the bed with her phaser trained on him. Her posture, her demeanor—everything about Carson had changed. No longer the timid medic, she carried herself with the cold poise of a professional killer. "As a privateer, I'm sure you understand these things."

"Sure," he scoffed, while she motioned him toward the door. Casari wasn't sure what she planned to do with him once they got there, but he wasn't going to wait long enough to find out. As he turned away from Thayer, he snatched up the instrument tray, using his back to conceal his actions. "It's all about the score, isn't it?"

Carson, growing impatient, jabbed at Casari to get him moving. Seizing the initiative, he spun around with the tray in his hands and clubbed her across the side of the head.

A loud clang marked the point of impact, scalpels and forceps raining down on Carson as she smashed into the deck. Casari broke into a run, making it less than two steps before she grabbed him by the leg and tripped him. Losing his balance, he careened into the bulkhead next to the door, bouncing off the edge before it slid open and he fell through. Carson was on him in an instant, pouncing on Casari as he crawled into sickbay. He clawed at her, trying to push her off, but came up with fistfuls of empty air. Carson, meanwhile, wrapped her arm around Casari's throat, jerking him backward so hard that he heard his own vertebrae cracking.

"Let him go, Nicole!"

The voice came out of nowhere, making time stand still. Oxygen flowed back into Casari's brain, but the chokehold on him remained, even as Carson hauled him to his feet. A moment later, he felt the hard point of her phaser against his temple, along with Carson's perfectly controlled breathing on the back of his neck.

"I said, let him go."

Jenna Reed stood at the entrance to sickbay, with Nick Locarno next to her. Both of them pointed phasers at Carson, though their only line of fire was through Casari.

"Then what?" Carson asked.

"We sort things out."

Carson laughed.

"I'll give you props for honesty, Reed," she said. "For a minute I thought you were going to say we could talk it over."

"This ends the way you want it to end, Nicole," Reed told her. "We're all stuck on this ship together. Nobody else has to die."

"The hell with that!" Casari spat, not caring anymore. "*Shoot* her!"

Reed did just the opposite, holstering her weapon.

"You see?" she said, holding up her hands. "We can all walk out of here."

"It's too late for that," Carson said, detached from any trace of emotion or empathy. "Nobody was supposed to walk out of here at all. That was the plan."

"*What* plan?" Locarno demanded. "Who are you working for?"

"People like that don't have names. They just give orders."

"And you follow them without question," Reed finished. "But reviving *the Borg*? What kind of insanity is that?"

"A very useful kind," Locarno proffered. "Think about it. After everything that's happened—Wolf 359, Sector 001, the Dominion War—all the devastation that left this quadrant vulnerable to God knows what. Then throw in a weaponized Borg, under strict control—ready to fight and die at a moment's notice." He scowled at Carson. "Sounds to me like your handlers have big plans for the future. The only question is, how do *we* fit in?"

A sudden, dark realization settled over all of them.

"We're the test subjects," Reed said.

She started walking toward Carson, each step a provocation. The medic—or whatever she really was—pulled Casari closer.

"Harlow tried to tell us," Reed continued, "but I didn't want to hear it. 'We are kindred,' he said—all of us except you." She stopped, flexing her voice like a weapon. "What did you do to us, Nicole?"

Carson smiled, cold and reptilian.

"The shots I gave you prior to the mission," she admitted. "They contained a modified strain of Borg nanoprobes."

Reed bored into her, eyes flickering black over green. Already, the nanites were at work—manipulating her, changing her.

"How do we stop it?"

"You don't," Carson answered. "This was a one-way ticket. Walsh saw to that."

Hatred flared behind Reed's fixed expression.

"No way the skipper would sell us out."

"I admit it took a little push," Carson said, "but once he saw how much money was at stake, he couldn't sign on fast enough. He was a privateer, after all." She laughed softly, mockingly. "Of course, he didn't plan on becoming a victim of his own greed—but it's just as well. Knowing what he knew, Walsh would have been a dangerous loose end."

"And what about *you*?"

"Oh, I'm a survivor."

"Not for long," Locarno said. "Once Starfleet gets here, they'll kill you just as dead as the rest of us."

"We'll see," Carson retorted—insinuating so much more.

"They'll get their chance," Reed assured her—and jumped out of the way.

Hidden behind her, Locarno had already zeroed in on Carson. He fired a short burst, ionizing the space between them with a stun beam on a wide aperture, enough to take down both her and Casari. Carson reacted with skill and speed, tossing her hostage into the field of fire while she ducked and rolled away. Casari took the brunt of the hit, which spun him around and dropped him on the deck. Carson, meanwhile, dove behind a nearby rack and peppered Locarno with phaser fire, her own weapon set to kill. The air around him crackled with coherent energy, exploding against the wall as he ran, beams dogging his movements like tracers as they closed in on their target. He leapt over a desk before the last shot could find its mark, taking cover underneath as a computer console detonated above his head.

Reed, meanwhile, threw herself over Casari. He was still conscious, but in serious pain, his left arm nearly paralyzed from the stun beam. He swore out loud, grabbing Reed by the collar and pulling her face-to-face.

"She's getting away," he grunted.

Reed looked up and saw Carson bolting for the door. She disappeared before Reed could draw her phaser again.

"Come on," she said.

By the time they got off the floor, Locarno had emerged from his hiding place. He quickly checked the corridor, then ran over to join them. "She's gone," he said. "Where's Thayer?"

"Back there," Casari told them, pointing toward the lab. "He's in bad shape."

"Check on him," Reed said.

Casari limped off. At the same time, Locarno grabbed Carson's bag off the shelf and dumped the contents out over one of the beds. The gridstalker rifled through the things with a practiced eye, searching for something specific.

"What are you looking for?" Reed asked.

"If this *is* a black-bag job," Locarno explained, "then Carson would make sure she had an insurance policy. Spooks don't do anything without a backup plan." He lingered for a moment on her tricorder, which he popped open and examined closely. Removing one of the circuit boards, he found a small card wedged in where it shouldn't have been. Prying it loose, he held it up for both of them to see.

"Looks like an isolinear chip," Reed said.

"It is," Locarno agreed, "but this one is a multidimensional prototype—not exactly standard issue." He went over to a nearby console and inserted the chip, while Reed watched over his shoulder. "This is some major storage—enough to cold-boot one of the computer cores if she wanted."

"Is that what she had in mind?"

"Tell you in a flash," Locarno said, navigating the intricate data paths that appeared on the display. He breached the security layers in a matter of seconds, which released a torrent of code. Locarno, however, immediately found what he wanted and pointed it out to Reed. "This is a control subroutine—engines, navigation, deflectors—everything you need to fly this ship."

"Can you use it to get us out of here?"

Locarno read further, his face hardening. "No," he said, with an edge of finality. "Nothing works without the interaction of an actual Borg crew. The core matrix won't allow it."

Reed pounded a fist on the desk.

"We were going to be that crew," she seethed. "After we turned, Carson was going to use *us* to handle the goddamned ship."

"That explains why she moved on Chief Harlow. She needed to speed up assimilation before Starfleet got here."

"A lot of good it did her," Reed muttered, glancing toward the lab. "Where the hell is Casari? He should have been back by now." Raising her voice, she started in that direction herself. "Jimmy! What's going on in there?"

No answer. Locarno followed her as an ominous pall descended, a sudden realization that something was horribly, dangerously *wrong*. Phasers in hand, they approached the door to the pathology lab. An unnatural silence reigned within, stirred only by the low, steady flow of the reclamation tanks. Reed signaled for Locarno to hang back and cover her, while she slipped over to the edge of the door, the pounding of her heart and the adrenal surge in her veins somehow alien to her.

I'm losing myself, she thought. *It won't be long—for any of us.*

And right there, the concept of risk suddenly lost all meaning.

Reed thrust herself inside, staying low and staring down the sight of her weapon. Locarno appeared behind her, taking the high ground and sweeping the area while Reed pushed in farther. She immediately found the diagnostic bed empty, its restraints torn to shreds—the only trace that Thayer had ever been there. On the floor between the tanks, however, she saw a pair of legs sticking out. It would have been bad enough if they belonged to a dead man—but these legs jerked like flesh on a live wire, as did the rest of the body, in some kind of diseased frenzy.

"Nick!" Reed called out.

Neither of them dared touch Casari. They could feel the heat coming off him even at a distance, as his face contorted into a sound-less scream. Holes extended into his temples from where the nano-probes had gone in, red blood coagulating to black. It was as if the Borg inside was tearing him apart to get out.

Reed's communicator sounded off.

"Skipper, bridge," Rayna Massey said. *"You better get up here."*

She mouthed the word at first, unable to speak as she witnessed Casari's assimilation. This was her future. *Their* future.

"Report," she finally spoke.

"Unidentified contact, max range. I think it's Starfleet."

Locarno turned to Reed, like a condemned man facing his executioner. Reed, meanwhile, drew a long breath as she weighed their limited options.

"Best evasive," she ordered. "We're on our way."

Locarno motioned toward Casari. "What about him?"

Her thumb caressed the trigger of her phaser. One more blast would end Casari's misery—and make it that much easier when it was her turn. But something inside her, some species memory, wouldn't allow it.

"Leave him," she said, and left without looking back.

The corridor compressed into a jumble of illusory artifacts and points of light, every detail flashing past in stop-motion continuity. Nicole Carson could taste her body's reaction to that imperative, survival asserting itself just as her training had taught her, and she used it to fuel her flight, focusing every impulse on her objective. She had memorized the way to auxiliary control, long before coming aboard, and could find it in total darkness if needed; and she had made provisions for just this contingency, with a stockpile of small arms and a thruster suit she had scavenged from *Reston*'s emergency stores.

Carson ran toward her destination with mechanical efficiency, moving swiftly but never in a panic, stopping every few meters to check her six in case the others had decided to pursue. When the alert klaxon sounded, blaring through the narrow space with its doomsayer wail, she thought it was a bluff at first, some attempt by Reed to slow her down or flush her out; but it soon became apparent that nobody was coming after her, and that the alarm—which sounded a call to general quarters—was *real,* probably triggered automatically by the ship's defensive systems. That kind of alert could only mean one thing: an enemy vessel in close proximity.

The Feds are here.

Carson picked up the pace, bypassing her precautions so she could cover more ground. Auxiliary control was still two full sections away, and she didn't have much time. By her calculations, it would take at least seven minutes to suit up and get to the shuttlebay, which she had already programmed to open on a delay once she sent the command. A starship within sensor range wouldn't take much longer than that to ascertain *Reston*'s identity and begin its attack run, and by then Carson had every intention of blasting through space with a thruster strapped to her back.

The ship lurched to port, a hard evasive turn. Carson grabbed hold of a support pylon, fighting off a sudden wave of vertigo. The going wasn't easy with the corridor starting to spin around her, and she squeezed her eyes shut for the brief moment it took for the sensation to pass. She thought about the odds against her, the chances that the Feds would ignore her distress signal even if they picked up on it—but even so, they were better than the odds of remaining on board.

And Carson had no desire to die for the likes of the man who had sent her here.

She pushed off, making it a few steps before the ship reeled again. This time *Reston* spiraled downward, gravity taking less than a second to compensate—but that was enough to knock Carson off balance and send her careening toward the deck. She dropped her phaser, both hands reaching out to blunt the impact—until something yanked her back, a grip so strong that it dug into her shoulders like a pair of sharp hooks. Her feet left the deck entirely, kicking through empty air before her body traversed the full width of the corridor and slammed into the bulkhead.

Head cracking against cold metal, Carson felt her legs melt beneath her—but she didn't crumble. Instead, she remained hanging on the wall, pinned there by some immutable force. She blinked several times, the blur before her eyes resolving itself into a gothic visage. It regarded her not with the impassive detachment that she expected, but a smoldering fury that metastasized into something far more malevolent because it could not find release. In that countenance, Carson saw pure, distilled evil—a perfect reflection of her own.

Chris Thayer, a Borg shell of himself, twisted his mouth into a vampiric snarl.

"Go ahead," Carson rasped. "Assimilate me."

Thayer didn't.

But before the screaming stopped, before he finished with her, Carson begged him to.

The turbolift doors opened onto an abandoned bridge, with just Rayna Massey left to man the conn. Reed felt a palpable emptiness as she walked in, even with Locarno at her side, each of them taking solemn measure of one another. Her team had numbered seven when they beamed over, and now there were only three—*three* of them left to handle the ship, against whatever approached through the electrified mists of the Korso Spanse.

"What's our status, Rayna?" Reed asked, circling around to the command chair.

"Contact appears to be a *Nova* class," Massey said, as Locarno relieved her at the conn. She patched the image to the main viewer before heading back up to tactical. "Bearing three-two-zero, parallel to our flank."

"Probably the same ship we tangled with before," Locarno observed.

"Persistent bastards," Reed said. "Any idea if they've seen us?"

"Negative," Massey replied, checking her own display. "Looks like he's heading toward *Celtic*'s last position. Picking up active sensor sweeps in the area of the debris field."

Reed tossed a sideways glance toward the ready room, and the large gash where there used to be a door. Inside, hidden away in the dark, she could sense a crippled Tristan Harlow without seeing him—the same way she sensed a growing connection with Casari and Thayer, something that stirred her blood and plugged her in to a wider consciousness. Reed shook her head and tried to clear it, using the sights and sounds around her like white noise—for as long as that lasted.

"We can only make like a hole in the sky for so long," she decided. "Once they pick up our fuel trail, we've had it."

Massey stared at the tiny moving dot on the screen. "What do we do?"

Locarno tried his controls, the useless panel refusing every trick.

"I got nothing," he breathed. "We're out of options."

"No," Reed countered. "We're not."

Both of them looked at her, their faces a cross between hope and terror.

"But it all depends on how much you want to live."

Massey and Locarno had a silent exchange. If either one of them showed the slightest doubt, Reed would call it off and accept their fate at the hands of Starfleet—but neither of them did. As they turned back toward her, she knew they had made up their minds. Dying wasn't the issue. They just didn't want their lives to end like this.

And neither did Reed.

"The control routine," she said to Locarno. "Can you modify it so that all command functions are routed through the crew instead of the main computer?"

Locarno thought about it for a moment. "Yes."

"Then you better hurry."

Locarno nodded, understanding. He then rushed over to the engineering station to complete the programming, while Massey looked on, confused and anxious. "What's that supposed to do?" she asked. "I thought we couldn't do anything with the ship's computer."

"We can't. Not until he drops the firewall."

"And what happens then?"

"What was always going to happen," Reed told her. "We assimilate."

Massey shivered inside the regeneration chamber, more scared and vulnerable than Reed had ever seen her. All the bravado, all the posturing that had made her the toughest privateer in Evan Walsh's crew, was gone. She was just a woman now, exactly like Reed—human, but only in the present tense. What awaited beyond that, nobody could know.

As Reed strapped Massey in, the chamber's circuitry began to hum and pulsate. The core matrix sensed Massey's presence, matching her body's rhythms in a display of eager anticipation, biometric fields cascading over her like water in a drowning pool. She reached out and touched Reed's arm, pleading with her eyes.

"Will I still be me?" Massey asked. "Even if it's just a piece?"

Reed smiled. "You can't put out that kind of fire, Rayna."

Massey nodded, preparing herself for what came next. Slowly, Reed closed the door and sealed her in, watching from behind the glass as Massey closed her eyes. Her features softened, assuming a kind of peace—or, at the very least, acceptance. Perhaps it was only what Reed wanted to see, but if so, she was grateful for the illusion.

She moved on to Locarno. He appeared the same as when she first met him, projecting that same reckless confidence. In that moment, Reed felt as if she had known him for years—and wondered if she would remember him the same way after they changed.

"It's kind of fitting when you think about it," Locarno said. "The man becomes machine. Not a bad way to go for a gridstalker."

"We'll find out who did this, Nick."

He gave her a sympathetic look.

"I *mean* it," she implored. "Promise me you'll hold on to that."

Locarno couldn't refuse her.

"I promise," he said. "We won't let anybody stop us."

Reed took his hand and squeezed it tight. She didn't want to let go, but he was fading already, along with her capacity to connect with him on a flesh-and-blood level. For her, the world had narrowed to an interface, bits of data coalescing into a new reality. As Reed closed the door on him, severing her final human contact, she cast off the last of her emotions—except for her anger, which burned like a glowing ember in an endless night.

That was her anchor, her purpose. And she swore never to lose sight of it.

Stepping into her own chamber, Reed didn't need to seal herself in. The others had gathered there, as she knew they would, to await her transcendence. Thayer and Casari did it with a care and precision akin to reverence, acknowledging Reed's previous incarnation while ushering her into the next. And when the assimilation began, she borrowed their strength and made it her own, even as the core matrix ripped the consciousness from her body and merged it with the collective whole.

The agony spanned time and space, then collapsed in on itself.

And on the other side emerged *hunger,* the kind that devoured worlds.

★　★　★

Captain Rivellini saw past *Norfolk*'s viewscreen, probing the Spanse with his own instincts and taking measure of the wreckage that drifted past his ship. He already had the vessel identified by the time the sensor sweep was done, but waited for his people to confirm.

"Mass and dimensions match the merchant vessel we intercepted," the ops officer reported. "So do the markings. It's definitely *Celtic*, Captain."

Rivellini maintained an outward detachment, but the destruction of any vessel—even one he was hunting—made him nervous. He stood up from the command chair, walking toward the screen while the bridge crew looked on. Blast patterns on the remains of *Celtic*'s hull indicated phaser fire, but not conclusively. The way the rest of the ship had broken apart, with entire sections separated from one another at the seams, could just as easily have been caused by a massive structural failure.

"What the hell happened here?" Rivellini muttered.

"Captain," the tactical officer said, his panel beeping. "I just detected a stream of ionized gases. Could be a thruster trail."

"Direction?"

"Off the starboard."

"Defensive posture," Rivellini ordered, returning to his chair as Yellow Alert sounded. "Full active sweep. If something's out there, I want to see it."

"Aye, sir," tactical replied, and almost immediately his panel lit up. "Positive contact, bearing zero-four-zero—range, five hundred thousand kilometers."

"Identify."

The tactical officer looked at his display, eyes darting back and forth in confusion. "This can't be right," he said, running through the scan again—and coming up with the same result. "Captain, our sensors are picking up what appears to be a Federation starship. There's some interference from the cloud . . . but it looks like a *Nebula* class, sir."

Rivellini frowned. "That's impossible."

"Verified, sir. She's the real deal."

"One-half impulse power!" the captain snapped. "Plot an intercept course!"

A proximity alarm went off.

"Contact is already moving to intercept *us,*" the conn officer said. "Closing fast."

"Raise shields!"

"Incoming!" tactical shouted—half a second before the first salvo hit.

Norfolk rocked under the blunt force of impact, her frame groaning from stem to stern. As she began to roll, the starship roared past on the viewscreen, releasing aft torpedoes in her wake. One of them struck *Norfolk* amidships, while the others exploded fore and aft. The resulting shock wave shattered consoles across the bridge, gravity and inertia canceling each other out and tossing crewmen back and forth. Rivellini grabbed hold of his chair and hauled himself up, smoke burning his eyes as he tried to make sense of it all.

"Emergency power!" he ordered. "Give me some room to maneuver!"

"I can't get engineering!" ops answered. "Nobody's responding!"

"Then get me a weapons lock!"

"Fire control is down!" tactical replied. "I need a minute to bypass!"

Looking up through the static on the viewer, Rivellini knew they didn't have that kind of time. *Reston* had swung around and now approached on a kill vector, her weapons locked. He kept going over the reasons why a Federation starship would want to destroy them—and it was only then that he noticed the starship's true configuration.

"No," he whispered, as the Borg ship coasted to a halt.

It hung there, suspended over them, as an abject quiet settled over the bridge. Everyone stared at that image, nobody daring to move or make a sound, as the seconds ticked into minutes. But still nothing happened. Rivellini picked himself up, straightening his uniform jacket while he cleared his throat, speaking the words no captain ever wanted to utter.

"Signal enemy vessel," he said. "Is it their intention to discuss terms?"

The comm officer opened a channel, but received no response.

"Ask them what they want."

Again, the Borg ship refused to answer. After a few moments, however, it broke off from *Norfolk* and pushed into the debris field, where it drifted among the *Celtic*'s remains and collected all the pieces. One by one, it assimilated them all—and when it finished, the Borg ship turned about and withdrew. It shrank into the distance as it left the Korso Spanse, farther and farther until it was only a speck.

Then it disappeared into warp, gone in a relativistic shimmer.

"Alert Starfleet Command," Rivellini intoned. "Inform them that the Borg are back."

Sloth

sloth

Work Is Hard

Greg Cox

Historian's Note

This story takes place in the year 2370 (ACE) just after the discovery of the interphasic organisms infecting the *U.S.S. Enterprise* NCC-1701-D warp core ("Phantasms") and before Ambassador Lwaxana Troi comes aboard the ship with the Cairn ("Dark Page").

Captain's book, today.
Went a long way. Will go more tomorrow. We are far from home.

N ot right now."
Aadnalurg, captain of the Pakled freighter *Rorpot,* waved away Snollicoob, his chief engineer. A comfy chair supported his ponderous bulk as he rested in his stateroom, adjacent to the bridge. The delta-shaped chamber was dominated by a squat, cluttered desk made of dull orange metal. Outside a metal porthole, distant stars streaked past at warp speed. The captain scowled at Snollicoob for intruding on his privacy; he did not feel like looking over any boring maintenance reports at the moment. It was time for his lunch and then maybe a nap. A tray of replicated leviathan blubber rested on top of his desk, next to a mug of steaming *raktajino.* The refreshing Klingon beverage was just one innovation that the Pakleds had adopted as their own. A nearby couch beckoned to him.

He stifled a yawn. It was hard work being a captain, telling people what to do. He would look at those reports tomorrow. Or maybe the day after that.

"But the reports are ready," Snollicoob protested. He stood before the captain, holding out a padd full of data. Like the captain, he was a heavyset humanoid clad in a layered brown uniform made of thick, quilted fabric. Bushy brown eyebrows, meeting above his nose, climbed toward a receding hairline, giving him a perpetually bemused expression. What little hair he had was slicked back from his forehead. Squinty brown eyes were sunken beneath the heavy brows. Horizontal facial folds creased his cheeks. A tool belt girded his waist. Typical of Pakleds, his verbal abilities were distinctly limited. "You should read them. Now."

"Later." Aadnalurg disliked repeating himself; it was too much work. A medallion upon his chest proclaimed his rank. He took the padd from Snollicoob and put it aside, atop a stack of navigational reports and sensor readings he was going to look at sometime soon. When he found the time. The padd teetered precariously atop the pile. "My eyes are tired."

Maintenance reports always put him to sleep. Besides, he would rather play with his pet slug. Snirgli wriggled upon his lap. Its tentacles protruded over the edge of the desk, sniffing the captain's lunch. Aadnalurg plucked a tiny morsel of blubber from the tray and fed it to the greedy mollusk. Its mottled yellow skin glistened wetly. Over ten centimeters long, from head to tail, Snirgli stretched eagerly for the treat. Aadnalurg chuckled at the slug's appetite. He licked his greasy fingertips. The replicated blubber tasted almost as good as the real thing.

"You said that yesterday," Snollicoob reminded him. "And the day before."

Aadnalurg frowned. The engineer was smarter than average. Maybe too smart. He could be exhausting.

"I am worried about the warp engine," Snollicoob persisted. He appeared to be in no hurry to leave the captain alone with his meal. "It is getting old. We should replace it."

Warp technology was new to the Pakleds. *Rorpot* had stolen its engine from a derelict Cardassian scout ship abandoned during a border skirmish with the Federation. Aadnalurg did not really understand how the engine worked, but Snollicoob had always made it go before. Replacing it would be hard. The captain groaned at the prospect, but he supposed he would have to get around to it someday. Snollicoob was smart. He understood how the ship worked better than anyone. Aadnalurg wondered if maybe he should listen harder.

"Will it go?" he asked.

"Yes," Snollicoob admitted. "But it is old. It needs repairs. And new parts."

"Soon," the captain promised. The tantalizing aroma of the raw blubber tickled his nostrils; he wanted to stop talking and eat. His stomach rumbled. "You think too much. Relax." He gestured at the tray of food. "Sit down. Help yourself."

Snollicoob hesitated. He glanced briefly at the ignored padd. But, as Aadnalurg had hoped, the generous offer—and the enticing odor of the fatty blubber—proved too tempting to resist. The engineer pulled over a stool and sat down opposite his captain. He licked his lips. "Thank you. I *am* hungry."

"Uh-huh." Aadnalurg fed Snirgli another bite of leviathan. He grinned at the engineer, pleased to have changed the subject at last. Buck teeth protruded from his upper lip. "You are a good crewman, Snollicoob. Later we play a game of *broogola.*" The demanding board game, copied from a Terran game known as tic-tac-toe, was a favorite pastime aboard the ship. "All right?"

Snollicoob grinned back at him. "Yes. I will enjoy that."

The captain looked forward to the game. Maybe he would even beat Snollicoob for once.

The two Pakleds dug into their meal. They tore lumps of blubber apart with their bare hands, disdaining utensils, and talked with their mouths full. Snirgli squirmed onto the table, leaving an adorable trail of mucus behind. Both men laughed at the pet.

The engine could wait. . . .

"Sub-captain?"

First officer Frojuhpwa awoke with a start upon the bridge. Disoriented, he looked about in confusion, momentarily uncertain where he was. He had been dreaming about a sunny beach on Risa, before the intrusive voice snatched him back to reality. His bleary eyes took in the familiar sights and sounds of *Rorpot*. A soothing orange light radiated from the glowing power column at the rear of the bridge, illuminating the rust-colored steel bulkheads. A low ceiling gave the bridge the feel of a cozy den. Arched doorways led to adjoining corridors and compartments. Crewmen huddled around scattered control pedestals, looking over each other's shoulders as they stood at their stations. The only chair upon the bridge, which Frojuhpwa now occupied, was behind the command console in the center of the chamber. The forward viewscreen displayed the inky blackness of interstellar space. Stars and nebulae sparkled in the distance. They looked very far away.

Uh-huh, Frojuhpwa thought, rubbing his eyes. He realized that he must have dozed off in the command chair. *Hope nobody saw.*

The equipment on the bridge was awkwardly cobbled together from a wide variety of sources. A Jaradan-style keyboard was hot-wired to an Andorian transducer matrix. The knobs and switches on the control panel in front of Frojuhpwa were cannibalized from a twenty-third century Bajoran sleeper ship; minuscule prayer symbols were still etched on the components. The Pakleds had figured out long ago that inventing their own technology took too long. It was faster—and easier—to "borrow" their hardware from other civilizations and species. People thought this meant that Pakleds weren't smart, but they were wrong. It was the humans and the Vulcans and the Klingons and the others who were stupid. Pakleds were smart enough to let everyone else think up new things. It was a good plan. A smart plan.

If you could stay awake when you were supposed to be in charge.

Frojuhpwa thought he heard the crew chuckling at his expense. "What is it?" he bristled, sitting up straight in the chair. He tugged his rumpled tunic into place. "You interrupted my thinking!"

"Sorry, Sub-captain," a helmsman named Byzeppoz apologized. He kept his eyes on his display panel. "We crossed into Sector 004-B. I wanted you to know."

"Uh-huh." Frojuhpwa settled back into his seat. "How far to Deep Space 9?"

The helmsman counted on his fingers. "Four more cycles. I think."

"That is too long," Frojuhpwa grumbled. They were taking a shortcut through an unfamiliar region of space, but he was already bored with this run. The sooner they reached their destination and dropped off their load of unprocessed magnesite ore, the sooner he could take some time off. He shifted impatiently in the chair. "Increase speed to warp four."

"Uh-huh," Byzeppoz assented. A burst of acceleration trumped the inertial dampers, shoving Frojuhpwa back against the seat cushions. The bridge vibrated in a somewhat worrying manner, but the crew was used to such minor wobbles. The helmsman grinned. "Warp speed four, you bet."

"Good." Frojuhpwa squinted at the tiny stars, willing them to get bigger soon. Confident that he had not missed anything important while napping, he allowed his mind to wander. Let the crew steer the ship; he would rather daydream about what he would do while on shore leave at Deep Space 9. Probably plant himself in Quark's bar, he expected, and not budge until it was time to report back to the ship.

Maybe play a little dabo or visit a holosuite. It had been a long time since he had visited the space station; there would probably be some fun new programs by now. Or perhaps he would just sit at the bar and catch up with his friend Morn. The Lurian pilot was good to drink with. Frojuhpwa thought Morn was the most interesting talker he had ever met.

Mostly, though, he just wanted to do nothing.

Being first officer is hard, he thought. *I need a break.*

Warp four was too slow. They needed to go faster. He leaned forward. "Increase speed—"

Before he could complete the order, however, a tremendous shock jolted the entire ship. Frojuhpwa was thrown forward, smashing his torso into the edge of the command console hard enough to bruise his ribs. He grunted in pain, even as the other crewmen were hurled across the bridge. They slammed into the bulkheads and viewscreen, landing in heaps upon the floor. Startled curses competed with fearful cries. White-hot sparks erupted from the command pedestals. Jagged shards of steel and crystal flew like shrapnel. An emergency klaxon wailed like a Caldonian banshee. The overhead lights flickered on and off. Energy surges caused the transparent power column to strobe alarmingly. Dust and debris rained down from the ceiling, bouncing off the first officer's head and shoulders. A smoky haze filled the bridge. Injured Pakleds, sprawled upon the floor, whimpered out loud. Thin pink blood smeared the bulkheads. The floor bucked violently. Rubble rolled across the bridge.

Huh? Frojuhpwa grabbed onto the console for dear life. The jarring impact caused him to bite down on his own thick tongue. He tasted blood. The floor tilted forward, which could only mean that the artificial gravity was not working the way it was supposed to. Dazed, the first officer looked around in confusion. He did not understand what was happening. It was like *Rorpot* had suddenly crashed into a wall of solid duranium. *What did we hit?*

A guilty expression came over his face. "I was not sleeping! I was not!"

Or was he?

The rocking stabilized for a moment. The blaring siren, added to crackling flames and moaning crewmen, hurt his ears. He reached out to silence it. A stubby finger stabbed a button. *It is too loud. I need to think!*

Mismatched circuits shorted. Sparks flared from the console. A high-voltage jolt caused his whole body to stiffen in shock. Short brown hair stood on end. The smell of burnt hair further polluted the smoky atmosphere. A hoarse gasp tore itself from his lungs. His eyes rolled upward until only the whites were visible. Smoke rose from his uniform. His jaws clenched together involuntarily. Convulsions shook him from head to toe.

Ouch! That hurts!

Frojuhpwa toppled backward into the captain's chair. His eyelids drooped shut. A low groan escaped his lips. Froth trickled from the corner of his mouth. The spasms subsided, leaving him limp and motionless. Unconscious once more, he would not be waking up anytime soon.

The bridge went away. A lightning storm raged over a beach in Risa.

"What is it?"

Captain Aadnalurg lumbered through an archway onto the bridge. His head was ringing. Blood seeped from an ugly gash on his scalp, where he had smacked his head into his desk. Spilled *raktajino* stained the front of his uniform. His face was smeared with blubber grease. Snirgli perched upon his shoulder; the frightened slug waved its feelers in alarm. It squealed in the captain's ear. He placed a hand over the slug to keep it safe.

"Uh-oh."

He looked about in dismay. The bridge was in shambles. Small fires danced atop broken pedestals and consoles. Gases vented from ruptured conduits. Battered crewmen were strewn across the chamber. Smoke obscured his vision. The screaming klaxon scraped at his nerves. Rubble littered the floor. *Rorpot* looked as though it had been struck by a photon torpedo—or something.

No one answered his initial query, so he shouted louder. "What did this?" He spit a broken tooth onto the floor. "What hit us?"

"Nothing!" Byzeppoz sat up on the floor. His face was bruised. One eye was swollen shut. Soot blackened his face. Wincing, the helmsman grabbed onto the nearest pedestal and pulled himself to his feet. He teetered unsteadily before pointing at the viewer. "Look! Nothing is there!"

Aadnalurg squinted through the haze. A wounded crewman was slumped at the foot of the viewer. The screen was cracked right down the middle, but still working . . . sort of. Visual static distorted the image on the viewer, which wavered like a malfunctioning hologram. Despite the problems, however, he could still make out the view. There was nothing but empty space ahead of them for light-years. He blinked and rubbed his eyes to make sure they were working right.

Where is it? What did we hit?

He had expected to see the shattered remains of an asteroid or comet or something, but Byzeppoz was right. There was nothing in front of them. He noticed that the distant stars were stationary now. *Rorpot* was not moving anymore. The ship had come to a halt, but its captain had no idea why. He scratched his head.

Maybe they had hit a cloaked Klingon warship? Or a Romulan?

"Explain!"

He searched for his first officer, only to find Frojuhpwa slumped in the command chair. His short hair and bushy eyebrows were singed. Scorch marks charred his uniform. His mouth hung open slackly. Drool trickled down his chin. Only the steady rise and fall of his chest indicated that he was still breathing. Aadnalurg was almost disappointed.

"Stupid, not-smart person!" He glared at the unconscious subcaptain, furious at Frojuhpwa for letting this catastrophe take place on his watch. He had to blame someone, and the other Pakled was the easiest target. "What did you do to my ship?"

Frojuhpwa merely gurgled in response.

The more Aadnalurg looked, the worse it was. The automated fire-suppression systems were working erratically, forcing the crew to put out the flames with portable extinguishers and loose sheets of debris. Disheveled crewmen tended to their more injured comrades, applying hyposprays and bandages. A junior navigator was carted away on a stretcher. Another shrieked as a broken leg was splinted into place. There was no medical officer aboard, only a handful of crewmen trained in the rudiments of first aid. A quick glance around revealed no actual fatalities on the bridge, but it was hard to be certain. And what about the rest of the ship?

"Emergency stations! Fix broken things!"

He stumbled across the bridge, almost tripping over a fallen ceiling tile. None too gently, he shoved Frojuhpwa out of the captain's chair onto the floor. The first officer's inert form landed with a thump upon the chipped ceramic tiles. Aadnalurg took his seat behind the smoking command console. A well-meaning midshipman sprayed the top of the console with a fire extinguisher, splattering the captain with chemical foam. He choked and sputtered. Acrid fumes stung his nostrils.

"Report!" He pounded his fist on the armrest, which promptly broke off and clattered onto the floor, only a few centimeters from Frojuhpwa's head. Aadnalurg wiped the foam and grease from his lips. "Somebody give me a report!"

"Uh-huh!" Snollicoob followed the captain onto the bridge. He limped over to one of the few control pedestals still in one piece. The engineer himself was in need of repairs. A split lip thickened his voice. He favored his left leg, flinching with every step. His brown uniform was torn at the collar. "Just a minute!"

Panting, he worked the knobs and dials. The klaxon fell silent, much to the captain's relief. Snollicoob called up a status report on the pedestal's display screen. He shook his head dolefully as he scanned the readouts. "It is bad."

Aadnalurg did not like the sound of that. "How bad?"

"Propulsion is gone. We cannot go." That was bad enough, but Snollicoob kept on reading from the screen. "Shields are weak. The hull has buckled belowdecks. There are breaches. We have lost some of our air."

"How much?"

"Too much." Snollicoob fidgeted uneasily. "Life support is breaking down. The air generators will not work."

"Fix it!" the captain demanded. Was he just imagining it, or did the air on the bridge already seem stale and thin? He tried not to breathe too deep. "Make it go!"

Snollicoob gulped. "I can try. But things are broken. It will be hard. Maybe too hard."

An energy surge lit up the power column, causing it to flare more brightly than it ever had before. For a moment, the bridge was as sunny as Vulcan's Forge at noon. More light leaked through a web of hairline cracks in the vertical cylinder. Snollicoob threw up a hand to shield his eyes from the glare, lowering it only when the flash faded back to normal. He shook his head. Watery eyes widened in alarm. "That is not good."

Bright blue spots danced in the captain's vision. He was going to ask Snollicoob what he meant, but another jolt rocked the ship before he had the chance. Aadnalurg clutched his remaining armrest to keep from being thrown from his chair. Crewmen staggered across the bridge, grabbing the nearest convenient handholds. The second jolt was less severe than the first, more like an aftershock, but it was enough to knock the ship for a loop. Fresh gusts of coolant burst from pipes. The viewer went dark for several seconds, then rebooted itself. Random gravity fluctuations caused Aadnalurg's stomach to flip. Byzeppoz vomited onto his boots. The captain could barely keep his own blubber down, let alone conceal his frustration. Snirgli lifted off from his shoulder. He grabbed onto the levitating pet to keep it from floating away.

"What is doing that?" He glared at the cracked viewer. "I do not see anything!"

Snollicoob's screen went dead. He whacked the controls, but the display did not return, forcing him to relocate to another pedestal. He had to step over a whimpering bosun to do so. Shifting g forces tugged his fleshy face out of shape, as though he was trapped inside a spinning centrifuge. He made a gagging noise. His complexion turned green.

"Talk to me!" Aadnalurg ordered "Tell me what to do!"

The engineer adjusted his controls. Aadnalurg felt the gravity stabilize a little. Snirgli settled down into his lap. Smelly secretions advertised its fear. Aadnalurg knew how it felt.

"Passive sensors only," Snollicoob reported. His brow furrowed in concentration as he attempted to analyze the data before his eyes. Puzzlement beamed onto his face. "Readings are strange. It is hard to put into words."

What is not? Aadnalurg thought. Words were tricky. "Try to explain."

Snollicoob took a deep breath. "Subspace is all . . . swirly? There are many very small particles around us. They are very hot. They go too fast. They have too much energy. It is not normal. I do not understand. Except . . ." His voice trailed off. He smacked himself on the side of the head. "Of course! That is it!" A momentary look of triumph was swiftly supplanted by alarm. His eyes widened in fear. "Oh no! That is bad!"

"What is it?" Aadnalurg pressed. He could tell that the engineer had figured something out. He was smart. "Tell me!"

"A quantum filament." Snollicoob spoke slowly and carefully, his thick lips struggling to form the unwieldy phrase. "We hit a quantum filament. Maybe more than one."

"Huh?" The captain greeted the theory with befuddlement. He had heard the term before, but had never really understood it. He swallowed his pride and admitted his confusion. Now was no time to worry about looking smart. "What is that?"

Snollicoob tried to explain. "It is like a cosmic string, but different." He gesticulated awkwardly with his hands, laboring to convey what he meant. His limited vocabulary was not equipped to express such a difficult concept. "It is very long, but less than an atom across. It has more energy than mass. Too much energy."

Aadnalurg peered into the darkness on the viewer. He did not see any strings. "Why didn't we see it? What about our sensors?"

"They have almost no mass," Snollicoob repeated. "They are hard to detect, even with sensors. It is very hard if you are going too fast." He looked at the captain. "Was there any warning in the sensor reports? Or in the star charts for this sector?"

Aadnalurg blushed as he remembered the navigational reports and long-range sensor readings he had been meaning to look at. The neglected padds now littered the floor of his stateroom, along with all the other boring reports he been ignoring lately. He wished he had paid more attention to them. *I was not smart.*

"Never mind about that!" he blustered. He changed the subject. "Is it over? Have we passed the fil-fila—that thing?"

Another collision answered his question. The entire ship lurched to port. Dislodged pedestals toppled over onto the floor. A deafening roar drowned out the shouting of the crew as straining bulkheads wailed in protest. A jet of hot vapor scalded a crewman, who fell backward over a broken pipe. Fresh debris pelted Aadnalurg before *Rorpot* finally righted itself. Snirgli wriggled in alarm. Its antennae retracted.

"No," Snollicoob answered redundantly. He clung to his pedestal. "There are too many filaments, all around us." He seized on an image to get the idea across. "Like a jungle of hanging vines, but the vines are poison. They sting us when we brush against them!"

Aadnalurg thought he understood, a little. "We need to get away from them." He looked urgently at the engineer. "Can you make us go?"

The power column flared brightly again. "Dung!" the captain swore, averting his eyes. The blinding glare lasted longer this time, almost half a minute. The brilliant orange glow edged toward red. He blinked the tears from his eyes.

Snollicoob gazed at the column in horror. "That is very bad." He turned back toward his pedestal's display screen and called up more data in a hurry. The computer did not respond fast enough, so he kicked it hard. Beeping noises suggested that the blow had done the trick. Snollicoob looked over the readouts. "Uh-oh." His voice grew hushed. "The warp engine is getting too hot. I cannot cool it down. The force field bubble is going to pop."

Aadnalurg understood the internal workings of the warp engine about as much as he comprehended quantum filaments. He knew that matter and antimatter collided in the engine and made the ship go, but that was about it. He glanced nervously at the column behind him, which took its power from the engine two decks below. "What does that mean?"

"We are going to blow up," Snollicoob said. "Soon."

The captain understood that part. "Shut it down!"

Snollicoob fiddled with the knobs. "It is not working. The safety controls are old. They are broken." A hint of an accusation crept into his voice. "I told you. We needed repairs."

"That was before!" Aadnalurg barked, a little defensively. "Forget about that. What are we going to do *now*? Can you stop the engine?"

The engineer shook his head. He threw up his hands. "I do not think so. Sorry."

"But you are smart!" the captain protested.

Snollicoob's head drooped. He stepped away from the useless controls. "Not smart enough."

Aadnalurg believed him. Despite what he'd just said, the engineer was the smartest Pakled aboard. He knew things. If he said the ship was going to blow up, it was going to blow up. There was only one thing left to do.

"Abandon ship." He rose from the chair. The thought of leaving *Rorpot* and its load of precious magnesite behind made him sick to his stomach. He would need to work a long time to recover from this loss. Pakleds considered insurance a waste of credits. He lumbered toward the emergency exit. "Get to the escape pods!"

Nobody moved. Snollicoob and the others stayed where they stood. Nobody tried to help the wounded to their feet. Crewmen murmured furtively to each other. They shuffled their feet. Aadnalurg was baffled by their behavior. What was wrong with the men? Did they want to blow up with the ship?

"Did you hear me?" He stamped his foot. "Hurry! We need to go!"

The men exchanged sheepish looks, avoiding the captain's eyes. A few of the men sagged against the bulkheads, looking defeated. Others squatted on the floor to await their fate.

"What is the matter?" Aadnalurg bellowed. "Come with me! That is an order!"

Snollicoob finally spoke up. "There are no escape pods. We left them in the shop on Honvali Trice. Remember?"

Oh.

It came back to him now. In the commotion, he had completely forgotten. The escape pods had been broken, but the Pakled mechanics at their last port of call had been too slow to get the pods fixed in time for *Rorpot*'s scheduled departure. After much hard thinking, he had left the pods behind in order to get the magnesite to Deep Space 9 on time. It had seemed like a good idea at the time; he had never needed to use the pods before. Why not just pick them up again on the return trip? He was not planning on any emergencies.

"Oops," he murmured. Maybe that was not smart.. He looked over at Snollicoob. "We cannot get off the ship?"

"Uh-uh," the engineer confirmed. "We are stuck here. There is no way to go."

Aadnalurg dropped back into his chair. He kicked Frojuhpwa's comatose form, taking out his frustration on the stunned first officer, who groaned faintly in response. A fresh layer of debris coated the prone figure. "Now what?" Aadnalurg asked bleakly. His sullen gaze drifted toward the cracked viewer. He could think of only one more option.

"Call for help."

Snollicoob fired up the communications circuits. The captain hoped they were working better than the engine. A lighted display panel encouraged him.

"Now?" Snollicoob asked.

Aadnalurg looked at the other Pakled like he was stupid.

"Yes, now!"

He kicked the first officer again.

It didn't make him feel any better.

Chief engineer's log, stardate 47235.9.
I am personally supervising an upgrade to the bridge's aft engineering work-station, taking advantage of the damage inflicted on the Enterprise's *systems by a recent infestation of interphasic life-forms to replace aging subprocessors and optical data trunks . . .*

"Captain," Lieutenant Worf announced from his tactical station. His gruff voice somehow made even the most routine statements sound like a call to arms. "We are receiving a mayday signal from Sector 004-B."

Geordi La Forge looked up from an illuminated console at the rear of the bridge. He had just run one last diagnostic on the modified station and was getting ready to return to his usual haunts in engineering, but curiosity tempted him to linger. As proud as he was of his current duties and titles, he sometimes regretted that he wasn't able to spend as much time on the bridge as he used to. He wouldn't trade his position as chief engineer for all the gold-pressed latinum on Ferenginar, but he still occasionally missed being where the action is.

Wonder what's up with this SOS?

"On-screen," Captain Picard ordered. He leaned forward in the captain's chair. It was the first shift, so the bridge was manned by the entire senior staff. Commander Riker and Counselor Troi flanked the captain. Commander Data had the ops station, while Ensign Wruum, who had recently transferred over from the *Ephrata*, took the conn. Downy azure feathers carpeted her scalp. A pointed beak proclaimed the avian roots of her people. Wruum's owl-like features were the only new face in sight.

Just like old times, Geordi thought, feeling nostalgic for his own days at the helm. If he squinted through his VISOR, he could almost imagine Wesley Crusher on the bridge. Had he really been serving on the *Enterprise* for seven years now? The time seemed to have flown by at warp speed. . . .

The streaking stars on the main viewer gave way to a blurry, visually incoherent image. Phosphorescent "snow" obscured the picture, so that Geordi could barely make out a stocky humanoid figure at the center of the screen. Static distorted the audio component of the signal. Vid tiling hid the identity of the speaker. Not even the universal translator could make sense of the random crackles and buzzes. Geordi couldn't even tell what species was at the other end of the message.

Picard frowned. "Can you improve the transmission, Mister Worf?"

"I am attempting to do so, Captain." The Klingon growled at the uncooperative hardware. "There appears to a great deal of subspace interference at the signal's point of origin."

La Forge wondered if the interference had anything to do with the nature of the emergency. "Try increasing power to the primary array," he suggested. Worf wrestled with the control panel, but the pixels on the screen stubbornly refused to resolve. Geordi stepped up to the rail. "Mind if I give it a go?"

Thankfully, Worf did not consider the balky technology a challenge to his honor. He gladly moved aside to make room for Geordi. "I would welcome your assistance."

La Forge scanned the data streaming across the control panel, immediately seeing the problem. Worf hadn't been exaggerating when he'd complained about all the interference. Massive amounts of quantum fluctuations had virtually shredded the transmission en route to the *Enterprise*. A flurry of subatomic particles created a storm of static. Trying to distinguish the signal packet from the turbulent background noise was like trying to read white subtitles against a holographic blizzard. *Where are they hailing us from?* Geordi wondered. *The other side of a quasar?*

"It is urgent that we discover the nature of the emergency without further delay," Captain Picard stressed. His stern gaze was fixed on the maddeningly indistinct image before him. "Time may well be of the essence."

"Understood, sir." Geordi's fingers danced across the control panel. A few deft keystrokes called up a more sophisticated user interface that granted him a greater degree of hands-on control over the *Enterprise*'s ship-to-ship communications network. His VISOR allowed him to observe minute variations in the graphic displays. Advanced procedural menus offered him a range of specialized options. "If I bring the auxiliary preprocessors online and reconfigure the clutter filters, I might be able to reduce the phase variance enough to give the compensation algorithms enough to work with . . ."

The chaos on the screen resolved into a coherent image, revealing the lumpen head and shoulders of a middle-aged male Pakled wearing a captain's medallion. Geordi recognized the species immediately.

"Oh great," he muttered. "Those guys."

He did not have a terrific history with Pakleds.

"Help us!" the Pakled said. Static still abraded his voice, but at least he was audible now. *"We need help!"*

La Forge snorted. "I've heard that before."

Five years ago, the *Enterprise* had responded to a distress signal from another Pakled vessel. La Forge had personally beamed aboard to help the Pakleds repair their ship, only to discover that the supposed malfunctions were just a ruse. The duplicitous aliens had taken Geordi hostage in hopes of extorting advanced Starfleet technology from the *Enterprise*. To make their point, they had repeatedly stunned Geordi with his own phaser, to the extent that he had required medical attention once Commander Riker and the others had finally rescued him. He winced at the memory. All those phaser blasts had *hurt*.

He hadn't trusted a Pakled since.

"So I recall," Picard assured him. The captain had not actually been present during their first contact with the Pakleds, having been away on personal business at the time, but he was no doubt familiar with the incident. He addressed the screen. "This is Captain Jean-Luc Picard of the Federation *Starship Enterprise*. You issued a distress signal?"

"Enterprise!" Relief, or perhaps a treacherous facsimile thereof, flooded the Pakled's face. A fresh cut scarred his forehead. He was missing a tooth. His chair appeared to be broken. *"Good. You can help us. We need help."*

Riker sighed. "I've missed this sparkling repartee," he said dryly.

"Please identify yourself," Picard requested.

"I am Aadnalurg, the captain. My ship is Rorpot." Only a small portion of the vessel's bridge could be glimpsed behind him. A smoky haze veiled the scene, but charred bulkheads and severed cables added some credence to his claims, along with the captain's apparent injuries. *"It is broken. We need help."*

"So you say," Riker challenged him. He had been in command when the Pakleds had taken Geordi hostage. His suspicious tone made it clear that he was not about to be fooled again. "Is this a trick?"

"No trick!" Aadnalurg insisted. *"We are in danger. You must help us!"*

"Yeah, right." La Forge shook his head in disbelief. *Did the Pakleds really expect them to fall for the same ploy twice?* The damage in the background was probably just stage dressing. This was an insult to their intelligence. "Shall I terminate this transmission, Captain?"

"Not so fast, Mister La Forge." Picard signaled Geordi to mute their response to the hail, so they could converse freely without being heard by the Pakleds. "I admit the circumstances invoke a distinct sense of déjà vu, but we should not jump to conclusions. It is entirely possible that the Pakleds are not crying wolf this time." He settled back into his seat. "Let us hear what they have to say."

"Yes, sir." Geordi restored the audio connection.

Riker began the interrogation. "What is the nature of your emergency?"

"We hit a . . . a . . ." Aadnalurg seemed to fumble for the words. Another Pakled, who appeared to be a bit younger, whispered into his captain's ear. *" . . . quantum filament."*

A gasp escaped Deanna's lips. La Forge didn't have to be a telepath to guess that she was remembering the time, a few years back, when the *Enterprise* had collided with an invisible quantum filament. The unexpected disaster had wreaked havoc on the ship and briefly placed Deanna in command of the bridge—at the worst possible moment.

That can't have been fun, Geordi thought.

"Are you all right, Counselor?" Picard asked.

"Yes, Captain." She quickly regained her composure.

Aadnalurg ignored Deanna's outburst. *"Our ship is broken,"* he repeated. *"We cannot go. The engine is too hot. It is burning up. Help us."*

Picard looked to Deanna for confirmation. "Counselor?"

"It is difficult to truly sense his emotions from so far away," she answered. "But his anxiety strikes me as sincere." Her dark Betazoid eyes took in the Pakled's expression and body language. "I believe they are truly in danger."

Worf disagreed. He rejoined La Forge at the tactical station. "They have deceived us before," he snarled. "They are without honor."

"Perhaps," Picard conceded. "But even scoundrels can sometimes be in genuine need of assistance." He came to a decision. "By all means, we should stay on our guard, but I do not believe that we can turn our back on these individuals simply because of our unfortunate history with others of their species."

He held up a hand to ward off any further objections from Worf. "Mister Data, estimated time to Sector 004-B?"

The android officer swiftly performed the calculations in his head. "At maximum warp, we should be able to reach *Rorpot*'s coordinates in approximately six-point-two-four-eight hours. If there are indeed quantum filaments in the vicinity, however, we may be forced to navigate the sector at a slower speed to avoid a disaster of our own. This could significantly delay our arrival."

"Good point," Riker said. "We don't want to collide with the same filaments that damaged the Pakled vessel. *If* they even exist."

"Are there any other Federation ships in the region?" Picard inquired. "Who might be able to reach *Rorpot* more quickly?"

Data consulted his ops terminal. "No, sir. The nearest other vessel is the *Lorentz,* currently patrolling Sector 2001-G. We are indeed the closest ship available."

"Very well, then," Picard said. "Warp speed seven. Proceed with caution." He hailed Aadnalurg once more. "We are prepared to offer you whatever assistance we can provide, Captain, but I fear it will be some time before we can arrive at your coordinates. Can you hold out until then?"

"*Umm . . . maybe. I don't know.*" Aadnalurg tugged another Pakled into the frame. He looked like the same crewman who had whispered to the captain before. Aadnalurg prodded his subordinate. "*Talk to them!*"

The second Pakled waved clumsily. His cropped brown hair had not receded as far. His facial creases were less pronounced. A split lip looked painful. His torn uniform had seen better days. "*Uh. Hello.*"

"And you are?" Picard asked.

"*I am Snollicoob. I am the number one engineer.*"

The chief engineer? Geordi contemplated his Pakled counterpart. He wasn't impressed.

"What is your status?" Picard inquired.

"*You must hurry!*" Snollicoob exclaimed. "*Life support is breaking down. Our air is going bad. We have no escape pods. The warp engine is too hot.*" He wrung his hands. "*The force field bubble is going to pop!*"

Bubble? It took La Forge a moment to realize that Snollicoob was referring to the magnetic containment field. The full implications of the report sank in. "Captain, I think he's talking about a possible warp core breach!"

Despite his doubts regarding the Pakled's honesty, he felt a chill run down his spine. *What in the world were the Pakleds doing with warp technology?* Just the idea of them messing with matter/antimatter reactions made him nervous. They could barely manage impulse engines!

"*Yes!*" Snollicoob confirmed. "*Warp core breach! We will blow up!*"

Picard's frown deepened. The situation appeared to be growing more dire by the moment. "Can you shut it down?"

"*I am trying!*" Snollicoob insisted. "*But it will not work.*" La Forge got the definite impression that the Pakled engineer was in over his head, dealing with borrowed alien technology that he didn't fully understand. Snollicoob lowered his head in shame. "*I don't know how.*"

"How much time do you have?" Picard asked.

Snollicoob shrugged. *"Not a lot."*

His answer lacked precision, but got the idea across. Riker turned to the captain. He lowered his voice. "If they can't shut down that runaway warp core, there could be nobody to rescue by the time we get there."

"His fear seems authentic as well," Deanna reported. "We should assume he's telling the truth. If not, the results could be truly tragic."

Picard nodded. "Captain Aadnalurg. How many crewmen are aboard your vessel?"

The Pakled captain needed to think about it for a minute. *"Eighty-five. Maybe."* He massaged his wounded brow. *"Many of us are hurt."*

"I understand." Picard considered his options. "Mister La Forge, can you talk the Pakled engineer through the procedure?"

"I can try," he said dubiously. He remembered coaching the clue-less Pakleds on the workings of their own freighter years ago. "They're not exactly easy to explain things to."

"Please make every effort, Mister La Forge." Picard made it clear that failure was not an option.

"Yes, sir." Geordi turned the communications panel over to Worf. He figured it might be easier to converse with Snollicoob away from the commotion of the bridge. It was also possible that the Pakled engineer might speak more freely away from the presence of his own captain. Geordi headed for the turbolift. "Patch him through to engineering," he instructed Worf. "I'll talk to him there."

"Good luck, Mister La Forge," Picard called out to him.

Thanks, he thought. *I'm probably going to need it.*

The angled display screen atop Geordi's desk in engineering was smaller than the main viewer on the bridge, but Snollicoob looked just as distressed. Fearful brown eyes gazed up at Geordi, who had cleared his office of extraneous personnel in order to give Snollicoob his full attention. A reinforced window of transparent aluminum offered a view of the *Enterprise*'s own matter/antimatter reaction assembly. The familiar thrum of the engine room penetrated the walls of the office. After so many years in charge of the engines, Geordi could sometimes detect subtle irregularities in the intermix just by ear. He wondered what the Pakled's engine sounded like now.

"Are you smart?" Snollicoob asked him. *"Can you help me?"*

La Forge rolled his eyes behind his VISOR. It would be easier talking to little Molly O'Brien, and she was just two years old!

I can't believe I'm doing this, he thought. *Probably just a scam anyway.*

"Why don't you start by sending me your data," he suggested.

"Uh-huh," Snollicoob agreed. Like La Forge, the Pakled had relocated to the engineering section of his own vessel. Geordi heard much hubbub and commotion in the background. Tools banged against metal pipes and valves. Welding lasers hissed and sizzled. Nerve-jangling buzzers and alarms sounded with aggravating frequency. Worried Pakleds stomped back and forth, seemingly engaged in frantic repair operations. If it was all an act, they were putting on quite a show. Snollicoob, who apparently did not have an office of his own, hunched over a blocky tabletop console that looked like a cruder version of Geordi's own master systems display. He fiddled with some knobs. "I am sending it now."

To La Forge's slight surprise, the requested data appeared promptly on the screen alongside Snollicoob's image. By now, Geordi had the *Enterprise*'s computers working overtime to compensate for the subspace interference. He swiftly inspected the readings.

Damn!

It was even worse than he had imagined. As nearly as he could tell, a quantum resonance had caused a polarity shift in the antimatter containment field, while the reaction chamber itself was building toward a full-scale meltdown. It was only a matter of time before the increasing temperature overwhelmed the weakened shields, at which point *Rorpot* would be reduced to atoms. Assuming that the data hadn't been cooked up to fool him.

"Okay, we've got to lower the temperature right away," Geordi said, getting down to business. "Flood the assembly with coolant."

Snollicoob shook his head. *"I cannot do that. The tank broke open when we hit the filament. It leaked into space."*

"Really?" La Forge found that hard to believe. Redundant baffles should have prevented a leak of that magnitude, as they would have on the *Enterprise*. "All right. Can you activate the backup cooling systems?"

Snollicoob cocked his head. *"What are backups?"*

Is he serious? La Forge felt a headache coming on. "You know, backups. Secondary systems that duplicate the functions of the primary apparatus."

"I do not understand," Snollicoob said. *"Why build two systems when all you need is one?"*

He really doesn't get it, La Forge thought. This was going to be harder than he thought. "So you have it if the first one breaks."

A lightbulb flickered dimly above Snollicoob's head. His eyes lit up. *"That is a good idea!"* Then reality sunk in and his shoulders slumped. *"We have no backups,"* he said sheepishly. *"I am sorry."*

Despite his growing frustration, La Forge was starting to feel sorry for the hapless engineer. It wasn't his fault his people relied on technology they barely understood. "Never mind," Geordi said. "We'll try something else." He searched his brain for an effective stopgap measure; unfortunately, five years had left his memory of the Pakleds' layout pretty fuzzy. He could use Data's computerized recall right now. "How about you send me a schematic of your engine?"

"Uh-huh!" Snollicoob hurried to oblige. Within seconds, a detailed diagram of *Rorpot*'s engineering section appeared on La Forge's screen. He was impressed by the level of the detail, which actually approached Federation standards.

That's more like it, he thought. Maybe the Pakleds were better with blueprints and numbers than with words. *They aren't stupid,* he reminded himself, *or they would never have made it out into the galaxy in the first place. They just have undeveloped language skills.*

Fine. He didn't need Snollicoob to write a sonnet, just to get his overheating engine under control.

"You get the pictures?" the Pakled asked.

"Yes," La Forge said. "Thanks. They're just what I needed."

Snollicoob grinned, pleased to be of service. *"You are welcome."*

A rapid analysis revealed that *Rorpot*'s single warp engine was of basic Cardassian design, albeit a few generations out of date. La Forge wondered briefly how the Pakleds had gotten their hands on the technology; he couldn't imagine the Cardassians falling for the same "samaritan snare" the *Enterprise* had been suckered into years ago. The Cardassians were not exactly known for their benevolent nature, as Ro Laren had always been quick to remind people. They'd be more likely to seize a stalled freighter than render assistance.

There's got to be a story there.

At the moment, however, it didn't matter *how* the Pakleds had attained warp capacity. He just had to keep it from incinerating them. If that was even possible.

"Mister La Forge!" Snollicoob blurted. The Pakled stared at his own monitors in alarm. *"The bubble is halfway gone!"*

"I can see that." According to the readouts, the containment field was down to forty-nine percent and falling. The *Enterprise*'s own safety margin was fifteen percent; anything below that, and a warp core explosion was inevitable. La Forge had to assume that *Rorpot*'s primitive engine was even more unstable. "Stay calm. We can handle this."

Maybe they could dampen the matter/antimatter reaction to buy some time? "Increase the flow of deuterium to the reaction chamber," he suggested. If they smothered the antihydrogen with an excess of gaseous matter, severely skewing the annihilation ratio, they might be able to slow the chain reaction long enough for the *Enterprise* to arrive in time to evacuate the freighter. Conscious of the Pakled's limitations, he attempted to explain his plan as simply as possible. "Give the engine too much of one fuel, so that it chokes."

"Good idea!" Snollicoob beamed. *"You are smart!"*

"So they tell me."

La Forge crossed his fingers as the other engineer went to work. He wasn't going to relax until he knew this desperate improvisation was going to work. His spirits sank as Snollicoob's hopeful expression collapsed only slightly faster than the containment field itself. *This doesn't look good.*

"It is not working. The valves are stuck." Snollicoob twisted his controls so hard one of the knobs broke off. He gaped at the broken component in chagrin. *"I cannot make the flow go faster!"*

Great, La Forge thought sarcastically. He guessed that the injector nozzles were fused or pinched. The *Enterprise* was equipped with redundant cross-fed injectors, but at this point, he knew better than to expect that the Pakleds had built in the same precautions. *This is why we have the Prime Directive,* he thought irritably, biting down on his tongue to keep from saying something rude. *Some species just aren't ready for warp drives. . . .*

He found himself wishing he was on board *Rorpot* in person, so he could deal directly with the malfunctions, then caught himself. *What am I thinking?* He went back to advising Snollicoob long-distance. "You're going to have to open those valves manually. With a wrench if you have to!"

"We are trying!" Snollicoob insisted. A ladder crashed loudly in the background. Banging noises almost drowned out the engineer's words. A bright flash briefly bleached out the Pakled's features. *"They will not open! They are stuck!"*

A sudden jolt tossed him to one side. The screen blanked out abruptly.

"Snollicoob!" La Forge's heart skipped a beat. He tried to restore communications with *Rorpot*, only to discover that the transmission had been cut off at the other end. Grisly scenarios flashed through his brain. What had happened to *Rorpot*? Had the warp core exploded prematurely?

C'mon, Snollicoob. Don't do this to me.

A burst of static heralded the resumption of the signal. La Forge let out a sigh of relief as he answered the hail. Snollicoob's mournful face reappeared on the screen. The Pakled's hair was badly mussed. Fresh black soot smudged his features. His eyebrows were singed. Shouts and alarms sounded all around him.

"Hello, Mister La Forge. I am sorry for the interruption."

"Forget it." Geordi was surprised at just how relieved he was to see that his Pakled counterpart was still among the living. He thought he had lost him for good. "What happened to you?"

"We bumped into another filament," he explained. *"It shook us up."*

"I can tell," La Forge said. At least *Rorpot* was not traveling at warp speed anymore. The only good thing about the freighter's being stalled in deep space was that it could no longer collide into the quantum filaments at high velocity. "How are you doing?"

"It is bad," Snollicoob reported. *"The hull is buckling. There are fires everywhere. The galley is gone."* He shook his head dourly. *"I do not like quantum filaments."*

"You and me both." La Forge sympathized with what the Pakleds were going through. He and Beverly Crusher had been trapped in a burning cargo hold after the *Enterprise*'s own run-in with the deadly

interstellar hazard. They were both lucky to have survived the confla-
gration. "Trust me, I've been there."

"You have?" Snollicoob was surprised to hear it. *"But you are still
alive?"*

"You bet," La Forge encouraged him. "And you're going to get
through this, too."

The Pakled looked unconvinced. *"I don't know. It is bad here."*

A quick glance at the reactor readings lent some validity to Snollicoob's gloomy prognosis. Containment field integrity was down to
thirty-four percent. Geordi wasn't sure how far they were from a total
collapse, but he figured they were running out of time. There was only
one sensible course of action.

"You need to eject the warp core."

Expelling the overheating reaction assembly might spare *Rorpot*
from the catastrophic explosion. Granted, there was still a danger that
the core might detonate too near the freighter, but that was a chance
they would have to take. Better that the core explode right outside the
ship than inside its hull.

Snollicoob hesitated. *"But we will lose our engine. The captain will not
like that."*

"You don't have any choice," La Forge informed him. "It's extreme, I know, but you have to do it. Now."

"Uh-huh." Snollicoob gulped. *"You are smart. I trust you."*

The nervous Pakled took a deep breath, then keyed the emergency codes
into his console. La Forge hoped Snollicoob wouldn't get into too much
trouble for doing this without his captain's say-so, but they didn't have
time to conduct a lengthy debate on the pros and cons of the procedure.
At least, if this worked, the captain and the crew would still be alive.

Snollicoob flipped a switch.

Nothing happened.

"Uh-oh," the engineer said.

"What is it?" La Forge asked, afraid he already knew the answer.
Let me guess. It's not working.

"I cannot eject the core," Snollicoob confirmed. *"The hull doors will
not open."*

La Forge wanted to hit something. "Doesn't anything work right
on that ship of yours?"

"I do not know," Snollicoob confessed. He wrung his hands. Greasy tears leaked from the corners of his eyes. *"We are broken."*

"All right. Let's keep our cool." La Forge didn't have to be an empath to see that Snollicoob was on the verge of panic. He emulated Counselor Troi's comforting tone. "We just have to get those doors apart. Can you force them open from inside?"

Snollicoob pulled himself together. He wiped the tears from his eyes. *"I do not think so."* He consulted his gauges. *"The ejection chute is too hot. It is not safe. We would burn up."*

La Forge saw what he meant. A leak in the EPS conduits had flooded the interior of the ejection chute with superenergized gases. The blazing plasma would fry any Pakled technicians before they had a chance to pry open the exterior hull plates.

"Okay then," he concluded. "You're going to have to do it from outside."

"Outside the ship?" Snollicoob's eyes widened in fear. *"That will be dangerous."*

"Dangerous is better than dead," La Forge said bluntly.

Snollicoob looked like he wasn't quite sure that was so.

"Uh-huh."

Space was cold. And dark. And scary.

Snollicoob squeezed through an airlock as he exited the ship. The sliding doors had not opened all the way, forcing him to turn sideways to slip through the gap. He held his breath, hoping that his modified Tellarite spacesuit would not catch or tear on anything. The ill-fitting suit, which was one size too small for him, hampered his movements. He had looked for a better fit, but this suit had been in the best condition. In the end, he had chosen safety over comfort. In space, leaks were bad.

He stepped nervously out onto the hull. A tinted visor hid his face. A searchlight built into the top of his helmet cut through the darkness before him. A fully charged phaser was affixed to his tool belt. His heart pounded loudly. He was afraid.

The vast openness of empty space was profoundly intimidating, especially after weeks aboard the cozy confines of the freighter. Despite the protective spacesuit, he felt uncomfortably naked and exposed, like a newborn cub shoved out of the den into the threatening world outside. Vertigo sent his head spinning, and he realized that he had forgotten to exhale. He gulped down air until the light-headedness passed. The sound of his own breathing echoed inside the helmet.

"Mister La Forge, are you there?"

"Call me Geordi," the human engineer answered via the headset in Snollicoob's helmet. His voice was scratchy and faint, but reassuring nonetheless. Snollicoob did not want to do this alone. An optical connection linked Geordi's VISOR to a camera in the helmet, so he could see what Snollicoob saw. *"I'm not going anywhere. We engineers have to stick together, right?"*

"Uh-huh," Snollicoob answered uncertainly. He looked longingly back at the airlock entrance, tempted to turn back. "I do not like this, Geordi."

"You ever spacewalked before?"

"No," he admitted. He could not remember the last time the hull had been inspected from the outside. If only he could change places with Geordi . . . !

"You can do it," the human said. *"Just put one foot in front of the other."* Geordi sounded tense. *"But you had better get going. I don't want to rush you, but that containment field is not looking good."*

Snollicoob understood. Bolstering his courage, he set out across the hull. The magnetized soles of his boots clung to the weathered metal surface; he had to strain against the attraction to lift his feet. The helmet light illuminated his patch. He flinched at the scarred appearance of the outer plating. The rust-colored tritanium was scorched and dented, as though it had been lashed by a Ferengi plasma whip. Countless score marks and fissures cried out to be patched. Vapor jetted through a pin-sized puncture below the ventral impeller. He paused briefly to plug the hole with a wad of thermoconcrete, all too aware that there were probably many more punctures elsewhere. *Rorpot* was going to need serious repairs—if it didn't blow up.

Maybe it would be easier to let it explode?

"Are we almost there yet?" Geordi asked anxiously. *"You need to hurry."*

"Uh-huh." Snollicoob quickened his pace. Unfortunately, the nearest working airlock had been on *Rorpot*'s starboard flank, a long hike from the ejection chute doors, which were located on the underbelly of the freighter. He had to make his way along the ravaged hull, detouring around mangled fins and twisted metal clamps, to get to where he needed to go. An enormous barrel of slush deuterium, hitched to the freighter's side, blocked his path, forcing him to take the long way around. A jagged wound in the side of the metal drum had already released its contents to the void. *Rorpot*'s losses were mounting, but Snollicoob was too worn out to care. Walking in the magnetized boots was exhausting. His legs were already tired by the time he reached the bottom of the ship. He wasn't used to moving this fast, let alone in sticky boots and a clumsy suit. Breathing hard, he forced himself to keep on going.

He was going to need a vacation after this, if he survived.

Walking upside-down beneath *Rorpot* was disorienting. Empty space stretched endlessly above him—or was it below? Worried eyes searched the vast expanse. He couldn't see the quantum filaments, but he knew they were still there, all around him.

What if the ship bumps into one while I am out here?

He shuddered at the thought.

"How are you doing?" Geordi nagged him. *"Can you go any faster?"*

The human's obvious impatience worried Snollicoob. He wondered how close the warp core was to exploding. His helmet could not provide him updates on the ship's status; he was cut off from his gauges. "How weak is the bubble?"

"Trust me, you don't want to know." Geordi's reticence was not reassuring. *"Just get a move on."*

"I am almost there." By his reckoning the chute doors were only seven meters away. He shone his searchlight in the right direction. His jaw dropped. "Uh-oh."

An immense hull breach gaped between him and his destination. From the looks of things, the magnesite in the cargo hold had ignited, blowing open the hull. Only what remained of *Rorpot*'s structural integrity field was holding the ship together. Over four meters across, the breach was like a mountain ravine, directly in his path.

"Geordi, there is a problem."

"I see," Geordi sighed. *"Is there any way around it?"*

Snollicoob swept the searchlight along the length of the fissure. It appeared to stretch quite a ways across the width of the ship, for many meters in both directions. There was no way to bridge the gap; the flickering SIF would not support his weight.

"I do not think so, Geordi." He peered down into the chasm. The blackened interior of the vault was large enough to hold many kilotons of solid ore. "Maybe I can climb down into the hold and back up again?"

"There's no time for that," the human declared. *"You're going to have to jump."*

Snollicoob's mouth went as dry as . . . a very dry thing. He hoped he hadn't heard Geordi right.

"Jump?"

"If you get a running start," Geordi said, as though the idea were not the craziest thing Snollicoob had ever heard, *"then demagnetize your boots at the last minute, your momentum should carry you across the gap. Then you just need to grab onto something on the other side before you go too far."*

Snollicoob spotted a docking strut jutting out from the hull just beyond the crevasse. The metal rail protruded ten centimeters from the underside of the ship; it was bent at an angle, but looked like it was still riveted in place. Geordi's plan *could* work, but . . .

"I am afraid. What if I miss?"

"You can't think about that now." Geordi was obviously not going to take no for an answer. *"You can do it, Snollicoob. I believe in you."*

"You do?"

"Absolutely." Geordi sounded oddly bemused by his own declaration. *"You can fly if you have to. You just need to move!"*

Snollicoob decided to take his word for it. Geordi was smart. *If he thinks I can do this, maybe I can.*

He backed up as far as he could. As with their technology, the Pakleds had appropriated most of their religious beliefs from other species, so he offered up a silent prayer to the Prophets, Kahless, the Overseer, the Blessed Exchequer, and the Q Continuum before sprinting toward the gap faster than any Pakled had probably ever run before. His soles pounded against the warped tritanium plating. Adrenaline rushed through his veins.

It was an unusual feeling.

The yawning abyss looked bigger and bigger the nearer he got to it. He was tempted to close his eyes and let Geordi look instead, but instead he kept his gaze fixed on the life-saving strut on the other side of the gap. Before he knew it, he was only paces away from the brink of the crevasse.

"Demagnetize your boots!" Geordi reminded him. *"Now!"*

Oh right, he thought. *I almost forgot.*

A trigger in the palm of his spacesuit shut off the magnets. He threw himself over the edge, his arms outstretched before him. Just as Geordi had predicted, he soared weightlessly over the chasm. A broad grin broke out across his face.

"I am doing it! It is working!"

He crossed the gap in a heartbeat. The docking strut seemed to come racing toward him. He reached out to snag it . . . and missed!

"Uh-oh!"

Snollicoob went flying past the hull doors into the void. Gloved fingers groped for something—anything!—to hold on to, but grasped only vacuum. Floating free and untethered, he tumbled helplessly away from the ship. He frantically switched his boot magnets back on, but it was already too late. The attraction was too weak; he had to be in contact with the hull for the magnets to work.

"Help me, Geordi! I am lost in space!"

"What's that? I can't hear you!" Geordi's voice was barely audible. He sounded like he was shouting from very far away. *"You're breaking up—"*

The transmission faded into silence. Snollicoob guessed that he had drifted too far away from *Rorpot*'s main antenna array. He tapped the side of the helmet, but Geordi's voice did not return. Snollicoob swallowed hard. He was on his own now.

What can I do?

He was in big trouble. His spacesuit's air supply would run out in hours, long before he died of thirst and hunger or cold. He did not know if that was a good thing or not. He looked longingly at *Rorpot* as it receded into the distance. What if he hit a filament first? How much would that hurt?

"Do not give up," he told himself. "Geordi would not."

He fumbled with the tools on his belt. There had to be something he could use to save himself. He conducted a quick inventory of his equipment: a phaser, a tricorder, an all-purpose wrench, a portable bi-polar torch, a pouch of small-gauge self-sealing stem bolts . . .

If only he had some kind of thruster!

Wait! His fingers went back to the phaser. An idea occurred to him. It was risky, but, like Geordi had said, dangerous was better than dead. More important, he didn't have any better ideas. *What can I lose?*

Unhitching the phaser from his belt, he set the angle of the beam for maximum dispersion, then fired back over his shoulder at the seemingly empty void behind him. He swept the vacuum with the crimson beam, which penetrated the icy blackness at the speed of light. Snollicoob braced himself.

At first, nothing happened. The phaser beam was not solid enough to propel him through space. He sighed in defeat. His desperate plan had not worked after all.

Maybe it was just as well. . . .

Just when he was going to give up, however, a blinding flash lit up the void. There was no sound, but, nanoseconds later, a shock wave slammed into Snollicoob from behind. He yelped loudly, in both fear and exhilaration.

I did it, he realized. *I hit a filament!*

The energy discharge hurled him back toward *Rorpot.* The underside of the freighter seemed to surge toward him like a tidal wave. He threw out his hands and feet to cushion the impact, even as he crashed into the bottom of the ship with bone-jarring force. His face rebounded painfully against the inside of his helmet, squashing his nose. The phaser was almost knocked from his grip, but he held on to to it tightly. Magnetic soles locked onto the metal plating.

He was back!

"—icoob? Snollicoob!" Geordi's voice greeted him. *"Can you read me?"*

"Yes, Geordi!" He wobbled atop his boots, dazed by his collision with the ship. He shook his head to clear it and blinked the tears from his eyes. His nose felt broken. Blood dripped from his nostrils. He reached to wipe it, only to find the helmet's visor in the way. He sniffled loudly. His swollen lip had split open again. "I was lost, but not anymore."

"You'll have to tell me all about it later," Geordi said. *"Can you get to the hull doors now?"*

Snollicoob groaned. He really wanted to rest for a minute, after his harrowing ordeal, but the inconsiderate warp core was not going to wait for him to catch his breath. His spotlight surveyed the ship's exterior as he tried to figure out exactly where he was. *Do not let me be back on the wrong side of the gap.* He knew he did not have the nerve to jump over it again.

To his relief, he spied the hull doors only a few meters away. Hope gave him a second wind and he limped across the hull to the balky steel plates. The glow of the searchlight quickly revealed that the double doors had been fused shut by the energized lashings of a quantum filament. He could tell at glance that it would take a long time, and a lot of work, to pry them open again.

So he lifted the phaser and disintegrated them instead.

A brilliant red glow suffused the solid tritanium doors before they dissolved into atoms, exposing an open shaft that ascended to the blazing heart of the ship. An incandescent cobalt radiance emanated from the top of the chute. Snollicoob backed away from the shaft entrance. He put plenty of distance between himself and the seething warp core.

"It is done," he reported. "The doors are gone."

"Good job!" Geordi said. *"And just in time. I've established remote control of your emergency safety system. I'm going to jettison the core now."*

"No!" Snollicoob froze, terrified by the human's announcement. He had planned to be safely inside *Rorpot* again before the core was ejected. "Wait! I am too close!"

"Sorry," Geordi said. *"Shield strength is twenty-one percent and plummeting. The temperature inside the reaction chamber is off the charts. It's going to blow any minute now. We're out of time!"*

Snollicoob believed him. "But what can I do?"

"Get out of there!"

He did not need to be told twice. Huffing and puffing, he dashed for the nearest available shelter: the hull breach above the cargo hold. An intense vibration shook the plating beneath his feet as the warp core came loose inside the chute. Glancing back over his shoulder, he saw the entire reactor assembly rocket out of the open chute, followed almost immediately by the antimatter containment pods. The warp core was glowing as brightly as a supernova; it was impossible to look at directly, even through the tinted visor. Geordi was right; the core was about to explode. Averting his eyes, Snollicoob dived headfirst into the chasm, his mass and momentum easily penetrating the feeble integrity field covering the opening. He shot down into the murky cargo hold.

It is not fair, he thought. *I saved the ship!*

Nothing but charred ashes now filled the empty vault, all the magnesite having been consumed during the earlier explosion. Floating embers reminded him that they had never bothered to install artificial gravity in the hold, to make stowing the cargo easier. The beam from his helmet fell upon the handle of a reinforced metal door at the far end of the vault. He kicked off from a floating piece of debris and ricocheted toward the door. He crossed the length of the cargo hold in an instant. His fingers closed around the handle. He seized it with both hands.

Made it!

The warp core exploded soundlessly outside the ship. The pristine flash of an uncontrolled matter/antimatter reaction flooded the unlit hold, briefly turning Snollicoob's entire world white. He squeezed his eyes shut, turning his face toward the door to keep from being blinded. He could feel the scorching heat even through the force field and his spacesuit. Sweat drenched the inner layers of the suit. He whimpered in fear.

How far away had the core gotten before it exploded? Was it far enough?

"Hold on!" Geordi said. *"Here it comes!"*

A shock wave, several times more powerful than the one that had propelled Snollicoob back to *Rorpot,* buffeted the freighter. He clung to the door handle as the ship tilted on its axis, rolling over onto its side. The charred remnants of the magnesite were flung across the vault. Bits of ash pelted his spacesuit. He flapped like a flag in an interstellar gale.

And then, abruptly, it was over. The intense effulgence blinked out. Shadows reclaimed the interior of the hold. *Rorpot* kept rotating slowly, but Snollicoob was able to fasten his boots to the floor in front of the door. In the absence of gravity, he felt as though he was standing still. He trembled uncontrollably, almost afraid to open his eyes. His rubbery legs felt about as steady as glop-on-a-stick.

"Snollicoob!" Geordi's anxious voice hurt his ears. *"Are you okay?"*

He peeked at his surroundings. The torched vault did not look like Sto-Vo-Kor or Sha Ka Ree, so he guessed he was still alive. "I think so."

Geordi laughed out loud. *"You did it. Just like I said you could!"*

"Yes," Snollicoob realized. Relief mingled with pride as his racing heart began to settle down. He sagged against the vault door, every muscle aching. "You *are* smart!"

"We both are," Geordi said. *"Now you just need to hold on for a little while more. Help is on the way."*

Snollicoob hoped the *Enterprise* would get there soon.

"Estimated time to our destination?"

Picard sat on the bridge, resisting an urge to pace impatiently. Space travel had never felt so slow.

"Three-point-eight-seven-seven hours, Captain," Data reported, "assuming we can maintain our present course of speed. Sensors confirm, however, a dense accumulation of quantum filaments directly ahead. We may be forced to further reduce our velocity before we reach *Rorpot*'s coordinates."

Merde, Picard thought. This was taking too long. They were already far behind their original estimates. Geordi had bought *Rorpot* much-needed time by resolving their warp core crisis, but the Pakled freighter and its crew remained in jeopardy. Time was the enemy.

"Well, the presence of those filaments certainly adds credence to the Pakleds' story," Riker noted. "Maybe this isn't a trap after all."

Worf grunted behind them. "I still do not trust them."

"Duly noted, Mister Worf," Picard said. He mulled over their options. "How much farther to the filaments, Data?"

The android reviewed the sensor readings. "The filaments themselves remain difficult to detect by conventional means, but an excess of subspace distortions and high-energy particles suggests that we are nearing the perimeter of the phenomenon. Tau neutrino levels exceeding ordinary probability levels by twenty-three-point-five-nine-eight percent. Meson proliferation increasing as well."

"Understood," Picard said grimly. "Reduce speed to warp five. Increase power to the forward shields. Yellow Alert."

"Aye, aye, sir," Ensign Wruum reported from the conn. Descended from seabirds, her people had a strong nautical tradition. "Warp factor five."

Picard scowled. He had issued the command reluctantly, but saw no alternative. They could not rescue the Pakleds if the *Enterprise* itself ran afoul of an invisible filament. Like everyone else who had survived that day, he still recalled the last time they had flown head-on into disaster. He had found himself trapped in an unstable turbolift with three small children—and a broken ankle to boot. Only the valiant assistance of those youngsters had allowed him to live to see another day. As he recalled, Jay Gordon's parents had since transferred off the *Enterprise,* but the other two children were still aboard the ship. He could not endanger them, and the other one-thousand-plus souls in his care, by recklessly charging into the hazardous filaments.

But could the Pakleds survive the delay?

"Hail *Rorpot*," he instructed Worf. It was imperative that he stay informed of the imperiled freighter's status.

"Yes, sir."

Captain Aadnalurg appeared upon the viewer. *"Where are you,* Enterprise?" he wailed, visibly distraught. He wrung his hands, while a sluglike creature squirmed restlessly atop his shoulder. An ugly scab had formed over the captain's head wound. *"Our life support is breaking. We are running out of air!"*

"We are proceeding as fast as we are able," Picard assured him. "What is your status? How much longer can you hold out?"

Aadnalurg hastily consulted with a subordinate. His face went pale. *"What? Do not say that!"* He angrily dismissed the unfortunate crewman before turning back toward the screen. He appeared even more rattled than before. *"It is bad. We cannot make any more air. We have only an hour left. Maybe not that much."*

"Oh, no," Deanna gasped, feeling the Pakled's fear. "Captain, we have to do something!"

"I know," Picard said. He wished he could promise Aadnalurg that they would get there in time, but that was looking increasingly unlikely. "We appreciate the urgency of your situation, Captain. Rest assured, we are making every effort to reach your coordinates."

His calm tone did little to reassure the other captain. *"You must hurry,* Enterprise!" Aadnalurg trembled noticeably. *"Our heat is broken, too. It is very cold!"*

Picard hoped that Geordi's heroic efforts had not been in vain. "We are on our way. *Enterprise* out." He signaled Worf to terminate the transmission. The captain looked to his crew for a solution to their current dilemma. "Data, is there any way we can increase our speed?"

"I would not advise it," the android said. "The extent of the subspace disturbances indicate a sizable concentration of quantum filaments. Navigating them safely will be difficult, especially since the *Enterprise* is considerably larger than the Pakled vessel."

"For once our size is working against us," Riker observed. "Too bad we're not smaller and more maneuverable."

Inspiration struck like a photon torpedo. "Perhaps we can make it so," Picard said. "Suppose we separate the saucer from the drive section?"

"That could work." Riker instantly saw the advantages. "Without the saucer, the drive section might be able to weave through the filaments more easily."

"And with less risk to the rest of the *Enterprise*, including the support staff and families aboard." Picard thought again of the children who had survived the previous collision; he had no desire to subject them to the same ordeal again. A saucer separation was a drastic move, which he had resorted to only a handful of times over the course of his career, but it might be just what the circumstances called for in this instance. *We have the capacity. We might as well use it.*

He rose from his chair. "Number One, the saucer is yours." He did not entrust this responsibility to Riker lightly; the enormous saucer contained the vast majority of the *Enterprise*'s crew and facilities. "Take care of our people."

"You can count on me, sir." Riker took the captain's chair, while Data and the others prepared to turn over their stations to the relief crew. A dedicated turbolift connected the bridge with the battle bridge in the drive section. "I just wish I was going with you."

"You're needed here." He clapped Riker on the shoulder. "Inform Captain Aadnalurg he can expect us shortly."

Provided they got there at all . . .

The battle bridge was located on Deck 8, at the top of the stardrive section. Its basic configuration resembled that of the main bridge in the saucer, but it was smaller and more streamlined, stripped down for combat and other hazardous situations. There were fewer workstations and less elegant decor. The conn and ops stations were positioned closer together. The captain's chair sat alone on an elevated platform at the center of the bridge. The tactical post was confined to a single compact console instead of the sweeping rail that graced the main bridge It was lean and mean, like the bridge of an old *Constitution*-class starship.

La Forge hurried onto the battle bridge and took his place at the aft engineering station. He noticed that Doctor Crusher had joined the rescue mission as well. Her usual post in sickbay was back on the saucer, but he recalled that there was an auxiliary medical facility elsewhere in the drive section. No doubt she and her staff would be busy once they reached *Rorpot*. According to Snollicoob, many of the Pakleds were in need of prompt medical treatment. Beverly nodded at Geordi as he arrived on the bridge. Counselor Troi was seated nearby, behind a plain metal guardrail. Like the rail, the overall look of the battle bridge was stark and utilitarian. It had not been designed with aesthetics in mind.

"Slow to impulse," the captain commanded Ensign Wruum. It was a shame that they had to reduce speed again, if only temporarily, but separating from the saucer at warp speed was against all the rules. They had done it before, in the most dire of emergencies, but they would be pushing their luck to try it again. "What is the progress of the evacuation?"

Even at full alert, it took time to transfer all nonessential personnel to the saucer. On his way to the battle bridge from engineering, Geordi had personally witnessed the orderly stampede going on in the corridors and turbolifts right now, as hundreds of crew members and their families rushed for safety aboard the saucer, leaving the drive section to the designated duty staff. Geordi had placed Miles O'Brien in charge of engineering in his absence. Keiko and little Molly had hurried past Geordi en route to the saucer. He hoped they were secure in their own quarters by now.

"Evacuation complete," Data reported. "Linking turbolifts sealed and retracted."

"Very good, Mister Data." Picard supervised the operation from his chair. "Proceed with separation."

Eighteen docking clamps, made of diffusion-bonded titanium

carbide, disengaged as the saucer lifted off from the top of the drive section. Onboard computers and inertial damping systems ensured a smooth transition, so that only a slight shudder was felt aboard the battle bridge. All eyes were fixed on the viewscreen as they watched the massive saucer sail away on impulse power; the saucer lacked warp capacity, but could rendezvous with another starship should anything happen to the drive section. La Forge felt a twinge of unease at the sight of the departing saucer. As chief engineer, he knew he would not entirely relax until the *Enterprise* was back in one piece again.

He had to imagine the captain felt the same—and then some.

They waited until the saucer was safely distant before engaging the warp drive once more. "Warp speed six," Picard instructed. "Maintain Yellow Alert."

The headless starship quickly left the saucer behind, accelerating into deep space. Geordi impatiently tracked their progress; even warp six seemed far too slow given *Rorpot*'s extreme jeopardy. Despite his past experience with the Pakleds, he no longer anticipated any treachery at the end of this voyage. There was no way they could have staged everything poor Snollicoob had gone through, nor would they have sacrificed their warp core just to lure the *Enterprise* into a trap. He had bonded with Snollicoob, engineer to engineer. All he was worried about now was making sure Snollicoob and the other Pakleds were okay. His skeptical attitude had done a complete turnaround.

Imagine that.

Long hours passed without incident until a sudden bump rocked the *Enterprise*. Geordi almost slipped from his seat. Deanna caught hold of the guardrail to keep from falling. The lights flickered briefly. Worf snarled at the disturbance. Ensign Wruum hooted shrilly.

Picard reacted promptly. "A filament?"

"Yes, Captain," Data confirmed. "A glancing blow off our starboard nacelle."

"Damage?"

"Shields holding, sir," Worf stated. "Hull integrity intact."

Damage reports started coming in from all over the ship. "Minor fires and ruptures in engineering and elsewhere," Geordi informed the captain. "Nothing too serious . . . yet."

"No major injuries," Doctor Crusher added. She scanned her display panel for casualty reports. "Although sickbay is standing by."

Deanna stared at the viewer. "But I don't *see* anything."

"You would not, Counselor," Data said, "but it is clear that we have entered the midst of the filaments."

Worf glared at the deceptive emptiness. His fingers were poised over the weapons controls. "Can't we just blast our way through?" He made a slashing gesture, as though blazing a trail with a machete or *bat'leth*.

"That would be inadvisable," Data stated. "The resulting quantum energy discharges could be formidable. It is uncertain if our shields could withstand them for long."

Picard's face grew even grimmer. "Reduce speed to warp four."

Damn, Geordi thought. *We just can't get a break!*

"The Pakleds are hailing us again," Worf announced with more than an touch of irritation. "They are being most insistent."

"If only we had better news to tell them," Picard said. "Put them through."

Aadnalurg was in bad shape. His lips were blue and his teeth chattered. A heavy blanket was draped over his stocky torso in a desperate attempt to preserve his body heat. Snollicoob could be glimpsed behind him, still wearing his insulated spacesuit, minus the helmet. The engineer hugged himself to keep warm.

"You are too slow!" Aadnalurg accused them. He gasped for breath. *"Our air is thin. We are freezing!"* He reached beneath his blanket and pulled out what looked like a lifeless lump of slug. *"Look! See how cold it is! Snirgli has gone to sleep! It thinks it is winter!"*

Geordi gathered that the oversized mollusk was hibernating, not dead.

Too bad the Pakleds couldn't do the same. . . .

"Wait!" he blurted. "That's it."

Picard turned around. Worf muted the transmission. "What is it, Mister La Forge?"

"Let them freeze," Geordi suggested. "Shut down all the heating on *Rorpot* and turn the entire ship into one big cryosatellite—like that sleeper ship we ran into way back when." Six years ago, during one of the *Enterprise*'s earliest missions, they had stumbled onto an ancient

Earth vessel holding three cryogenically frozen human beings from the late twentieth century. Much to La Forge's astonishment, the specimens had been revived by Doctor Crusher after three hundred years of suspended animation, despite an almost total lack of life support. "If we lower the Pakleds' metabolisms enough, there might be enough oxygen left aboard *Rorpot* to keep them alive until we can get there to revive them."

In other words, the Pakleds could save themselves by taking a long nap!

"A bold idea." Picard looked at Beverly. "Doctor, your thoughts?"

She thought it over. "It's risky, but doable, I suppose." Her tone was none too enthusiastic. "They'll need to be thawed out carefully, under controlled conditions."

"It may be their only chance, Captain," Geordi entreated.

Picard made his decision. "Very well." He returned his attention to the screen, where Aadnalurg and Snollicoob anxiously awaited any sort of hopeful tidings from the tardy starship. "Mister La Forge, I believe you have already established a good working relationship with the Pakleds. Would you care to explain your plan to them?"

"I can try, Captain." LaForge left his post at the rear of the bridge and approached the screen. He signaled Worf to restore the audio. "Snollicoob. It's me, Geordi. We have an idea that might buy us some more time. You just have to trust us."

"Uh-huh," Aadnalurg wheezed. Both Pakleds nodded eagerly. *"You are smart. Tell us what to do."*

"It's easy," Geordi said. "You just have to go to sleep for a while. That's all."

The Pakleds grinned.

"We can do that."

Warp four felt like a crawl.

At this rate, we'll never *get there,* Geordi thought. Data had warned, however, that the subspace distortions around them were only increasing. The seemingly empty space was aswarm with invisible currents and subatomic particles.

A second jolt eliminated any possibility that the first collision had been a freak event. The *Enterprise* jerked to one side, as though the port nacelle had caught on something. Straining shields crackled and hissed. Sparks arced across Crusher's control panel, forcing her to jump backward to avoid being shocked. Thrown to one side, La Forge whacked his elbow against the edge of his workstation. It stung like disruptor fire.

"Full reverse!" Picard ordered "One-third speed!"

"Aye, aye!" Wruum chirped.

The bridge stabilized as the ship backed away from the filament that had snagged them. Automated fire-suppression measures kicked in; a force field generator mounted on the ceiling projected an airtight containment field around Crusher's burning console, cutting off its supply of oxygen. Thick white smoke swirled inside the field, defining its borders, until the trapped carbon dioxide suffocated the blaze. The field remained in place for several minutes, to ensure the fire was fully extinguished.

"Full stop," Picard commanded. The *Enterprise* came to rest, still nowhere near *Rorpot*. The captain's frustration could no longer be contained. "This is intolerable. Even without the saucer, it's like trying to weave through a Tholian web blindfolded!"

"I'm sorry, sir," Wruum said. "I wish there was some way I could avoid them."

"It's not your fault, Ensign," he assured the avian helmsman, who looked like she was on the verge of molting. "We just need a means to chart a safe course through this minefield."

Geordi lifted his gaze from his controls and gauges. He turned his VISOR toward the viewer. His brow furrowed. Was it just his imagination, or could he almost see something out there . . . at the outer ranges of the electromagnetic spectrum? A faint, almost infinitesimal shimmer?

"Captain, call me crazy, but I think my VISOR might be picking up something the sensors are missing." The sophisticated optical prosthesis, which operated on a subspace field pulse, allowed him a much wider visual range than most humanoids. In the past, he had even managed to detect neutrino emissions invisible to ordinary sensors. Geordi squinted into the blackness of space. "Maybe some indication of the filaments?"

Picard gave Geordi his full attention. "Enough to navigate by?"

"I don't know," he said honestly. "It's awfully faint. More like a ripple than anything else." The mysterious shimmer seemed to waver in and out of view. "Or a mirage."

"Is there any way to enhance your vision?" Worf asked. "Perhaps by linking your VISOR to a tricorder, as you did on Galorndorn Core?"

La Forge had a better idea. "The interface unit, the one I used to control that probe." Just a few weeks earlier, he had tested an experimental new telepresence process that had linked his VISOR inputs to a remote probe, allowing its sensory data to be transmitted directly to his cerebral cortex. The interface connection had been instrumental in the rescue of a Federation starship trapped in the crushing depths of a gas giant. "Suppose we use that technology to hook my VISOR directly to the primary sensor array? That might amplify what I'm seeing. Or what I *think* I'm seeing."

"I don't know, Geordi," the doctor objected. "That interface provoked an unhealthy degree of neural stimulation. And remember the feedback problems?"

La Forge hadn't forgotten. The interface had let him experience everything the probe had encountered in a very tactile way, to the extent that he had been physically burned when the probe had passed through a fire. He glanced down at his palms. Thanks to Doctor Crusher's expert ministrations, they were no longer scarred, but the searing pain was still fresh in his memory. Did he really want to risk getting hurt like that again? Or worse?

What other choice is there?

"Please, Captain. Let me do this." Geordi called up the specs for the interface unit. "Like you said before, lives are at stake."

Picard nodded. "Make it so." He looked over at Beverly. "Doctor Crusher, I want you to monitor Mister La Forge very carefully."

"Count on it," she promised.

Thankfully, the interface apparatus was stored in engineering and not in the saucer. Data and Ensign Wruum worked quickly to assemble the equipment, which resembled a portable metal cage, around the conn station, while Geordi changed into a full-body, matte-black VR suit, composed of overlapping sensor pads, that covered him from the neck down. Multicolored cables were strung along the outside of the suit like exposed veins and arteries. Wireless antennae connected his VISOR to the conn terminal. He sat down at the helm.

Just like old times, he thought once more. It had been a long time since he had served as pilot, but regular practice simulations in the holodeck had kept him fully certified. Ordinarily the *Enterprise*'s flight controls were heavily automated, so that the conn officer was mostly overseeing the computer's piloting, but he switched to full manual control. He eased the ship forward cautiously, just to refamiliarize himself with the controls. The starboard nacelle felt a little sluggish, probably from grazing that filament earlier. He'd have to compensate for that.

"All right," he said. "Patch me into the sensors."

Beverly hovered nearby, brandishing a medical tricorder. "You let me know the minute it gets to be too much for you," she instructed. "This technology is by no means bug-free."

"Understood, Doctor," Picard said. "Proceed with implementation, Mister Data."

"Yes, sir." The android had resumed his seat at ops. La Forge found his lack of trepidation encouraging, even though he knew intellectually that Data was incapable of fear or anxiety. "Linking interface to primary sensor array."

La Forge braced himself for the transition, but it still blew him away. There was no way to prepare for the astonishing new vistas that opened up before him. As the sensors merged with the unique neural properties of his VISOR, Geordi literally became the eyes and ears of the *Starship Enterprise.* Subspace fluctuations and gravitational tides coursed before his eyes in all the colors of the rainbow . . . and beyond. Solar winds, wafting across the cosmos from distant stars, brushed against his skin. He could see for light-years in every direction. He heard the music of the spheres. Goosebumps sprouted beneath the suit. His pulse raced at the wondrous sights and sounds and sensations.

"I don't like this," Crusher declared. Her tricorder beeped in his ear. "His neural activity is already climbing."

"I can handle it," he insisted. Any ordinary human would have been overwhelmed by the awesome sensory overload, but he was used to coping with more visual input than other people. He declined to mention that his eyes were already throbbing. "Just give me a moment to adjust."

"What about the filaments?" Picard asked urgently. "Can you see them?"

La Forge tried to make sense of the myriad shapes and colors. Coruscating silver strands emerged from the background like a thicket of hanging vines. As thin as cobwebs, they were deceptively delicate in appearance . . . and worryingly plentiful. They pulsed with quantum energy, throwing off subatomic particles like sparks.

"Yes!" he reported. "They're all around us."

Picard stared at the viewer, unable to see for himself. "Can you make your way through them?"

"Just watch me," Geordi said.

Despite his bravado, navigating the threads was a nerve-racking challenge. The densely packed threads offered little margin for error. As he wove through the tangles, cruising at warp five, he was grateful that they had left the colossal saucer behind; this was tricky enough as it was. Perspiration beaded on his forehead and glued the inner layer of the interface suit to his back. His mouth went dry. Sweat seeped beneath his VISOR where he couldn't wipe it away. The cumbersome metal prosthesis could be a real pain sometimes. Maybe, when this was over, he needed to look into getting some of those new optical implants. . . .

Still, at least they weren't flying blind anymore.

"Neutrotransmitter levels elevated," Beverly reported ominously. La Forge recognized her worried tone; he had sounded just like her while monitoring *Rorpot*'s unstable warp engine. "Heart rate and respiration beyond recommended parameters."

His eyes were burning, too, but he wasn't going to admit it. A pounding headache squeezed his temples, right where his VISOR inputs were surgically implanted. It felt like stem bolts were being driven into his skull.

Work through it, he thought. The VISOR had always hurt a little; he was accustomed to pain. *Snollicoob is depending on us.*

A thick clump of filaments forced him to take a frustrating detour. Even now that he could see them, the lethal strands were still slowing them down. Trying to make up a little lost time, he cut a corner too close.

The stern of the drive section brushed against a vibrating strand, causing the ship's shields to flare up at the point of contact. The *Enterprise* was tossed about like on old-fashioned sailing ship atop a stormy sea.

A feedback loop seared La Forge's nervous system. Crying out in agony, he toppled from his seat onto the floor. Spasms shook his body. Blisters formed on his face and hands.

"That's it!" Beverly announced. "I'm pulling the plug."

"No!" La Forge blurted. The convulsions abated, and he scrambled back into his seat before the anxious doctor could intervene. "I can do this. Just a little longer!"

Beverly disagreed. "Captain Picard, as chief medical officer, I must protest. You saw what just happened. Mister La Forge suffered a severe neurological shock. His vital signs are spiking. We *have* to call off this dangerous experiment."

"It's too late now," Geordi pointed out. "We'll never find our way out of this maze unless I stay hooked up to the interface. It's the only way."

Picard turned to Deanna. "Counselor?"

"Geordi believes he can do it," she informed him. La Forge appreciated her vote of confidence.

"Very well then." The captain focused on the way ahead. "I appreciate your concerns, Doctor, but Mister La Forge is correct. We cannot turn back now."

The doctor bowed to the inevitable. She extracted a hypospray from the pocket of her long blue lab coat and applied it to La Forge's carotid artery. "This will help with the pain."

"Thanks," he murmured. The open blisters stung like blazes; his hands felt like he had been petting a Horta. He winced every time he touched the control panel. Straightening out the stern, he pushed forward through the daunting obstacle course ahead. "Only a little farther."

Without warning, a glowing filament drifted directly into the *Enterprise*'s path, forcing Geordi to veer hard to port. Picard and the others were thrown to the side, almost tumbling from their posts. A loose padd crashed to the floor. Deanna gasped. Worf snarled in annoyance. The ship glided past the filament, missing it by less than fifty meters. Geordi shook his head at their narrow escape. That had been a close one.

"A little more warning next time, Mister La Forge." Picard tugged his rumpled uniform back into place. "If you please."

"Yes, sir," LaForge said. "Sorry, sir."

This had better not be another trap, he thought irritably. But, no, he didn't really think that anymore. He trusted Snollicoob. *Like I told him, we engineers have to stick by each other.*

"We are within visual range of *Rorpot,*" Data announced.

About time, Geordi thought. *It felt like we were never going to get here.*

"On-screen," Picard ordered. "Full magnification."

The ill-fated freighter appeared on the viewer, drifting rudderless in space just as the Pakleds had claimed. *Rorpot* bore a definite resemblance to the vessel Geordi had visited years ago. Its triangular contours lacked the graceful lines of the *Enterprise,* looking crude and clunky by comparison. Its dull orange hull was scored and charred. Unpatched hull breaches appalled the engineer in Geordi. A torn metal canister was clamped to one side. An open chute beneath the freighter revealed where the warp core had been ejected; there was no trace of the core itself, which had presumably been atomized by the violent matter/antimatter explosion. The entire ship, which was dwarfed by the *Enterprise,* was rotating slowly on its axis. No running lights were evident along the freighter's exterior. Its transparent portholes and windows were dark. *Rorpot* looked like a ghost ship.

"It would appear," Picard observed, "the Pakleds were not malingering."

Data scanned *Rorpot* to be sure. "Shields are down. Impulse power inoperative. Life-support functioning only at a minimal level."

"Weapons?" Worf asked suspiciously.

"Rudimentary and disabled," Data reported. "As expected."

"Or so they would have us believe," Worf growled. "What of the masking field they employed before?"

During their previous encounter, the Pakleds had employed a sophisticated masking field that made them appear much more damaged than they actually were. It had concealed their offensive capabilities in a way that Worf had clearly not forgotten.

"Sensors do not indicate the presence of such a field," Data stated, "although, of course, masking fields are elusive by design."

"Indeed," Picard said. "Maintain shields, Mister Worf."

"What about life signs?" Beverly asked.

"I am detecting many faint life signs aboard the freighter," Data said, much to Geordi's relief. "Subspace interference makes attaining an exact count problematic."

Deanna closed her eyes in concentration. "I am sensing muted fears and apprehension. The impressions are foggy and incoherent, like bad dreams." She opened her eyes. "The Pakled crew are sleeping uneasily."

"I don't blame them," La Forge said. "I'd be nervous, too, in their shoes."

At least they're still alive. Barely.

He slowed to impulse. The *Enterprise* came to a stop within transporter range of the smaller vessel. He was tempted to turn off the interface and switch back to normal vision, but decided against it. He needed to stay alert for any drifting filaments.

"Well done, Mister La Forge," Picard said. "Let us hope we have arrived in time to revive Captain Aadnalurg and his crew." He contemplated the seemingly lifeless ship on the viewer. "Can we beam them directly to sickbay?"

"I would not advise it, sir," Data replied. "The extreme subspace fluctuations preclude locking onto multiple individuals with any degree of accuracy. I would recommend attaching combadges to each subject before attempting to transport them aboard."

"Let me do it, Captain." La Forge rose from the conn. He was anxious to check on Snollicoob. "Beam me over there."

"With all due respect, Geordi," Data said, "I believe I am better suited to endure the inhospitable conditions aboard *Rorpot* at the moment. The extreme cold and thin atmosphere will not impair my performance as they would an organic life-form."

Picard agreed. "Data will beam over first. Once he's gotten the lay of the land, and perhaps brought the life-support systems back up to speed, we can send over reinforcements to assist him."

La Forge had to admit that Data's plan made more sense. He nodded at his friend. "Take care of yourself over there."

"I will endeavor to do so." Data turned ops over to Ensign Wruum. He marched briskly toward the turbolift. "I will procure a quantity of surplus combadges en route to the transporter room."

Worf scowled. "I remind you, Captain, that it will be necessary to lower our shields to transport Commander Data over to the Pakled vessel."

"A necessary risk, Mister Worf," Picard said gravely. "We have not come this far only to hesitate upon the brink."

The Klingon conceded the point. "In that case, Captain, might I suggest a reasonable precaution . . ."

"I'm listening, Mister Worf."

The dazzle of the transporter beam briefly illuminated the darkened bridge. Data materialized upon *Rorpot* with his phaser raised and ready, in the unlikely event that an ambush was in store. The probability of a hostile reception was extremely low, given the lack of life support, yet Data did not intend to be taken unawares. He swept the bridge with the beam from a handheld light. A pouch of combadges was slung over his shoulder.

He found the bridge both silent and deserted. Frost coated the abandoned pedestals and consoles. Frozen blood spackled the floor and walls. Extensive damage confirmed the Pakleds' account of their difficulties. The wreckage was real and tangible, not an illusion generated by a masking field or holoprojector. The main viewscreen had gone black. His footsteps echoed in the sepulchral gloom. A deep breath confirmed that oxygen levels were far below that needed to sustain most humanoid beings.

Sometimes there were advantages to being an android.

Data lowered his phaser. He tapped his combadge. "Data to *Enterprise*." He reported his findings to Captain Picard. "The bridge is unoccupied. Life support is barely functioning. I will now commence a search for the captain and crew."

"Very good, Mister Data." Picard's voice emanated from Data's badge. *"Stay on your guard. We don't want another hostage situation."*

"That would not be advantageous to our mission," the android agreed. "Data out."

He attached his phaser to his side. A tricorder picked up faint life signs coming from deeper inside the freighter. He followed the readings until he came to what appeared to be the crew's barracks. Rows of sturdy metal bunks, stacked two high, ran along both sides of a wide corridor in a cramped tunnel aft of the bridge. The spartan quarters lacked the amenities available aboard the *Enterprise*. A metal grille clattered beneath his boots as he walked the length of the barracks. He observed the occupants of the bunks with interest.

The Pakleds appeared to have retired to their bunks to await the *Enterprise*'s arrival. They lay flat upon their backs, their arms at their sides. Frost glazed their bodies, which were cold and rigid to the touch. According to the tricorder, their respective metabolisms had indeed been slowed to a remarkable degree. If not for the readings before him, confirming almost negligible evidence of life, the motionless bodies could have been easily mistaken for corpses. The barracks were as cold and inhospitable as a morgue. Data suspected that a human would have found the atmosphere distinctly eerie. He understood the concept, if not the emotion.

"Data to *Enterprise*. I have located the Pakleds." He placed his fingers gently against a sleeping Pakled's throat. It was several seconds before he felt a pulse. "As anticipated, they are frozen in a state of suspended animation."

"*Excellent,*" Picard responded. "*Doctor Crusher and her staff are standing by in sickbay, ready to revive them. Are all the Pakleds accounted for?*"

Data surveyed the long rows of bunks. "I do not see Captain Aadnalurg at this location. It is probable that he has separate quarters elsewhere aboard the ship."

"*Rank has its privileges,*" Picard acknowledged. "*I suspect you will find him in a private stateroom.*"

La Forge intruded on the discussion. "*What about Snollicoob? The chief engineer? Is he okay?*"

"I have not yet attempted to identify every Pakled at this site," Data admitted. He understood that Geordi was concerned about his fellow engineer. "I will notify you as soon as I come across him."

"*Thanks, Data,*" Geordi said. "*I'm sure he's in good hands now.*"

"*Begin preparing the Pakleds for transport to sickbay,*" Picard instructed. "*You can locate Captain Aadnalurg later. If he is any captain at all, I am certain that he would wish us to see to his crew's safety first.*"

"You may be giving him too much credit, sir." Data had formed his own impression of Aadnalurg's character by observing his conduct during the crisis. "But I will proceed as ordered. Data out."

He put away the tricorder and opened the pouch of combadges.

The generic badges, which were intended for visiting civilians, lacked many of the advanced functions available to Starfleet personnel, but would allow the *Enterprise*'s transporters to lock onto the wearers despite the subspace interference outside. He walked to the end of the barracks, intending to work his way back to the bridge. Chances were, Captain Aadnalurg's personal quarters were located near the freighter's command center.

But before he could affix the first of the combadges to a hibernating Pakled, Data spotted an inert figure lying atop a metal grille at the rear of the barracks. A closer look revealed that the sprawled Pakled was in fact Snollicoob, the engineer. Unlike his compatriots, Geordi's colleague had not made it safely to his bunk. He was sprawled on the floor as though he had collapsed without warning. Data noted that Snollicoob was no longer wearing the spacesuit he had donned earlier. He hoped, for Geordi's sake, that the engineer was not dead or injured.

Data hurried forward to investigate. He did not wish to alarm Geordi until he had fully ascertained Snollicoob's condition. He was less than a meter away from the stricken Pakled, however, when the grille beneath his feet gave way. Gravity seized him and he plunged through the trapdoor, landing hard on a scuffed steel floor one deck below. The impact jarred him all the way to his artificial, polyalloy endoskeleton. Internal gyros failed to preserve his balance. He found himself face-down on the floor.

His positronic brain, securely cradled in a skull of solid duranium, quickly recovered from the fall. Conducting a rapid self-diagnostic, he determined that he had suffered no significant damage to any major component, although a more thorough inspection would be in order once he returned to the *Enterprise*. He rolled onto his back and sat up. Cool golden eyes surveyed his surroundings, which appeared to be a communal mess hall. Tables and chairs were scattered haphazardly around the unlit chamber. Fallen plates and cutlery littered the floor. Tilting his head back, he observed the open gap through which he had fallen. The loose grille hung down on one side. Data made a mental note to be more careful of his footing in the future.

"Do not move, Starfleet!" an electronically amplified voice sounded behind him. The muzzle of a disruptor pistol was pressed against the nape of his neck. "You are my prisoner."

Data recognized the voice, and uncomplicated speech patterns, of Captain Aadnalurg. The Pakled commander, who was evidently not hibernating like the rest of his crew, confiscated Data's phaser and combadge. The android did not resist.

"The threat of violence is unnecessary," he stated calmly. "We are here to assist you."

"Turn around," Aadnalurg said. "Let me see who you are."

Raising his hands above his head so as not to provoke the armed Pakled, Data did as instructed. He saw that Aadnalurg had donned the primitive spacesuit that Snollicoob had worn before. The suit shielded him from the subzero temperature and oxygen-deficient atmosphere. A built-in microphone allowed him to threaten Data despite the thin air. He kept the disruptor pointed at his prisoner as he crossed the room to a lighted control panel by the door. He keyed a command into the panel. A low hum indicated that *Rorpot* was not completely without power.

"Snollicoob fixed the shields," Aadnalurg explained, "before I hit him. He is smart."

Data found his use of the present tense encouraging.

Confused brown eyes squinted at Data.

"You are not a human." Aadnalurg tapped Data's golden countenance with a gloved finger. "What are you?"

"I am an android," Data explained. He realized that he had fallen for a rudimentary snare, employing Snollicoob's unconscious form as bait. His brain wasted not a nanosecond on regret, but instead began calculating a number of probable outcomes. A preliminary analysis indicated that his situation was serious but not critical. Careful handling of the volatile captain might yet defuse the situation. "Lieutenant Commander Data of the *Starship Enterprise.*"

"A machine?"

"That is correct," Data said.

Aadnalurg grinned broadly. "I like that idea. Make machines to do all the work."

"You are mistaken," Data informed him. "I am an autonomous individual, not a labor-saving device."

The Pakled had a different view. "We need machines like you. To do our work." He examined Data from a safe distance. "That would be good."

Data chose not to debate the issue. "Your ship is in jeopardy," he reminded Aadnalurg. "Your efforts to hold me hostage are ill-timed."

"My ship is broken," the captain said. His grin faded. "I want yours."

"Captain!" Troi called out from the tactical station. "*Rorpot* has raised its shields."

"What?" Picard reacted. This did not bode well. In theory, the freighter's entire crew should have been cryogenically frozen.

"We're being hailed, Captain," Deanna said. "Via Data's combadge."

Picard eyed the screen warily. The *Enterprise* had restored its own shields immediately after beaming Data over to the freighter. "Put it through."

A familiar voice came over the loudspeakers. "*This is Aadnalurg. I have your machine. Do not try to take him back or I will break him.*"

"You've got to be kidding me!" La Forge exclaimed from the conn. "Not this again."

"He is serious, Captain," Deanna reported. "I can sense his hostility."

"I doubt it is any match for mine," Picard said, his indignation evident. "May I remind you, Captain Aadnalurg, that we have come in answer to your distress signal, and at no little risk to ourselves, I might add. Such treachery is unworthy of you . . . and reckless in the extreme."

But the Pakled captain could not be shamed. "*My ship is broken. I want yours. I will trade you the machine for the* Enterprise."

Picard was taken aback by the man's audacity. Surely he did not expect them to turn over a Federation starship in exchange for a single hostage? "First, I want proof that my officer is unharmed. Let me speak to Lieutenant Commander Data."

"*Uh-huh,*" Aadnalurg said. "*But no tricks!*"

Data's voice replaced the Pakled's. "*I am still intact and functional, Captain, but I'm afraid that Captain Aadnalurg has the upper hand at the moment. He is holding a disruptor pistol on me.*"

"I see." Picard was glad to hear that Data had not been injured yet, but he did not intend to let Aadnalurg get away with this betrayal.

Fortunately, he had thoroughly reviewed the *Enterprise*'s files on the Pakleds during the voyage here. "You are not smart, Aadnalurg. You are a fool to think that we would trade the *Enterprise* for a mere machine." He cringed inwardly at the deliberately callous words, but took comfort from the fact that Data had no feelings to hurt. "Surrender or I will unleash our dreaded crimson force field!"

The latter was a bluff that Commander Riker had successfully employed against the Pakleds during their first encounter. By back-flushing ionized hydrogen gas through the *Enterprise*'s Bussard collectors, he had produced a spectacular—if harmless—pyrotechnic display that had cowed the Pakleds into submission. Picard hoped the tactic would suffice a second time.

Aadnalurg laughed harshly. *"That is an old trick. You cannot fool me. I am too smart!"*

So much for that ploy, Picard thought. Apparently the Pakleds had seen through the ruse at some point. He fished for time . . . and information. "Where are you?" he demanded. "Why can't I see you?"

"We are not on the bridge," Aadnalurg admitted. *"We have no viewer."*

Interesting. Picard saw a way to turn that intelligence to their advantage. "You don't want the *Enterprise*, Captain. We hit too many quantum filaments on our way here. We are too badly damaged. Worse than your own ship."

"You are lying," Aadnalurg accused him. *"I do not believe you. The* Enterprise *is too strong."*

"See for yourself," Picard challenged him. "Go to your bridge."

"Careful. No tricks!"

Aadnalurg prodded Data with the muzzle of the disruptor as they climbed a series of metal stairways to *Rorpot*'s bridge. The android's own phaser was tucked into a pouch in the Pakled's uniform. A bag full of combadges dangled from Aadnalurg's other hand; he guessed he could get a good price for them on the other side of the Neutral Zone. He watched the artificial human as it climbed the steps ahead of him. The machine was impressively lifelike. It would be a shame to trade it back to the humans. He wondered if there was any way to keep Data as well.

I could program it to do all my work, he thought. *Even read all the boring reports!*

But first he had to make sure he got the *Enterprise* so he could get away from the filaments. He had it all worked out. He would have the Starfleet crew beam aboard *Rorpot* while he and his men claimed the Federation ship. Of course, he would have to thaw out his frozen crew on his own, but how hard could that be?

He hoped the *Enterprise* was not really as broken as Picard claimed. The human captain had to be lying. *He thinks he is smarter than me, but he is wrong. I will show him who is the most smart.*

They walked through an archway onto the bridge, which was just as dark and broken as he remembered. Aadnalurg frowned at the wreckage. Repairing *Rorpot* would be too much work. It would be easier to take another ship instead. That was the Pakled way.

He gestured toward a corner with the disruptor. "Stand over there," he ordered Data, while he lumbered over to a working control pedestal. Snollicoob had turned off the main viewer to save power, but Aadnalurg knew how to turn it back on. He would see just how damaged the *Enterprise* really was. Examining the controls, he kept one eye on Data. "Do not move or I will shoot you!"

"I am not the individual you need to worry about," Data replied.

A shadowy figure emerged from an unlit alcove. Aadnalurg got a fleeting glimpse of a reflective visor before a phaser blast lit up the bridge. His spacesuit was no protection from the beam. The phaser's energy shocked his system.

Uh-oh.

The Pakled captain joined his crew in restless slumber.

Worf stepped forward to inspect his fallen foe. A Starfleet environmental suit maintained his life functions. He prodded Aadnalurg's body with the toe of his boot. The unconscious Pakled did not stir.

"I told you he was without honor," the Klingon said.

As planned, Worf had covertly beamed aboard *Rorpot* at the same time as Data, albeit to a different location. Data assumed that the security officer had been monitoring Aadnalurg's communications with the *Enterprise*—and hence had known where to lie in wait for the duplicitous Pakled commander. Captain Picard had done his own part by luring Aadnalurg to the bridge.

"It appears your suspicions were well-founded," Data said. He reclaimed his phaser, pouch, and combadge. "I am grateful for your timely intervention." A quick inspection revealed that his supply of extra badges had not been damaged by Worf's phaser blast. He was ready to resume the rescue mission. "Perhaps you would care to assist me in tagging the Pakled crew members?"

Worf grunted in assent. "Let's get to work."

Snollicoob was very cold when he woke up. His head hurt, too.

He opened his eyes and looked around. He saw at once that he was no longer aboard *Rorpot,* but was instead resting in a bio-bed in a very impressive medical facility. A shiny silver blanket trapped his body heat. Blinking screens monitored his vital signs. An overhead sensor cluster hummed softly. Doctors and nurses in Starfleet uniforms went about their business. For a second, Snollicoob thought he was still dreaming, but then he heard himself yawning. He felt too tired to be asleep.

"Where am I?"

"Welcome to the *Enterprise,*" Geordi said. The Starfleet engineer was lying in the bed next to his. He was the only human patient present. The rest of the beds were occupied by sleeping Pakleds. Geordi looked exhausted as well. Healing salves were smeared on his face and hands. "How are you feeling?"

"I am confused," Snollicoob admitted. "My head hurts."

"I'll bet. Your captain clocked you but good." Geordi brought him up to speed. It seemed that the *Enterprise* had finally arrived to take the frozen Pakleds aboard. Most of *Rorpot*'s crew were now resting comfortably in the starship's various sickbays, although Captain Aadnalurg was currently confined to the brig. A tractor beam had been employed to tow *Rorpot* out of the danger zone. Now back in one piece, the *Enterprise* would drag the freighter to Deep Space 9, where the Pakleds could see about getting *Rorpot* a new engine. "We also left a subspace beacon to warn any future ships away from the filaments."

Snollicoob listened carefully. "All that happened while I was sleeping?"

"Yep," Geordi said. "And that's not all. With Aadnalurg in custody, and your first officer taking the blame for the crash, that puts you in charge. Congratulations, my friend. You're the new captain of *Rorpot!*"

Oh no! Snollicoob thought. This was the last thing he wanted to hear.

"If you want," Geordi volunteered, "I can help you shop for a new engine when we get to Deep Space 9."

"Uh-uh," Snollicoob said. He decided right then and there to sell the derelict freighter for scrap. He bet Quark would give him a good price. "No, thank you!"

Being captain was too much work!

About the Authors

Dayton Ward. Author. Trekkie. Writing his goofy little science-fiction stories and searching for a way to tap into the hidden nerdity that all humans have. Then, an accidental overdose of Mountain Dew altered his body chemistry. Now, when Dayton Ward grows excited or just downright geeky, a startling metamorphosis occurs. Driven by outlandish ideas and a pronounced lack of sleep, he is pursued by fans and editors, as well as funny men in bright uniforms wielding Tasers, straitjackets, and medication. In addition to the numerous credits he shares with friend and co-writer Kevin Dilmore, Dayton is the author of the *Star Trek* novels *In the Name of Honor* and *Open Secrets* and the science fiction novels *The Last World War* and *The Genesis Protocol,* as well as short stories that appeared in the first three *Star Trek: Strange New Worlds* anthologies, the Yard Dog Press anthology *Houston, We've Got Bubbas, Kansas City Voices* magazine, and the *Star Trek: New Frontier* anthology *No Limits.* Dayton is believed to be working on his next novel, and he must let the world think that he *is* working on it, until he can find a way to earn back the advance check he blew on strippers and booze. Though he currently lives in Kansas City with his wife and two daughters, Dayton is a Florida native and maintains a torrid long-distance romance with his beloved Tampa Bay Buccaneers. Visit him on the web at http://www.daytonward.com.

Kevin Dilmore has found ways to turn geek into cash for more than a decade. It all started with his eight-year run as a contributing writer to *Star Trek Communicator,* for which he wrote news stories and personality profiles for the bimonthly publication of the Official *Star Trek* Fan Club. Then he teamed with writing partner and heterosexual life mate Dayton Ward on *Interphase,* their first installment of the *Star Trek: S.C.E.* series. Since then, the pair has put more than one million words into print together. His solo story "The Road to Edos" was published as part of the *Star Trek: New Frontier* anthology *No Limits.* By day, Kevin works as a senior writer for Hallmark Cards in Kansas City, Missouri, doing about everything but writing greeting cards (including helping to design *Star Trek*–themed Keepsake Ornaments). His first children's book, *Superdad and His Daring Dadventures,* with illustrations by Tom Patrick, was published by Hallmark in May 2009. A graduate of the University of Kansas, Kevin lives in Overland Park, Kansas. Keep up with his shameful behavior and latest projects on Facebook and Twitter.

David A. McIntee has written far too much Doctor Who for his own good; comics including *William Shatner Presents: Quest for Tomorrow*; several other books, both fiction and non; as well as the *Star Trek: The Next Generation* story "On the Spot" for *The Sky's the Limit.* He is outnumbered by five females: his wife, Lesley, and the cats Katya the Cannonball, Mistress B'Elanna, Seven of Nine Lives, and Foxy Cleopatra.

James Swallow is proud to be the only British writer to have worked on a *Star Trek* television series, creating the original story concepts for the *Star Trek: Voyager* episodes "One" and "Memorial"; his other associations with the *Star Trek* saga include the *Titan* novel *Synthesis, Day of the Vipers,* the novella "Seeds of Dissent" for *Infinity's Prism,* the short stories "Closure," "Ordinary Days," and "The Black Flag" for the anthologies *Distant Shores, The Sky's the Limit*, and *Star Trek: Mirror Universe—Shards and Shadows*, scripting the video game *Star Trek Invasion*, and writing over four hundred articles in thirteen different *Star Trek* magazines around the world.

Beyond the final frontier, as well as a nonfiction book *(Dark Eye: The Films of David Fincher)*, James also wrote the *Sundowners* series of original steampunk westerns, *Jade Dragon, The Butterfly Effect*, and fiction in the worlds of *Doctor Who, Warhammer 40,000, Stargate*, and *2000 AD*. His other credits include scripts for video games and audio dramas, including *Battlestar Galactica, Blake's 7*, and *Space 1889*.

James Swallow lives in London, and is currently at work on his next book.

Keith R.A. DeCandido is well-known for his Klingon-focused fiction, but this is the first time that he has written about twenty-third-century Klingons in detail. His previous forays into the wild and wacky world of the Klingons include the short stories "Family Matters" in *Mirror Universe: Shards and Shadows* and *"loDnI'pu' vavpu' je"* in *Tales from the Captain's Table;* the *Alien Spotlight: Klingons* comic book; and the novels *Diplomatic Implausibility, The Art of the Impossible, A Good Day to Die, Honor Bound, Enemy Territory, A Burning House, Articles of the Federation, A Singular Destiny*, and *A Time for War, a Time for Peace*, as well as the two-book series *The Brave and the Bold*. His other work is in media universes ranging from TV shows to video games to comic books. Find out less at Keith's web site at DeCandido.net, read his tiresome ramblings at kradical.livejournal.com, or listen to him babble as a contributor to the podcast *The Chronic Rift* (www.chronicrift.com).

Keith would also like to thank the following: Michael Ansara, William Campbell, John Colicos, Charles Cooper, Susan Howard, and Michael Pataki for their portrayals of Kang, Koloth, Kor, Korrd, Mara, and Korax on screen; Scott & David Tipton, who created Jurva, Kohlar, and Morglar in the magnificent *Blood Will Tell* comic book miniseries; and Dr. Lawrence M. Schoen and the Klingon Language Institute for the terms *QuchHa'* (literally "the unhappy ones," hence the story's title) and *HemQuch* ("the proud forehead").

Britta Burdett Dennison is a writer who lives in Portland, Oregon. Her previous publishing credits include two *Star Trek* novels with S. D. Perry, and a novelization of an original screenplay with S. D. Perry. She is currently at work on an original novel.

Marc D. Giller wrote his first science-fiction novel at the tender age of sixteen, with the certainty of fame and riches before him. When that plan didn't work out he went to college instead, earning a bachelor of science degree in journalism from Texas A&M University. Over the years, Marc has worked as a photographer, producer, computer trainer, and even had a one-night stint as a television news reporter. For the last several years, he has worked in information systems management. He is the author of the books *Hammerjack* and *Prodigal,* and makes his home in the Tampa Bay area of Florida with his wife and two children.

Greg Cox is the *New York Times* bestselling author of numerous *Star Trek* novels, including *The Q Continuum, To Reign in Hell, The Eugenics Wars* (Volumes One and Two), *Assignment: Eternity,* and *The Black Shore.* He wrote the official movie novelizations of *Daredevil, Ghost Rider, Death Defying Acts, Underworld, Underworld: Evolution,* and *Underworld: Rise of the Lycans,* as well the novelizations of three popular DC Comics miniseries, *Infinite Crisis, 52,* and *Countdown.* In addition, he has written books and short stories based on such popular series as *Alias, Batman, Buffy, C.S.I., Farscape, Fantastic Four, The 4400, X-Men, Iron Man, Roswell, Terminator, Underworld, Xena,* and *Zorro.* Recent short fiction can be found in such anthologies as *Star Trek: Mirror Universe—Glass Empires, Star Trek: The Sky's the Limit,* and *Timeshares.*